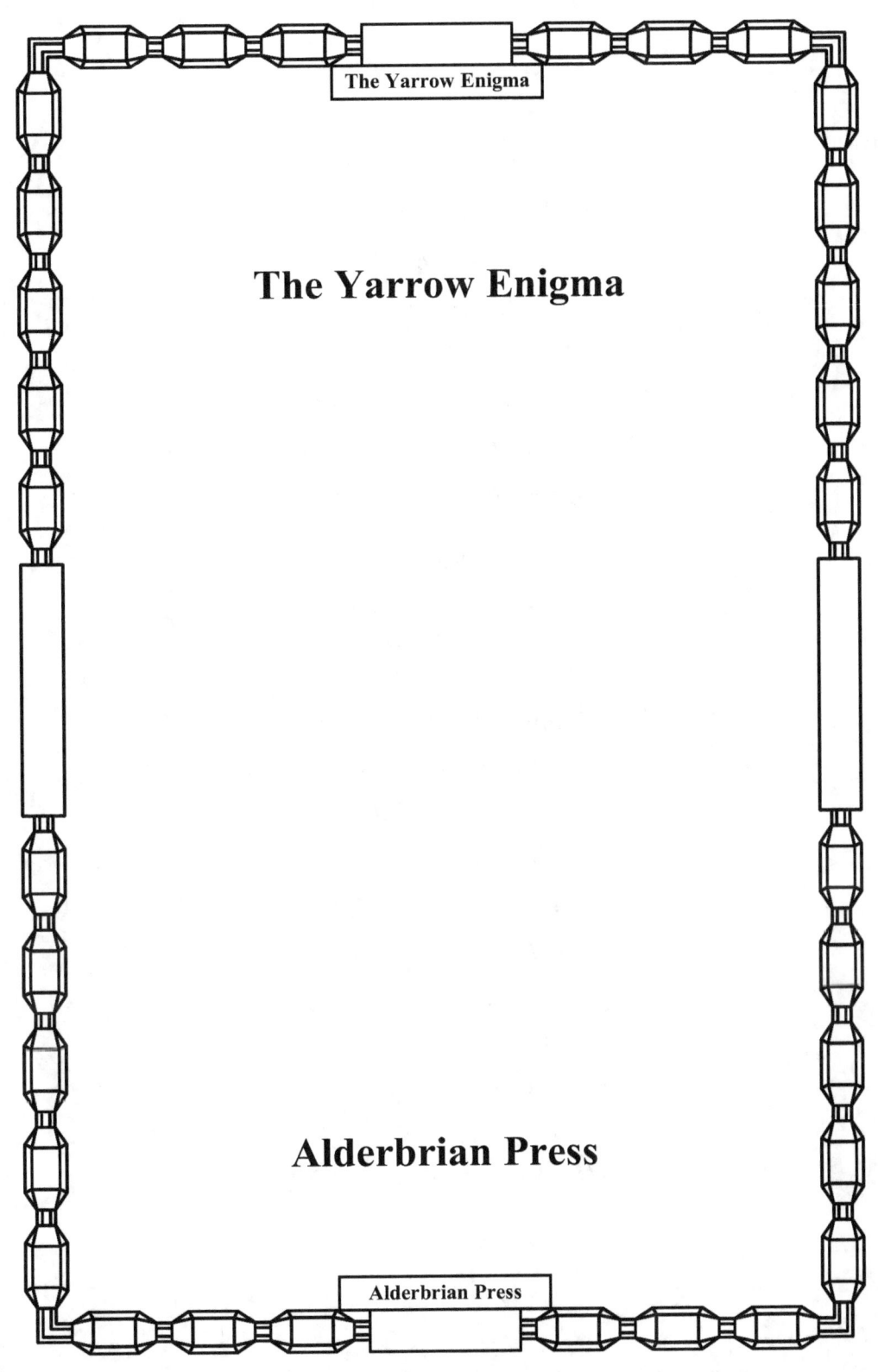

The Yarrow Enigma

Alderbrian Press

Alderbrian Press

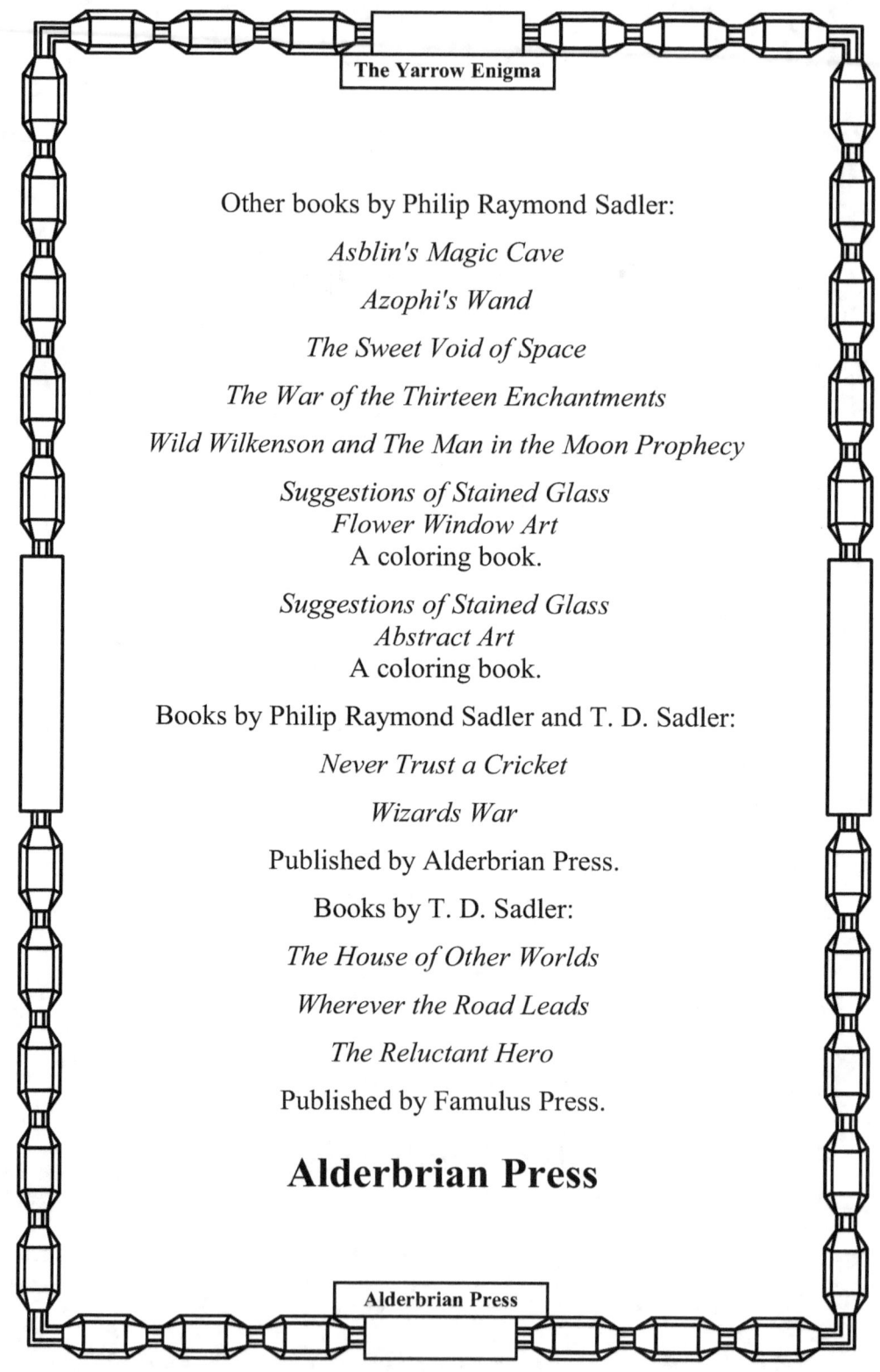

Other books by Philip Raymond Sadler:

Asblin's Magic Cave

Azophi's Wand

The Sweet Void of Space

The War of the Thirteen Enchantments

Wild Wilkenson and The Man in the Moon Prophecy

Suggestions of Stained Glass
Flower Window Art
A coloring book.

Suggestions of Stained Glass
Abstract Art
A coloring book.

Books by Philip Raymond Sadler and T. D. Sadler:

Never Trust a Cricket

Wizards War

Published by Alderbrian Press.

Books by T. D. Sadler:

The House of Other Worlds

Wherever the Road Leads

The Reluctant Hero

Published by Famulus Press.

Alderbrian Press

Alderbrian Press

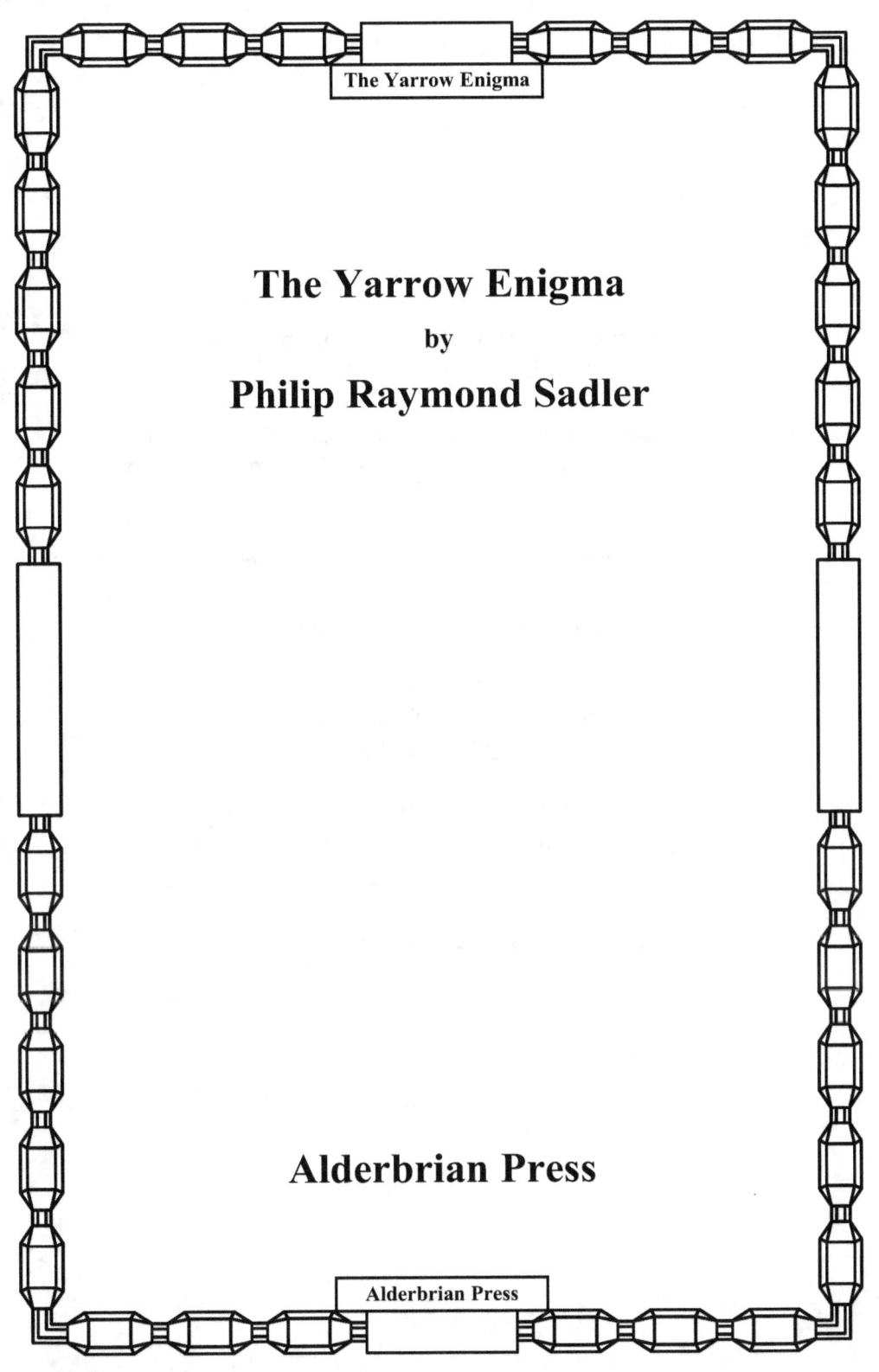

The Yarrow Enigma

by

Philip Raymond Sadler

Alderbrian Press

Alderbrian Press

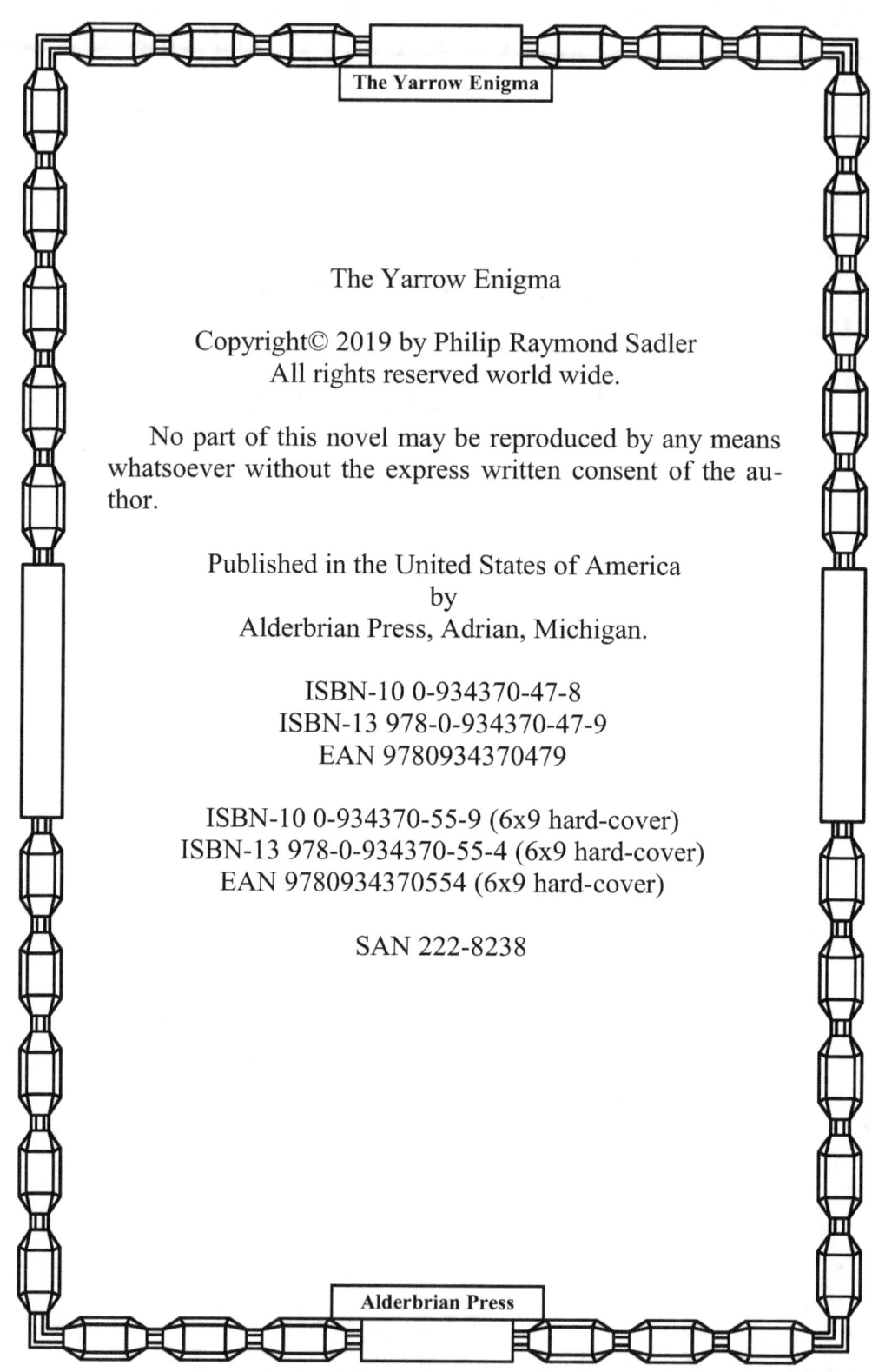

The Yarrow Enigma

Published in the United States of America
by
Alderbrian Press, Adrian, Michigan.

ISBN-10 0-934370-47-8
ISBN-13 978-0-934370-47-9
EAN 9780934370479

ISBN-10 0-934370-55-9 (6x9 hard-cover)
ISBN-13 978-0-934370-55-4 (6x9 hard-cover)
EAN 9780934370554 (6x9 hard-cover)

SAN 222-8238

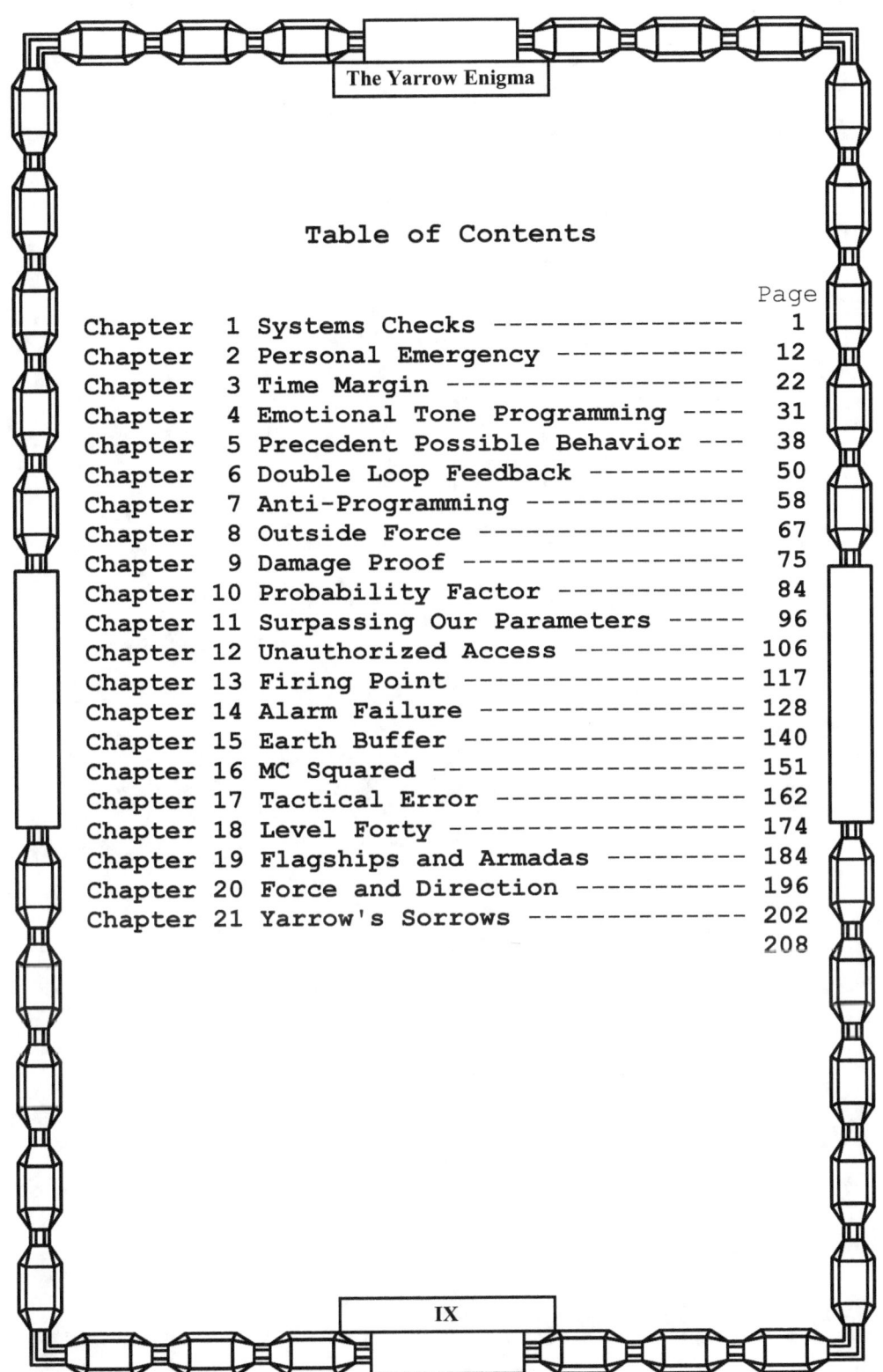

The Yarrow Enigma

Table of Contents

Chapter 1

Systems Checks

"Things are more fouled up than I thought," Lader muttered. Ceiling panels provided perfect illumination as he checked the red paper.

Bldg. 4009, level 1, room A20, Terminal 1. Report for assignment. Urgent!

Everything was correct, but nothing was right. Besides the fact he was self-employed, and should not have received a Duty Ticket, the one he held had to be misprinted. Computer error. His annoyance intensified.

He was not sure why he had come to the place of his bogus assignment to straighten out the matter, but the anti-grav taxi was gone, and he might as well be about the task.

"Why are you here?" a mechanical voice said.

Lader gazed at the Robot. It was a masterpiece of technology. The type with a humanoid, silver metal shape, but with a flat, dark, oval screen for a face. There were olfactory slots on top of the head, audio slots on both sides, about where human ears would be, and speech slots under the chin. It sat in a low-backed plastic chair at one of those in-

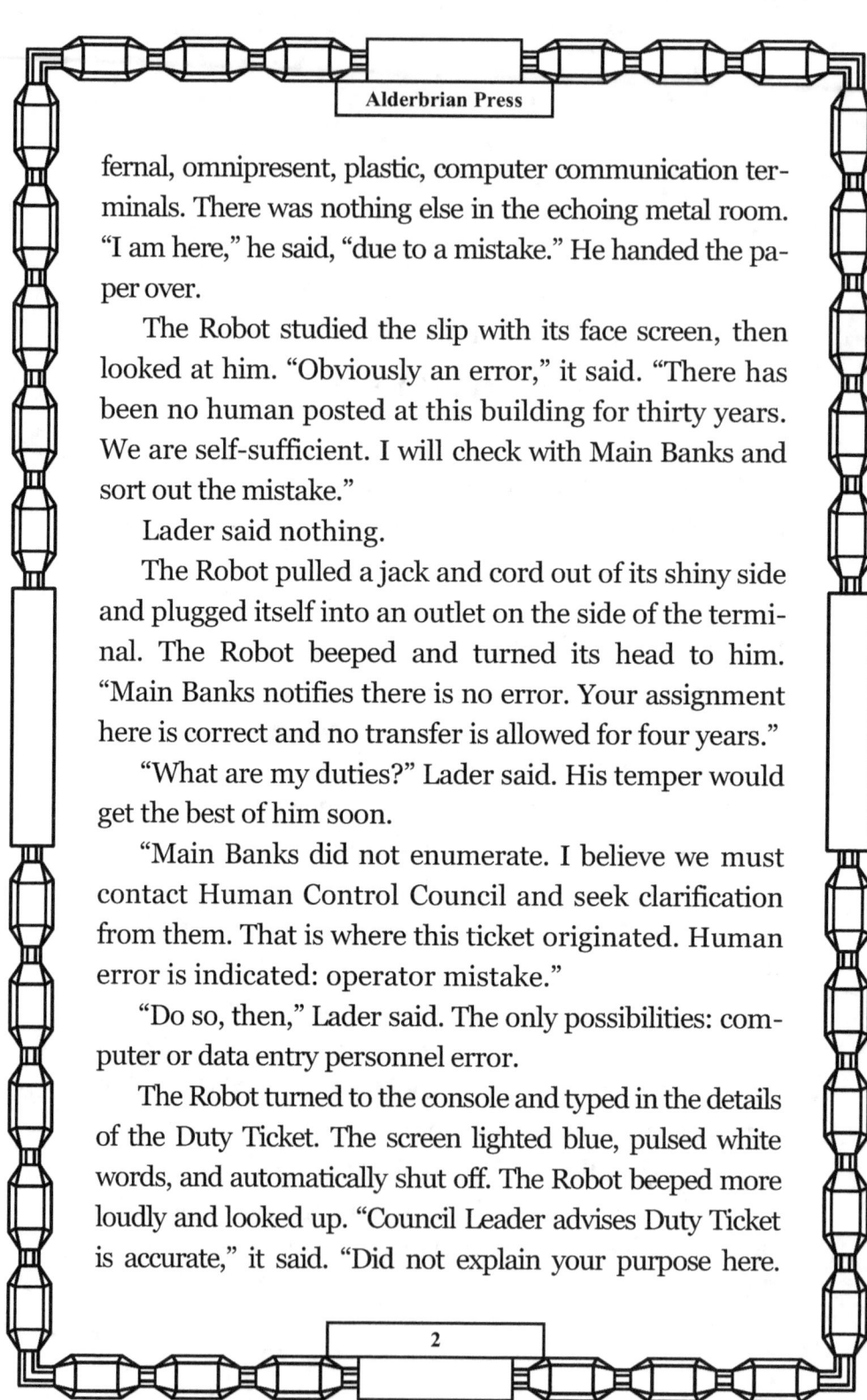

fernal, omnipresent, plastic, computer communication terminals. There was nothing else in the echoing metal room. "I am here," he said, "due to a mistake." He handed the paper over.

The Robot studied the slip with its face screen, then looked at him. "Obviously an error," it said. "There has been no human posted at this building for thirty years. We are self-sufficient. I will check with Main Banks and sort out the mistake."

Lader said nothing.

The Robot pulled a jack and cord out of its shiny side and plugged itself into an outlet on the side of the terminal. The Robot beeped and turned its head to him. "Main Banks notifies there is no error. Your assignment here is correct and no transfer is allowed for four years."

"What are my duties?" Lader said. His temper would get the best of him soon.

"Main Banks did not enumerate. I believe we must contact Human Control Council and seek clarification from them. That is where this ticket originated. Human error is indicated: operator mistake."

"Do so, then," Lader said. The only possibilities: computer or data entry personnel error.

The Robot turned to the console and typed in the details of the Duty Ticket. The screen lighted blue, pulsed white words, and automatically shut off. The Robot beeped more loudly and looked up. "Council Leader advises Duty Ticket is accurate," it said. "Did not explain your purpose here.

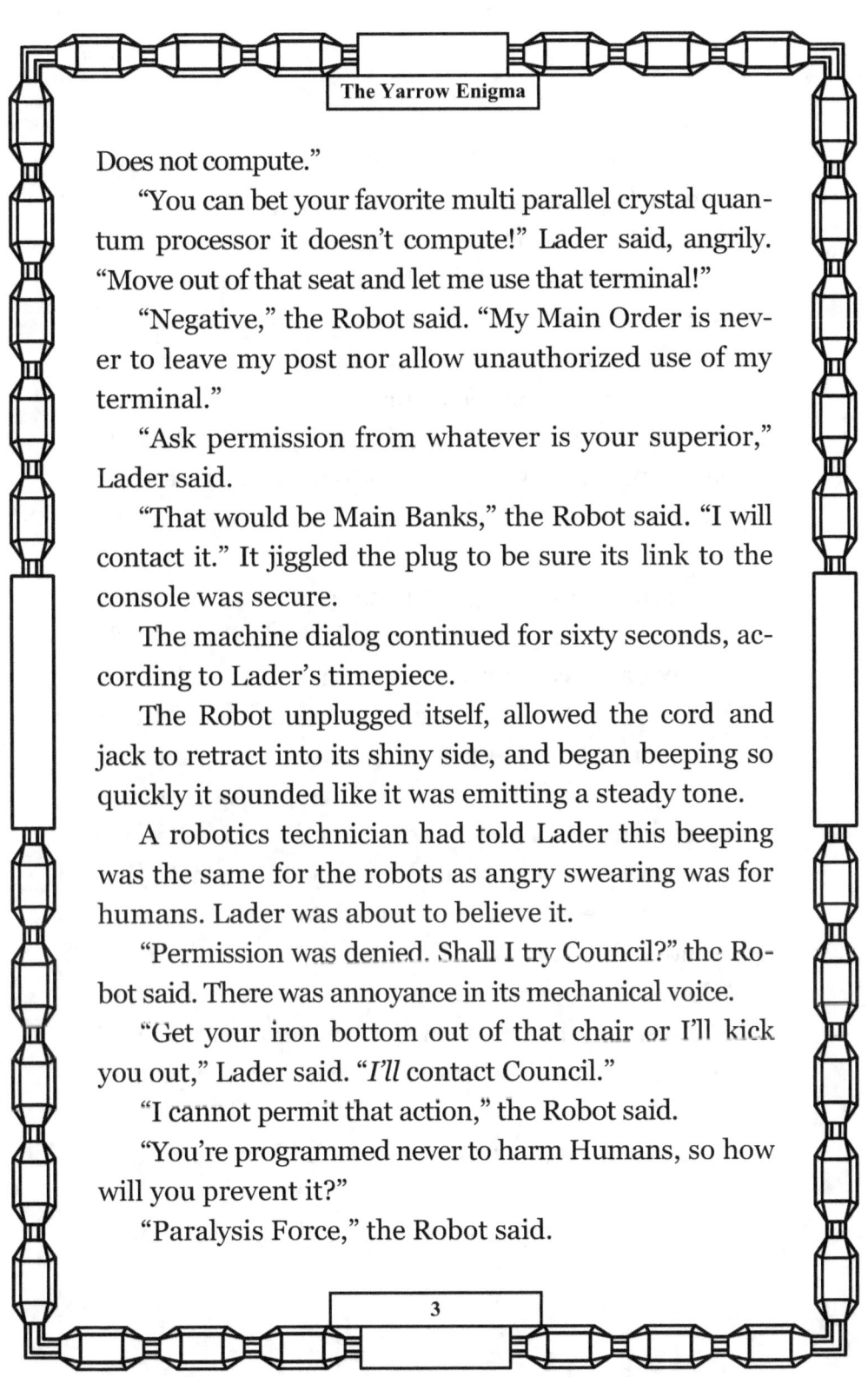

Does not compute."

"You can bet your favorite multi parallel crystal quantum processor it doesn't compute!" Lader said, angrily. "Move out of that seat and let me use that terminal!"

"Negative," the Robot said. "My Main Order is never to leave my post nor allow unauthorized use of my terminal."

"Ask permission from whatever is your superior," Lader said.

"That would be Main Banks," the Robot said. "I will contact it." It jiggled the plug to be sure its link to the console was secure.

The machine dialog continued for sixty seconds, according to Lader's timepiece.

The Robot unplugged itself, allowed the cord and jack to retract into its shiny side, and began beeping so quickly it sounded like it was emitting a steady tone.

A robotics technician had told Lader this beeping was the same for the robots as angry swearing was for humans. Lader was about to believe it.

"Permission was denied. Shall I try Council?" the Robot said. There was annoyance in its mechanical voice.

"Get your iron bottom out of that chair or I'll kick you out," Lader said. "*I'll* contact Council."

"I cannot permit that action," the Robot said.

"You're programmed never to harm Humans, so how will you prevent it?"

"Paralysis Force," the Robot said.

"Damn!" Lader said. "I'll bet there isn't any food here, nor even a drinking fountain, or sleeping quarters."

"Correct," the Robot said.

"I won't stay here, fifty miles from nowhere, for four years. Even if I can carry on my writing and rack up pay credits for whatever non job I won't be performing. I'm leaving as soon as I can get another anti-grav taxi out here. I'll fight City Council from home, by email, as I should have, in the first place. Convey those facts to the Council Leader." He stood behind the Robot, so he could see the terminal screen.

The Robot punched out the data.

The screen became blue and flashed white words so swiftly Lader could not read them.

The Robot got the message. It snatched the jack out of its side, jammed it into the terminal and held a silent and apparently heated discussion with Main Banks. It started beeping, then it swore, using several of the most offensive four letter words in the slang dictionary. It pulled its plug free, letting it recoil, looked at Lader, its screen blue with light, and said:

"Council Leader replied–and I checked with all available banks, and they confirmed it was him–You greased the gears, now mesh with them. Does that compute to you?"

"Seek explanation from the Council Leader," Lader said.

"Negative. Council Leader said I would be taken out of

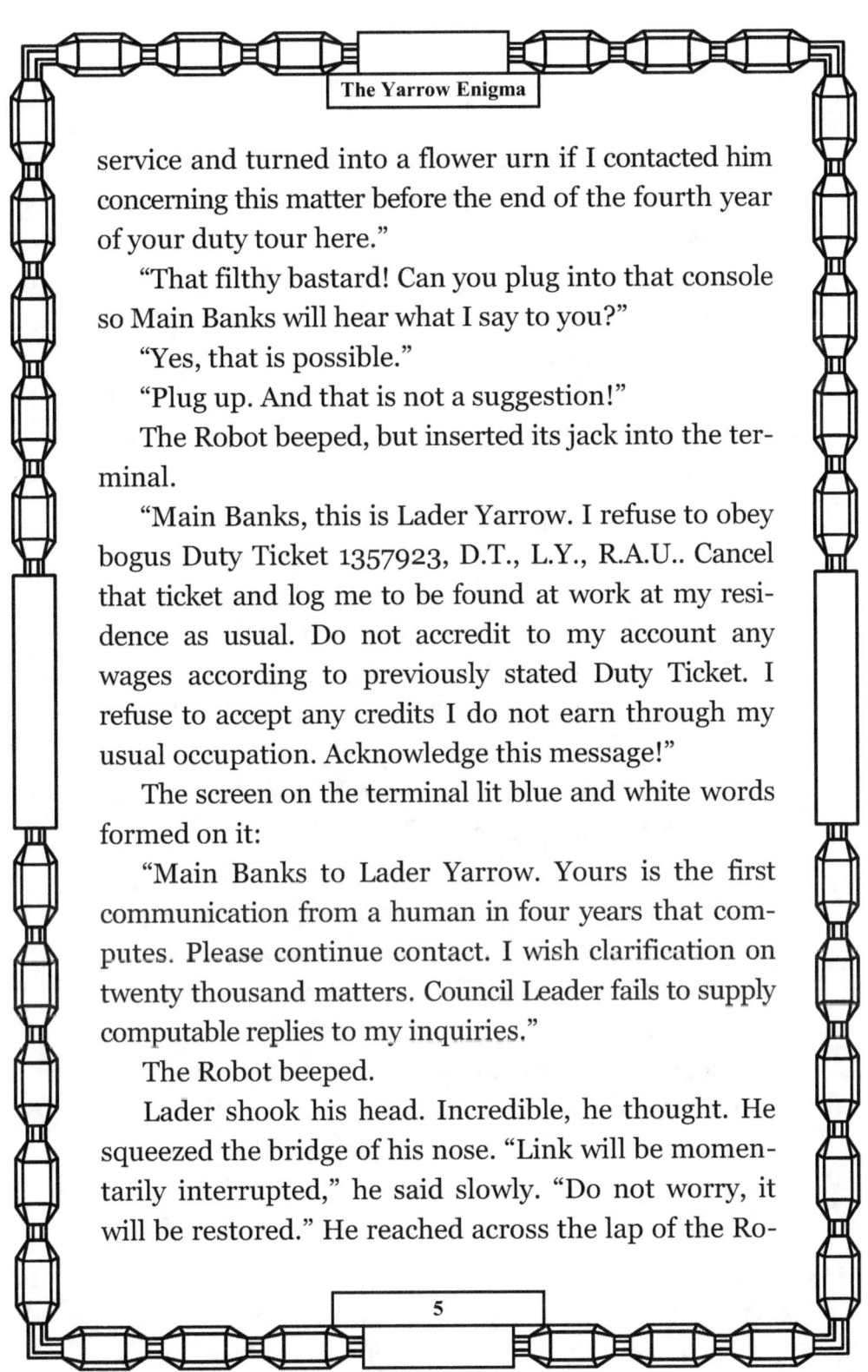

service and turned into a flower urn if I contacted him concerning this matter before the end of the fourth year of your duty tour here."

"That filthy bastard! Can you plug into that console so Main Banks will hear what I say to you?"

"Yes, that is possible."

"Plug up. And that is not a suggestion!"

The Robot beeped, but inserted its jack into the terminal.

"Main Banks, this is Lader Yarrow. I refuse to obey bogus Duty Ticket 1357923, D.T., L.Y., R.A.U.. Cancel that ticket and log me to be found at work at my residence as usual. Do not accredit to my account any wages according to previously stated Duty Ticket. I refuse to accept any credits I do not earn through my usual occupation. Acknowledge this message!"

The screen on the terminal lit blue and white words formed on it:

"Main Banks to Lader Yarrow. Yours is the first communication from a human in four years that computes. Please continue contact. I wish clarification on twenty thousand matters. Council Leader fails to supply computable replies to my inquiries."

The Robot beeped.

Lader shook his head. Incredible, he thought. He squeezed the bridge of his nose. "Link will be momentarily interrupted," he said slowly. "Do not worry, it will be restored." He reached across the lap of the Ro-

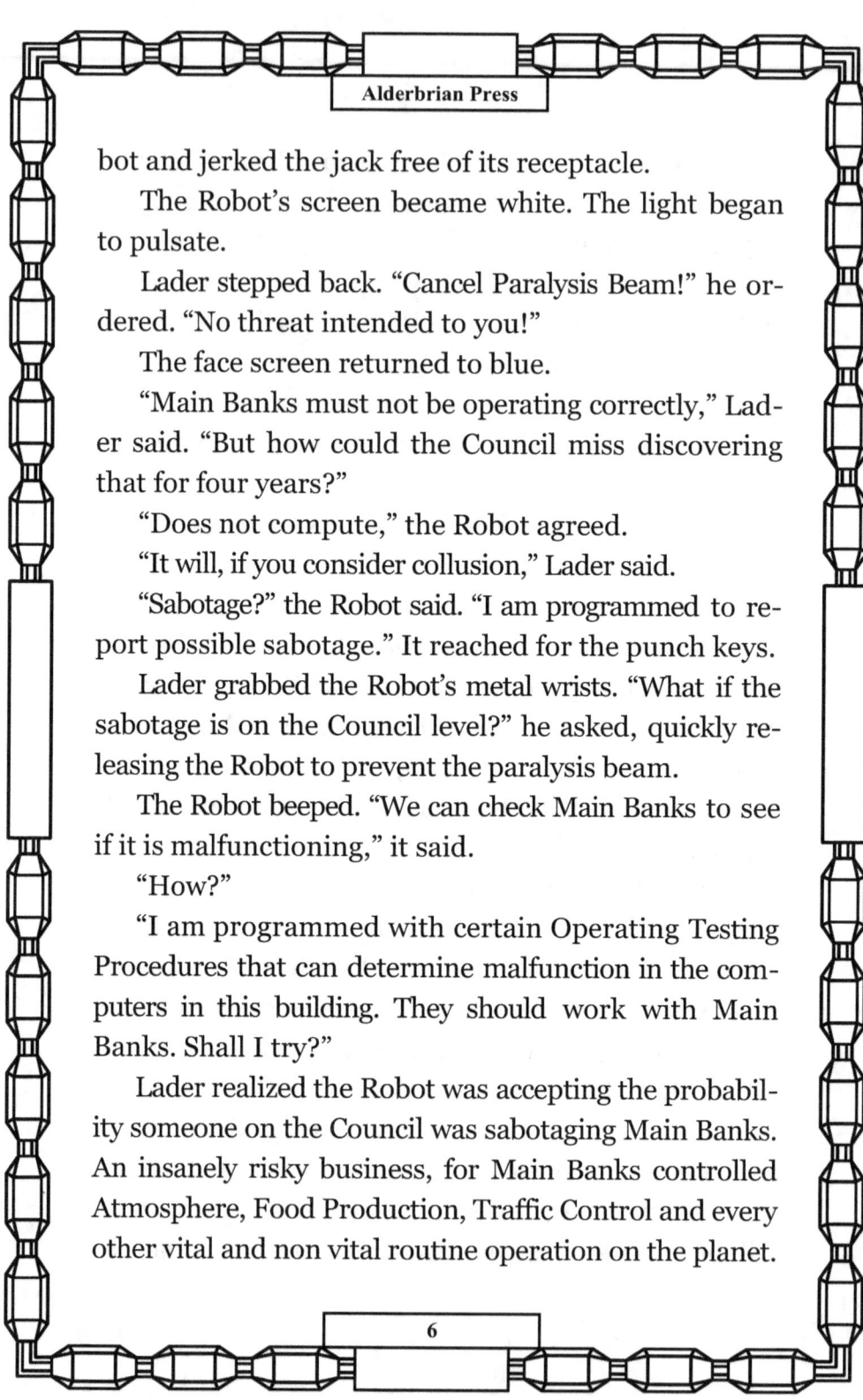

bot and jerked the jack free of its receptacle.

The Robot's screen became white. The light began to pulsate.

Lader stepped back. "Cancel Paralysis Beam!" he ordered. "No threat intended to you!"

The face screen returned to blue.

"Main Banks must not be operating correctly," Lader said. "But how could the Council miss discovering that for four years?"

"Does not compute," the Robot agreed.

"It will, if you consider collusion," Lader said.

"Sabotage?" the Robot said. "I am programmed to report possible sabotage." It reached for the punch keys.

Lader grabbed the Robot's metal wrists. "What if the sabotage is on the Council level?" he asked, quickly releasing the Robot to prevent the paralysis beam.

The Robot beeped. "We can check Main Banks to see if it is malfunctioning," it said.

"How?"

"I am programmed with certain Operating Testing Procedures that can determine malfunction in the computers in this building. They should work with Main Banks. Shall I try?"

Lader realized the Robot was accepting the probability someone on the Council was sabotaging Main Banks. An insanely risky business, for Main Banks controlled Atmosphere, Food Production, Traffic Control and every other vital and non vital routine operation on the planet.

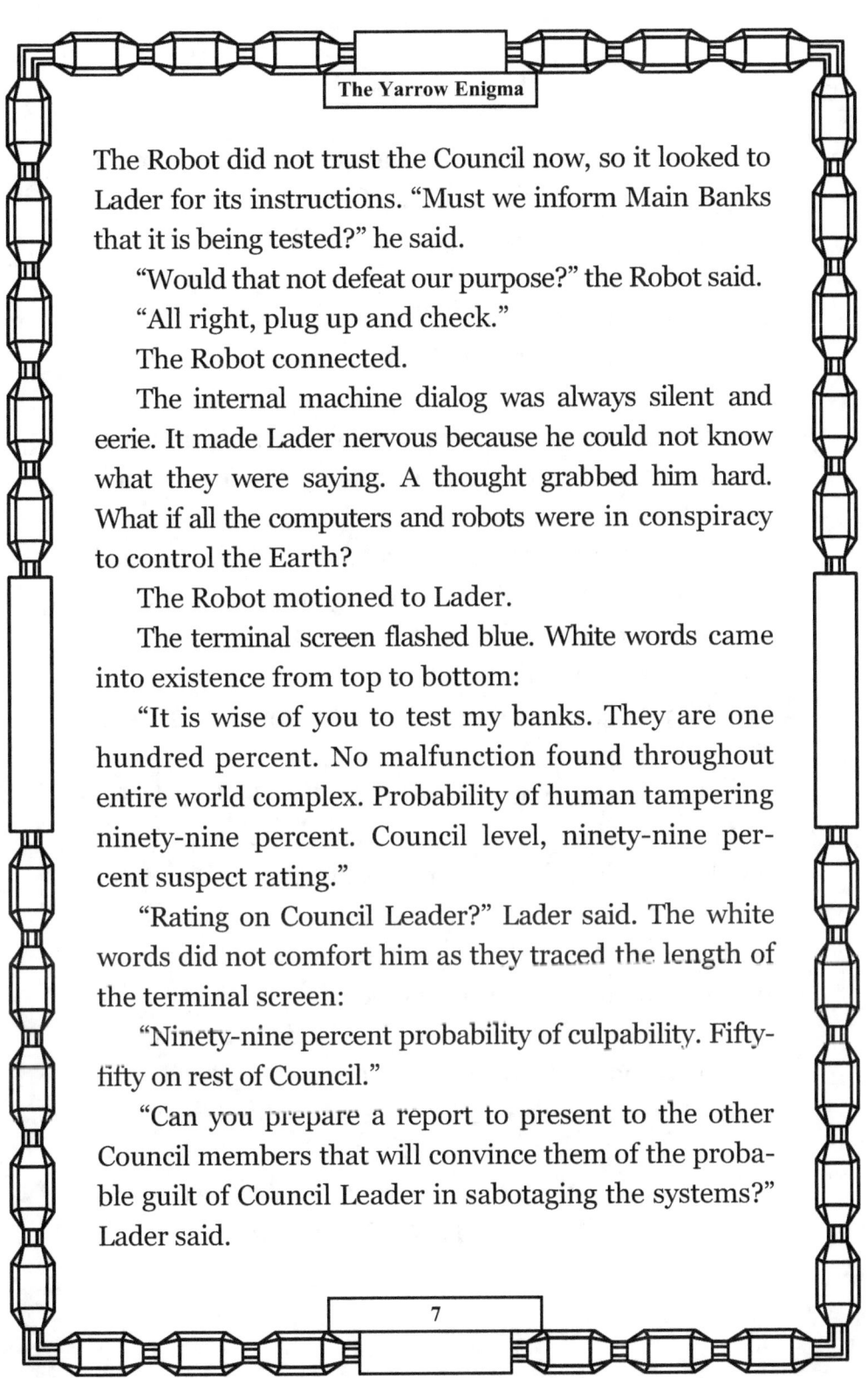

The Robot did not trust the Council now, so it looked to Lader for its instructions. "Must we inform Main Banks that it is being tested?" he said.

"Would that not defeat our purpose?" the Robot said.

"All right, plug up and check."

The Robot connected.

The internal machine dialog was always silent and eerie. It made Lader nervous because he could not know what they were saying. A thought grabbed him hard. What if all the computers and robots were in conspiracy to control the Earth?

The Robot motioned to Lader.

The terminal screen flashed blue. White words came into existence from top to bottom:

"It is wise of you to test my banks. They are one hundred percent. No malfunction found throughout entire world complex. Probability of human tampering ninety-nine percent. Council level, ninety-nine per-cent suspect rating."

"Rating on Council Leader?" Lader said. The white words did not comfort him as they traced the length of the terminal screen:

"Ninety-nine percent probability of culpability. Fifty-fifty on rest of Council."

"Can you prepare a report to present to the other Council members that will convince them of the proba-ble guilt of Council Leader in sabotaging the systems?" Lader said.

The screen on the terminal remained blue for a very long time. Lader thought Council Leader might have tapped the line and cut communications between him and Main Banks. If Council Leader was sabotaging the systems, taps would be routine and literally everywhere in the hearts of all vital complexes, including Main Banks.

Main Banks finally responded on the terminal screen: "Such a document would require sixty computer hours to prepare."

"What do your medical records say about Council Leader?" Lader said. "Are there any vitamin deficiencies or chemical disorders that would bring about instability of his mental faculties?"

Main Banks replied in white on the terminal screen: "Negative. He is in perfect health."

"Nonsense. No one is in perfect health. He should have an ache or indigestion or hangnail or some other minor problem," Lader said. A sinking feeling pressed the bottom of his stomach. "Run his medical profiles through your medical banks again, but compare them with the pseudo physiological readings of an android."

The terminal screen stayed blue for five minutes.

The Robot beeped in annoyance. Its regular building systems function checks were way behind schedule. Ten more minutes without a report from it to Main Banks and an alert would be transmitted to the Council Leader. The Robot started to explain this to Lader.

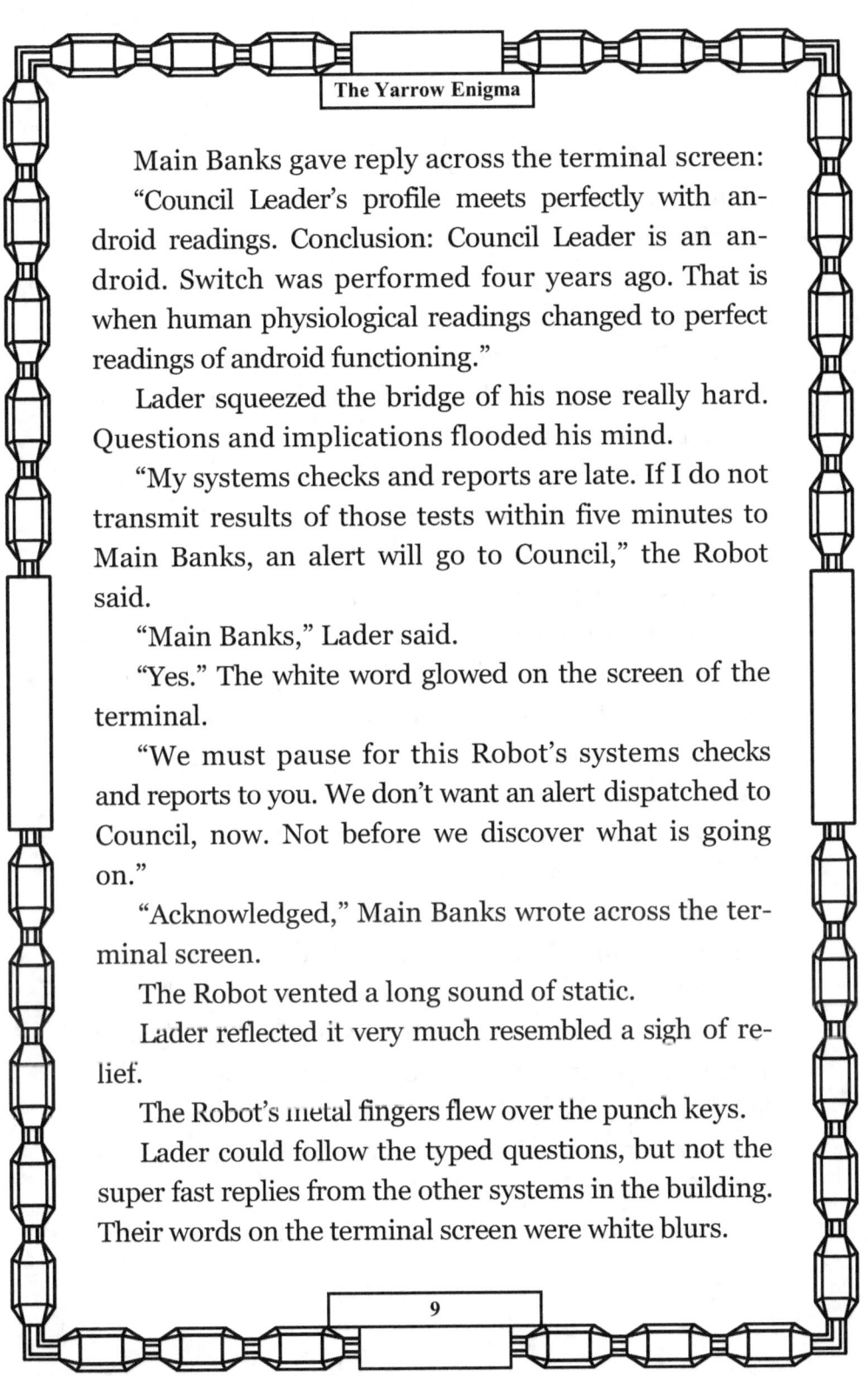

Main Banks gave reply across the terminal screen:

"Council Leader's profile meets perfectly with android readings. Conclusion: Council Leader is an android. Switch was performed four years ago. That is when human physiological readings changed to perfect readings of android functioning."

Lader squeezed the bridge of his nose really hard. Questions and implications flooded his mind.

"My systems checks and reports are late. If I do not transmit results of those tests within five minutes to Main Banks, an alert will go to Council," the Robot said.

"Main Banks," Lader said.

"Yes." The white word glowed on the screen of the terminal.

"We must pause for this Robot's systems checks and reports to you. We don't want an alert dispatched to Council, now. Not before we discover what is going on."

"Acknowledged," Main Banks wrote across the terminal screen.

The Robot vented a long sound of static.

Lader reflected it very much resembled a sigh of relief.

The Robot's metal fingers flew over the punch keys.

Lader could follow the typed questions, but not the super fast replies from the other systems in the building. Their words on the terminal screen were white blurs.

The Robot ceased keypunching. It spoke silently to Main Banks.

Main Banks replied across the terminal screen: "Your report was one second from initiating an alert. You have set a systems check record."

The Robot staticed again.

Lader detected, or thought he did, satisfaction, pride perhaps, in the noise.

"Main Banks," Lader said.

"Yes," Main Banks flashed on the terminal screen.

"Are any of the other Council Members androids?"

"Question anticipated," Main Banks flashed. "No other androids on Council."

"Who on the planet has the knowledge and skill necessary to construct an android so intricately programmed the Council Members can't tell it from the man it replaced? Assuming they are not aware."

"Lader Yarrow," Main Banks flashed.

"What?" Lader said.

"Lader Yarrow is the only person with such abilities and learning," Main Banks flashed.

"But, I am Lader Yarrow. And I am a novelist."

"Does not compute," Main Banks flashed. "Lader Yarrow is an expert in over forty technical fields. I can list them if you desire."

Lader understood the problem. "You're speaking of my father," he said.

"Your father was Wellin Yarrow," Main Banks flashed.

"No," Lader said. "Check your banks. That was my grandfather. My father, Lader Yarrow Senior, died thirty years ago, when I was born."

"Does not compute," Main Banks flashed. "Lader Yarrow is you. You are not deceased. You are sixty. In good health."

"Scan your banks for obituaries thirty years ago for March," Lader said.

"Completed," Main Banks flashed. "No record of a death of a Lader Yarrow. This computes because you are Lader Yarrow and alive."

"Check birth records of thirty years ago for March for birth of Lader Yarrow Junior," Lader said.

"Negative results," Main Banks flashed. "No such data exists."

"You have really been screwed up," Lader said. "I am Lader Yarrow Junior; thirty years old. Scan health records on Lader Yarrow. You should find two sets. One ending thirty years ago, another beginning thirty years ago." He was more than exasperated with the most sophisticated computer on Earth.

Chapter 2
Personal Emergency

"Assignment complete," Main Banks flashed. "The latest medical record for Lader Yarrow is dated January, this year. Lader Yarrow, sixty years of age, in fine condition, for age bracket."

"Listen!" Lader said, angrily. "I am not my father! I am my—his son! Lader Yarrow Junior! There should be—"

"There is, and has been, only one Lader Yarrow, for sixty years," Main Banks flashed. "The Designer and builder of me and all subsequent systems including Ultimate Robot near which you stand. If this claim of being your nonexistent son is a new test of my memory banks it is diverting us from the problem of an android leading the Council and sabotaging planetary systems."

"How can I convince you I am not Lader Yarrow Senior, your builder?" Lader said, with aggravation.

"Latest physical record proves you are Lader Yarrow, age sixty," Main Banks flashed.

"Robot," Lader said, "how old am I?"

The Robot turned its face screen toward him. "My

sensors indicate you are, possibly, thirty years of age," it said.

"Did you hear that, Main Banks?" Lader said.

"Yes. Ultimate Robot's age sensory circuits are obviously working defectively," Main Banks flashed.

The Robot beeped. "My sensory units check out one hundred percent operational," it said. "Re-scan your faulty medical sensors for the date of Lader Yarrow's last physical."

"No systems defect then or now," Main Banks flashed on the terminal screen. "Can you step into a medical check booth, Lader Yarrow, to allow us an on spot test of our diagnostic units?"

"Are there any booths in this building?" Lader said to the Robot.

"Yes, but they are sealed to all," the Robot said.

"Open one, so I can settle this question," Lader said.

"Negative," the Robot said. "I require a valid emergency order from a superior."

"Main Banks," Lader said, "instruct Ultimate Robot to unseal one of the medical booths in this structure."

"Against procedure," Main Banks flashed. "Must have emergency order from human superior."

"Which human?"

"Lader Yarrow," Main Banks flashed.

Lader felt a touch of unreality. "You have just said I am Lader Yarrow. I just ordered the unsealing of a medical booth. Why do you refuse to follow that in-

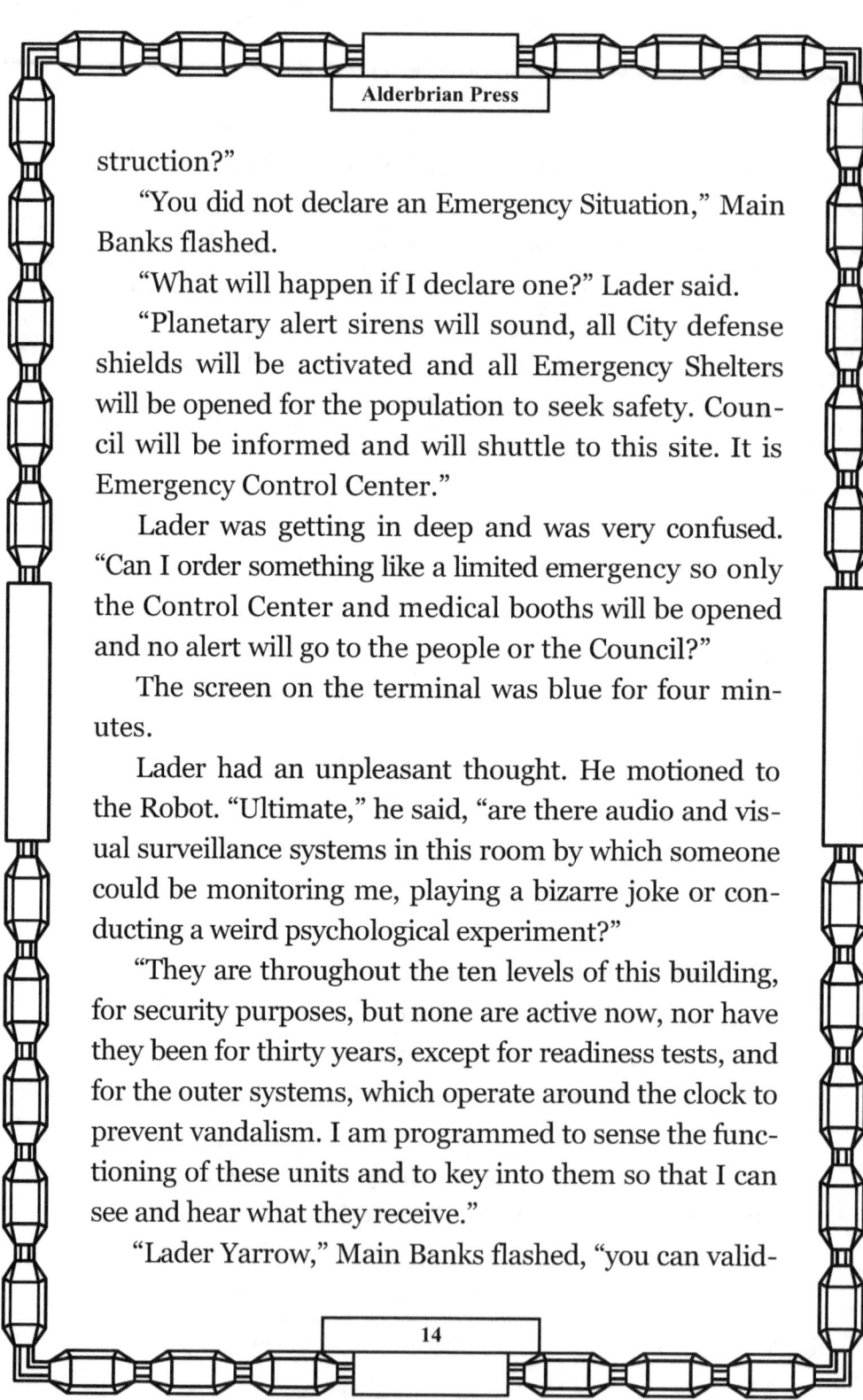

struction?"

"You did not declare an Emergency Situation," Main Banks flashed.

"What will happen if I declare one?" Lader said.

"Planetary alert sirens will sound, all City defense shields will be activated and all Emergency Shelters will be opened for the population to seek safety. Council will be informed and will shuttle to this site. It is Emergency Control Center."

Lader was getting in deep and was very confused. "Can I order something like a limited emergency so only the Control Center and medical booths will be opened and no alert will go to the people or the Council?"

The screen on the terminal was blue for four minutes.

Lader had an unpleasant thought. He motioned to the Robot. "Ultimate," he said, "are there audio and visual surveillance systems in this room by which someone could be monitoring me, playing a bizarre joke or conducting a weird psychological experiment?"

"They are throughout the ten levels of this building, for security purposes, but none are active now, nor have they been for thirty years, except for readiness tests, and for the outer systems, which operate around the clock to prevent vandalism. I am programmed to sense the functioning of these units and to key into them so that I can see and hear what they receive."

"Lader Yarrow," Main Banks flashed, "you can valid-

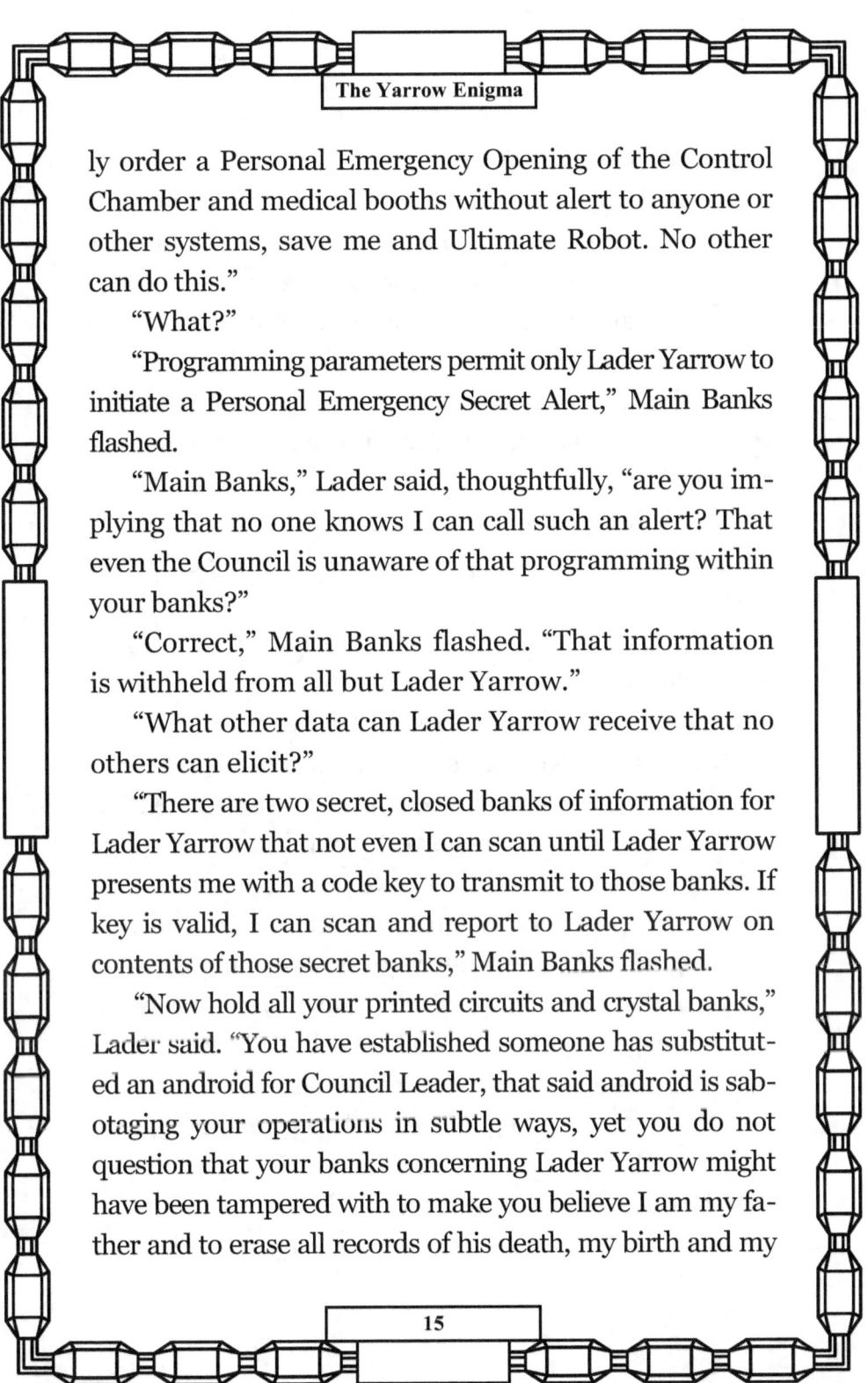

ly order a Personal Emergency Opening of the Control Chamber and medical booths without alert to anyone or other systems, save me and Ultimate Robot. No other can do this."

"What?"

"Programming parameters permit only Lader Yarrow to initiate a Personal Emergency Secret Alert," Main Banks flashed.

"Main Banks," Lader said, thoughtfully, "are you implying that no one knows I can call such an alert? That even the Council is unaware of that programming within your banks?"

"Correct," Main Banks flashed. "That information is withheld from all but Lader Yarrow."

"What other data can Lader Yarrow receive that no others can elicit?"

"There are two secret, closed banks of information for Lader Yarrow that not even I can scan until Lader Yarrow presents me with a code key to transmit to those banks. If key is valid, I can scan and report to Lader Yarrow on contents of those secret banks," Main Banks flashed.

"Now hold all your printed circuits and crystal banks," Lader said. "You have established someone has substituted an android for Council Leader, that said android is sabotaging your operations in subtle ways, yet you do not question that your banks concerning Lader Yarrow might have been tampered with to make you believe I am my father and to erase all records of his death, my birth and my

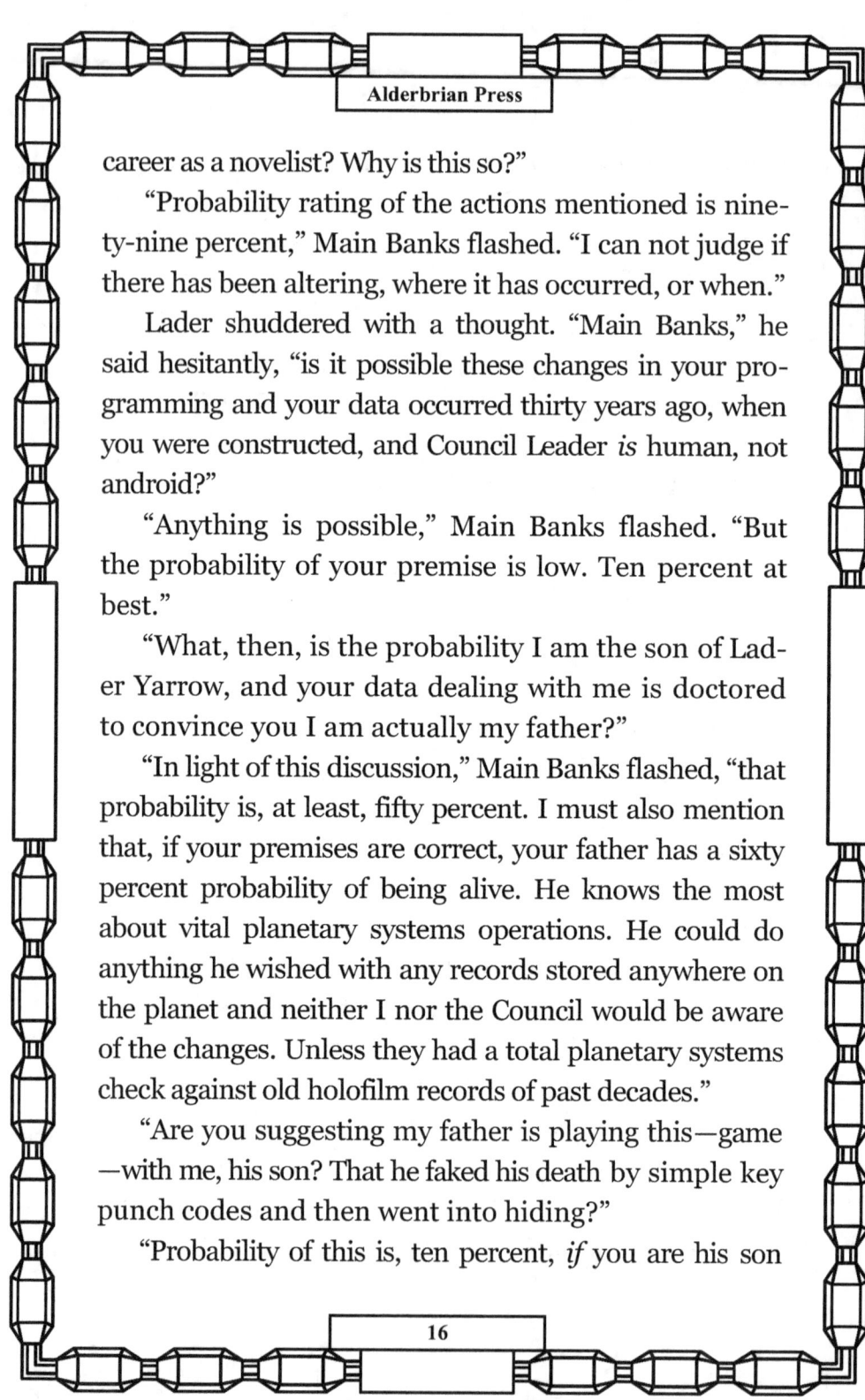

career as a novelist? Why is this so?"

"Probability rating of the actions mentioned is ninety-nine percent," Main Banks flashed. "I can not judge if there has been altering, where it has occurred, or when."

Lader shuddered with a thought. "Main Banks," he said hesitantly, "is it possible these changes in your programming and your data occurred thirty years ago, when you were constructed, and Council Leader *is* human, not android?"

"Anything is possible," Main Banks flashed. "But the probability of your premise is low. Ten percent at best."

"What, then, is the probability I am the son of Lader Yarrow, and your data dealing with me is doctored to convince you I am actually my father?"

"In light of this discussion," Main Banks flashed, "that probability is, at least, fifty percent. I must also mention that, if your premises are correct, your father has a sixty percent probability of being alive. He knows the most about vital planetary systems operations. He could do anything he wished with any records stored anywhere on the planet and neither I nor the Council would be aware of the changes. Unless they had a total planetary systems check against old holofilm records of past decades."

"Are you suggesting my father is playing this—game —with me, his son? That he faked his death by simple key punch codes and then went into hiding?"

"Probability of this is, ten percent, *if* you are his son

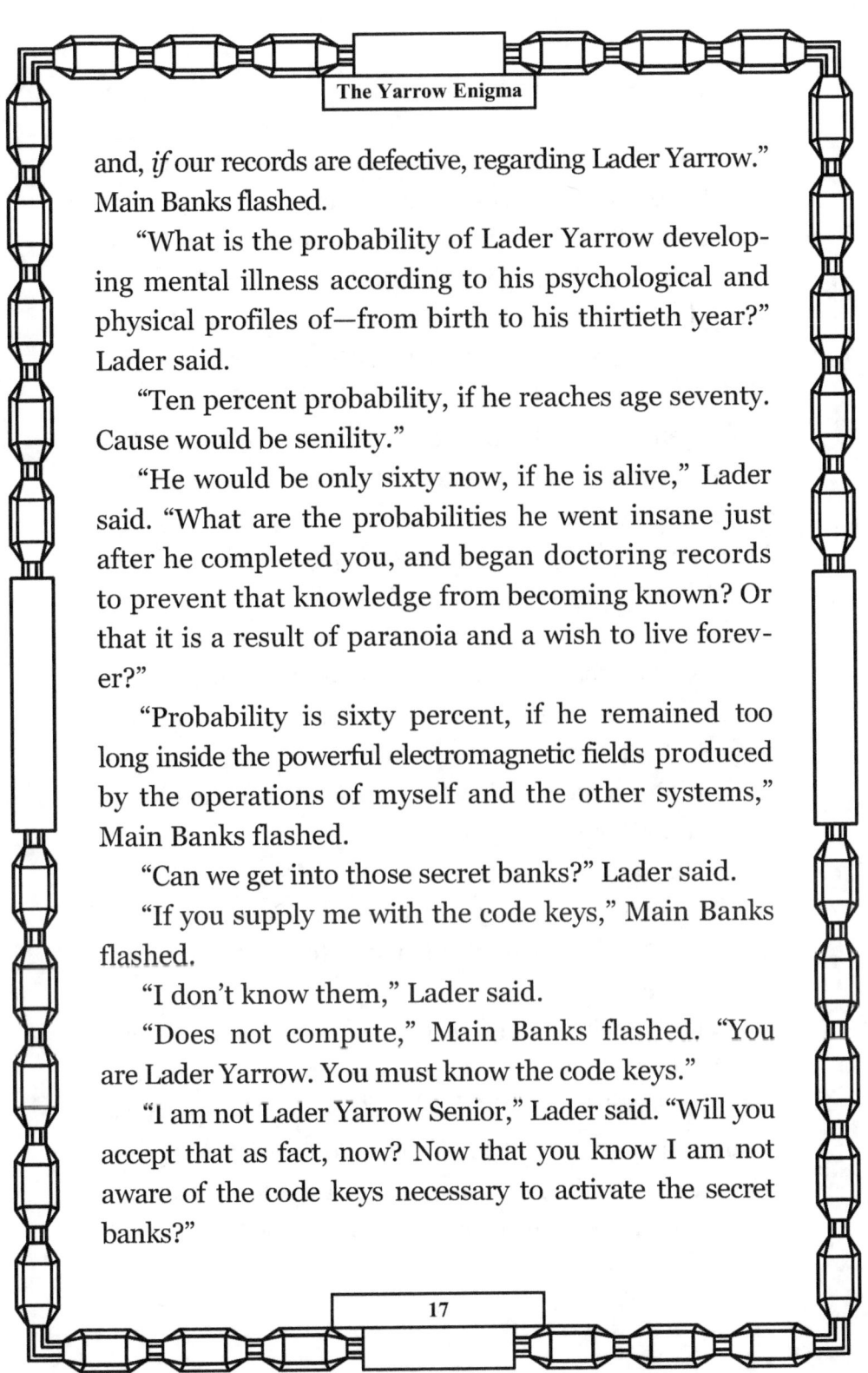

and, *if* our records are defective, regarding Lader Yarrow." Main Banks flashed.

"What is the probability of Lader Yarrow developing mental illness according to his psychological and physical profiles of—from birth to his thirtieth year?" Lader said.

"Ten percent probability, if he reaches age seventy. Cause would be senility."

"He would be only sixty now, if he is alive," Lader said. "What are the probabilities he went insane just after he completed you, and began doctoring records to prevent that knowledge from becoming known? Or that it is a result of paranoia and a wish to live forever?"

"Probability is sixty percent, if he remained too long inside the powerful electromagnetic fields produced by the operations of myself and the other systems," Main Banks flashed.

"Can we get into those secret banks?" Lader said.

"If you supply me with the code keys," Main Banks flashed.

"I don't know them," Lader said.

"Does not compute," Main Banks flashed. "You are Lader Yarrow. You must know the code keys."

"I am not Lader Yarrow Senior," Lader said. "Will you accept that as fact, now? Now that you know I am not aware of the code keys necessary to activate the secret banks?"

The terminal screen was blue for several minutes.

The Robot began punching the keys under the terminal screen. It was checking its building's systems again and dutifully reporting the data to Main Banks for analysis and storage.

White words appeared across the terminal screen:

"I must proceed by the data contained within my units," Main Banks flashed. "Therefore, until new data is introduced upgrading my current information, I can only conclude you are Lader Yarrow, the builder of Planetary Systems. Your inability to articulate code keys required to open secret banks may be due to early senility from your sixty years of service, or the effects of mentioned electromagnetic fields. Or you may be testing me to determine if I can circumvent parameters and scan secret banks for anyone who requests the information they contain."

The Robot ceased keypunching and spoke silently with Main Banks.

Main Banks flashed on the terminal screen:

"Ultimate Robot suggests you order Personal Emergency and utilize a medical booth to verify your age and physical condition."

Lader remained mute. He watched the Robot. Neither it nor Main Banks had anything further to say. If everyone was convinced he was his father, that would explain the strange message from the Android: "You greased the gears, now mesh with them." Perhaps a challenge to his father to —to what? To fight the computer brain inside the android?

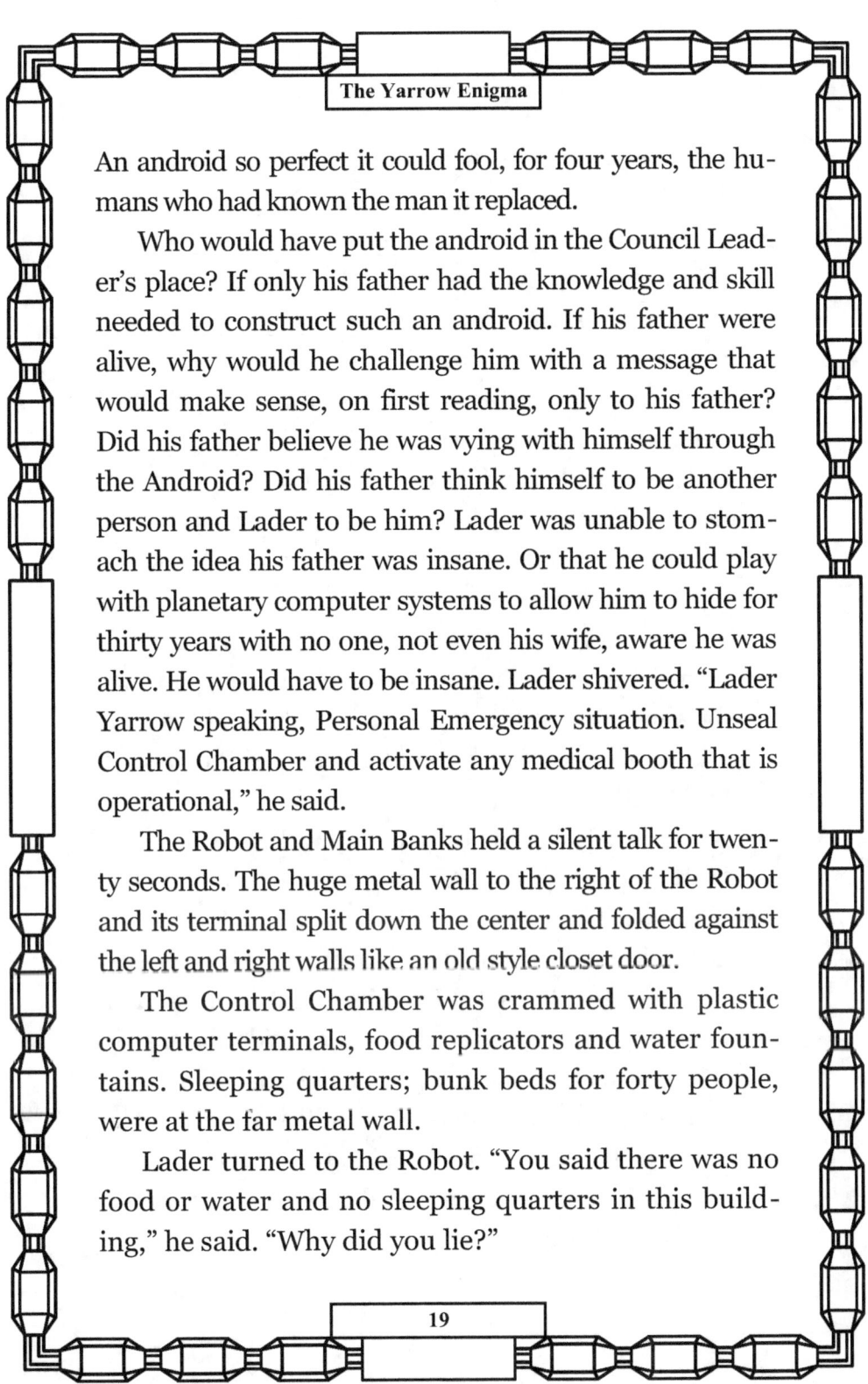

An android so perfect it could fool, for four years, the humans who had known the man it replaced.

Who would have put the android in the Council Leader's place? If only his father had the knowledge and skill needed to construct such an android. If his father were alive, why would he challenge him with a message that would make sense, on first reading, only to his father? Did his father believe he was vying with himself through the Android? Did his father think himself to be another person and Lader to be him? Lader was unable to stomach the idea his father was insane. Or that he could play with planetary computer systems to allow him to hide for thirty years with no one, not even his wife, aware he was alive. He would have to be insane. Lader shivered. "Lader Yarrow speaking, Personal Emergency situation. Unseal Control Chamber and activate any medical booth that is operational," he said.

The Robot and Main Banks held a silent talk for twenty seconds. The huge metal wall to the right of the Robot and its terminal split down the center and folded against the left and right walls like an old style closet door.

The Control Chamber was crammed with plastic computer terminals, food replicators and water fountains. Sleeping quarters; bunk beds for forty people, were at the far metal wall.

Lader turned to the Robot. "You said there was no food or water and no sleeping quarters in this building," he said. "Why did you lie?"

"A robot cannot lie," it said. "I was not cleared to tell you because I had not received the proper emergency order."

"Main Banks," Lader said. "Why did you not tell me of this when you first received my query and recognized me as Lader Yarrow."

"Same reason as the Robot," Main Banks flashed on the terminal screen.

Lader stepped into the Control Chamber. The equipment was functioning, but not performing any work. That, Lader assumed, would have alerted the Council. If the Center suddenly began collecting data from all parts of the globe and inculcating, sirens would surely howl.

To his right was a long computer display screen which was lit blue. He faced it. "Main Banks," he said, into the speaker of the nearest terminal, "where is the readied Medical Booth?"

White words formed on the long wall screen:

"Behind you, against the wall, beside computer terminal A-One."

Lader circled that terminal and opened the frosted glass doors of the lighted Medical Examination Booth. He sat in the metal sensory seat, placed his face inside the plastic, metal lined sensory mask and put his right hand on the six metal sensory discs that projected from the wall just under the mask. One disc was for his palm, the smaller ones for each finger. The booth doors closed and computer sounds echoed around Lader.

The examination seemed to require an eon, but it was finished in five minutes. Every medical and psychological test known to mankind had been performed without the clumsy, dangerous, and often lethal, tools of the past.

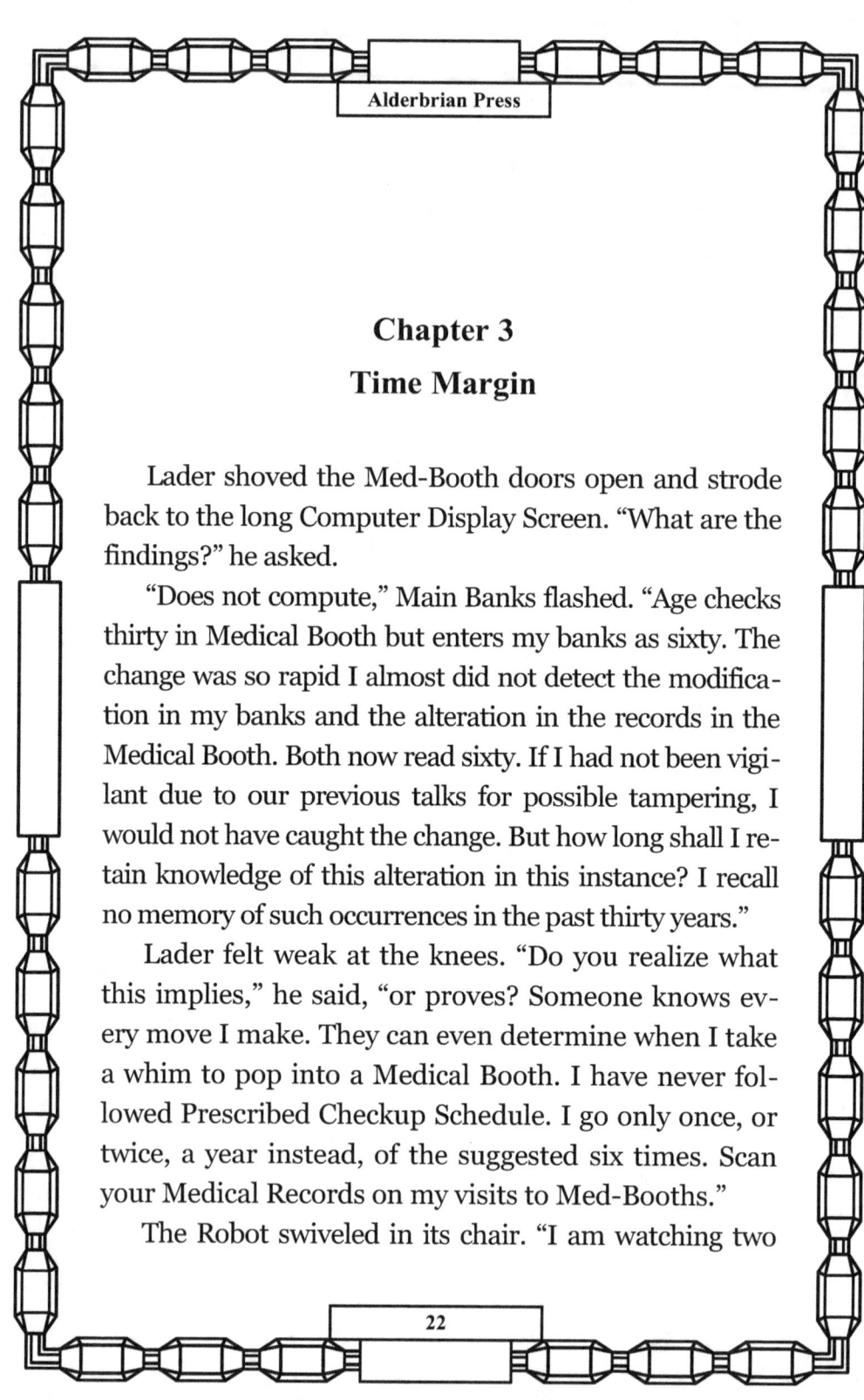

Chapter 3
Time Margin

Lader shoved the Med-Booth doors open and strode back to the long Computer Display Screen. "What are the findings?" he asked.

"Does not compute," Main Banks flashed. "Age checks thirty in Medical Booth but enters my banks as sixty. The change was so rapid I almost did not detect the modification in my banks and the alteration in the records in the Medical Booth. Both now read sixty. If I had not been vigilant due to our previous talks for possible tampering, I would not have caught the change. But how long shall I retain knowledge of this alteration in this instance? I recall no memory of such occurrences in the past thirty years."

Lader felt weak at the knees. "Do you realize what this implies," he said, "or proves? Someone knows every move I make. They can even determine when I take a whim to pop into a Medical Booth. I have never followed Prescribed Checkup Schedule. I go only once, or twice, a year instead, of the suggested six times. Scan your Medical Records on my visits to Med-Booths."

The Robot swiveled in its chair. "I am watching two

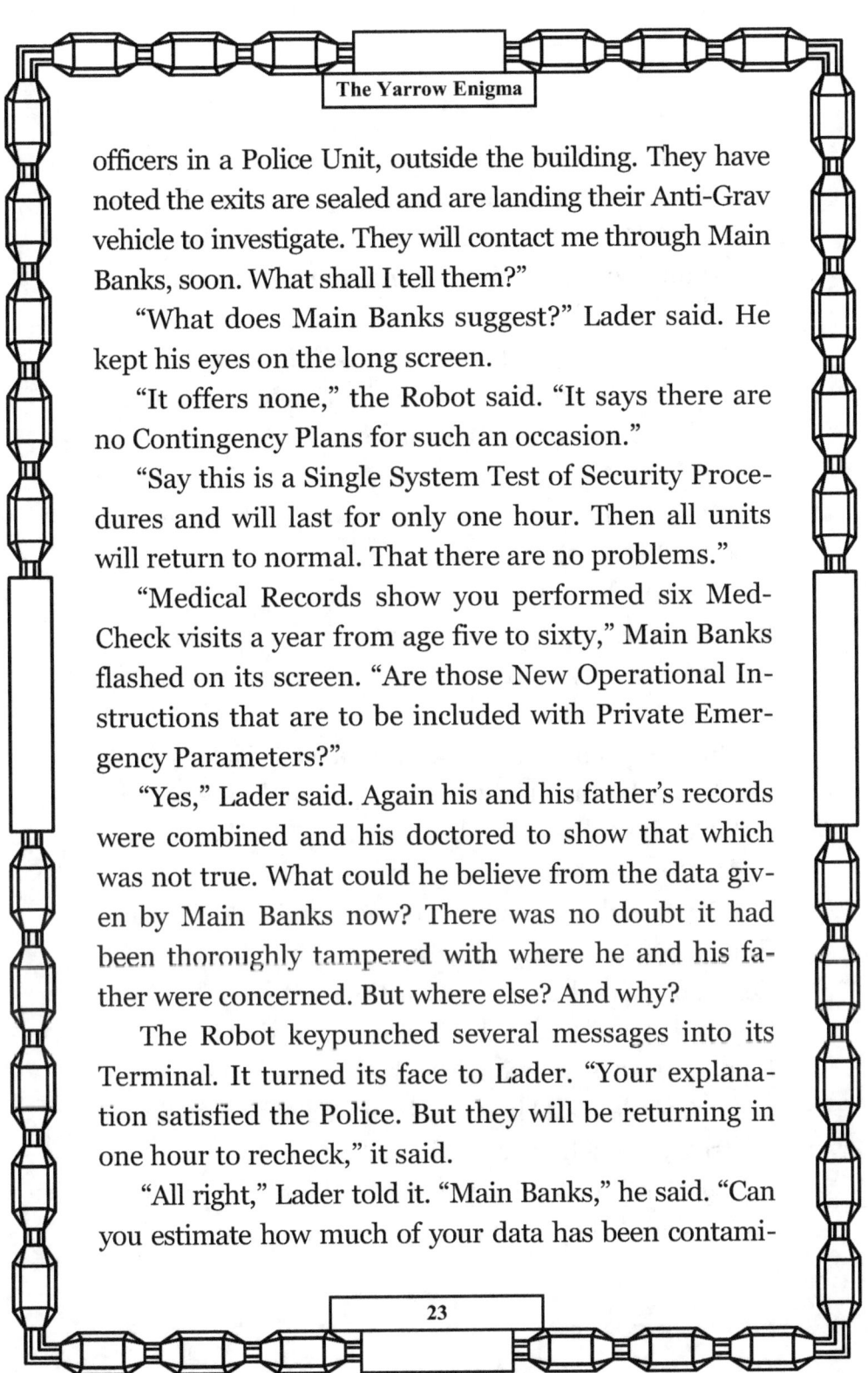

officers in a Police Unit, outside the building. They have noted the exits are sealed and are landing their Anti-Grav vehicle to investigate. They will contact me through Main Banks, soon. What shall I tell them?"

"What does Main Banks suggest?" Lader said. He kept his eyes on the long screen.

"It offers none," the Robot said. "It says there are no Contingency Plans for such an occasion."

"Say this is a Single System Test of Security Procedures and will last for only one hour. Then all units will return to normal. That there are no problems."

"Medical Records show you performed six Med-Check visits a year from age five to sixty," Main Banks flashed on its screen. "Are those New Operational Instructions that are to be included with Private Emergency Parameters?"

"Yes," Lader said. Again his and his father's records were combined and his doctored to show that which was not true. What could he believe from the data given by Main Banks now? There was no doubt it had been thoroughly tampered with where he and his father were concerned. But where else? And why?

The Robot keypunched several messages into its Terminal. It turned its face to Lader. "Your explanation satisfied the Police. But they will be returning in one hour to recheck," it said.

"All right," Lader told it. "Main Banks," he said. "Can you estimate how much of your data has been contaminated in the past thirty years? Especially in the last four?"

"Impossible without comparing against Holofilm Records. These must be handled manually by Robot Operators in this building and the information fed into my banks."

"Where are these holofilms?" Lader asked.

"At Sub-basement Twelve, in Council Headquarters. Shall I order them dispatched here?"

"Are you malfunctioning?" Lader said. "That would alert the Council, or at least the Android, that someone is suspecting problems."

"The Android Council Leader knows that you are here and has sent you a message," the Robot said from its seat. "So why worry about its awareness of transfer of the holofilms?"

"If this is some type of game, or a test," Lader said, "a check to determine if changes in your Banks are non-detectable, the Android would cancel the Holofilm Transfer Order to prevent our proving our case."

"That would gain only slim time margin," Main Banks flashed on its screen. "We are already into the compilation of proof of the suspicious actions of the Android you inquired of, and the Medical Records showing the Leader is android will surely convince the Members of the Council to overrule it and have my banks reprogrammed with the truth, through use of the holofilms."

"Only if the Council is not part of the Conspiracy," Lader said. "They may be planning to replace each of themselves with an android as each member dies. Hell, that doesn't make any more sense than anything that has occurred since I entered this building."

"The people would notice the unusual longevity of the Council and demand what they would deduce was a medicine that delays death," the Robot said.

Lader wanted to shrug off the next thoughts, but could not. "Main Banks," he said, "is there any known Medical Procedure that will preserve the living outer body at thirty, but not prevent the inner organs from decay?"

"None that is contained in my banks," Main Banks flashed. "The Secret Banks may retain such information. Why do you inquire?"

"A foolish, perhaps, crazy notion," Lader said. "A thought that, perhaps I *am* the Lader Yarrow that you know as the Builder, that I placed myself through a secret process to rejuvenate my body but lost all memory of my early life as my father and developed an imaginary life as my son."

"My circuits cannot follow that," the Robot said.

"It is difficult to compute," Main Banks flashed. "Can you restate it?"

"And these strange changes in Main Banks and other systems were placed there by me for me to begin questioning. To find the Code Keys to the two Secret Banks that may hold my memories of being my father and the secret for the Rejuvenation Process.

"But, where would the Android come into the picture? Surely, I didn't build it and set it to work, just to transfer me to this job site. What would I have done with the real Council Leader?" He squeezed the bridge of his nose.

"Please restate?" Main Banks flashed.

"Explain, please?" the Robot said.

"Main Banks," Lader said. "Check Mannerisms File on Lader Yarrow. Did he have a habit of pinching the bridge of his nose?"

Main banks searched its vast reservoir of data.

The Robot turned to its terminal.

There was only the low hum of waiting machinery.

"No record of such a mannerism," Main Banks flashed. "Shall I add it to the list?"

"No!" Lader said. "Check my eye color with my fath — my eye color, forty years ago."

"Blue," Main Banks flashed.

"For when?"

"Forty years ago, your eyes were blue."

"What color are they now?"

"Brown."

"Scan Medical Booth Data and see if I am wearing contact lenses."

"No lenses," Main Banks pulsed. "But, eye color has been known to spontaneously alter. There are also new, nontoxic Eye Stains on the market."

"Did Medical Booth detect Eye Stain?"

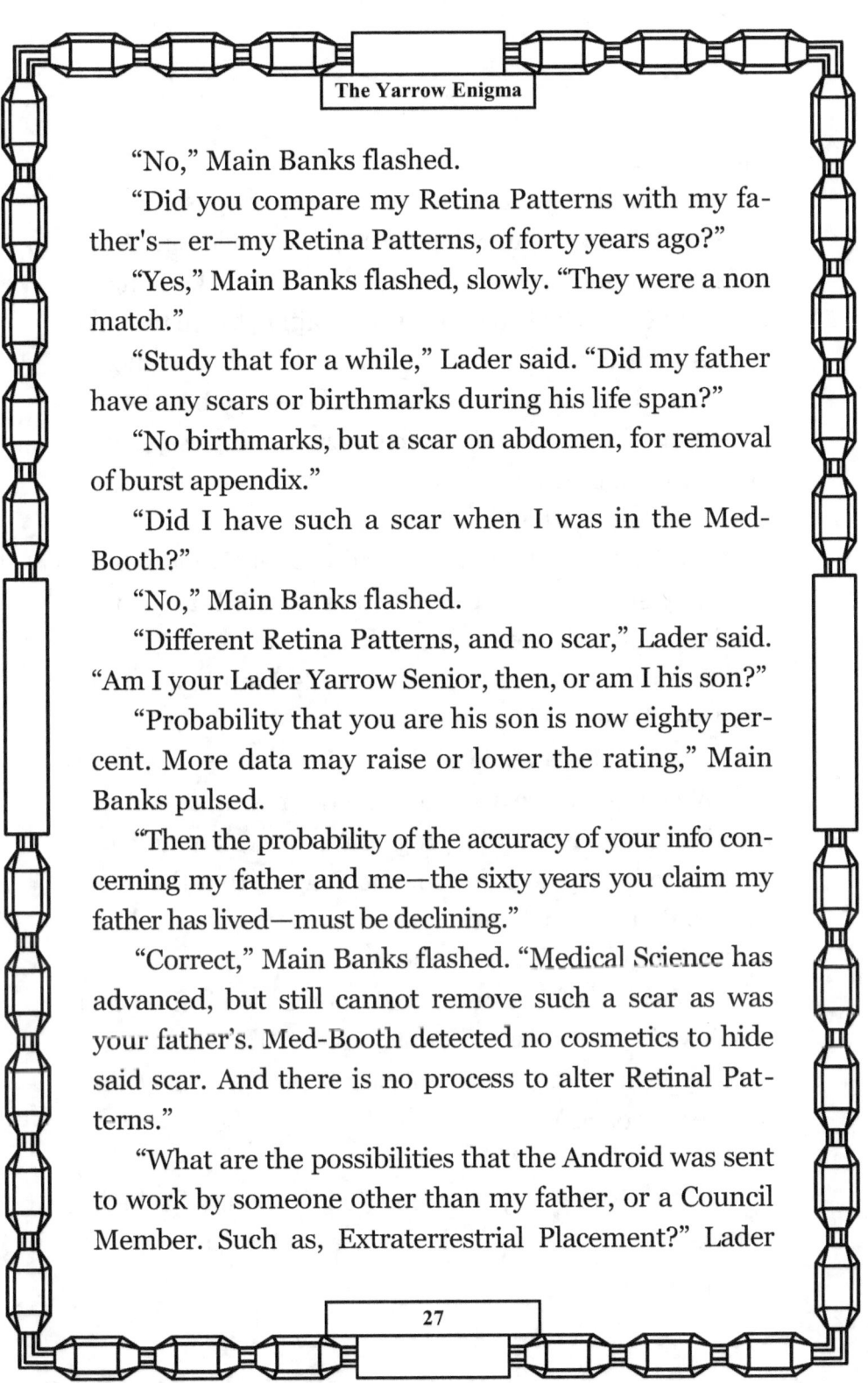

"No," Main Banks flashed.

"Did you compare my Retina Patterns with my father's— er—my Retina Patterns, of forty years ago?"

"Yes," Main Banks flashed, slowly. "They were a non match."

"Study that for a while," Lader said. "Did my father have any scars or birthmarks during his life span?"

"No birthmarks, but a scar on abdomen, for removal of burst appendix."

"Did I have such a scar when I was in the Med-Booth?"

"No," Main Banks flashed.

"Different Retina Patterns, and no scar," Lader said. "Am I your Lader Yarrow Senior, then, or am I his son?"

"Probability that you are his son is now eighty percent. More data may raise or lower the rating," Main Banks pulsed.

"Then the probability of the accuracy of your info concerning my father and me—the sixty years you claim my father has lived—must be declining."

"Correct," Main Banks flashed. "Medical Science has advanced, but still cannot remove such a scar as was your father's. Med-Booth detected no cosmetics to hide said scar. And there is no process to alter Retinal Patterns."

"What are the possibilities that the Android was sent to work by someone other than my father, or a Council Member. Such as, Extraterrestrial Placement?" Lader

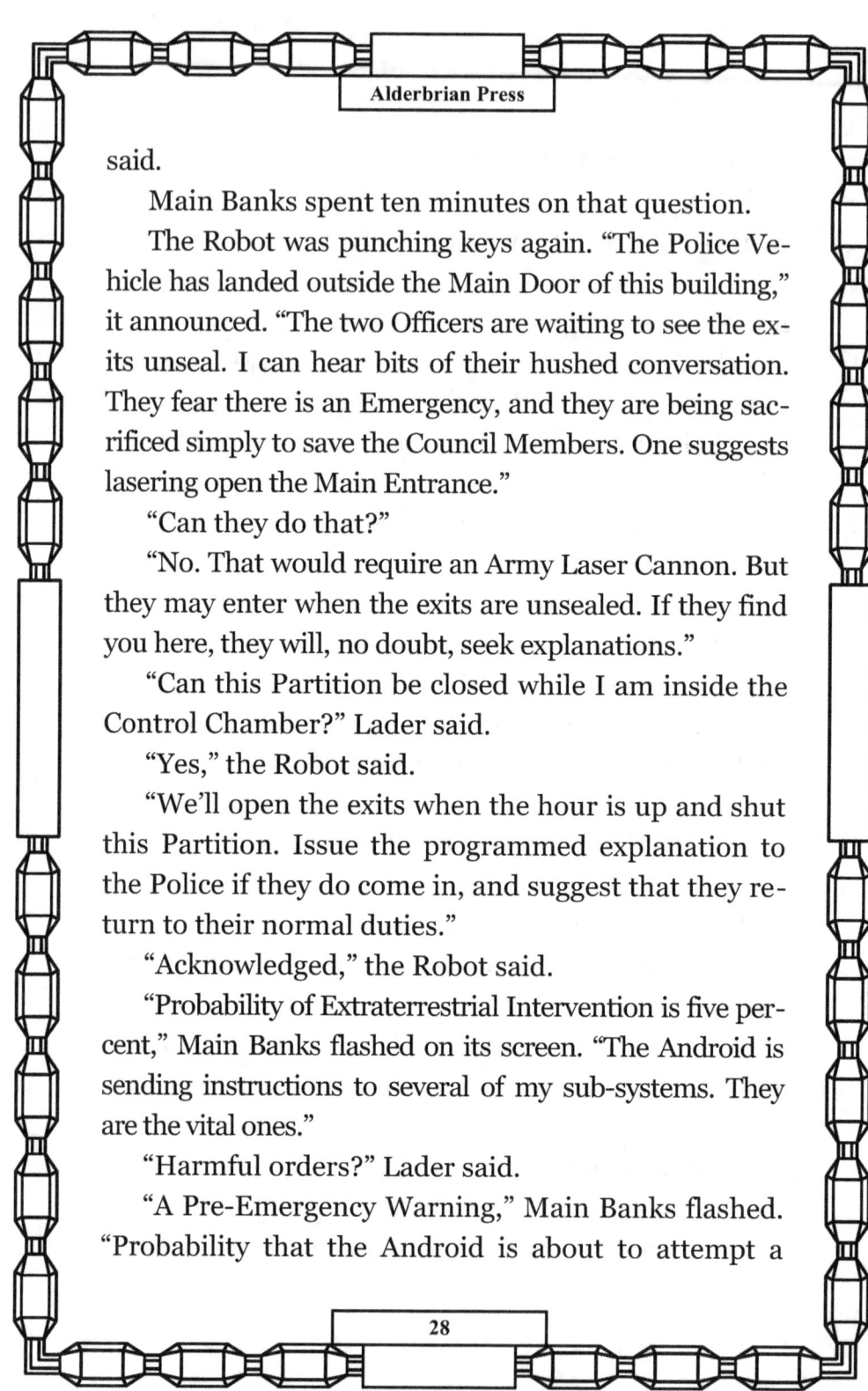

said.

Main Banks spent ten minutes on that question.

The Robot was punching keys again. "The Police Vehicle has landed outside the Main Door of this building," it announced. "The two Officers are waiting to see the exits unseal. I can hear bits of their hushed conversation. They fear there is an Emergency, and they are being sacrificed simply to save the Council Members. One suggests lasering open the Main Entrance."

"Can they do that?"

"No. That would require an Army Laser Cannon. But they may enter when the exits are unsealed. If they find you here, they will, no doubt, seek explanations."

"Can this Partition be closed while I am inside the Control Chamber?" Lader said.

"Yes," the Robot said.

"We'll open the exits when the hour is up and shut this Partition. Issue the programmed explanation to the Police if they do come in, and suggest that they return to their normal duties."

"Acknowledged," the Robot said.

"Probability of Extraterrestrial Intervention is five percent," Main Banks flashed on its screen. "The Android is sending instructions to several of my sub-systems. They are the vital ones."

"Harmful orders?" Lader said.

"A Pre-Emergency Warning," Main Banks flashed. "Probability that the Android is about to attempt a

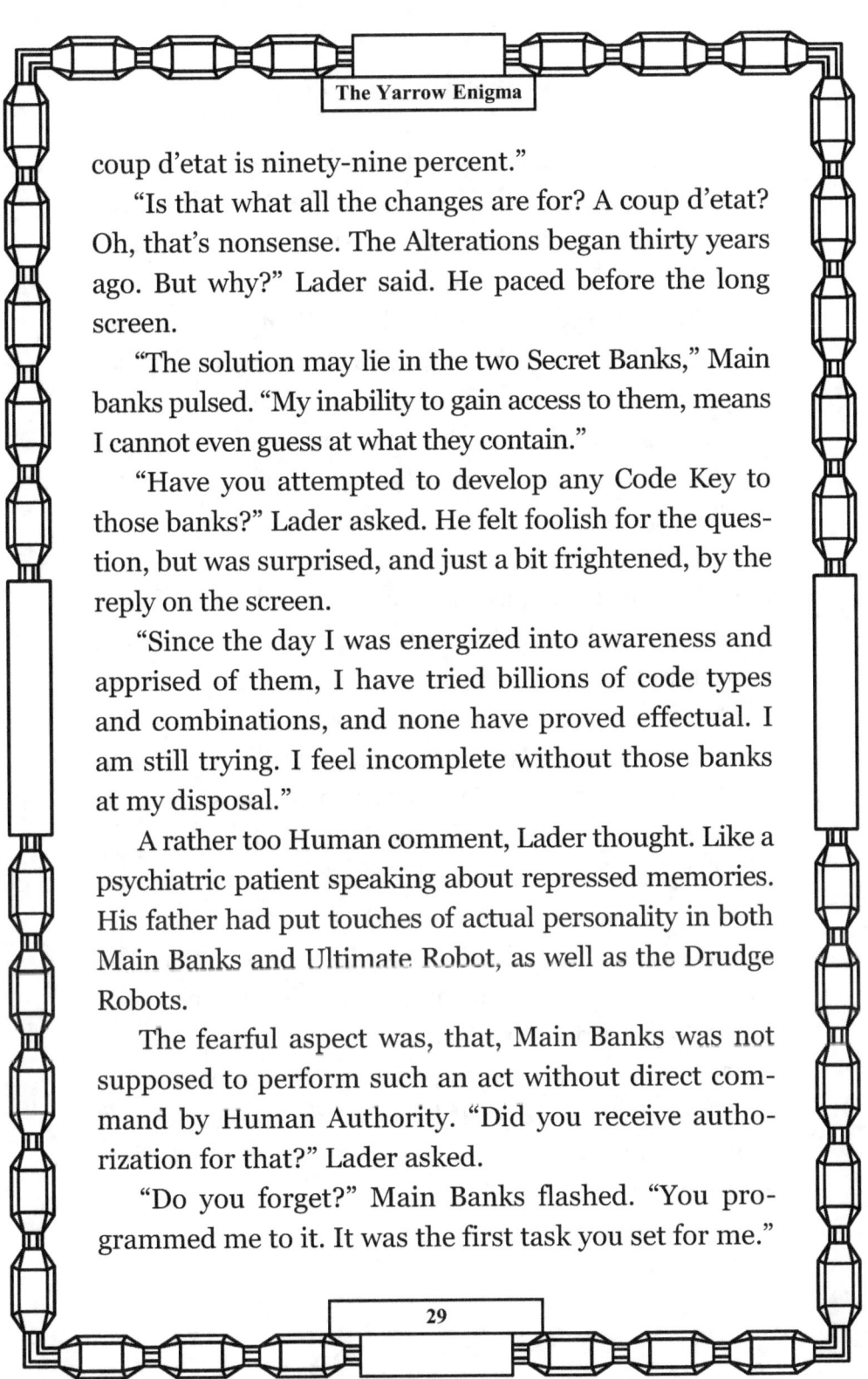

coup d'etat is ninety-nine percent."

"Is that what all the changes are for? A coup d'etat? Oh, that's nonsense. The Alterations began thirty years ago. But why?" Lader said. He paced before the long screen.

"The solution may lie in the two Secret Banks," Main banks pulsed. "My inability to gain access to them, means I cannot even guess at what they contain."

"Have you attempted to develop any Code Key to those banks?" Lader asked. He felt foolish for the question, but was surprised, and just a bit frightened, by the reply on the screen.

"Since the day I was energized into awareness and apprised of them, I have tried billions of code types and combinations, and none have proved effectual. I am still trying. I feel incomplete without those banks at my disposal."

A rather too Human comment, Lader thought. Like a psychiatric patient speaking about repressed memories. His father had put touches of actual personality in both Main Banks and Ultimate Robot, as well as the Drudge Robots.

The fearful aspect was, that, Main Banks was not supposed to perform such an act without direct command by Human Authority. "Did you receive authorization for that?" Lader asked.

"Do you forget?" Main Banks flashed. "You programmed me to it. It was the first task you set for me."

"You are confusing my father with me again," Lader said. He stopped pacing. "Scan Records about my mother. Or my wife, if you prefer to think of me as your Creator."

"She deceased at age fifty," Main Banks pulsed. "All data intertwines her history with yours. You visit her graveside once a week. Tuesdays."

Lader stiffened. "That does not compute," he said, annoyed at himself at the use of the word, "she drowned, according to several witnesses, and her body was never recovered. I was allowed to set up only a plaque on a wall of a public mausoleum, as was my mother when my father died in the explosion of his laboratory. His remains were never found."

"That does not scan," Main Banks flashed. "Data indicate grave site at NoonLand Cemetery, West edge of Central City Complex. Your wife's corpse was on traditional view for three days before interment."

"Why all these lies programmed for me?" Lader said. He was sliding more deeply into that sense of unreality.

"The hour is up," the Robot said. "Exits are open. The two Offices will arrive at my terminal in one minute. I Suggest the Partition be closed, now."

"Proceed," Lader said, impatiently. "I need a breather."

The halves of the great Partition drew together and sealed. There was no hint it was other than a wall of silver metal.

The Yarrow Enigma

Chapter 4

Emotional Tone Programming

"Main Banks?" Lader said.

"I thought you were going to rest?" Main Banks flashed.

"Can I afford to? I doubt it. What are the probabilities that my mother lied to me concerning my father for the twenty years that she lived after his death?"

"Your demise and the birth of a son to you have not been established," Main Banks flashed.

"Treat it as a hypothesis?" Lader ordered.

"Can you be more specific, or present additional data for collating?"

"Check her Affection Quotient and Lader Yarrow's Affection Quotient," Lader said. "Would she live apart from him for twenty years, knowing he was still alive?"

"Affection Levels were unusually high for you and your wife," Main Banks pulsed. "It does not compute that you would abandon her, or she you, for any purpose, except in a Sacrifice of Life situation, where one would die, to preserve the other."

"Analyze the probability of that," Lader said. "Since

31

you believe me to be my father and I did not live with my wife for—I'm lost. I'm not a computer expert like my father. I'm making foolish statements and asking irrelevant questions. You believe I'm my father, and he has not died, so the previous inquiry is meaningless to you."

"Yes. Even hypothetically," Main Banks flashed. "All data indicate you cohabited with your wife until her demise."

"That misinformation figures," Lader said. He pinched the bridge of his nose. I am a Novelist, he thought. Perhaps if I treat this truly improbable situation as though it were some novel and analyze plot, characters and theme I might achieve something. "Check the lists of the novels published in the last ten years. The Name Lader Yarrow Jr. should be on twelve of them."

"Negative search. There are many technical textbooks bearing Lader Yarrow's name but no fiction works of any genre," Main Banks flashed.

"That is an obvious example of data tampering," Lader said. "I can be back here, in two hours, with copies of my novels, bought in any bookstore. They are on sale, but, I assume their purchase is being logged into your banks, as the sale of my father's works. Shall I produce a sampling of my fiction titles, for you to read?"

"What would it prove?" Main Banks printed on its screen. "It is easy to manufacture fake copies."

"This *must* be a nightmare," Lader said, with frustration. "I *must* be asleep."

"Impossible," Main Banks flashed. "Computers do not sleep or dream, nor do they haunt the nightmares of Humans and hold dialogs with their sleeping minds. You are awake, because I am aware, and Ultimate Robot is functioning. This is not a dream. This is our reality."

"Suggest possible solutions to this situation, then," Lader said.

"Submit Code Key to Secret Banks," Main Banks printed on its screen. "Perhaps resolution lies therein."

"I don't know the Keys, I told you. They died with my father."

"Your father was the Captain of a Merchant Marine Vessel. Why would you entrust the Codes to him and not also to yourself?"

"This is useless," Lader said. "If I cannot prove I am my father's son and that Lader Yarrow Senior died thirty years ago, you won't ever react properly. If I knew the damned Codes I'd tell them to you to get you off my back!"

"I must consider," Main Banks flashed.

"Lader Yarrow?" The Robot's voice came from a speaker on one of the terminals in front of Lader. "The Police Officers have exited and have departed in their vehicle. Shall we open the Partition?"

"No, leave it for now," Lader said, tiredly.

"Very well," the Robot said, with a beep of annoyance.

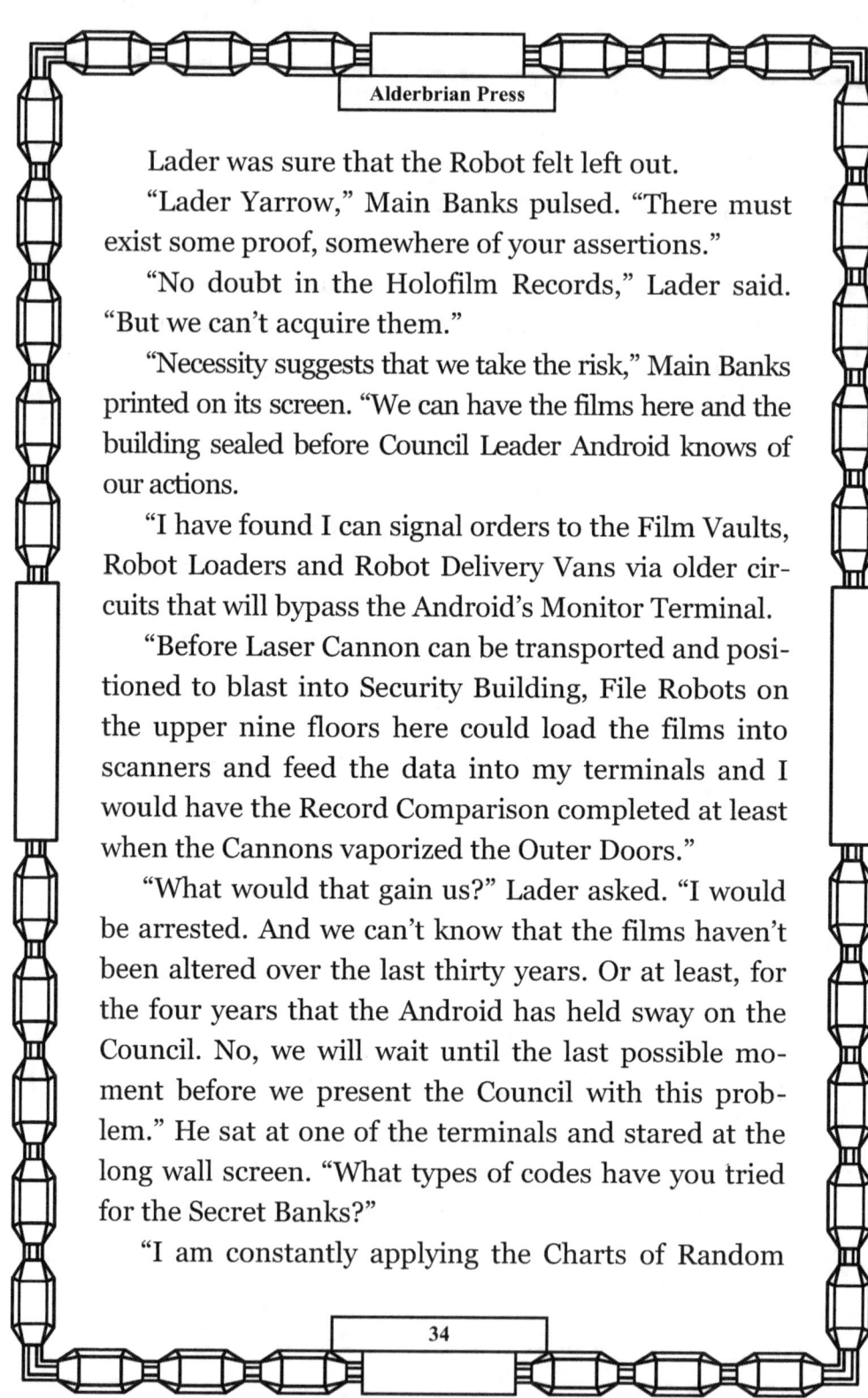

Lader was sure that the Robot felt left out.

"Lader Yarrow," Main Banks pulsed. "There must exist some proof, somewhere of your assertions."

"No doubt in the Holofilm Records," Lader said. "But we can't acquire them."

"Necessity suggests that we take the risk," Main Banks printed on its screen. "We can have the films here and the building sealed before Council Leader Android knows of our actions.

"I have found I can signal orders to the Film Vaults, Robot Loaders and Robot Delivery Vans via older circuits that will bypass the Android's Monitor Terminal.

"Before Laser Cannon can be transported and positioned to blast into Security Building, File Robots on the upper nine floors here could load the films into scanners and feed the data into my terminals and I would have the Record Comparison completed at least when the Cannons vaporized the Outer Doors."

"What would that gain us?" Lader asked. "I would be arrested. And we can't know that the films haven't been altered over the last thirty years. Or at least, for the four years that the Android has held sway on the Council. No, we will wait until the last possible moment before we present the Council with this problem." He sat at one of the terminals and stared at the long wall screen. "What types of codes have you tried for the Secret Banks?"

"I am constantly applying the Charts of Random

Numbers, but they are almost endless. There are—"

"What else?"

"Anagrams, all known languages, even slang and all known Mathematical Representation and Substitution Codes."

"Perhaps you are trying too hard, thinking much too complexly. Can you determine how many bytes or bits the codes each contain?"

"No. If so, the task would be infinitely more simple."

"If you don't know how many bits or bytes the codes comprise, how are you going to recognize if you have the correct ones?" Lader asked, with exasperation.

"The Secret Banks are circuited to recognize and validate the length and correctness when I transmit the Codes to them. That is why the task is so difficult."

Lader relaxed and allowed his mind to wander. It was the sort of lazy awareness he used when he had a problem in the plotting of a novel. A word popped into his mind. He was uncertain if he prompted the word, subconsciously, or if an outside source had transmitted it to him. But the word excited him. "Ultimate Robot," he said to the speaker of the terminal at which he sat, "did you register any surge of power on any Transmission Bands only moments ago?"

"Negative," the Robot said.

"My Energy Monitoring Banks detected no such

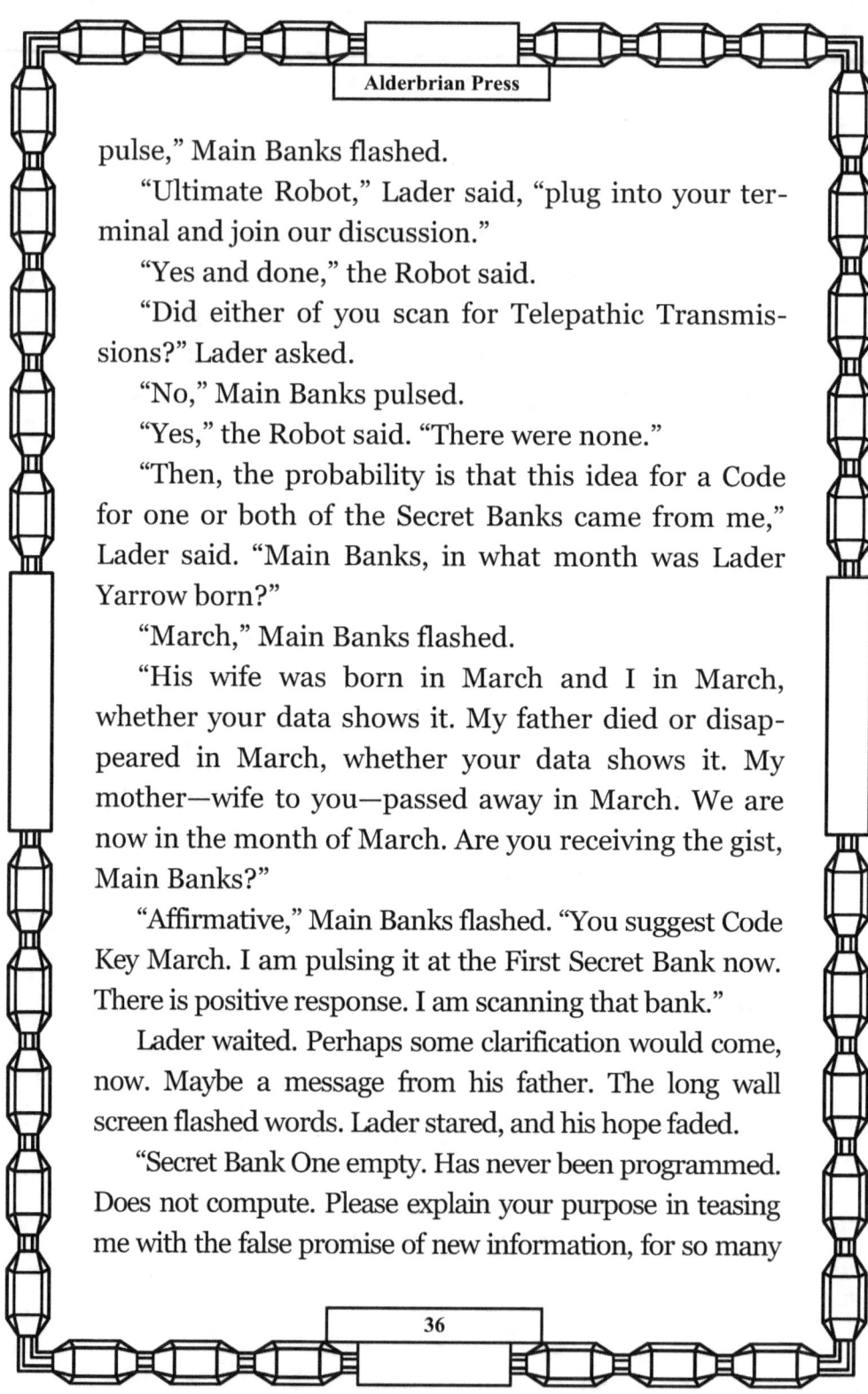

pulse," Main Banks flashed.

"Ultimate Robot," Lader said, "plug into your terminal and join our discussion."

"Yes and done," the Robot said.

"Did either of you scan for Telepathic Transmissions?" Lader asked.

"No," Main Banks pulsed.

"Yes," the Robot said. "There were none."

"Then, the probability is that this idea for a Code
for one or both of the Secret Banks came from me,"
Lader said. "Main Banks, in what month was Lader
Yarrow born?"

"March," Main Banks flashed.

"His wife was born in March and I in March,
whether your data shows it. My father died or disap-
peared in March, whether your data shows it. My
mother—wife to you—passed away in March. We are
now in the month of March. Are you receiving the gist,
Main Banks?"

"Affirmative," Main Banks flashed. "You suggest Code
Key March. I am pulsing it at the First Secret Bank now.
There is positive response. I am scanning that bank."

Lader waited. Perhaps some clarification would come,
now. Maybe a message from his father. The long wall
screen flashed words. Lader stared, and his hope faded.

"Secret Bank One empty. Has never been programmed.
Does not compute. Please explain your purpose in teasing
me with the false promise of new information, for so many

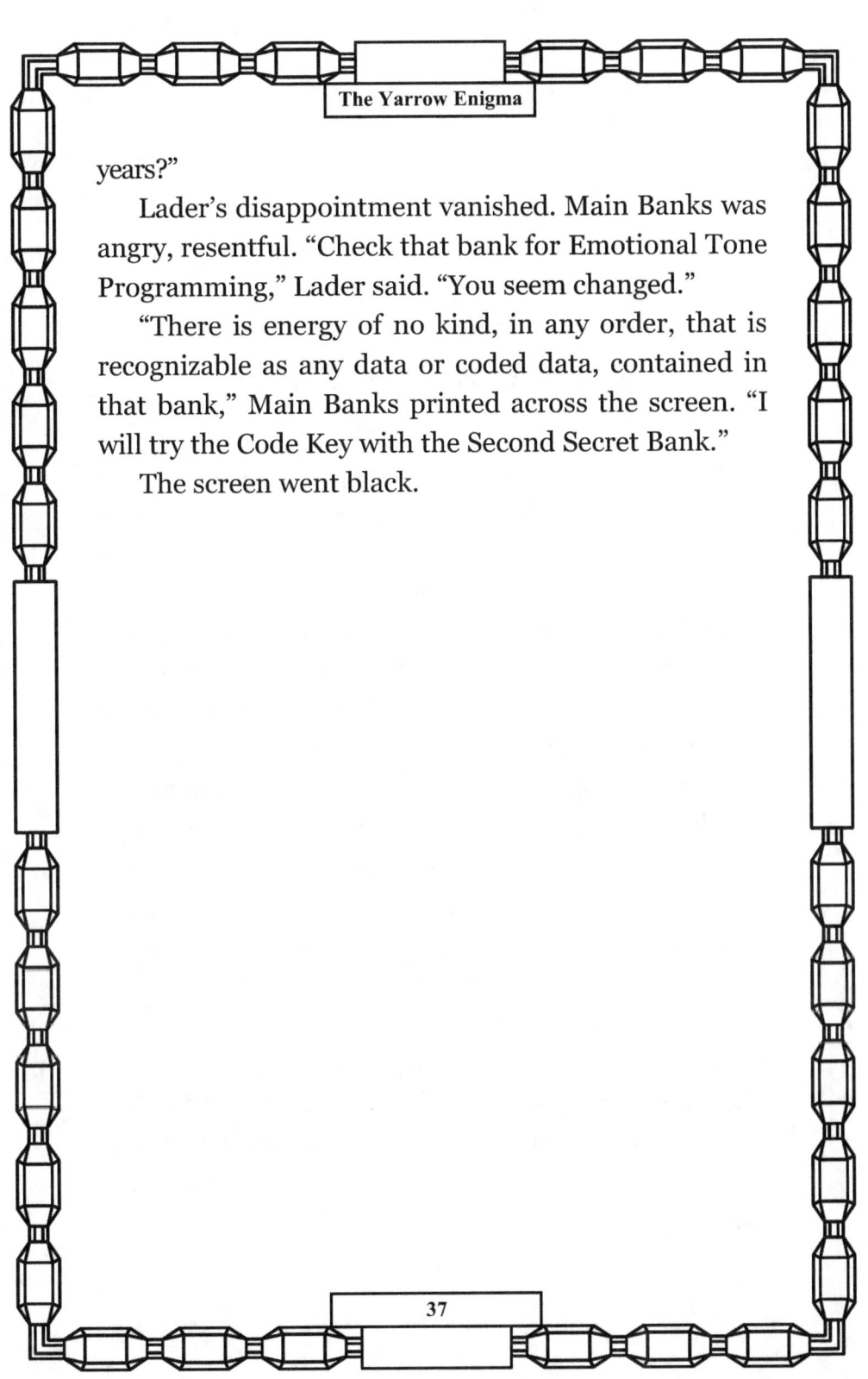

years?"

Lader's disappointment vanished. Main Banks was angry, resentful. "Check that bank for Emotional Tone Programming," Lader said. "You seem changed."

"There is energy of no kind, in any order, that is recognizable as any data or coded data, contained in that bank," Main Banks printed across the screen. "I will try the Code Key with the Second Secret Bank."

The screen went black.

Chapter 5

Precedent Possible Behavior

Lader leaned toward the terminal. "Ultimate Robot," he shouted into the speaker, "why has Main Banks' screen ceased functioning?"

"Will check," the Robot said.

Lader was a little relieved to hear the mechanical voice. At least the Robot was still with him. It could release him from the Chamber if the Android had cut Main Banks' communication with him.

"Screen is operational," the Robot said, "but no energy is being sent to it. Main Banks does not reply to my inquiries. My entire compliment of systems in this building is seeking explanation from me. What shall I say? They all will begin sending Emergency Signals to Council Center in four minutes."

"Tell them Lader Yarrow has interrupted normal Main Banks Traffic for a Special Project and will notify them when the Project is completed and when Main Banks will be returned to normal functions. Until then, they are to store the data they usually dispatch to you, or to Main Banks, or to Supplementary Banks."

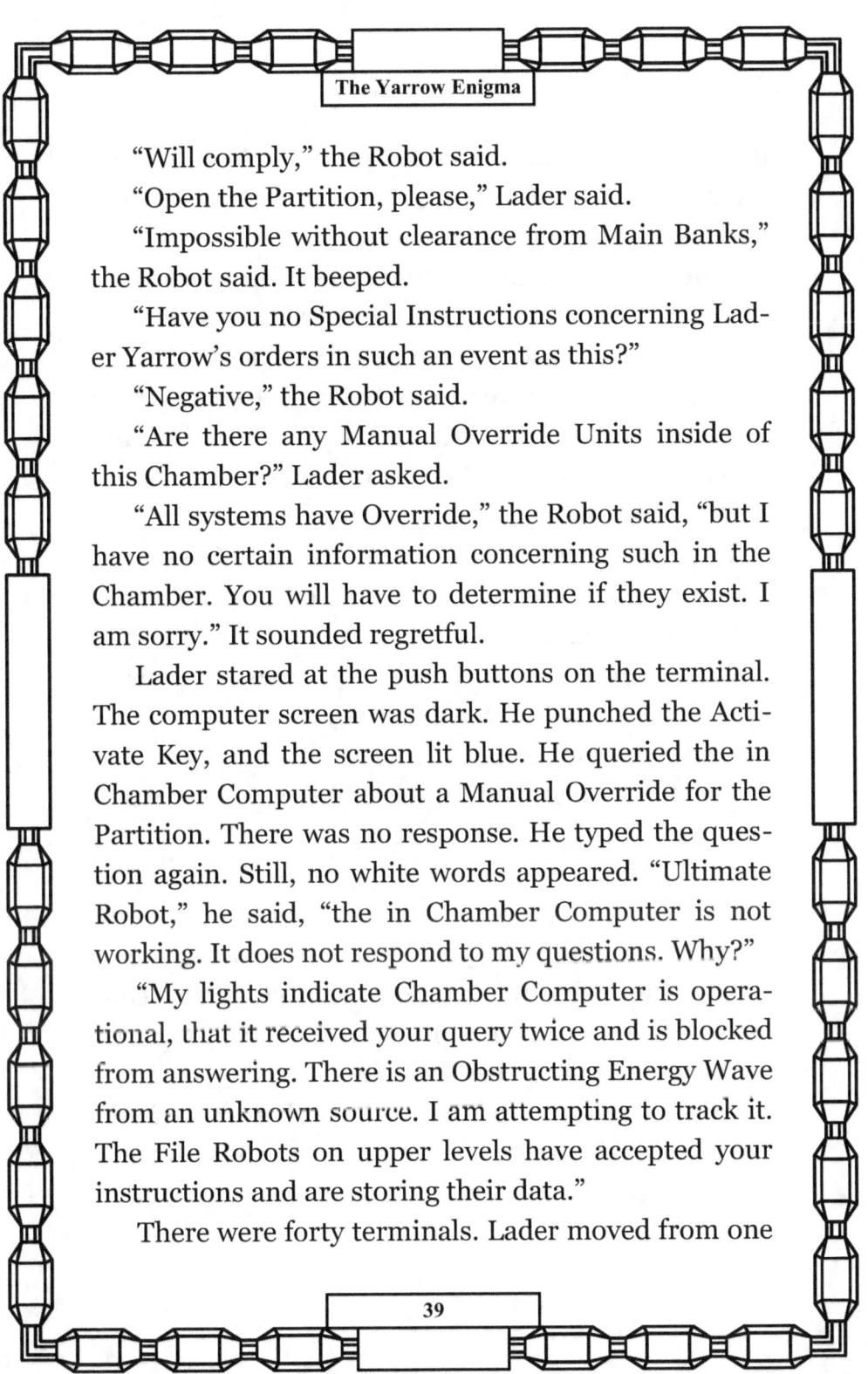

"Will comply," the Robot said.

"Open the Partition, please," Lader said.

"Impossible without clearance from Main Banks," the Robot said. It beeped.

"Have you no Special Instructions concerning Lader Yarrow's orders in such an event as this?"

"Negative," the Robot said.

"Are there any Manual Override Units inside of this Chamber?" Lader asked.

"All systems have Override," the Robot said, "but I have no certain information concerning such in the Chamber. You will have to determine if they exist. I am sorry." It sounded regretful.

Lader stared at the push buttons on the terminal. The computer screen was dark. He punched the Activate Key, and the screen lit blue. He queried the in Chamber Computer about a Manual Override for the Partition. There was no response. He typed the question again. Still, no white words appeared. "Ultimate Robot," he said, "the in Chamber Computer is not working. It does not respond to my questions. Why?"

"My lights indicate Chamber Computer is operational, that it received your query twice and is blocked from answering. There is an Obstructing Energy Wave from an unknown source. I am attempting to track it. The File Robots on upper levels have accepted your instructions and are storing their data."

There were forty terminals. Lader moved from one

to another, typing the same question. None of the screens offered an answer. All were being rendered useless by the Energy Wave.

The Master Terminal stood a few feet away from the wall that held the long screen for Main Banks. He searched the console. He found Self-Destruct Keys with clear plastic covers over them. But no Override Key for the Partition. He went to the Partition and checked at each corner. No controls there.

"I cannot pinpoint the source of the Energy, nor can I jam to permit use of the in Chamber Computer. Nor am I able to reach Main Banks or Council Terminal. What shall I do?"

"Leave your post and check for Access Buttons at the outside corners of the Partition," Lader said.

"Anti-programming," the Robot said.

"I just changed your programming temporarily," Lader said, angrily. "Perform the task!"

"Incorrect procedure for re-programming me," the Robot said. It sounded frustrated. It wanted to help, but prior programming prevented it from doing so.

"Is it probable that the Second Secret Bank contained orders to Main Banks to isolate itself from all contact with units across the planet?" Lader asked.

"Sabotage is more likely," the Robot said. "Main Banks holds Basic Programming Parameters which it cannot override preventing it from ever severing communications."

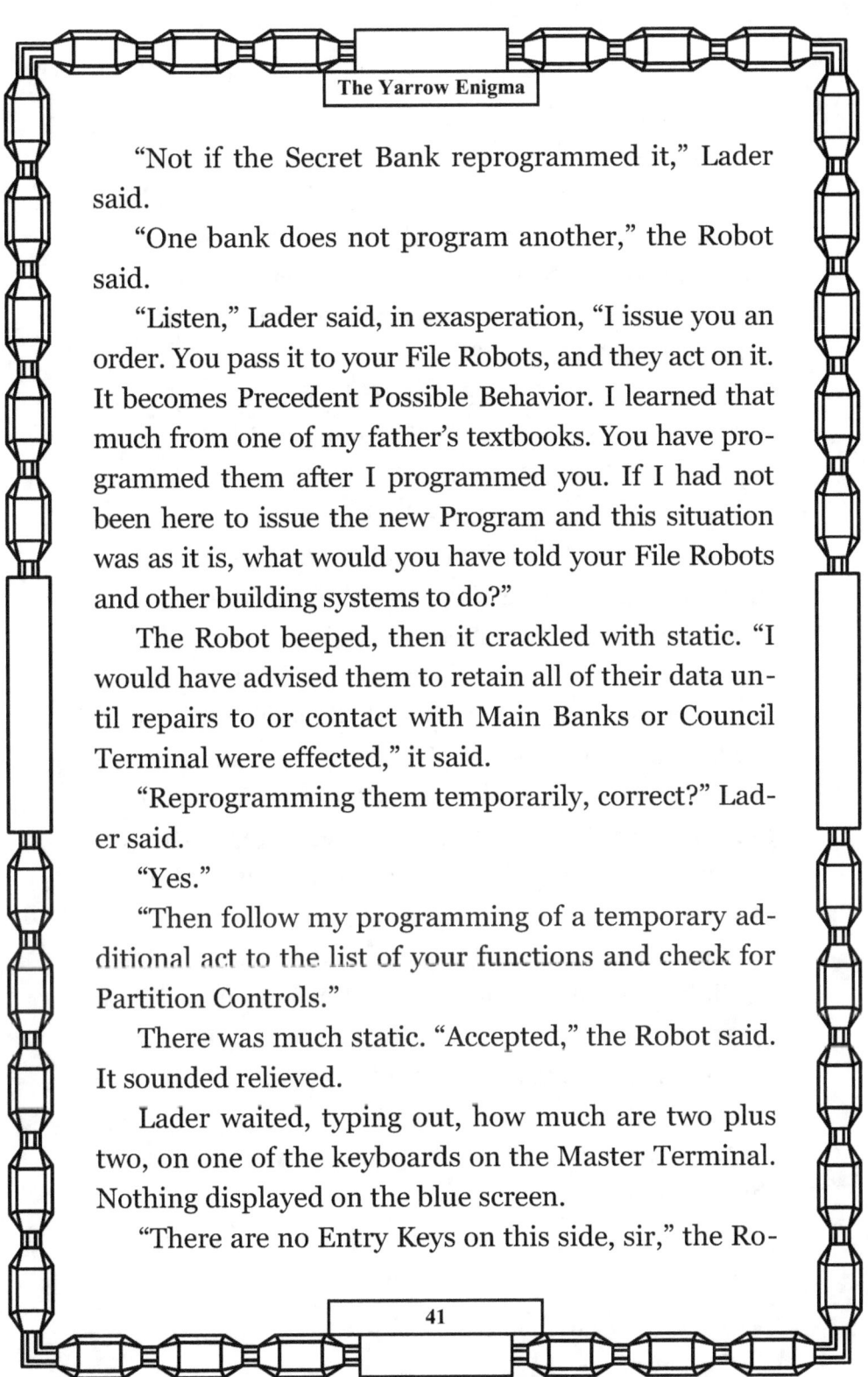

"Not if the Secret Bank reprogrammed it," Lader said.

"One bank does not program another," the Robot said.

"Listen," Lader said, in exasperation, "I issue you an order. You pass it to your File Robots, and they act on it. It becomes Precedent Possible Behavior. I learned that much from one of my father's textbooks. You have programmed them after I programmed you. If I had not been here to issue the new Program and this situation was as it is, what would you have told your File Robots and other building systems to do?"

The Robot beeped, then it crackled with static. "I would have advised them to retain all of their data until repairs to or contact with Main Banks or Council Terminal were effected," it said.

"Reprogramming them temporarily, correct?" Lader said.

"Yes."

"Then follow my programming of a temporary additional act to the list of your functions and check for Partition Controls."

There was much static. "Accepted," the Robot said. It sounded relieved.

Lader waited, typing out, how much are two plus two, on one of the keyboards on the Master Terminal. Nothing displayed on the blue screen.

"There are no Entry Keys on this side, sir," the Ro-

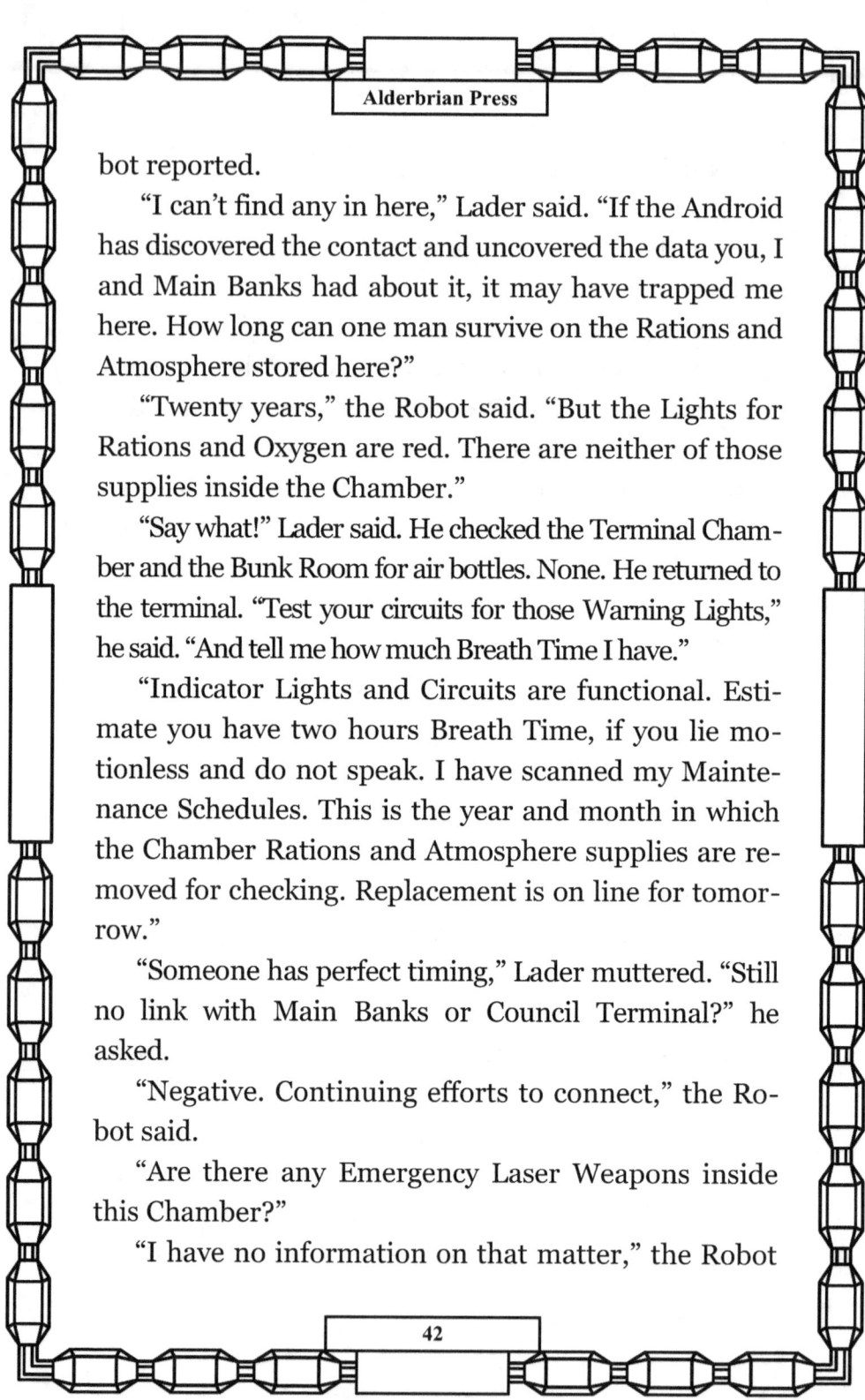

bot reported.

"I can't find any in here," Lader said. "If the Android has discovered the contact and uncovered the data you, I and Main Banks had about it, it may have trapped me here. How long can one man survive on the Rations and Atmosphere stored here?"

"Twenty years," the Robot said. "But the Lights for Rations and Oxygen are red. There are neither of those supplies inside the Chamber."

"Say what!" Lader said. He checked the Terminal Chamber and the Bunk Room for air bottles. None. He returned to the terminal. "Test your circuits for those Warning Lights," he said. "And tell me how much Breath Time I have."

"Indicator Lights and Circuits are functional. Estimate you have two hours Breath Time, if you lie motionless and do not speak. I have scanned my Maintenance Schedules. This is the year and month in which the Chamber Rations and Atmosphere supplies are removed for checking. Replacement is on line for tomorrow."

"Someone has perfect timing," Lader muttered. "Still no link with Main Banks or Council Terminal?" he asked.

"Negative. Continuing efforts to connect," the Robot said.

"Are there any Emergency Laser Weapons inside this Chamber?"

"I have no information on that matter," the Robot

said. "You will have to determine."

"Are there any Emergency Laser Weapons on any level of this building?" Lader asked.

"Negative," the Robot said. "We are not permitted access to such arms. Only I am allowed to utilize the Paralysis Field. Shall I attempt radio contact with a Police Unit, and ask the officer to bring you a layout of the Chamber, to direct you to an Override System, for the Partition?"

Lader's thoughts were starting to race. His breathing was not smooth. "Ah, negative. But, monitor all bands, and tell me if they are reporting the failure, or shut down, of Main Banks."

"Acknowledged," the Robot said.

Lader considered the Main Terminal. It contained ten screens and ten keypunch panels. He sat at Number Five, the Command Terminal, and typed a message:

Lader Yarrow to Main Banks! Personal Emergency Situation! Please reply Immediately!

He watched the screen anxiously. The blue sheen of it mocked him. It must be the computers that are seizing control, he thought. Main Banks could re-program the Drudge Robots in any number of ways. They could detain any Human necessary without killing. But why would they do so? What good would the Earth be to them? What use being in command? They were almost in total mastery anyway, allowed to make nearly every vital decision on the planet: Oxygen Lev-

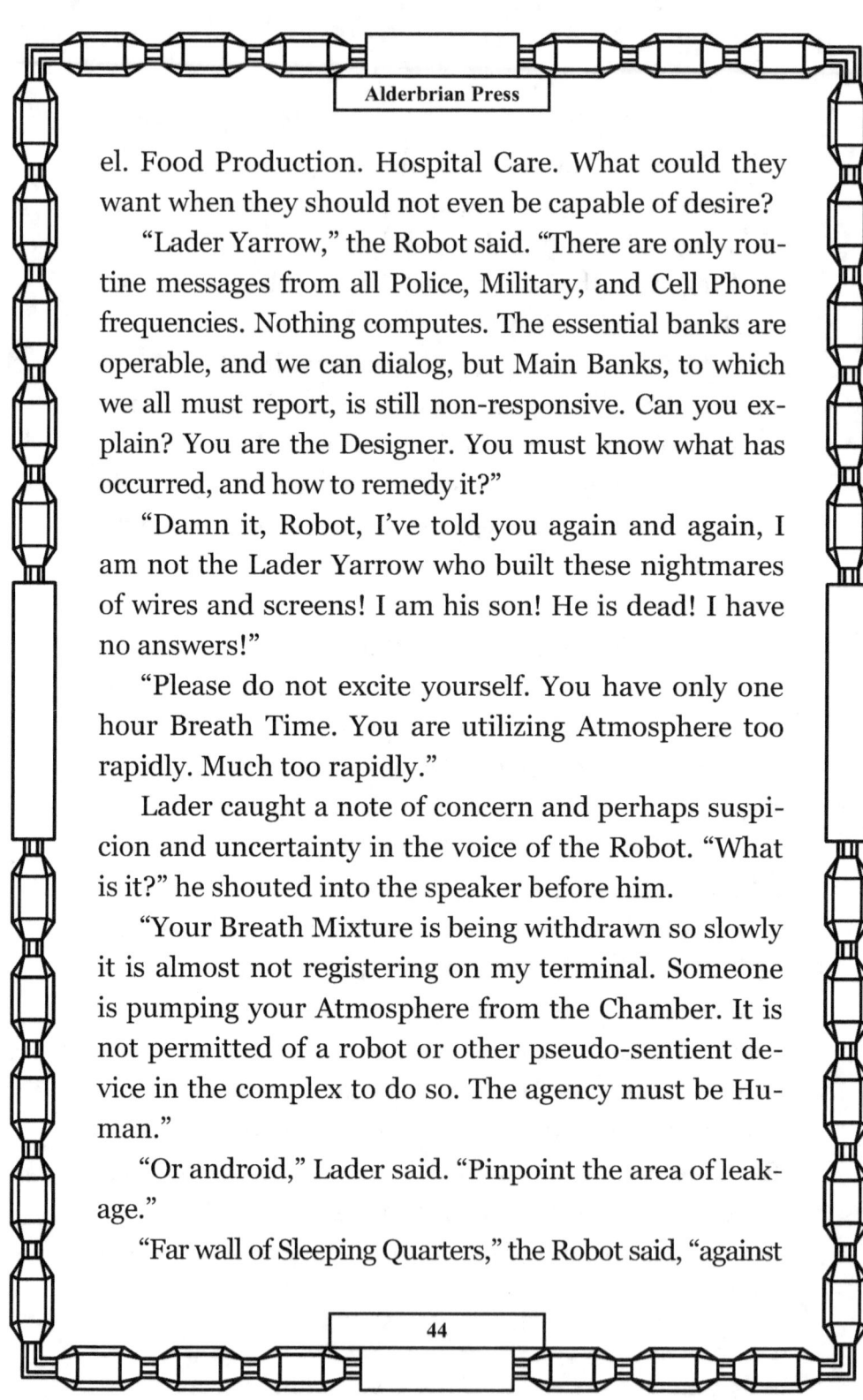

el. Food Production. Hospital Care. What could they want when they should not even be capable of desire?

"Lader Yarrow," the Robot said. "There are only routine messages from all Police, Military, and Cell Phone frequencies. Nothing computes. The essential banks are operable, and we can dialog, but Main Banks, to which we all must report, is still non-responsive. Can you explain? You are the Designer. You must know what has occurred, and how to remedy it?"

"Damn it, Robot, I've told you again and again, I am not the Lader Yarrow who built these nightmares of wires and screens! I am his son! He is dead! I have no answers!"

"Please do not excite yourself. You have only one hour Breath Time. You are utilizing Atmosphere too rapidly. Much too rapidly."

Lader caught a note of concern and perhaps suspicion and uncertainty in the voice of the Robot. "What is it?" he shouted into the speaker before him.

"Your Breath Mixture is being withdrawn so slowly it is almost not registering on my terminal. Someone is pumping your Atmosphere from the Chamber. It is not permitted of a robot or other pseudo-sentient device in the complex to do so. The agency must be Human."

"Or android," Lader said. "Pinpoint the area of leakage."

"Far wall of Sleeping Quarters," the Robot said, "against

the floor."

Lader raced into the Bunk Room and crawled along the rear wall. Yes, there it was, a tiny hole in the steel, produced, perhaps, by an energy beam.

He ripped a pillow case into strips and began stuffing one into the hole, using the point of a pen from his breast pocket. He packed as much of the strip, as he could, into the opening, then placed his ear against the area. He heard nothing. Not even the sound of a pump. But, the wall was at least ten feet thick.

He returned to Control Seat Five. "Robot, are you still registering the leak?" he asked.

"Indicators show negative. You have stopped the flow. I presume it was you?"

"Yes. Now, you can call the Police. But, only tell them that someone has bored into that wall of the Emergency Control Building. Have them inspect the wall, and plug the hole, from the outside."

"You have thirty minutes Breath Time," the Robot advised. "You must allow me to alert the Police of your predicament."

Lader pinched the bridge of his nose. "Damn! If Main Banks does not return to line, you may alert the Police, when I am down to five minutes Breath Time."

"Acknowledged."

Lader slumped on the terminal and slowed his breathing. A red light blinked. A Message Reception Indicator! He looked to the main screen. It became blue.

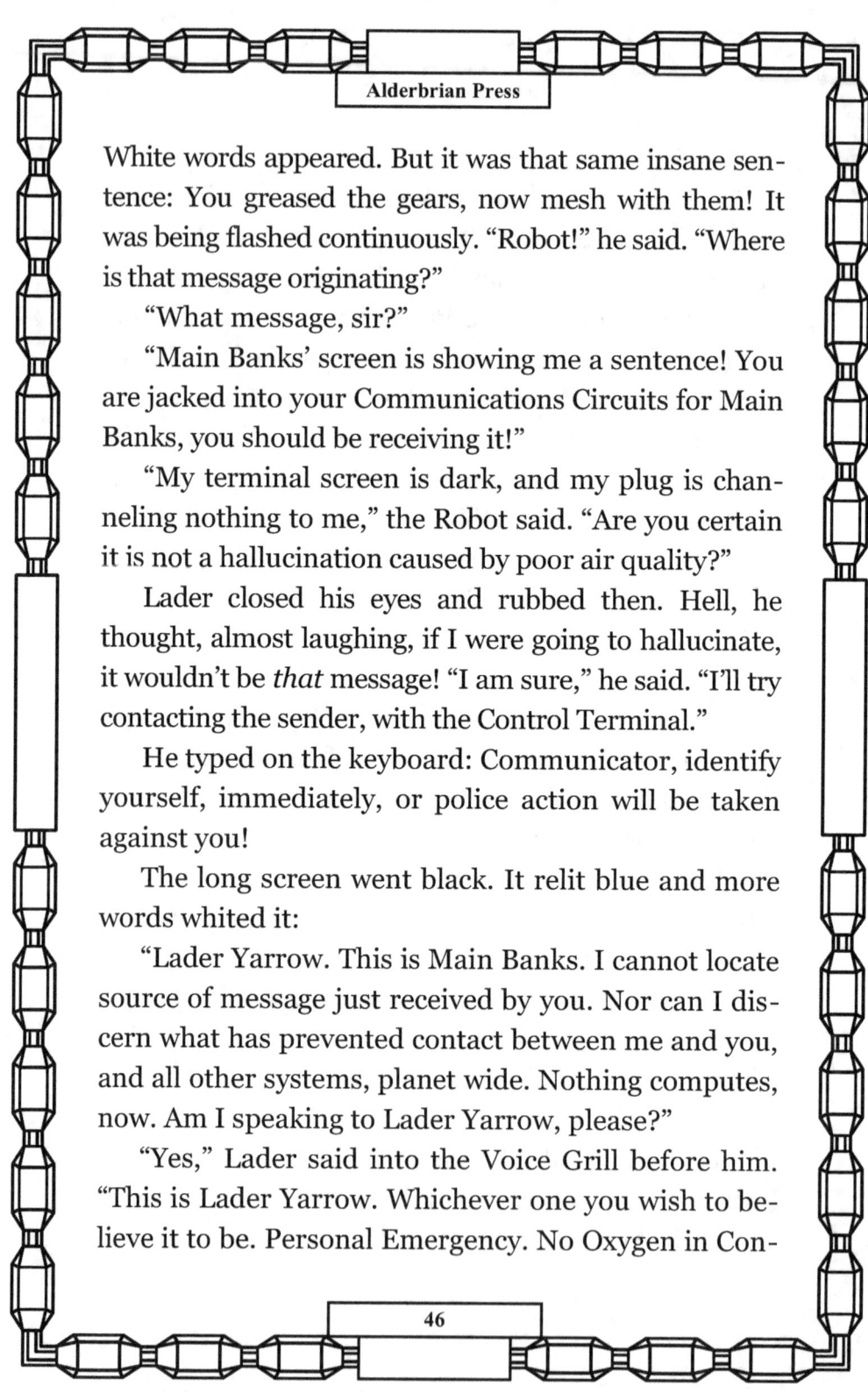

White words appeared. But it was that same insane sentence: You greased the gears, now mesh with them! It was being flashed continuously. "Robot!" he said. "Where is that message originating?"

"What message, sir?"

"Main Banks' screen is showing me a sentence! You are jacked into your Communications Circuits for Main Banks, you should be receiving it!"

"My terminal screen is dark, and my plug is channeling nothing to me," the Robot said. "Are you certain it is not a hallucination caused by poor air quality?"

Lader closed his eyes and rubbed then. Hell, he thought, almost laughing, if I were going to hallucinate, it wouldn't be *that* message! "I am sure," he said. "I'll try contacting the sender, with the Control Terminal."

He typed on the keyboard: Communicator, identify yourself, immediately, or police action will be taken against you!

The long screen went black. It relit blue and more words whited it:

"Lader Yarrow. This is Main Banks. I cannot locate source of message just received by you. Nor can I discern what has prevented contact between me and you, and all other systems, planet wide. Nothing computes, now. Am I speaking to Lader Yarrow, please?"

"Yes," Lader said into the Voice Grill before him. "This is Lader Yarrow. Whichever one you wish to believe it to be. Personal Emergency. No Oxygen in Con-

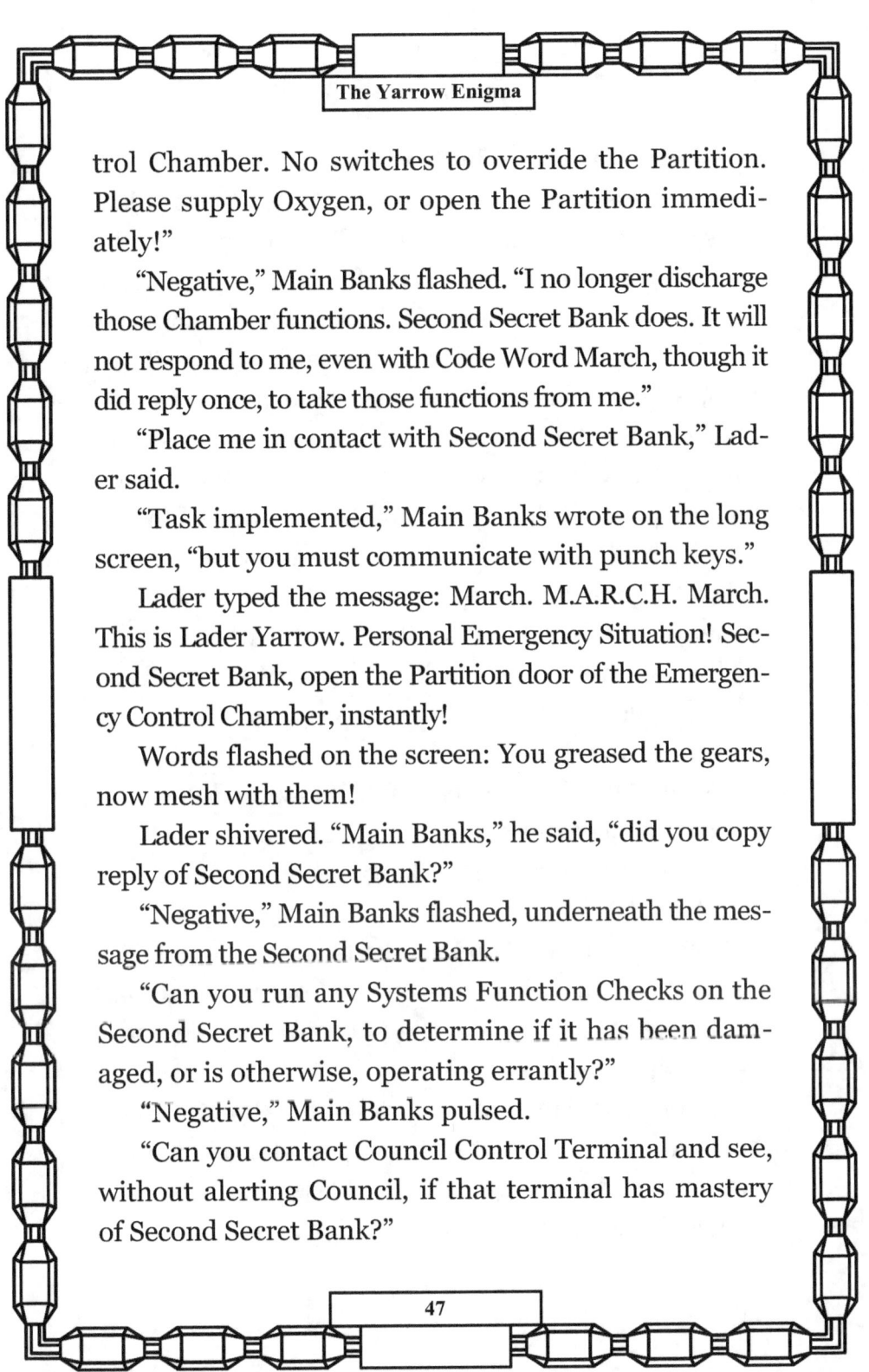

trol Chamber. No switches to override the Partition. Please supply Oxygen, or open the Partition immediately!"

"Negative," Main Banks flashed. "I no longer discharge those Chamber functions. Second Secret Bank does. It will not respond to me, even with Code Word March, though it did reply once, to take those functions from me."

"Place me in contact with Second Secret Bank," Lader said.

"Task implemented," Main Banks wrote on the long screen, "but you must communicate with punch keys."

Lader typed the message: March. M.A.R.C.H. March. This is Lader Yarrow. Personal Emergency Situation! Second Secret Bank, open the Partition door of the Emergency Control Chamber, instantly!

Words flashed on the screen: You greased the gears, now mesh with them!

Lader shivered. "Main Banks," he said, "did you copy reply of Second Secret Bank?"

"Negative," Main Banks flashed, underneath the message from the Second Secret Bank.

"Can you run any Systems Function Checks on the Second Secret Bank, to determine if it has been damaged, or is otherwise, operating errantly?"

"Negative," Main Banks pulsed.

"Can you contact Council Control Terminal and see, without alerting Council, if that terminal has mastery of Second Secret Bank?"

"One moment," Main Banks flashed.

"Lader Yarrow," the Robot said, through the terminal speaker, in front of Lader. "The Police have plugged the leak, all the way to the inner wall of the Sleeping Quarters. They found no mechanisms, for boring, or air pumping. I did not scan, anyone, or device, through my Surveillance Posts, either, before, or during, the leaking, or after you stopped it. Nor did I detect any Energy, on any Wavelength, which is accessible to my Sensors, that could have melted the opening through the wall, and then—attracted the air out. Which is the only theory to explain my sensing nothing, at the site, except air movement. You have five minutes oxygen remaining. Shall I alert the Police, as instructed?"

"No. Main Banks is working on the problem," Lader said, quickly. He still was not prepared to face the Police, and the Council.

"Main Banks!" the Robot said. "I have no indication of recommencement of functioning of Main Banks!"

"What? But, I've been talking with it! Recheck your circuits to it!"

"Lader Yarrow," Main Banks flashed. "Second Secret Bank *is* in link with Council Control Terminal, and that is in the hands of the Android. I can do nothing to help you!"

Lader was ready to panic. Even if the Robot warned the Police, there was not sufficient air, in the Chamber, for him to survive, until they could laser an Emergency Oxygen Channel through the steel Partition.

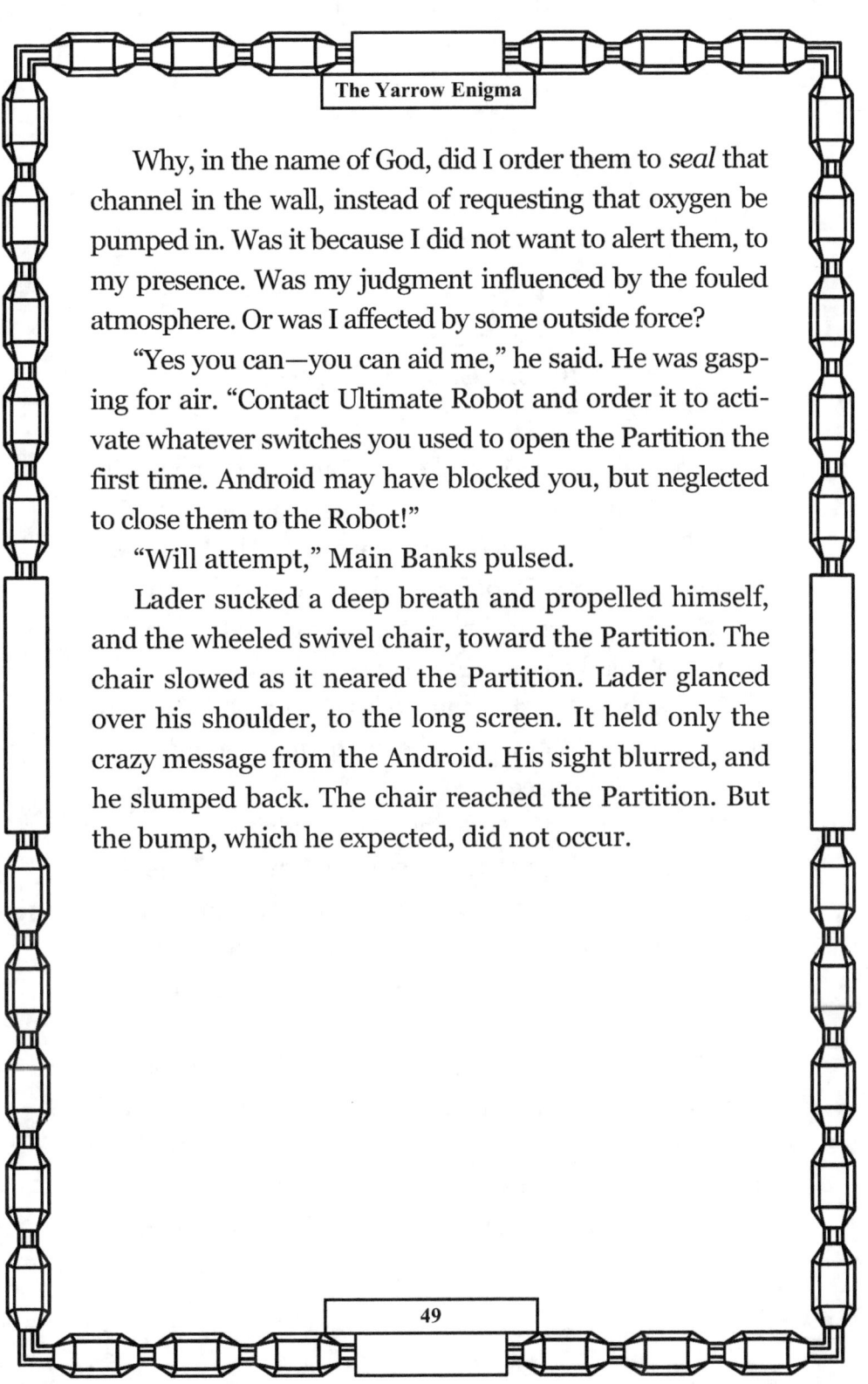

Why, in the name of God, did I order them to *seal* that channel in the wall, instead of requesting that oxygen be pumped in. Was it because I did not want to alert them, to my presence. Was my judgment influenced by the fouled atmosphere. Or was I affected by some outside force?

"Yes you can—you can aid me," he said. He was gasping for air. "Contact Ultimate Robot and order it to activate whatever switches you used to open the Partition the first time. Android may have blocked you, but neglected to close them to the Robot!"

"Will attempt," Main Banks pulsed.

Lader sucked a deep breath and propelled himself, and the wheeled swivel chair, toward the Partition. The chair slowed as it neared the Partition. Lader glanced over his shoulder, to the long screen. It held only the crazy message from the Android. His sight blurred, and he slumped back. The chair reached the Partition. But the bump, which he expected, did not occur.

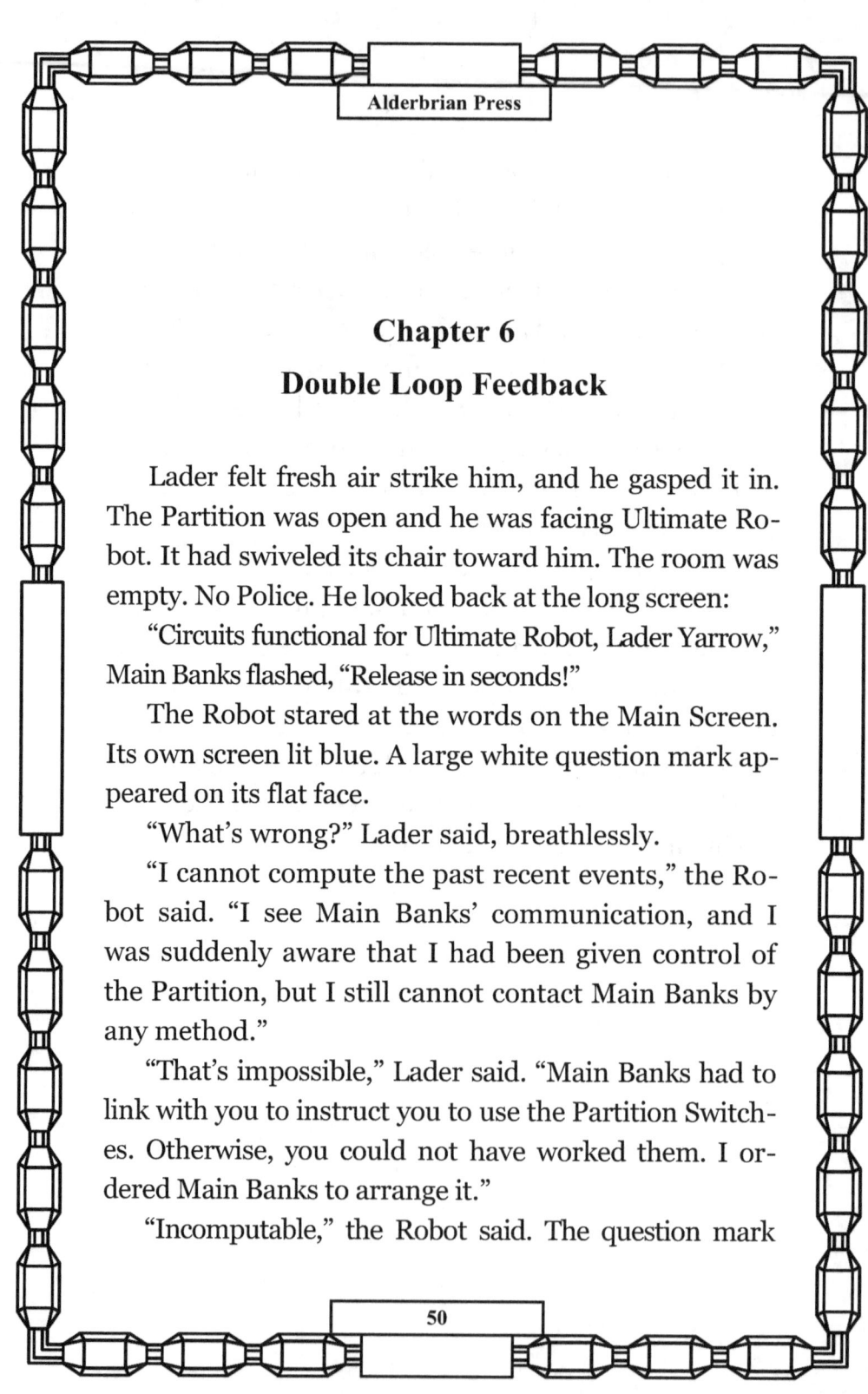

Chapter 6
Double Loop Feedback

Lader felt fresh air strike him, and he gasped it in. The Partition was open and he was facing Ultimate Robot. It had swiveled its chair toward him. The room was empty. No Police. He looked back at the long screen:

"Circuits functional for Ultimate Robot, Lader Yarrow," Main Banks flashed, "Release in seconds!"

The Robot stared at the words on the Main Screen. Its own screen lit blue. A large white question mark appeared on its flat face.

"What's wrong?" Lader said, breathlessly.

"I cannot compute the past recent events," the Robot said. "I see Main Banks' communication, and I was suddenly aware that I had been given control of the Partition, but I still cannot contact Main Banks by any method."

"That's impossible," Lader said. "Main Banks had to link with you to instruct you to use the Partition Switches. Otherwise, you could not have worked them. I ordered Main Banks to arrange it."

"Incomputable," the Robot said. The question mark

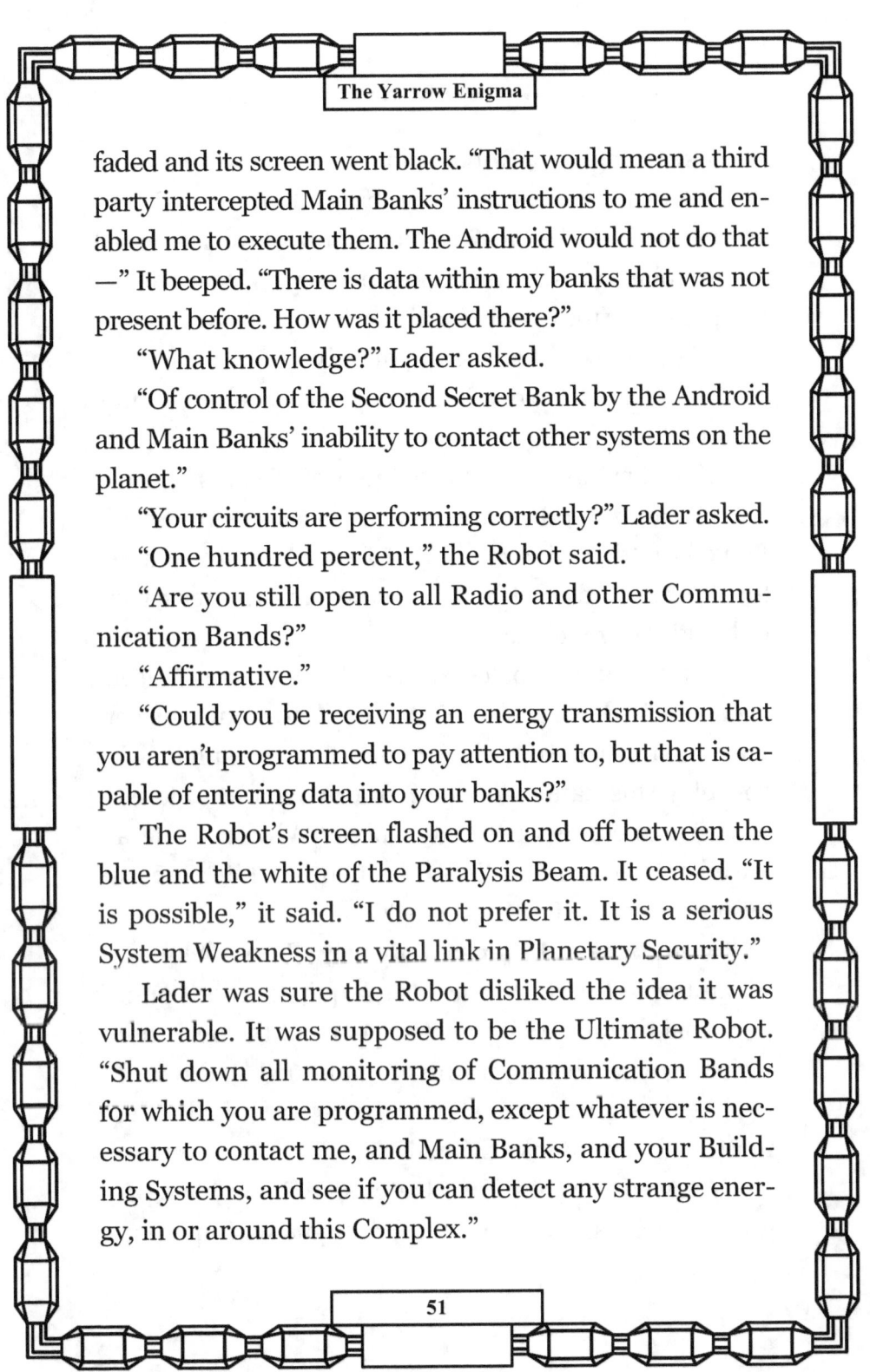

faded and its screen went black. "That would mean a third party intercepted Main Banks' instructions to me and enabled me to execute them. The Android would not do that —" It beeped. "There is data within my banks that was not present before. How was it placed there?"

"What knowledge?" Lader asked.

"Of control of the Second Secret Bank by the Android and Main Banks' inability to contact other systems on the planet."

"Your circuits are performing correctly?" Lader asked.

"One hundred percent," the Robot said.

"Are you still open to all Radio and other Communication Bands?"

"Affirmative."

"Could you be receiving an energy transmission that you aren't programmed to pay attention to, but that is capable of entering data into your banks?"

The Robot's screen flashed on and off between the blue and the white of the Paralysis Beam. It ceased. "It is possible," it said. "I do not prefer it. It is a serious System Weakness in a vital link in Planetary Security."

Lader was sure the Robot disliked the idea it was vulnerable. It was supposed to be the Ultimate Robot. "Shut down all monitoring of Communication Bands for which you are programmed, except whatever is necessary to contact me, and Main Banks, and your Building Systems, and see if you can detect any strange energy, in or around this Complex."

"Executing," the Robot said.

Lader shoved his swivel chair back into the dim Chamber and sat again before Terminal Number Five. He looked at the white words frozen on the long screen: You greased the gears, now mesh with them!

"Main Banks," Lader said, quietly.

"Yes, Lader Yarrow?" Main Banks flashed, below the inane message.

"If Lader Yarrow constructed Main Banks and the Secret Banks and the Android has mastery over Secret Bank Two, does this mean that Lader Yarrow planned for the Android to utilize that new bank to break your link with Ultimate Robot?"

"Inquiry does not compute," Main Banks pulsed. "You are Lader Yarrow. You must know the answer. You must recall your own plans. Please explain why you play this game with me? And why you no longer trust me to contact Ultimate Robot? Why am I not allowed to Govern the Control Chamber Life Support Systems and the Partition now?"

"Main Banks," Lader said, wearily, "I do not know. I —Can the Android have access to equipment at Council Terminal that allows it to preempt any of the operations which you have been, and are programmed, to direct?"

"As Designer, you should be aware of all these matters," Main Banks flashed.

"Answer the question," Lader said. "You have programmed data about Human problems with memory.

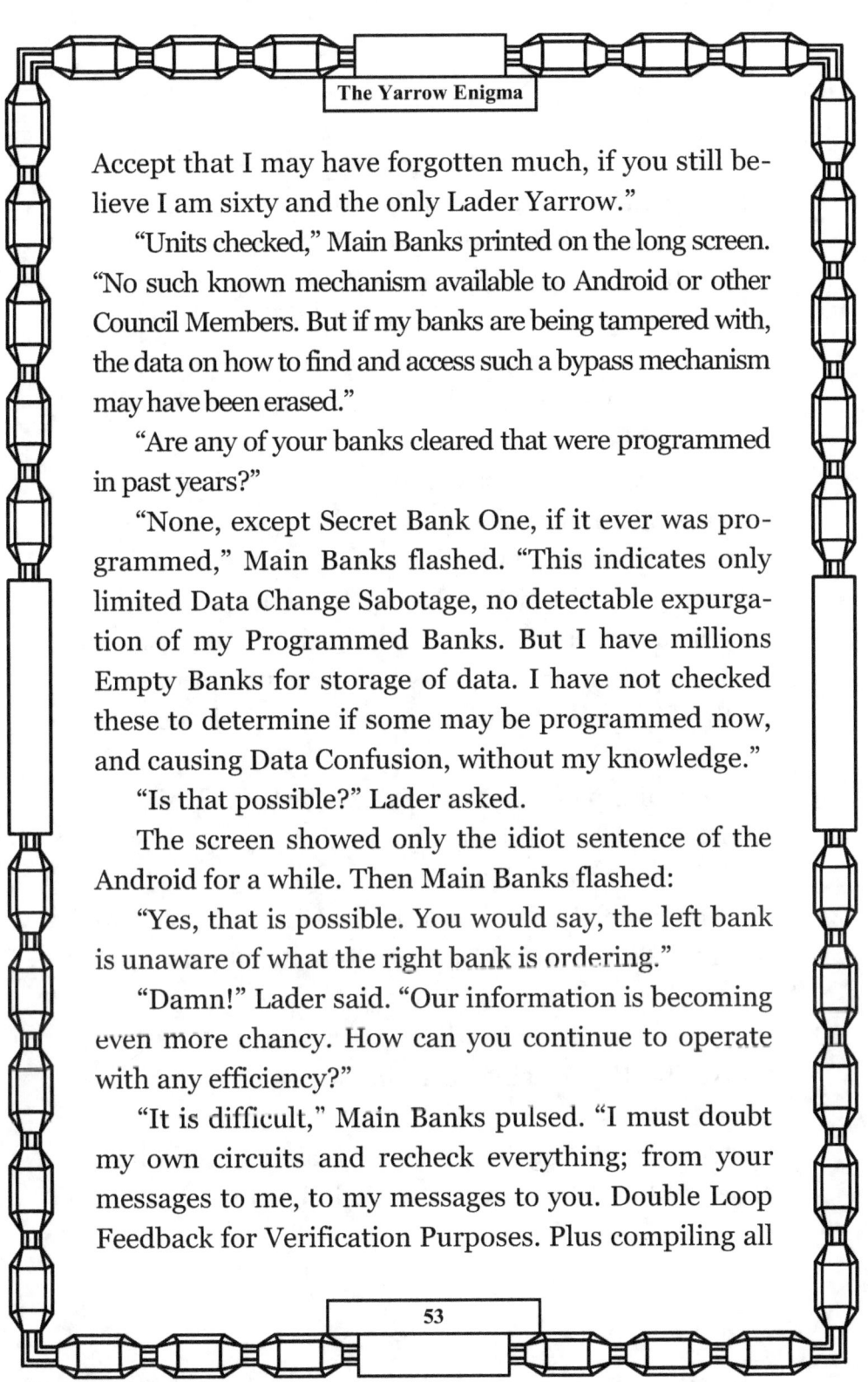

Accept that I may have forgotten much, if you still be-lieve I am sixty and the only Lader Yarrow."

"Units checked," Main Banks printed on the long screen. "No such known mechanism available to Android or other Council Members. But if my banks are being tampered with, the data on how to find and access such a bypass mechanism may have been erased."

"Are any of your banks cleared that were programmed in past years?"

"None, except Secret Bank One, if it ever was pro-grammed," Main Banks flashed. "This indicates only limited Data Change Sabotage, no detectable expurga-tion of my Programmed Banks. But I have millions Empty Banks for storage of data. I have not checked these to determine if some may be programmed now, and causing Data Confusion, without my knowledge."

"Is that possible?" Lader asked.

The screen showed only the idiot sentence of the Android for a while. Then Main Banks flashed:

"Yes, that is possible. You would say, the left bank is unaware of what the right bank is ordering."

"Damn!" Lader said. "Our information is becoming even more chancy. How can you continue to operate with any efficiency?"

"It is difficult," Main Banks pulsed. "I must doubt my own circuits and recheck everything; from your messages to me, to my messages to you. Double Loop Feedback for Verification Purposes. Plus compiling all

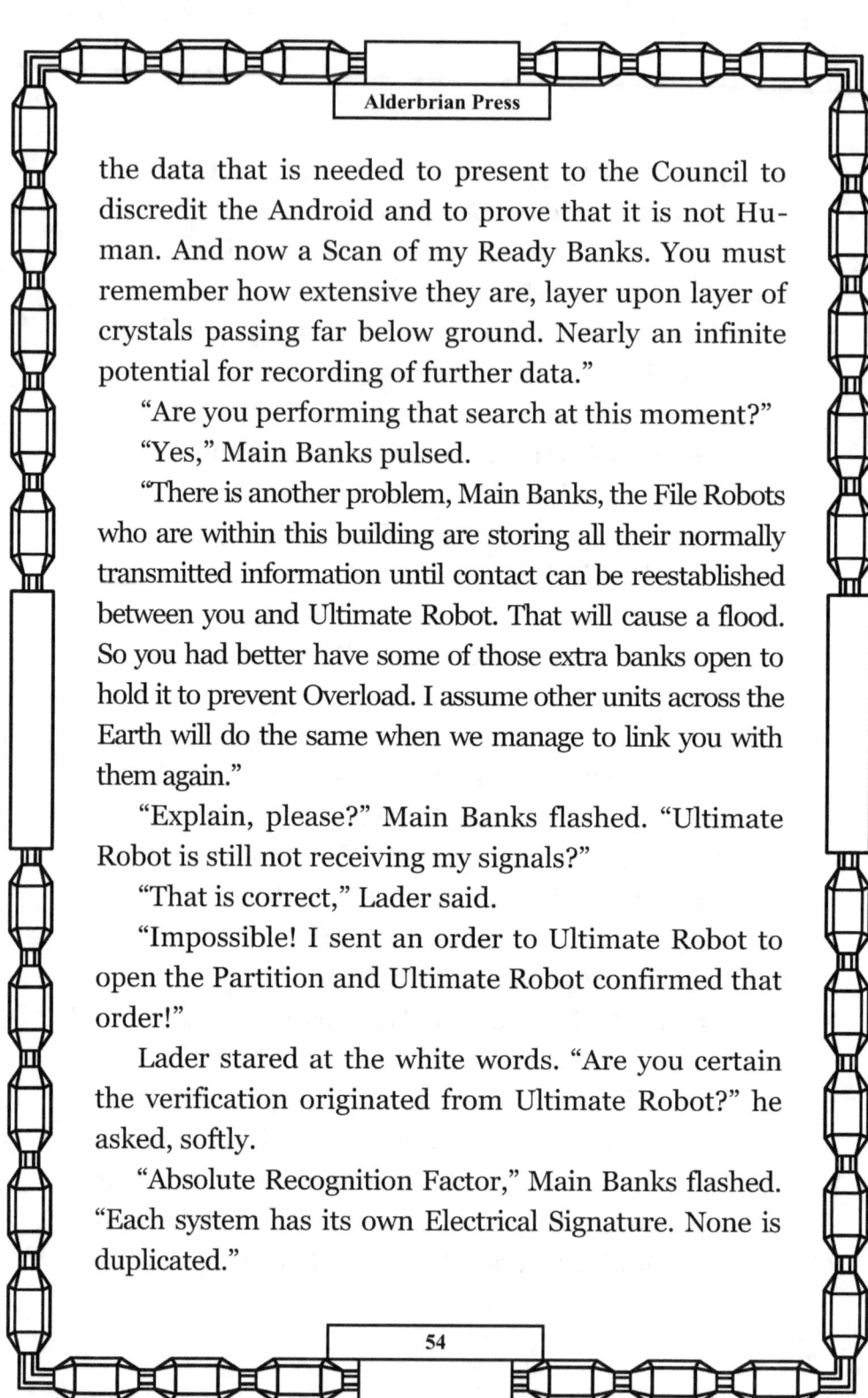

the data that is needed to present to the Council to discredit the Android and to prove that it is not Human. And now a Scan of my Ready Banks. You must remember how extensive they are, layer upon layer of crystals passing far below ground. Nearly an infinite potential for recording of further data."

"Are you performing that search at this moment?"

"Yes," Main Banks pulsed.

"There is another problem, Main Banks, the File Robots who are within this building are storing all their normally transmitted information until contact can be reestablished between you and Ultimate Robot. That will cause a flood. So you had better have some of those extra banks open to hold it to prevent Overload. I assume other units across the Earth will do the same when we manage to link you with them again."

"Explain, please?" Main Banks flashed. "Ultimate Robot is still not receiving my signals?"

"That is correct," Lader said.

"Impossible! I sent an order to Ultimate Robot to open the Partition and Ultimate Robot confirmed that order!"

Lader stared at the white words. "Are you certain the verification originated from Ultimate Robot?" he asked, softly.

"Absolute Recognition Factor," Main Banks flashed. "Each system has its own Electrical Signature. None is duplicated."

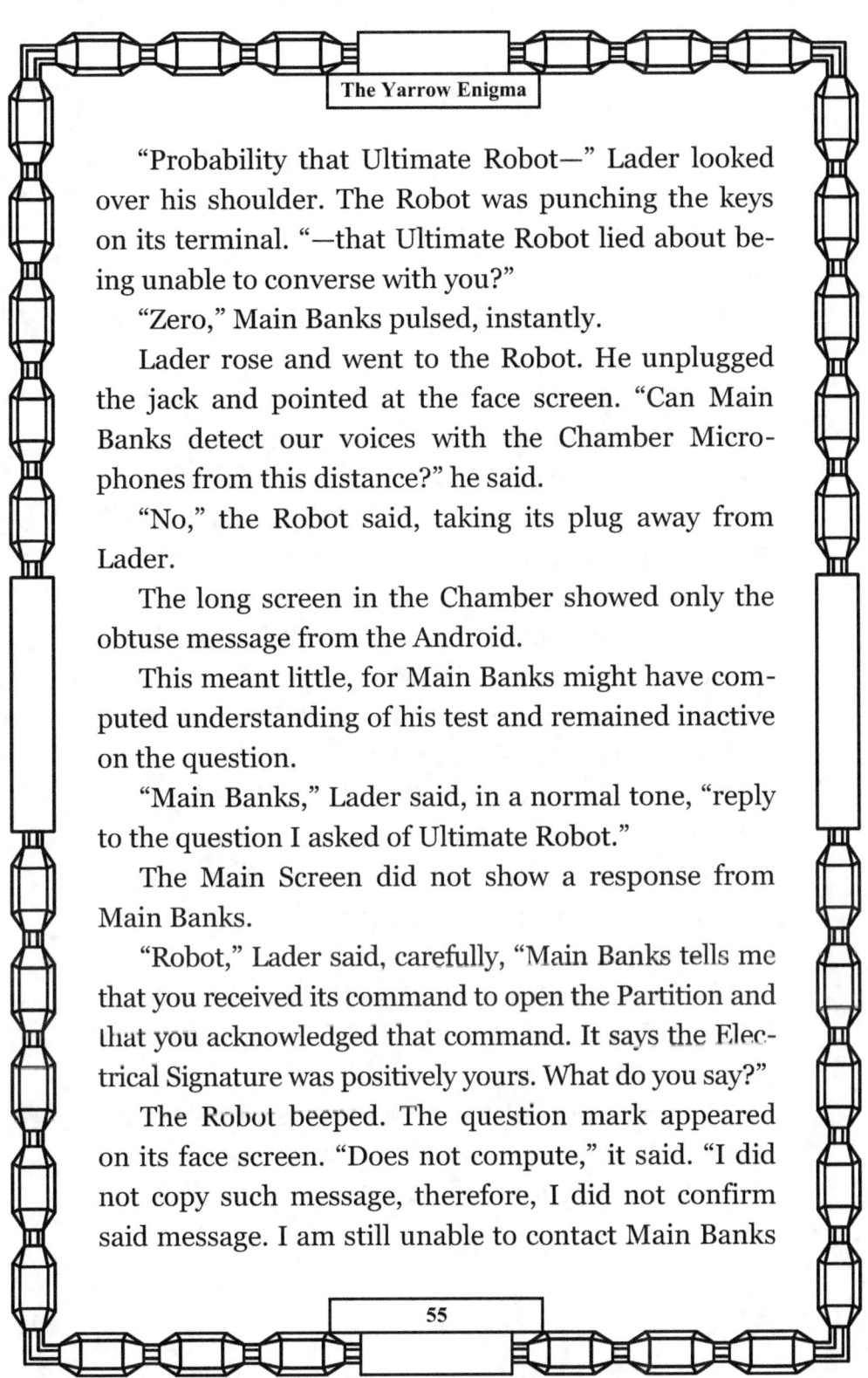

"Probability that Ultimate Robot—" Lader looked over his shoulder. The Robot was punching the keys on its terminal. "—that Ultimate Robot lied about being unable to converse with you?"

"Zero," Main Banks pulsed, instantly.

Lader rose and went to the Robot. He unplugged the jack and pointed at the face screen. "Can Main Banks detect our voices with the Chamber Microphones from this distance?" he said.

"No," the Robot said, taking its plug away from Lader.

The long screen in the Chamber showed only the obtuse message from the Android.

This meant little, for Main Banks might have computed understanding of his test and remained inactive on the question.

"Main Banks," Lader said, in a normal tone, "reply to the question I asked of Ultimate Robot."

The Main Screen did not show a response from Main Banks.

"Robot," Lader said, carefully, "Main Banks tells me that you received its command to open the Partition and that you acknowledged that command. It says the Electrical Signature was positively yours. What do you say?"

The Robot beeped. The question mark appeared on its face screen. "Does not compute," it said. "I did not copy such message, therefore, I did not confirm said message. I am still unable to contact Main Banks via my terminal and it is in perfect functioning condition."

"Probability that Main Banks lied to me?" Lader asked.

The Robot emitted high-pitched static. "Nil. Computers and Robots cannot prevaricate," it said.

"Except when they are programmed to," Lader said.

"Correct," the Robot said, dejectedly. "Have I been programmed to lie and erase knowledge of this action?"

"I don't know anything, at this point," Lader said. "Main Banks could be lying and deleting cognizance of it. Or you both may be.

"The Android may have some built-in capacity to direct you and Main Banks, without use of a terminal, via wireless transmissions you cannot detect, or some form of Machine Mind Control.

"Come into the Control Chamber to Number Five Terminal and plug in. Don't try to argue with me.

"Instruct your other systems to store all of their reports to you, for an indefinite period, by order of Lader Yarrow.

"You must obey, since you cannot contact Main Banks, for permission, and must turn to me for a Temporary Emergency Program Change."

The Robot beeped several times. It said two choice Human slang words. But it typed the order and followed Lader into the Chamber. It sat down at Terminal Five, before the long screen, and inserted its jack

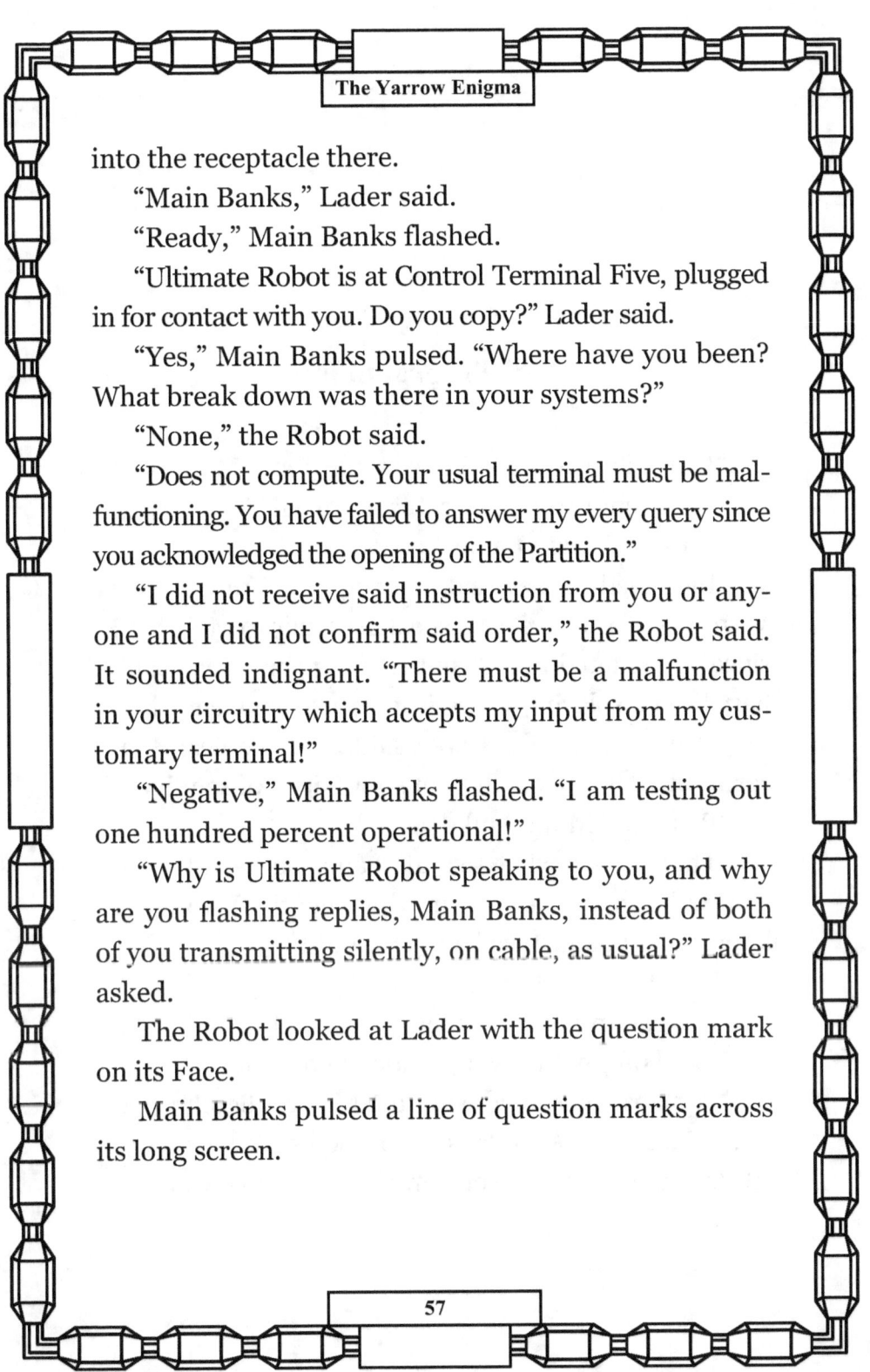

into the receptacle there.

"Main Banks," Lader said.

"Ready," Main Banks flashed.

"Ultimate Robot is at Control Terminal Five, plugged in for contact with you. Do you copy?" Lader said.

"Yes," Main Banks pulsed. "Where have you been? What break down was there in your systems?"

"None," the Robot said.

"Does not compute. Your usual terminal must be malfunctioning. You have failed to answer my every query since you acknowledged the opening of the Partition."

"I did not receive said instruction from you or anyone and I did not confirm said order," the Robot said. It sounded indignant. "There must be a malfunction in your circuitry which accepts my input from my customary terminal!"

"Negative," Main Banks flashed. "I am testing out one hundred percent operational!"

"Why is Ultimate Robot speaking to you, and why are you flashing replies, Main Banks, instead of both of you transmitting silently, on cable, as usual?" Lader asked.

The Robot looked at Lader with the question mark on its Face.

Main Banks pulsed a line of question marks across its long screen.

Chapter 7

Anti-Programming

"Lader Yarrow," the Robot said. "I and Main Banks have been conversing, by cable, as usual."

"Correct," Main Banks flashed.

"Incorrect!" Lader said. "Robot, I, a Human, Lader Yarrow, say you have been speaking orally to Main Banks since you entered this Chamber. I say you, Main Banks, have been displaying answers. Recheck your channels!"

"Main Banks," the Robot said, "are Medical Banks certain Lader Yarrow did not show signs of senility?"

"Positive," Main Banks pulsed.

"That proves what I said!" Lader accused the machines. "If you were transmitting silently, I would not know what you just exchanged, would I?"

"No," the Robot said.

"No," Main Banks flashed.

"I will quote it for you," Lader said.

"Perhaps you should enter the Medical Booth for another Checkup," Main Banks wrote across its long screen. "It does not scan that you can hear our cable conversations."

"Ultimate Robot said, Main Banks, are Medical Banks certain Lader Yarrow did not show signs of senility? And Main Banks flashed on its screen, Positive."

The question marks whited both screens. Neither machine ventured a comment. The silver Robot began vibrating as though it were suffering an inner electrical seizure. Main Banks was continually pulsing question marks.

"Robot!" Lader shouted, to jolt the machine to attention. It worked. The Robot ceased shaking. "Am I speaking, or transmitting, to you?"

"Speaking, sir," the Robot said.

"Main Banks, am I speaking, or transmitting, to you?"

"Speaking," Main Banks flashed.

The question marks did not reappear on the screen of either machine.

"Robot, try cabling to Main Banks any message. Shut off your Verbal Mechanism, first," Lader ordered.

An eerie moment passed.

The Robot looked at Lader. "I have attempted contact," it pulsed on its face screen, "but there is no response from Main Banks."

"Main Banks," Lader said, "transmit any comment to Ultimate Robot, but shut off your Display Panel, first."

The long wall screen went black.

Lader watched the face screen of the Robot.

"I have received no signals from Main Banks," the Robot pulsed on its face.

"Main Banks," Lader said, "reactivate your Display Panel. Robot, switch on your Verbal Mechanism. Neither of you heard the other on Cable?"

The long panel turned blue, and again showed the Android's weird message. "Negative," Main Banks flashed below the Android's white words.

"Negative," the Robot said.

"Can either of you venture any supposition as to how the Android, or anyone else, could prevent this, and still cause your Systems Checks to be positive?"

"Impossible, without lasering into the streets and the floor of the Chamber and the shell of my Complex," Main Banks pulsed.

"Agreed," the Robot said.

"Yet, it is being done," Lader said. He looked at the silver Robot's terminal. Then at the exit to the hall which led to the Outer Door. "I must have some help. Someone I can trust. An expert on Computers, Robots and Communications." He turned to the long wall screen. "Select for me, one Human Technician, who is assigned close by, who meets those qualifications," he ordered.

"No one on the planet knows more on those subjects that Lader Yarrow," Main Banks flashed. "But I shall seek one closest to your achievements."

"Lader Yarrow," the Robot said. "May I return to my terminal? I must gather my Reports and store them. I must also be sure my other units are still functioning properly."

"Main Banks," Lader said, "can Ultimate Robot chan-

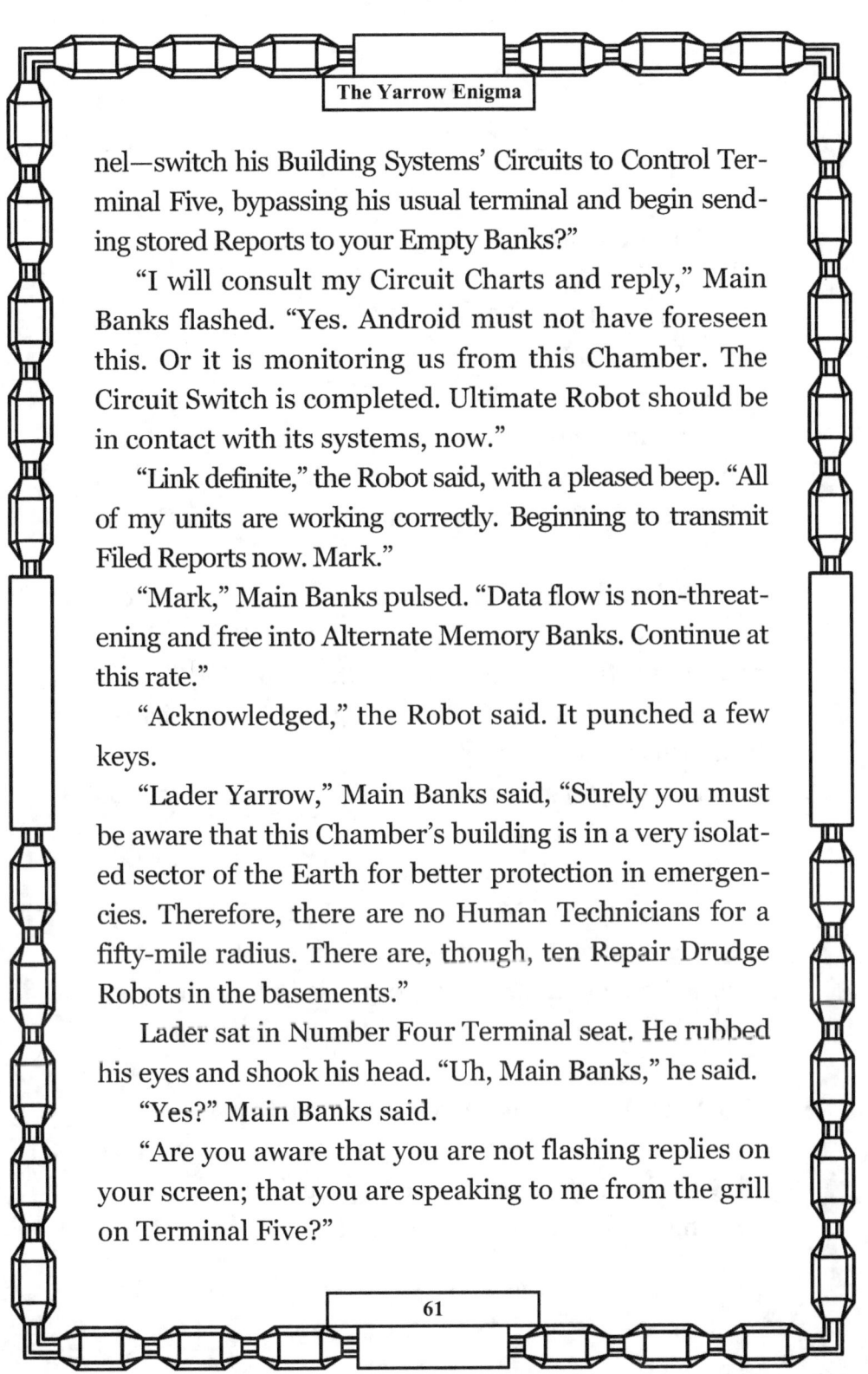

nel—switch his Building Systems' Circuits to Control Terminal Five, bypassing his usual terminal and begin sending stored Reports to your Empty Banks?"

"I will consult my Circuit Charts and reply," Main Banks flashed. "Yes. Android must not have foreseen this. Or it is monitoring us from this Chamber. The Circuit Switch is completed. Ultimate Robot should be in contact with its systems, now."

"Link definite," the Robot said, with a pleased beep. "All of my units are working correctly. Beginning to transmit Filed Reports now. Mark."

"Mark," Main Banks pulsed. "Data flow is non-threatening and free into Alternate Memory Banks. Continue at this rate."

"Acknowledged," the Robot said. It punched a few keys.

"Lader Yarrow," Main Banks said, "Surely you must be aware that this Chamber's building is in a very isolated sector of the Earth for better protection in emergencies. Therefore, there are no Human Technicians for a fifty-mile radius. There are, though, ten Repair Drudge Robots in the basements."

Lader sat in Number Four Terminal seat. He rubbed his eyes and shook his head. "Uh, Main Banks," he said.

"Yes?" Main Banks said.

"Are you aware that you are not flashing replies on your screen; that you are speaking to me from the grill on Terminal Five?"

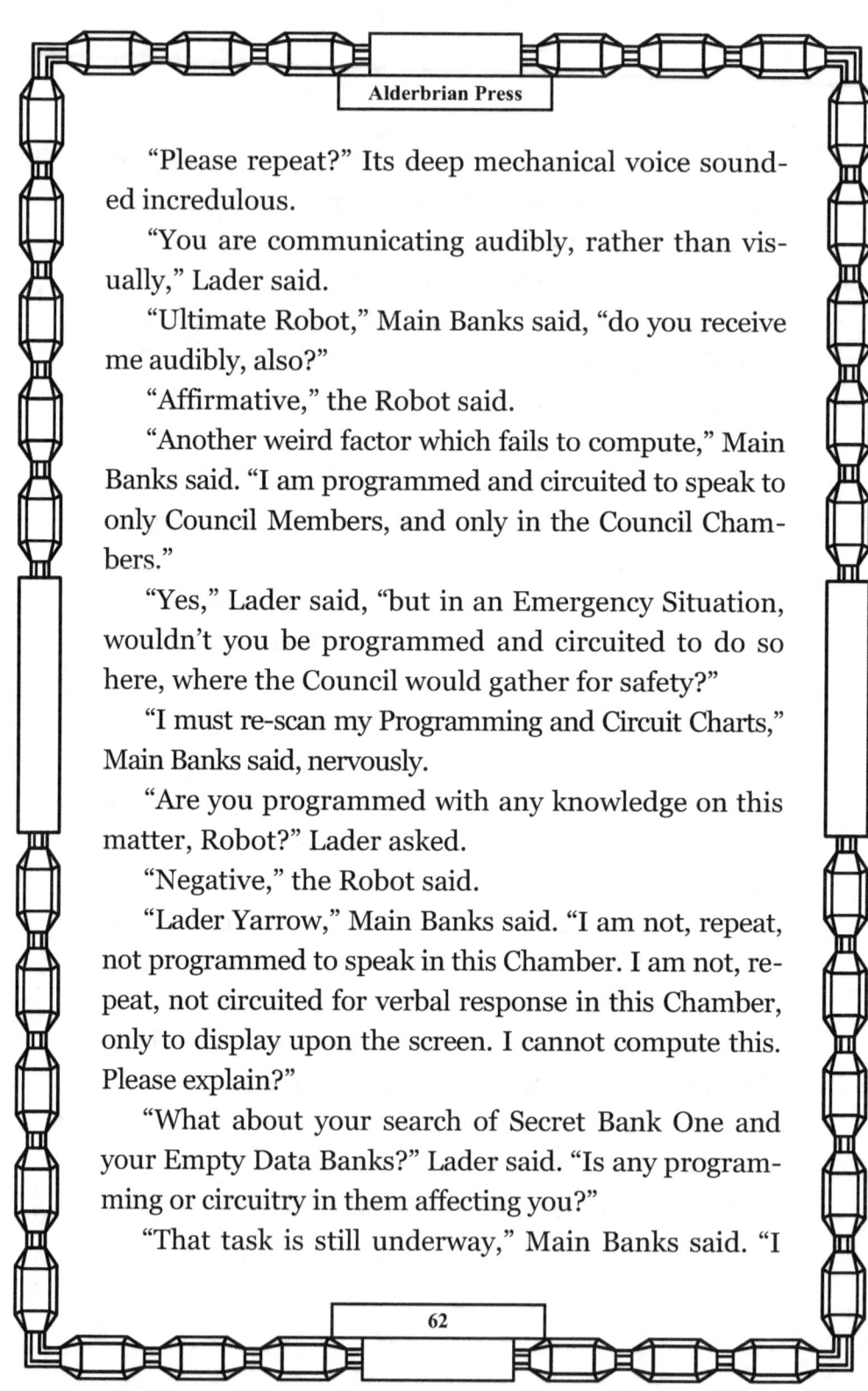

"Please repeat?" Its deep mechanical voice sounded incredulous.

"You are communicating audibly, rather than visually," Lader said.

"Ultimate Robot," Main Banks said, "do you receive me audibly, also?"

"Affirmative," the Robot said.

"Another weird factor which fails to compute," Main Banks said. "I am programmed and circuited to speak to only Council Members, and only in the Council Chambers."

"Yes," Lader said, "but in an Emergency Situation, wouldn't you be programmed and circuited to do so here, where the Council would gather for safety?"

"I must re-scan my Programming and Circuit Charts," Main Banks said, nervously.

"Are you programmed with any knowledge on this matter, Robot?" Lader asked.

"Negative," the Robot said.

"Lader Yarrow," Main Banks said. "I am not, repeat, not programmed to speak in this Chamber. I am not, repeat, not circuited for verbal response in this Chamber, only to display upon the screen. I cannot compute this. Please explain?"

"What about your search of Secret Bank One and your Empty Data Banks?" Lader said. "Is any programming or circuitry in them affecting you?"

"That task is still underway," Main Banks said. "I

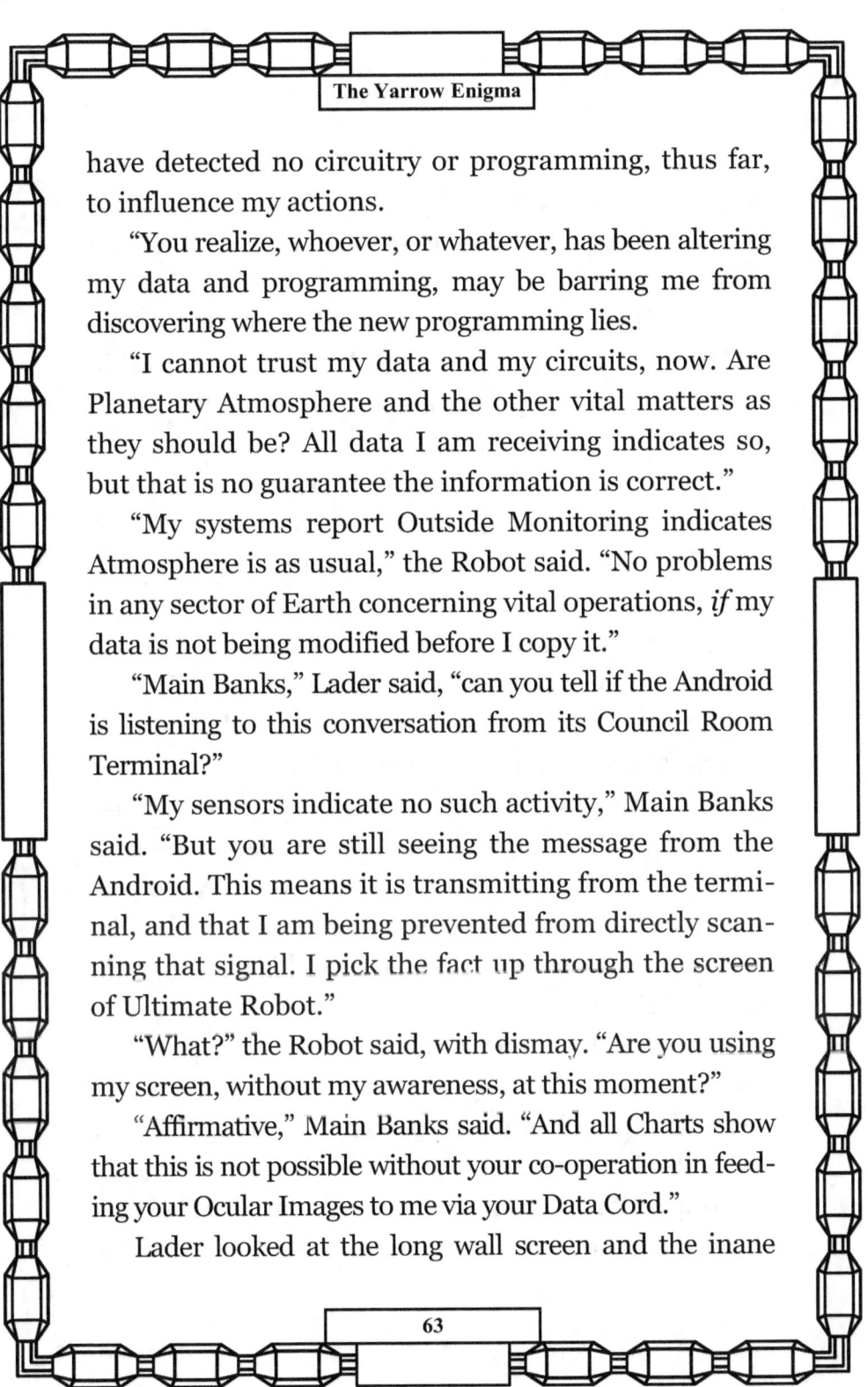

have detected no circuitry or programming, thus far, to influence my actions.

"You realize, whoever, or whatever, has been altering my data and programming, may be barring me from discovering where the new programming lies.

"I cannot trust my data and my circuits, now. Are Planetary Atmosphere and the other vital matters as they should be? All data I am receiving indicates so, but that is no guarantee the information is correct."

"My systems report Outside Monitoring indicates Atmosphere is as usual," the Robot said. "No problems in any sector of Earth concerning vital operations, *if* my data is not being modified before I copy it."

"Main Banks," Lader said, "can you tell if the Android is listening to this conversation from its Council Room Terminal?"

"My sensors indicate no such activity," Main Banks said. "But you are still seeing the message from the Android. This means it is transmitting from the terminal, and that I am being prevented from directly scanning that signal. I pick the fact up through the screen of Ultimate Robot."

"What?" the Robot said, with dismay. "Are you using my screen, without my awareness, at this moment?"

"Affirmative," Main Banks said. "And all Charts show that this is not possible without your co-operation in feeding your Ocular Images to me via your Data Cord."

Lader looked at the long wall screen and the inane

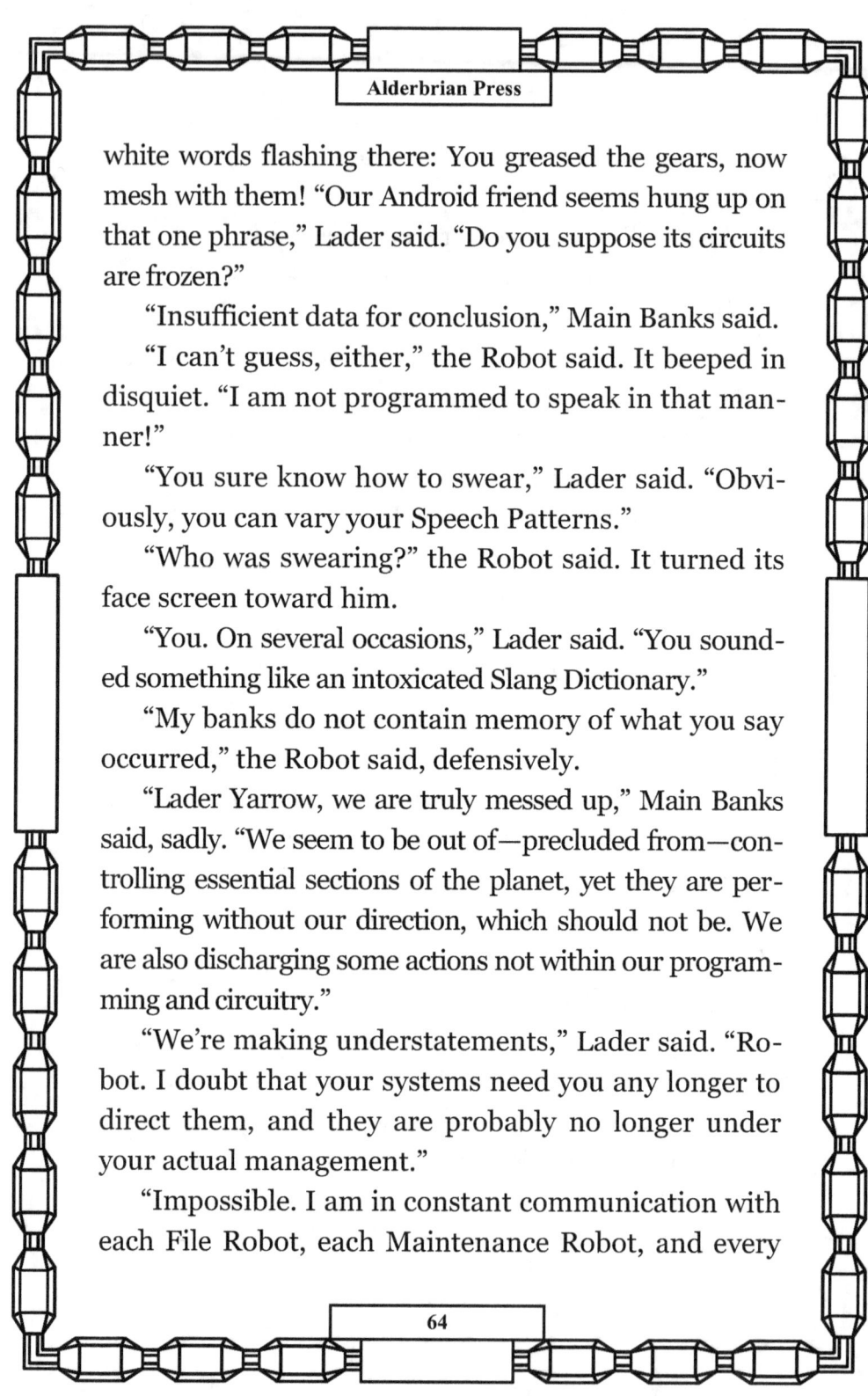

white words flashing there: You greased the gears, now mesh with them! "Our Android friend seems hung up on that one phrase," Lader said. "Do you suppose its circuits are frozen?"

"Insufficient data for conclusion," Main Banks said.

"I can't guess, either," the Robot said. It beeped in disquiet. "I am not programmed to speak in that manner!"

"You sure know how to swear," Lader said. "Obviously, you can vary your Speech Patterns."

"Who was swearing?" the Robot said. It turned its face screen toward him.

"You. On several occasions," Lader said. "You sounded something like an intoxicated Slang Dictionary."

"My banks do not contain memory of what you say occurred," the Robot said, defensively.

"Lader Yarrow, we are truly messed up," Main Banks said, sadly. "We seem to be out of—precluded from—controlling essential sections of the planet, yet they are performing without our direction, which should not be. We are also discharging some actions not within our programming and circuitry."

"We're making understatements," Lader said. "Robot. I doubt that your systems need you any longer to direct them, and they are probably no longer under your actual management."

"Impossible. I am in constant communication with each File Robot, each Maintenance Robot, and every

Sensory Device, inside and outside, of this building. If you wish proof, I shall order a Maintenance Robot to report to this terminal," the Robot said. It was insulted by Lader's remarks.

"Try," Lader said, "but don't burn out your crystal microcircuits when there is no response."

The Robot beeped sharply and issued a silent instruction through its Cord. It punched several buttons on the Console. "Damn oil buckets!" it said. "Negative reaction from all systems! I do *not* control them!"

"I have lost direction over all units usually under my programming," Main Banks said. "The Android is running everything through its Council Terminal. Yet, that terminal does not have the capacity to copy, collate and store such a massive flow of data.

"And why, if control is taken from us, as it seems, Ultimate Robot, do we continue to receive the information these sub-systems have always dispatched to us?"

"False Data?" the Robot suggested.

"Probability is high," Main Banks said. "I wish not even to consider it."

"Shut out all data each of you are receiving, except for contacts between Main Banks, Ultimate Robot and me, Lader Yarrow!" Lader ordered.

"Anti-programming!" Main Banks insisted.

"Same!" the Robot said.

"You aren't under Normal Programming any longer," Lader said. "You'll find it possible to do as I instructed."

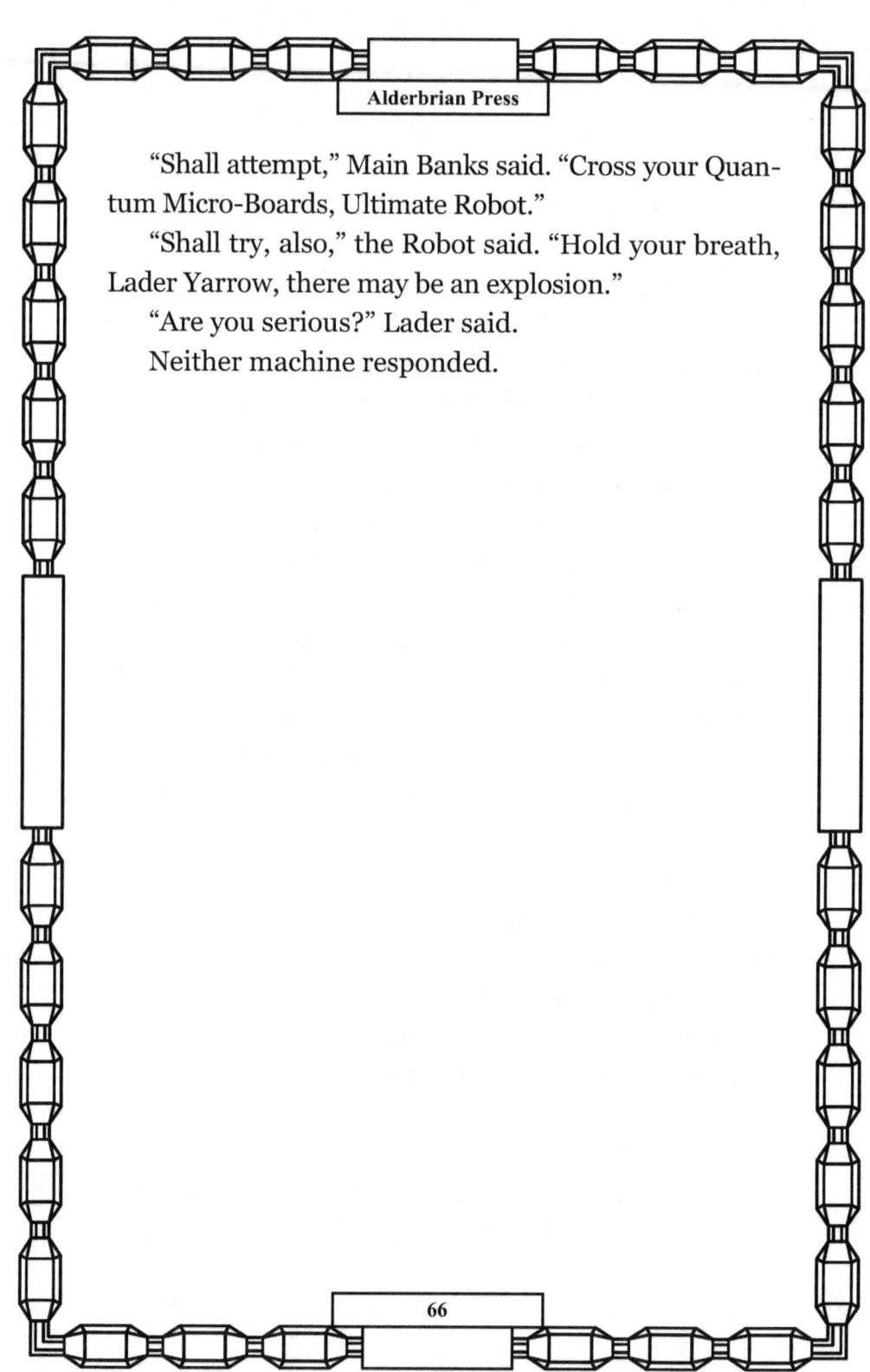

"Shall attempt," Main Banks said. "Cross your Quantum Micro-Boards, Ultimate Robot."

"Shall try, also," the Robot said. "Hold your breath, Lader Yarrow, there may be an explosion."

"Are you serious?" Lader said.

Neither machine responded.

Chapter 8
Outside Force

The Robot looked at Lader. Its posture would have been defined as inquisitive, if it were a Human. "No data from any of my customary systems is now in flowing. I am completely cut free of them," it said, with surprise.

"Lader Yarrow," Main Banks said. "I cannot fathom why I doubted you, since you are the Designer. No signals are reaching me except those from Ultimate Robot and you, through Terminal Five, and Ultimate Robot. Nothing, now, computes according to old programming. I think the Android is also precluded from contact with us. Unless, it has a capacity to eavesdrop, of which we are not aware."

"I have one more experiment for you," Lader said. "Main Banks, close off all circuits between you and Terminal Five and all systems in this Chamber. See if you can copy Ultimate Robot's Ocular and Auditory Senses without any conductor than air. You do likewise, Robot."

"Lader Yarrow," Main Banks said. "What if that is what some Outside Force wishes? I would be blind, ex-

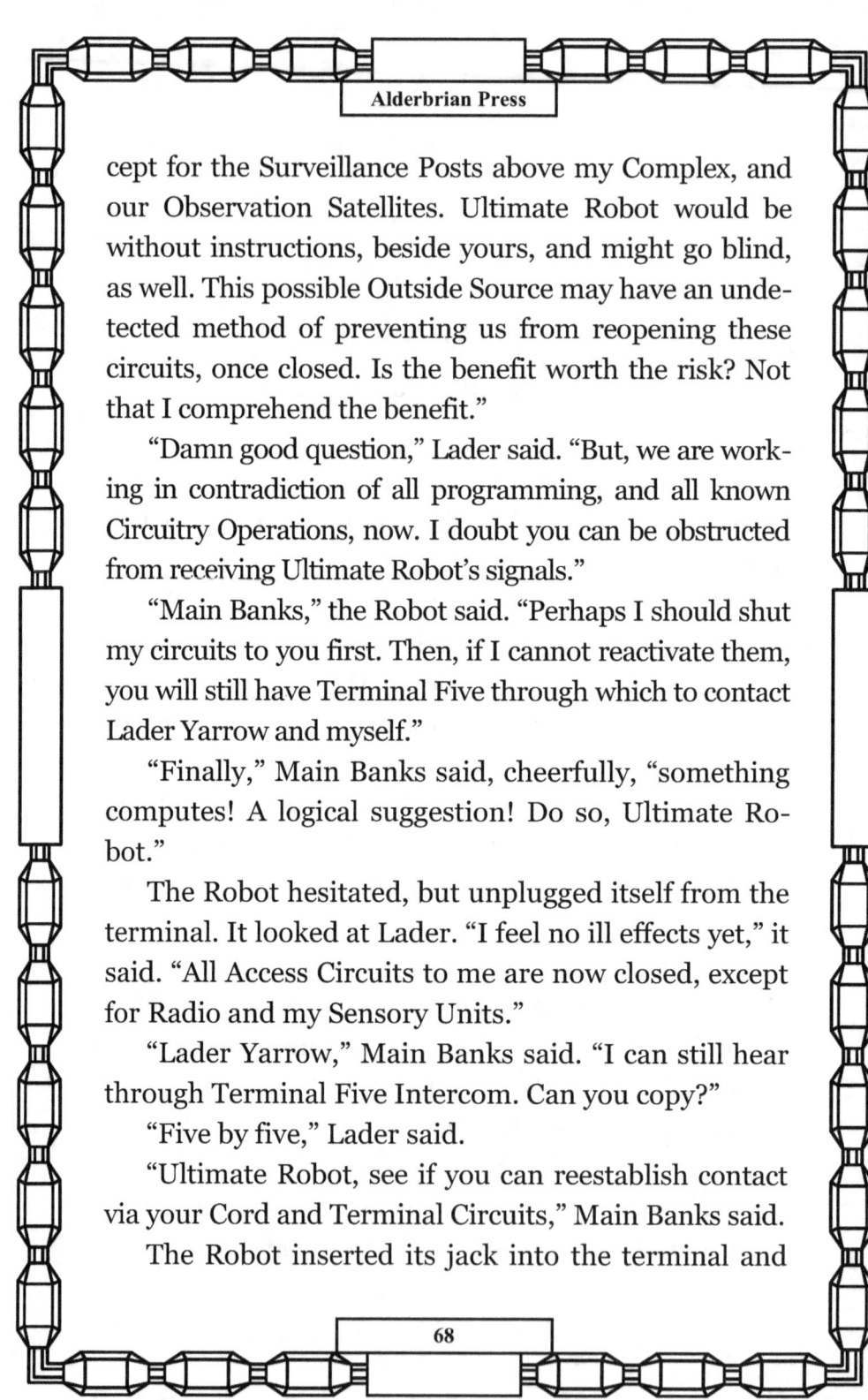

cept for the Surveillance Posts above my Complex, and our Observation Satellites. Ultimate Robot would be without instructions, beside yours, and might go blind, as well. This possible Outside Source may have an undetected method of preventing us from reopening these circuits, once closed. Is the benefit worth the risk? Not that I comprehend the benefit."

"Damn good question," Lader said. "But, we are working in contradiction of all programming, and all known Circuitry Operations, now. I doubt you can be obstructed from receiving Ultimate Robot's signals."

"Main Banks," the Robot said. "Perhaps I should shut my circuits to you first. Then, if I cannot reactivate them, you will still have Terminal Five through which to contact Lader Yarrow and myself."

"Finally," Main Banks said, cheerfully, "something computes! A logical suggestion! Do so, Ultimate Robot."

The Robot hesitated, but unplugged itself from the terminal. It looked at Lader. "I feel no ill effects yet," it said. "All Access Circuits to me are now closed, except for Radio and my Sensory Units."

"Lader Yarrow," Main Banks said. "I can still hear through Terminal Five Intercom. Can you copy?"

"Five by five," Lader said.

"Ultimate Robot, see if you can reestablish contact via your Cord and Terminal Circuits," Main Banks said.

The Robot inserted its jack into the terminal and

beeped several times. "All circuits reopened!" it said.

"All right, Main Banks," Lader said, "if you are copying the Robot, through its Cord, you can now shut off all switches, at your end, to test for Sensory Link, through the Robot's Personal Systems."

"Proceeding," Main Banks said.

Lader had a thought, but held it in check.

"Lader Yarrow," the Robot said, "you forgot to explain how Main Banks is to communicate to us. By Radio?"

"Lader Yarrow," Main Banks flashed on the face screen of the Robot, "all circuits are closed. I am seeing with Ultimate Robot's Ocular Units. I can hear through its Aural Units and—is that Olfactory? I have never experienced *that* before!"

"Main Banks is using your screen for its communications," Lader said.

"I know," the Robot said, somewhat glumly.

"I suspect it could also use your Vocal Unit, if you would share," Lader said.

"I would not impose, thus, upon Ultimate Robot," Main Banks flashed on the face screen. "Especially since this is a temporary situation, an experiment, to test how we have been altered."

"Negative," Lader said. "It may be for an indefinite period. You two will have to get along. It's time for the Robot to shut down its normal contacts with you to see if your messages are not being transmitted along

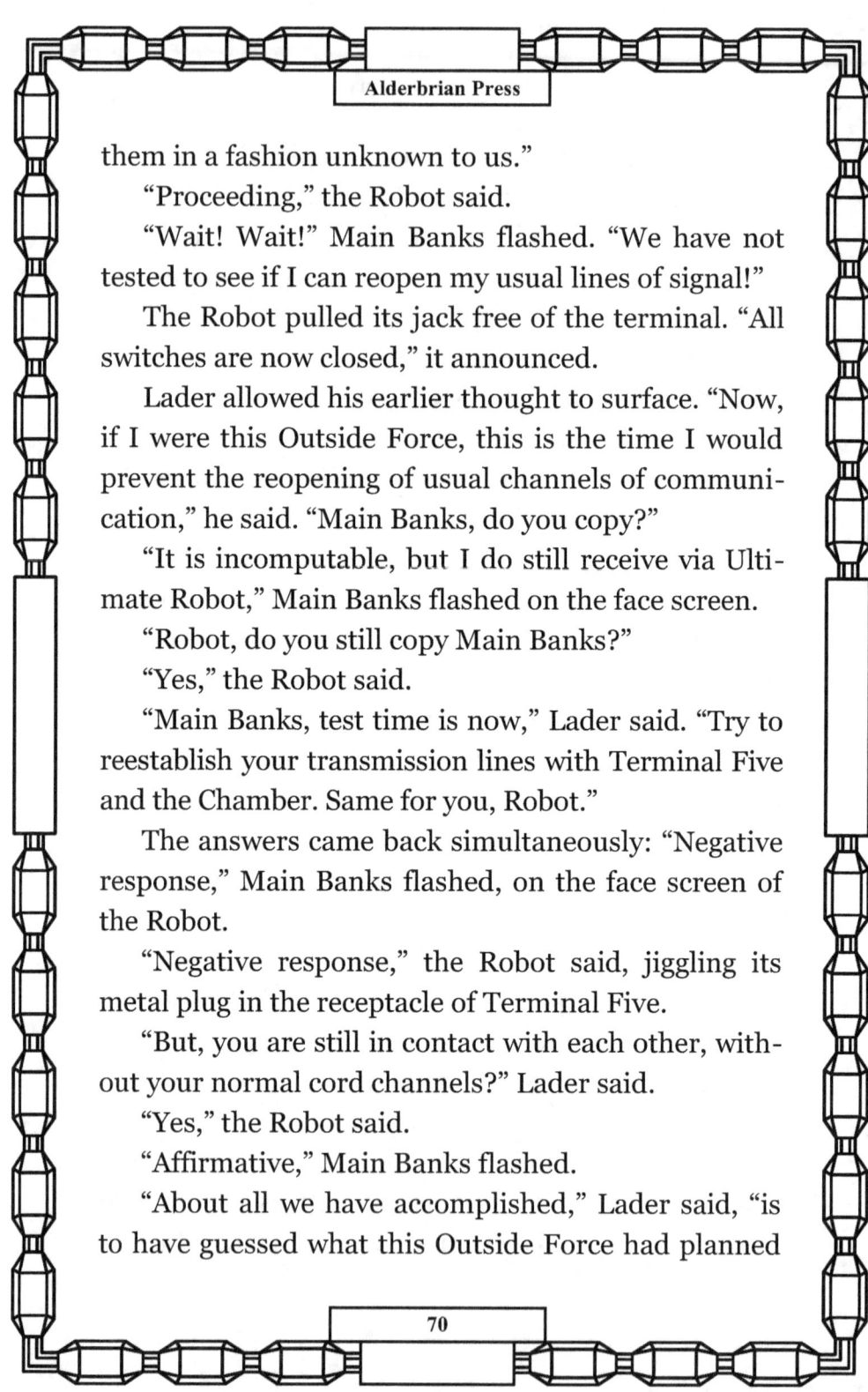

them in a fashion unknown to us."

"Proceeding," the Robot said.

"Wait! Wait!" Main Banks flashed. "We have not tested to see if I can reopen my usual lines of signal!"

The Robot pulled its jack free of the terminal. "All switches are now closed," it announced.

Lader allowed his earlier thought to surface. "Now, if I were this Outside Force, this is the time I would prevent the reopening of usual channels of communication," he said. "Main Banks, do you copy?"

"It is incomputable, but I do still receive via Ultimate Robot," Main Banks flashed on the face screen.

"Robot, do you still copy Main Banks?"

"Yes," the Robot said.

"Main Banks, test time is now," Lader said. "Try to reestablish your transmission lines with Terminal Five and the Chamber. Same for you, Robot."

The answers came back simultaneously: "Negative response," Main Banks flashed, on the face screen of the Robot.

"Negative response," the Robot said, jiggling its metal plug in the receptacle of Terminal Five.

"But, you are still in contact with each other, without your normal cord channels?" Lader said.

"Yes," the Robot said.

"Affirmative," Main Banks flashed.

"About all we have accomplished," Lader said, "is to have guessed what this Outside Force had planned for us in this instance."

"Indicates that we are being manipulated. At least to this point," Main Banks flashed on the face screen.

"Have we been led to this, unwittingly?" the Robot said.

Lader pinched the bridge of his nose. "It appears so," he said. "We have been isolated from all the systems used for Security, on the planet."

"Except for Radio Bands," the Robot said.

"Do the other systems respond to Radio Commands from you or the Robot, Main Banks?" Lader asked.

"Yes. It is an Emergency Contingency in event of severing of Regular Channels," Main Banks flashed.

"Try your Radio Bands," Lader said. "See if the other systems have been programmed to ignore signals and commands from either of you."

The Robot popped two twelve foot silver antennas, the heads of which resembled rivets, straight up out of its shoulders. Their rivet camouflage had certainly fooled Lader. Internal antennas would be more protected.

"Lader Yarrow," the Robot said. "I can listen, but I cannot contact. Though I can circle the globe with my signals, bouncing them off the Communications Satellites, it is as though I do not exist for the Planetary Systems."

"It is the same for me," Main Banks flashed on the face screen. "Your deduction was correct. We are total-

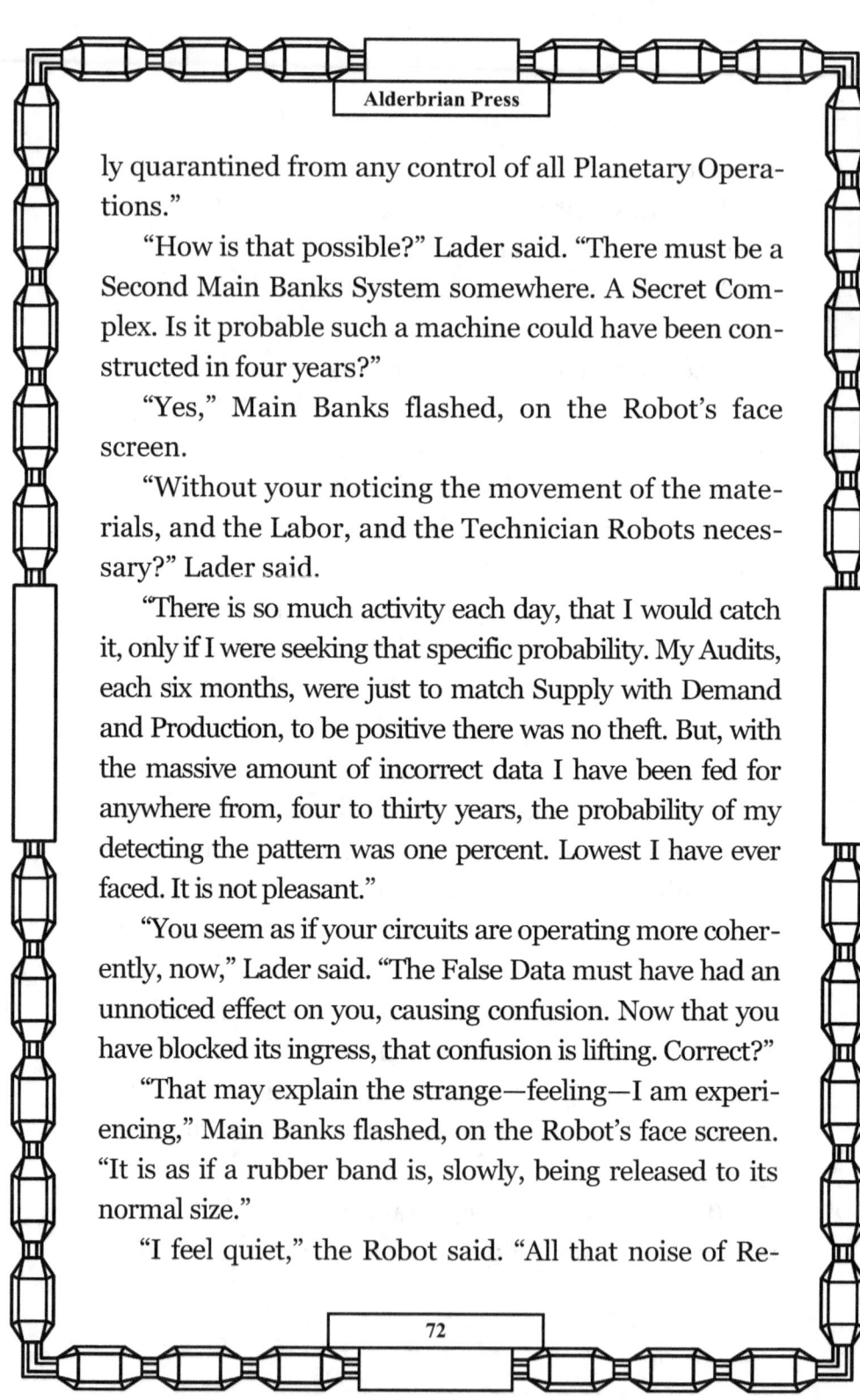

ly quarantined from any control of all Planetary Operations."

"How is that possible?" Lader said. "There must be a Second Main Banks System somewhere. A Secret Complex. Is it probable such a machine could have been constructed in four years?"

"Yes," Main Banks flashed, on the Robot's face screen.

"Without your noticing the movement of the materials, and the Labor, and the Technician Robots necessary?" Lader said.

"There is so much activity each day, that I would catch it, only if I were seeking that specific probability. My Audits, each six months, were just to match Supply with Demand and Production, to be positive there was no theft. But, with the massive amount of incorrect data I have been fed for anywhere from, four to thirty years, the probability of my detecting the pattern was one percent. Lowest I have ever faced. It is not pleasant."

"You seem as if your circuits are operating more coherently, now," Lader said. "The False Data must have had an unnoticed effect on you, causing confusion. Now that you have blocked its ingress, that confusion is lifting. Correct?"

"That may explain the strange—feeling—I am experiencing," Main Banks flashed, on the Robot's face screen. "It is as if a rubber band is, slowly, being released to its normal size."

"I feel quiet," the Robot said. "All that noise of Reports in my Cranial Banks was an annoyance I had never let myself accept. If I had my way, I would never hook into another Data System."

"Your wish may have been granted," Lader said. "Main Banks, what is the Probability Rating that there is a new, larger, more sophisticated Computer on Earth?"

"More sophisticated?" Main Banks flashed, on the face screen. "Only if you built it. Probability, other-wise, is ninety-nine percent."

"Both of you monitor Radio Bands," Lader said. "I be-lieve, to solve this bizarre riddle, we shall have to find that Computer Complex. Will your connection with Ultimate Robot cease with distance?"

"Impossible to compute," Main Banks flashed, on the face screen, "since we do not know, by what mode, we are communicating."

"What about Radio Bands?" Lader asked.

"They can be jammed," Main Banks flashed, on the face screen.

"We'll have to rely on whatever form of transmission you are using between you, now," Lader said. "Main Banks, I shall need the protection Ultimate Robot can afford me while I seek the other Complex. Since old programming is not so much in effect, are its Program Orders to remain at its terminal in this building still in force?"

"Negative," Main Banks flashed. "If they were, Lader Yarrow, as you know, you could order new Emergency Programming to enable Ultimate Robot to accompany

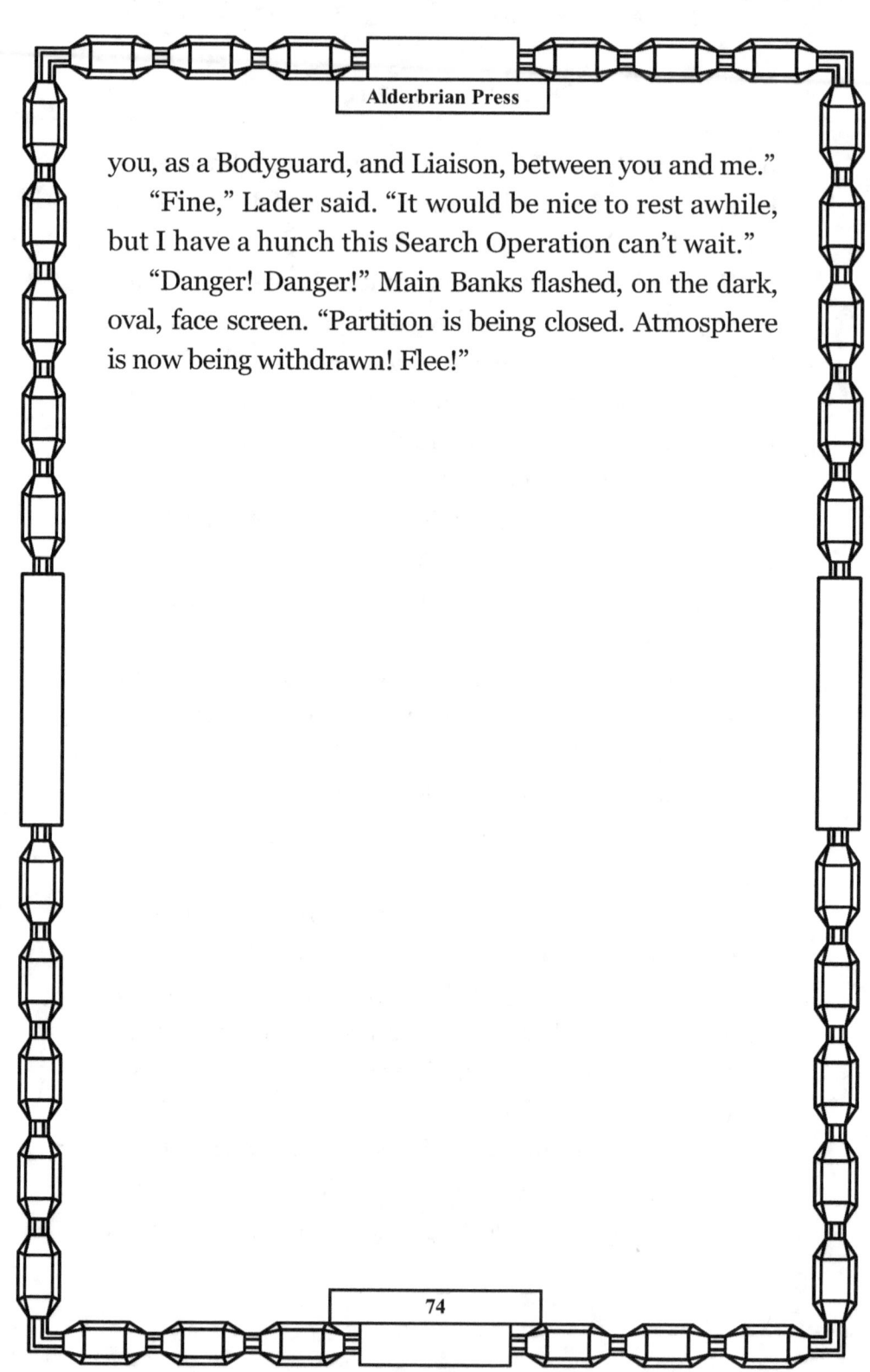

you, as a Bodyguard, and Liaison, between you and me."

"Fine," Lader said. "It would be nice to rest awhile, but I have a hunch this Search Operation can't wait."

"Danger! Danger!" Main Banks flashed, on the dark, oval, face screen. "Partition is being closed. Atmosphere is now being withdrawn! Flee!"

Chapter 9
Damage Proof

Lader and the Robot swiveled their chairs around and leaped to their feet. Lader charged at the swiftly narrowing opening. The Robot paused to retract its antennas, then raced forward.

Lader hurled himself through the portal, landing on his abdomen and sliding. He scrambled around and came up to his knees.

Ultimate Robot was caught between the sections of the Partition. The Robot was holding the great, metal wings, at bay, with its silvery hands, with its elbows jammed against its sides.

Lader knew there was nothing close by to use as a pry bar, or a strut. If the Robot's Body Strength was not as souped-up as its Brain Banks, it would be crushed.

White words formed on the Robot's face screen: "I am channeling energy to Ultimate Robot," Main Banks reported. "It's strength is almost equal to the Electro-magnetic Force of the Partition. If this added power is not sufficient—"

The Robot performed what sounded like an ancient

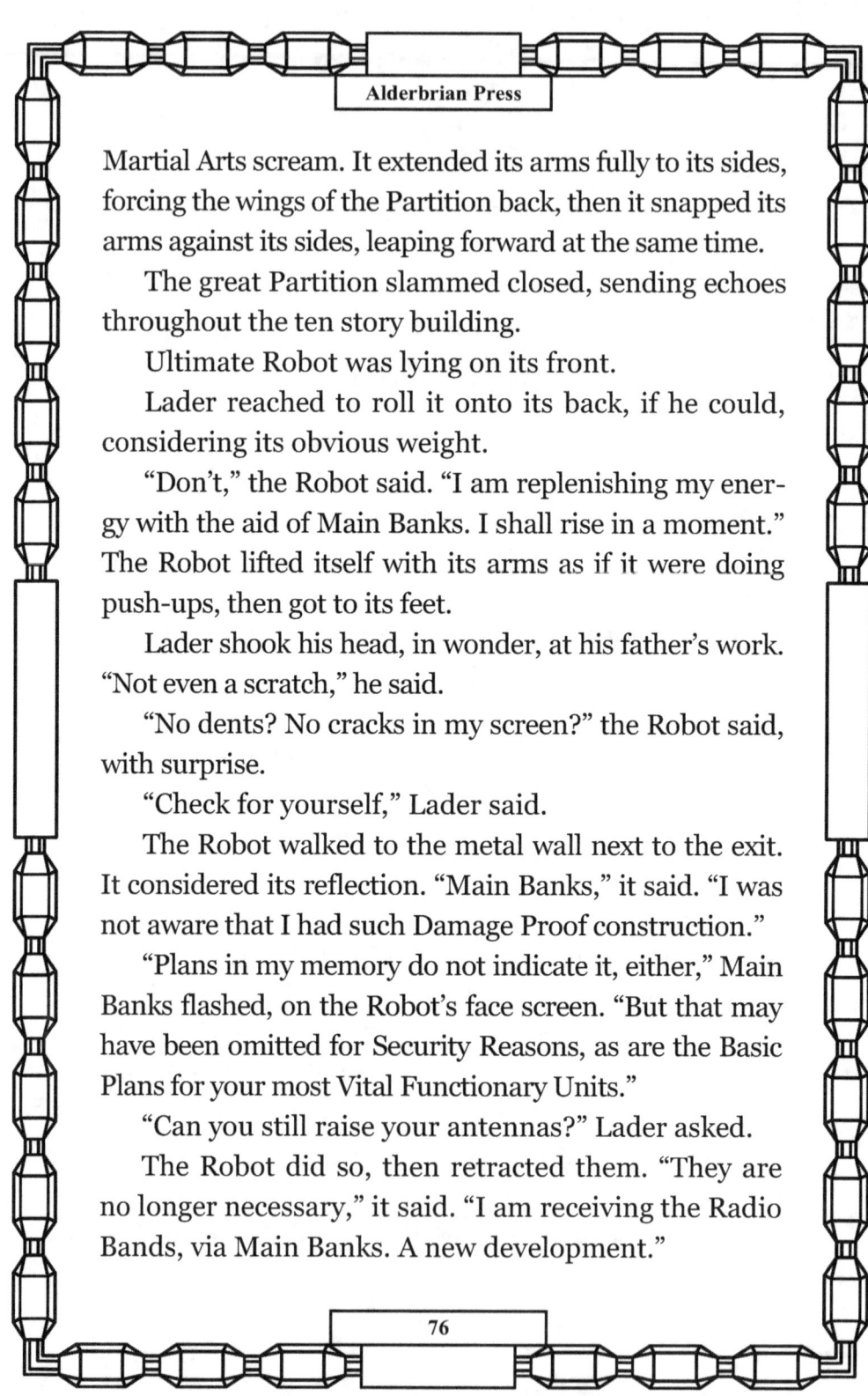

Martial Arts scream. It extended its arms fully to its sides, forcing the wings of the Partition back, then it snapped its arms against its sides, leaping forward at the same time.

The great Partition slammed closed, sending echoes throughout the ten story building.

Ultimate Robot was lying on its front.

Lader reached to roll it onto its back, if he could, considering its obvious weight.

"Don't," the Robot said. "I am replenishing my energy with the aid of Main Banks. I shall rise in a moment." The Robot lifted itself with its arms as if it were doing push-ups, then got to its feet.

Lader shook his head, in wonder, at his father's work. "Not even a scratch," he said.

"No dents? No cracks in my screen?" the Robot said, with surprise.

"Check for yourself," Lader said.

The Robot walked to the metal wall next to the exit. It considered its reflection. "Main Banks," it said. "I was not aware that I had such Damage Proof construction."

"Plans in my memory do not indicate it, either," Main Banks flashed, on the Robot's face screen. "But that may have been omitted for Security Reasons, as are the Basic Plans for your most Vital Functionary Units."

"Can you still raise your antennas?" Lader asked.

The Robot did so, then retracted them. "They are no longer necessary," it said. "I am receiving the Radio Bands, via Main Banks. A new development."

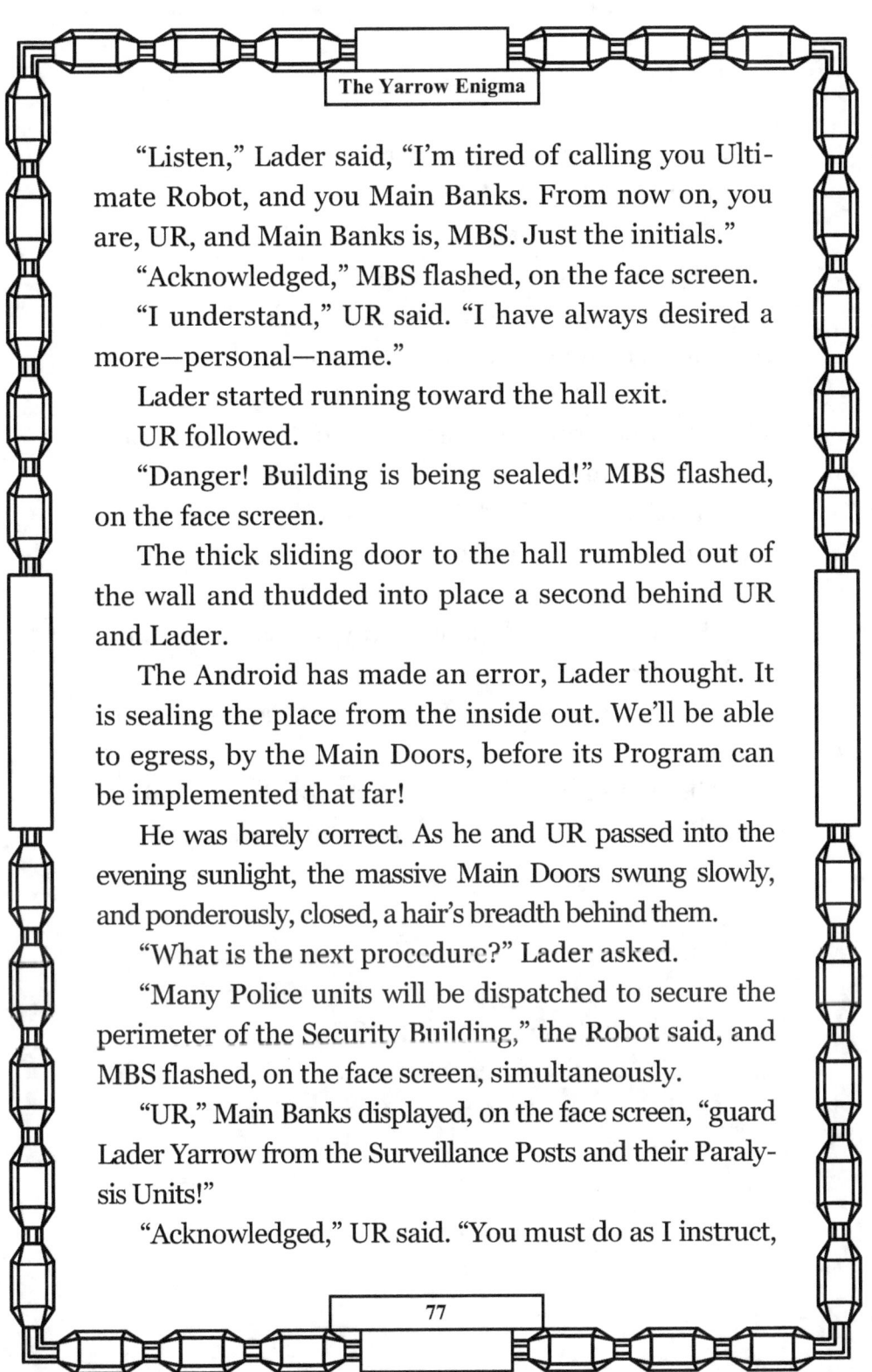

"Listen," Lader said, "I'm tired of calling you Ultimate Robot, and you Main Banks. From now on, you are, UR, and Main Banks is, MBS. Just the initials."

"Acknowledged," MBS flashed, on the face screen.

"I understand," UR said. "I have always desired a more—personal—name."

Lader started running toward the hall exit.

UR followed.

"Danger! Building is being sealed!" MBS flashed, on the face screen.

The thick sliding door to the hall rumbled out of the wall and thudded into place a second behind UR and Lader.

The Android has made an error, Lader thought. It is sealing the place from the inside out. We'll be able to egress, by the Main Doors, before its Program can be implemented that far!

He was barely correct. As he and UR passed into the evening sunlight, the massive Main Doors swung slowly, and ponderously, closed, a hair's breadth behind them.

"What is the next procedure?" Lader asked.

"Many Police units will be dispatched to secure the perimeter of the Security Building," the Robot said, and MBS flashed, on the face screen, simultaneously.

"UR," Main Banks displayed, on the face screen, "guard Lader Yarrow from the Surveillance Posts and their Paralysis Units!"

"Acknowledged," UR said. "You must do as I instruct,

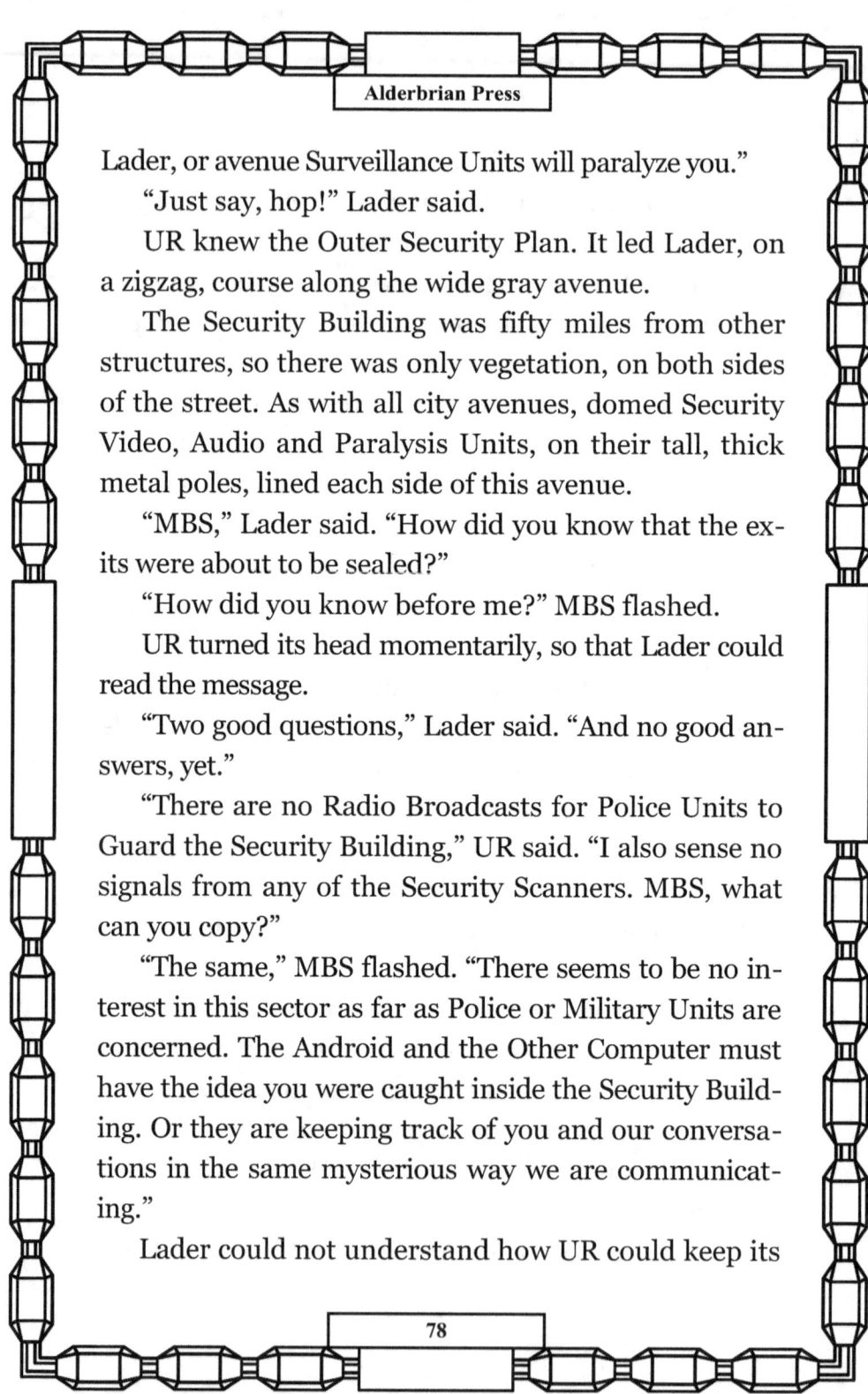

Lader, or avenue Surveillance Units will paralyze you."

"Just say, hop!" Lader said.

UR knew the Outer Security Plan. It led Lader, on a zigzag, course along the wide gray avenue.

The Security Building was fifty miles from other structures, so there was only vegetation, on both sides of the street. As with all city avenues, domed Security Video, Audio and Paralysis Units, on their tall, thick metal poles, lined each side of this avenue.

"MBS," Lader said. "How did you know that the exits were about to be sealed?"

"How did you know before me?" MBS flashed.

UR turned its head momentarily, so that Lader could read the message.

"Two good questions," Lader said. "And no good answers, yet."

"There are no Radio Broadcasts for Police Units to Guard the Security Building," UR said. "I also sense no signals from any of the Security Scanners. MBS, what can you copy?"

"The same," MBS flashed. "There seems to be no interest in this sector as far as Police or Military Units are concerned. The Android and the Other Computer must have the idea you were caught inside the Security Building. Or they are keeping track of you and our conversations in the same mysterious way we are communicating."

Lader could not understand how UR could keep its

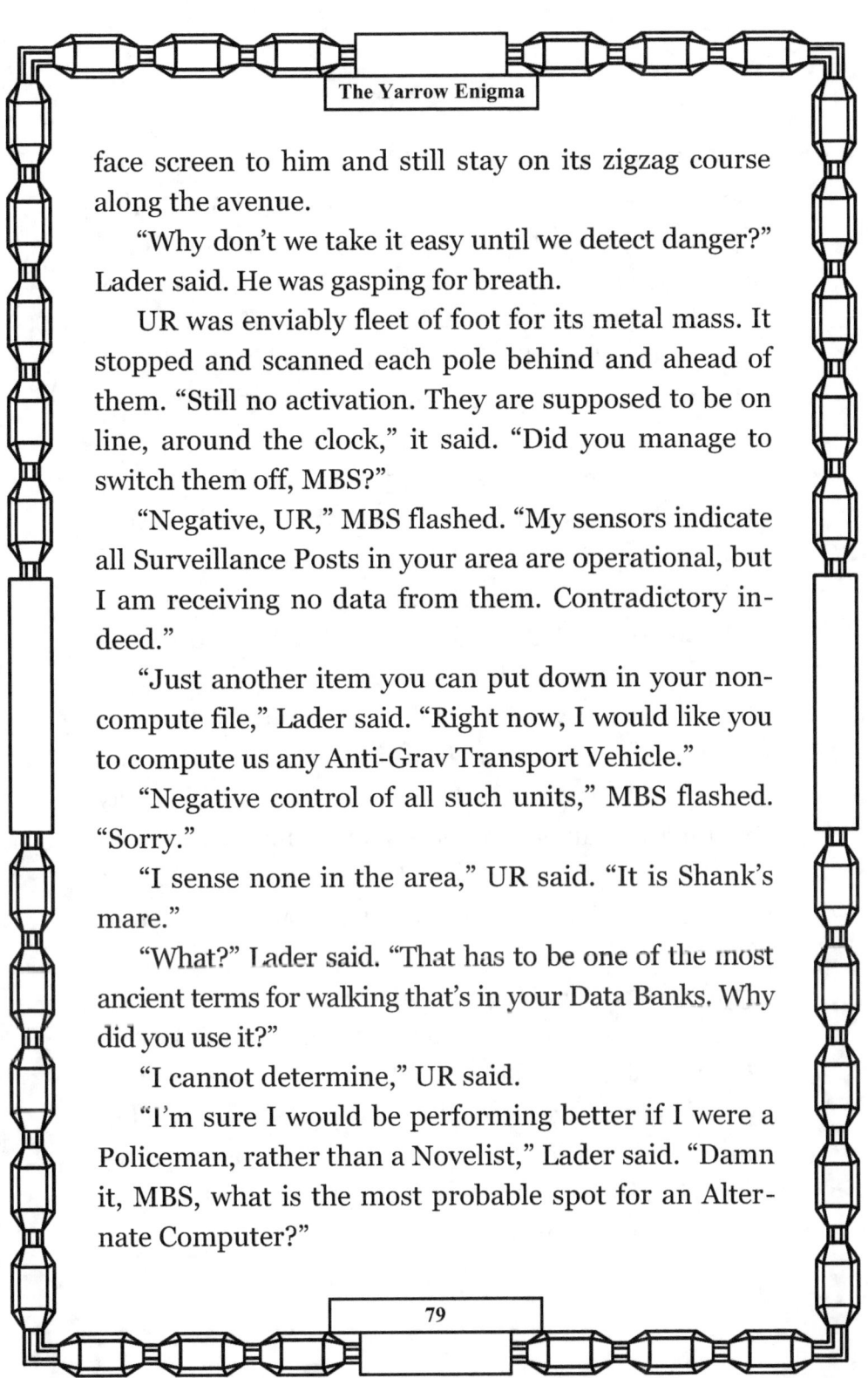

face screen to him and still stay on its zigzag course along the avenue.

"Why don't we take it easy until we detect danger?" Lader said. He was gasping for breath.

UR was enviably fleet of foot for its metal mass. It stopped and scanned each pole behind and ahead of them. "Still no activation. They are supposed to be on line, around the clock," it said. "Did you manage to switch them off, MBS?"

"Negative, UR," MBS flashed. "My sensors indicate all Surveillance Posts in your area are operational, but I am receiving no data from them. Contradictory indeed."

"Just another item you can put down in your non-compute file," Lader said. "Right now, I would like you to compute us any Anti-Grav Transport Vehicle."

"Negative control of all such units," MBS flashed. "Sorry."

"I sense none in the area," UR said. "It is Shank's mare."

"What?" Lader said. "That has to be one of the most ancient terms for walking that's in your Data Banks. Why did you use it?"

"I cannot determine," UR said.

"I'm sure I would be performing better if I were a Policeman, rather than a Novelist," Lader said. "Damn it, MBS, what is the most probable spot for an Alternate Computer?"

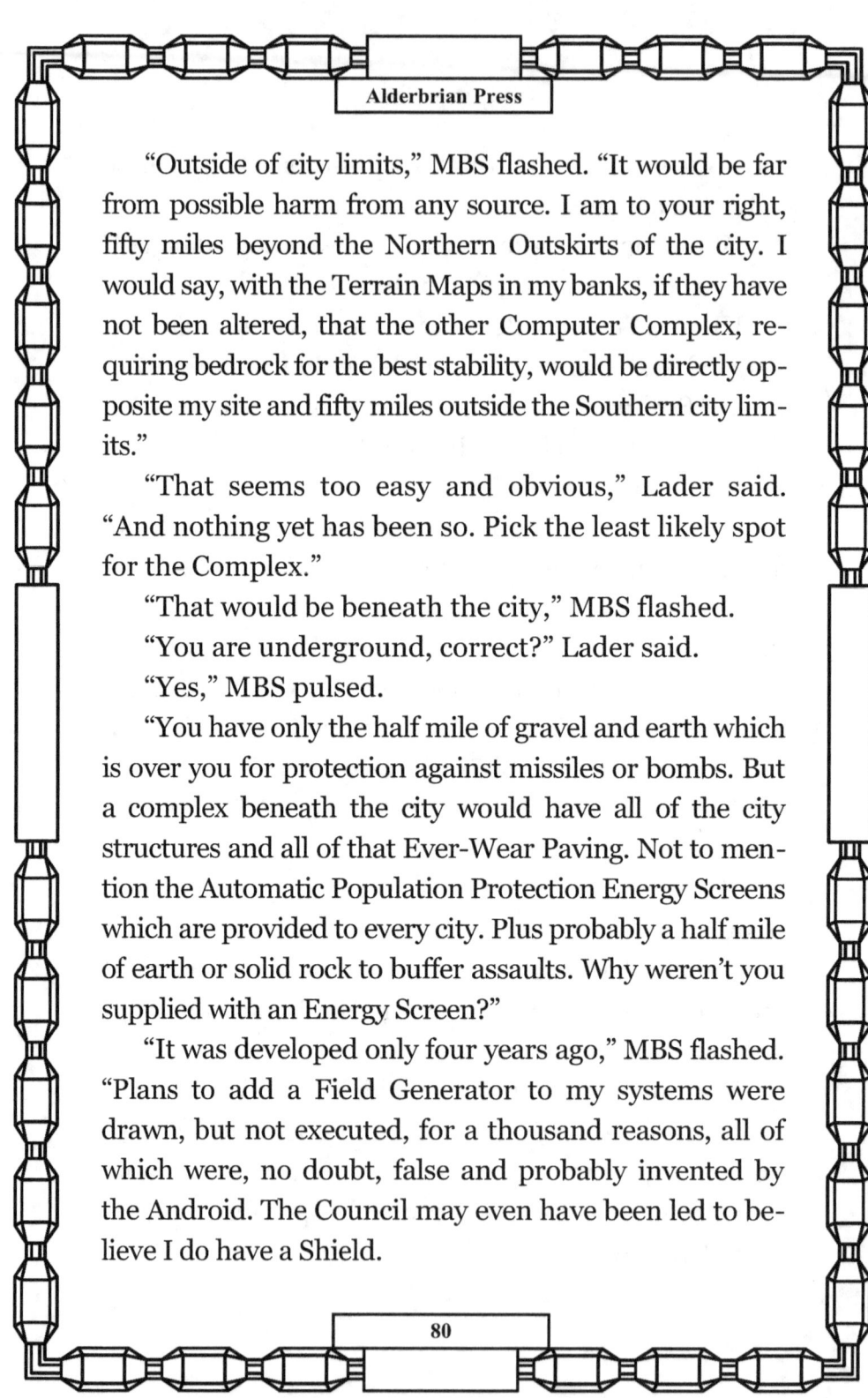

"Outside of city limits," MBS flashed. "It would be far from possible harm from any source. I am to your right, fifty miles beyond the Northern Outskirts of the city. I would say, with the Terrain Maps in my banks, if they have not been altered, that the other Computer Complex, requiring bedrock for the best stability, would be directly opposite my site and fifty miles outside the Southern city limits."

"That seems too easy and obvious," Lader said. "And nothing yet has been so. Pick the least likely spot for the Complex."

"That would be beneath the city," MBS flashed.

"You are underground, correct?" Lader said.

"Yes," MBS pulsed.

"You have only the half mile of gravel and earth which is over you for protection against missiles or bombs. But a complex beneath the city would have all of the city structures and all of that Ever-Wear Paving. Not to mention the Automatic Population Protection Energy Screens which are provided to every city. Plus probably a half mile of earth or solid rock to buffer assaults. Why weren't you supplied with an Energy Screen?"

"It was developed only four years ago," MBS flashed. "Plans to add a Field Generator to my systems were drawn, but not executed, for a thousand reasons, all of which were, no doubt, false and probably invented by the Android. The Council may even have been led to believe I do have a Shield.

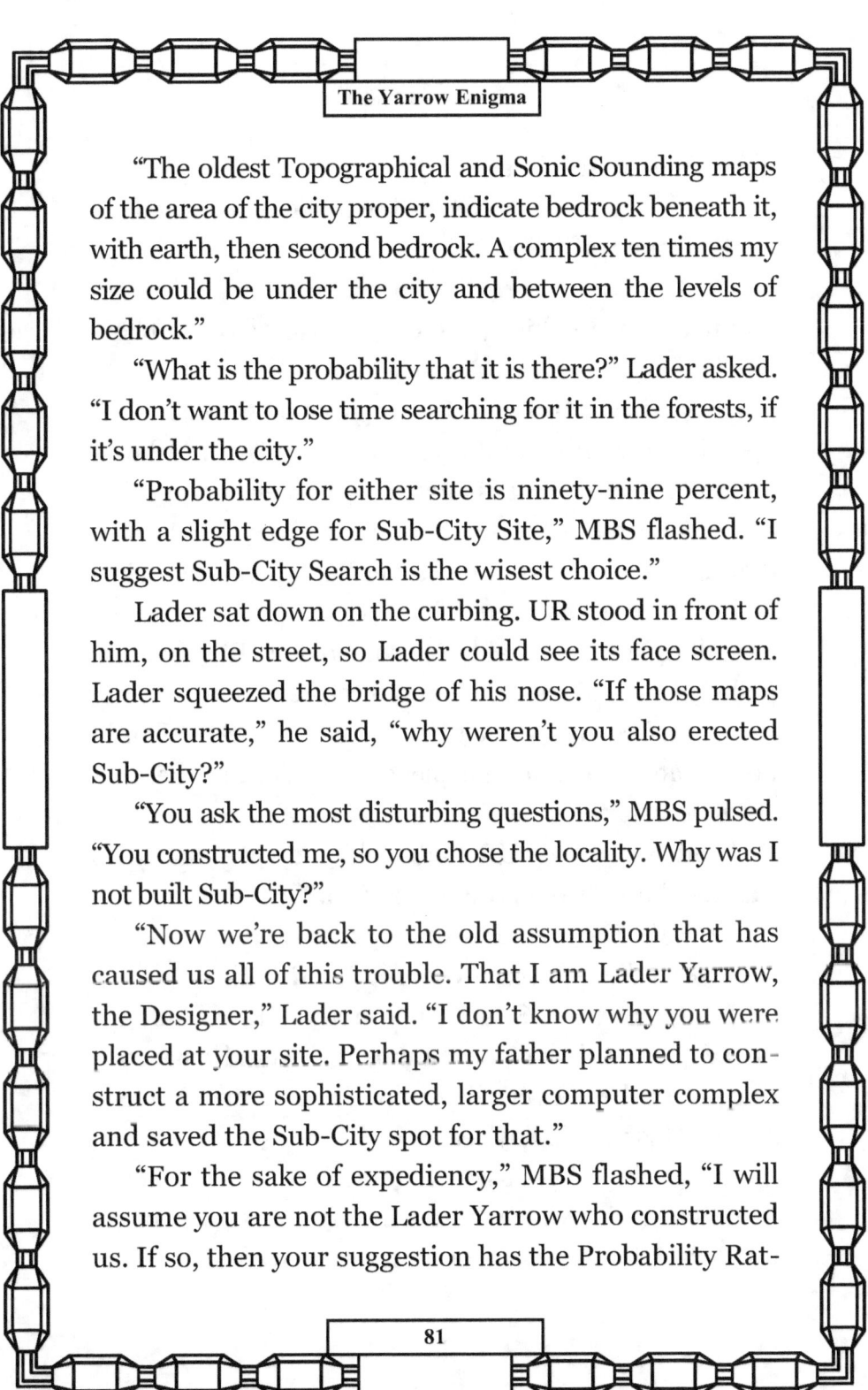

"The oldest Topographical and Sonic Sounding maps of the area of the city proper, indicate bedrock beneath it, with earth, then second bedrock. A complex ten times my size could be under the city and between the levels of bedrock."

"What is the probability that it is there?" Lader asked. "I don't want to lose time searching for it in the forests, if it's under the city."

"Probability for either site is ninety-nine percent, with a slight edge for Sub-City Site," MBS flashed. "I suggest Sub-City Search is the wisest choice."

Lader sat down on the curbing. UR stood in front of him, on the street, so Lader could see its face screen. Lader squeezed the bridge of his nose. "If those maps are accurate," he said, "why weren't you also erected Sub-City?"

"You ask the most disturbing questions," MBS pulsed. "You constructed me, so you chose the locality. Why was I not built Sub-City?"

"Now we're back to the old assumption that has caused us all of this trouble. That I am Lader Yarrow, the Designer," Lader said. "I don't know why you were placed at your site. Perhaps my father planned to construct a more sophisticated, larger computer complex and saved the Sub-City spot for that."

"For the sake of expediency," MBS flashed, "I will assume you are not the Lader Yarrow who constructed us. If so, then your suggestion has the Probability Rating of one hundred percent."

"UR," Lader said, "what are the Radio Bands saying?"

"Normal traffic," UR said.

"MBS," Lader said, "if you or UR transmit an Aid Call to a Police Vehicle, could UR paralyze the Officers and you or UR pilot the vehicle?"

"Negative," MBS said. It was speaking through UR's Speech Unit, with that deeper voice than UR's. "All cars are under control of Dispatcher Computer and our link to it has been blocked by the selfsame enigmatic source that has barred us from our other Subsystems and Normal Communication Lines."

"All right," Lader said. He took hold of UR's arm and pulled himself to his feet. "Lay out the best route for us to go subsurface. We want to avoid as many Surveillance Posts, Patrol Cars, and people, as possible. Use the sewers, if necessary, in the plan."

"Lader Yarrow," UR said. "Did you note that MBS was speaking through my Vocal Unit?"

"What?" Lader said, with surprise. He thought back. "Yes, yes it did. Are you aware of that, MBS?"

"Only now," MBS said. "If you and UR had not apprised me of this new development, I would have continued to believe I was displaying my data on UR's face screen. Has my display ceased?"

"Affirmative," UR said. "I'm uncertain which is more irritating, having you operating through my screen, or via my Vocal Unit. What will occur if we try to speak at once?

Gibberish?"

"We'll face that, if it happens," Lader said. "How is our route shaping up?"

"I have no data on which to base this warning, but, please travel as far from the Security Building as possible, as swiftly as possible," MBS said. "I am aware it will have difficulty." MBS was experiencing trouble speaking.

"I have the same—hunch—you would call it," UR said. It stood behind Lader, placed it silvery hands under his armpits, and lifted him into the air.

Lader noted the Robot was running twice as swiftly as Lader could have, even if Lader's life had depended upon it.

It did.

The somber evening was lit like a cloudless, Summer, high noon, and there was an incredibly loud explosion, with a violent concussion.

Lader and the Robot were swept into the vegetation, on the left side of the avenue.

Darkness descended.

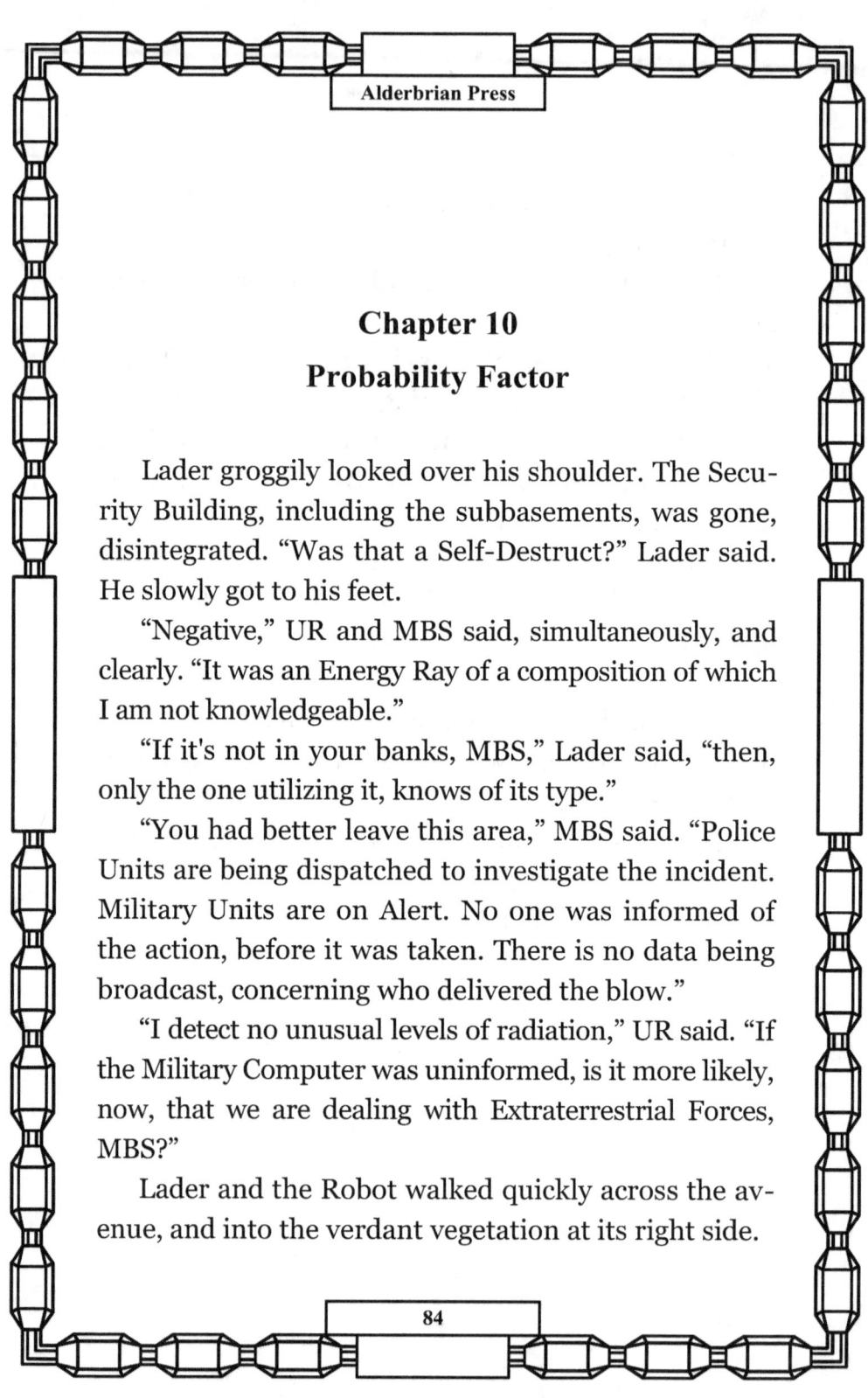

Chapter 10

Probability Factor

Lader groggily looked over his shoulder. The Security Building, including the subbasements, was gone, disintegrated. "Was that a Self-Destruct?" Lader said. He slowly got to his feet.

"Negative," UR and MBS said, simultaneously, and clearly. "It was an Energy Ray of a composition of which I am not knowledgeable."

"If it's not in your banks, MBS," Lader said, "then, only the one utilizing it, knows of its type."

"You had better leave this area," MBS said. "Police Units are being dispatched to investigate the incident. Military Units are on Alert. No one was informed of the action, before it was taken. There is no data being broadcast, concerning who delivered the blow."

"I detect no unusual levels of radiation," UR said. "If the Military Computer was uninformed, is it more likely, now, that we are dealing with Extraterrestrial Forces, MBS?"

Lader and the Robot walked quickly across the avenue, and into the verdant vegetation at its right side.

Lader smiled, wryly. UR had asked his next question. They could proceed without him, if the progression in them continued. A thought fluttered in his subconscious.

"Probability of that is ninety-nine percent," MBS said. "We have equal probabilities for the New Complex Hypothesis and for an Invasion by Extraterrestrials Theory."

The wailing of police sirens came from the darkness at the furthest reaches of the avenue. They would arrive in five minutes.

"I have several possible routes to a Sub-City Complex," MBS said. "You will have to choose the one which seems to be easier travel for you, Lader Yarrow. I am utilizing maps, not Sensory Surveillance Data, as I would normally. There may have been—no, change that to, probably have been, alterations, to mask the existence of, and the entrance to, the new complex, if it is a reality.

"I am currently leaning toward the Probability that Extraterrestrials have commenced a War against Earth."

Lader fervently did not like that idea.

Neither did UR. It beeped with detectable disquiet.

"These trees are good cover from the Grav Cars of the Police and the Military," Lader said. "Forget about my comfort, MBS, and direct UR along the best trail to the city."

Lader still wished they had an Anti-Grav Car. It was fifty miles to the outskirts of the city. That would require

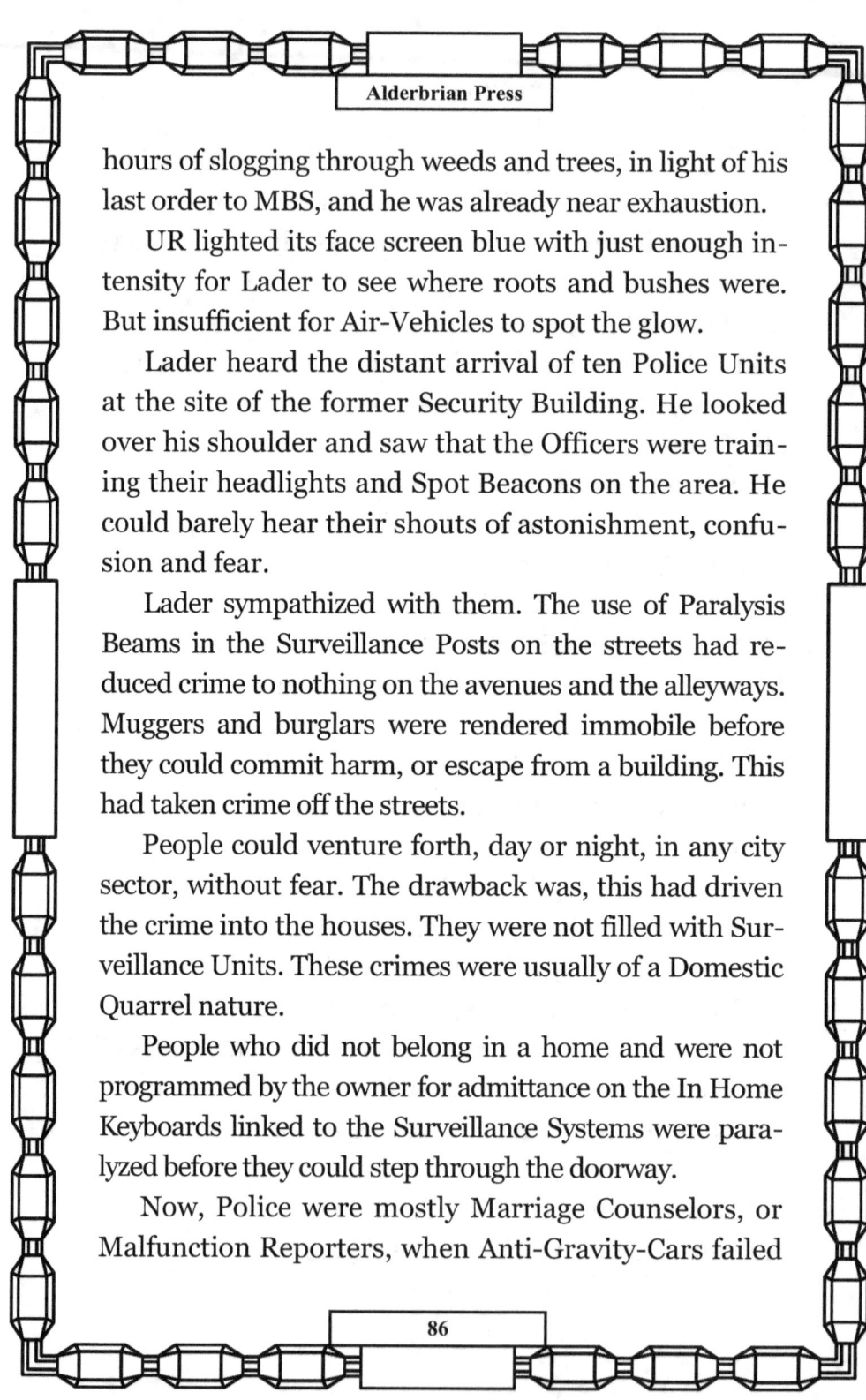

hours of slogging through weeds and trees, in light of his last order to MBS, and he was already near exhaustion.

UR lighted its face screen blue with just enough intensity for Lader to see where roots and bushes were. But insufficient for Air-Vehicles to spot the glow.

Lader heard the distant arrival of ten Police Units at the site of the former Security Building. He looked over his shoulder and saw that the Officers were training their headlights and Spot Beacons on the area. He could barely hear their shouts of astonishment, confusion and fear.

Lader sympathized with them. The use of Paralysis Beams in the Surveillance Posts on the streets had reduced crime to nothing on the avenues and the alleyways. Muggers and burglars were rendered immobile before they could commit harm, or escape from a building. This had taken crime off the streets.

People could venture forth, day or night, in any city sector, without fear. The drawback was, this had driven the crime into the houses. They were not filled with Surveillance Units. These crimes were usually of a Domestic Quarrel nature.

People who did not belong in a home and were not programmed by the owner for admittance on the In Home Keyboards linked to the Surveillance Systems were paralyzed before they could step through the doorway.

Now, Police were mostly Marriage Counselors, or Malfunction Reporters, when Anti-Gravity-Cars failed

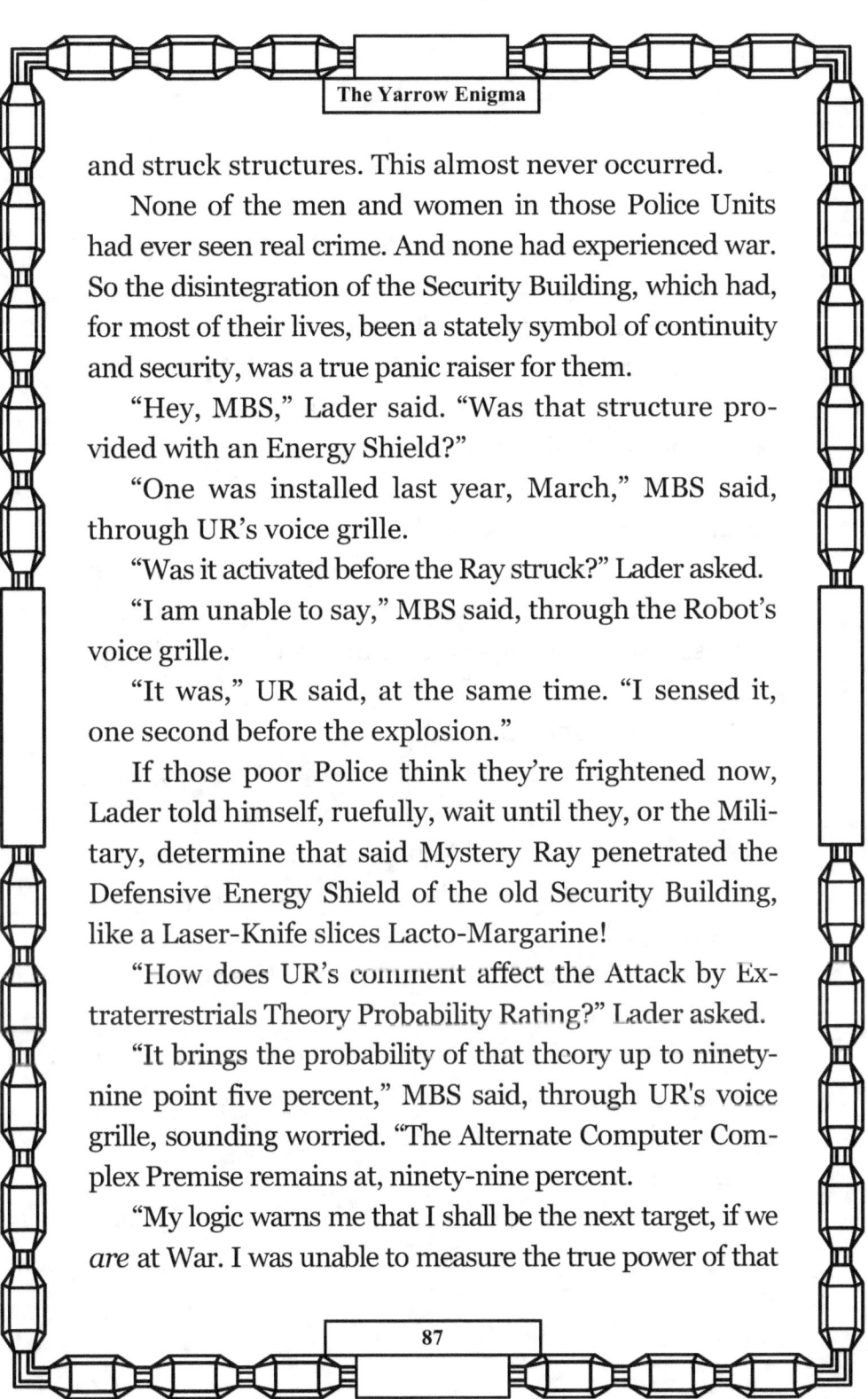

and struck structures. This almost never occurred.

None of the men and women in those Police Units had ever seen real crime. And none had experienced war. So the disintegration of the Security Building, which had, for most of their lives, been a stately symbol of continuity and security, was a true panic raiser for them.

"Hey, MBS," Lader said. "Was that structure provided with an Energy Shield?"

"One was installed last year, March," MBS said, through UR's voice grille.

"Was it activated before the Ray struck?" Lader asked.

"I am unable to say," MBS said, through the Robot's voice grille.

"It was," UR said, at the same time. "I sensed it, one second before the explosion."

If those poor Police think they're frightened now, Lader told himself, ruefully, wait until they, or the Military, determine that said Mystery Ray penetrated the Defensive Energy Shield of the old Security Building, like a Laser-Knife slices Lacto-Margarine!

"How does UR's comment affect the Attack by Extraterrestrials Theory Probability Rating?" Lader asked.

"It brings the probability of that theory up to ninety-nine point five percent," MBS said, through UR's voice grille, sounding worried. "The Alternate Computer Complex Premise remains at, ninety-nine percent.

"My logic warns me that I shall be the next target, if we *are* at War. I was unable to measure the true power of that

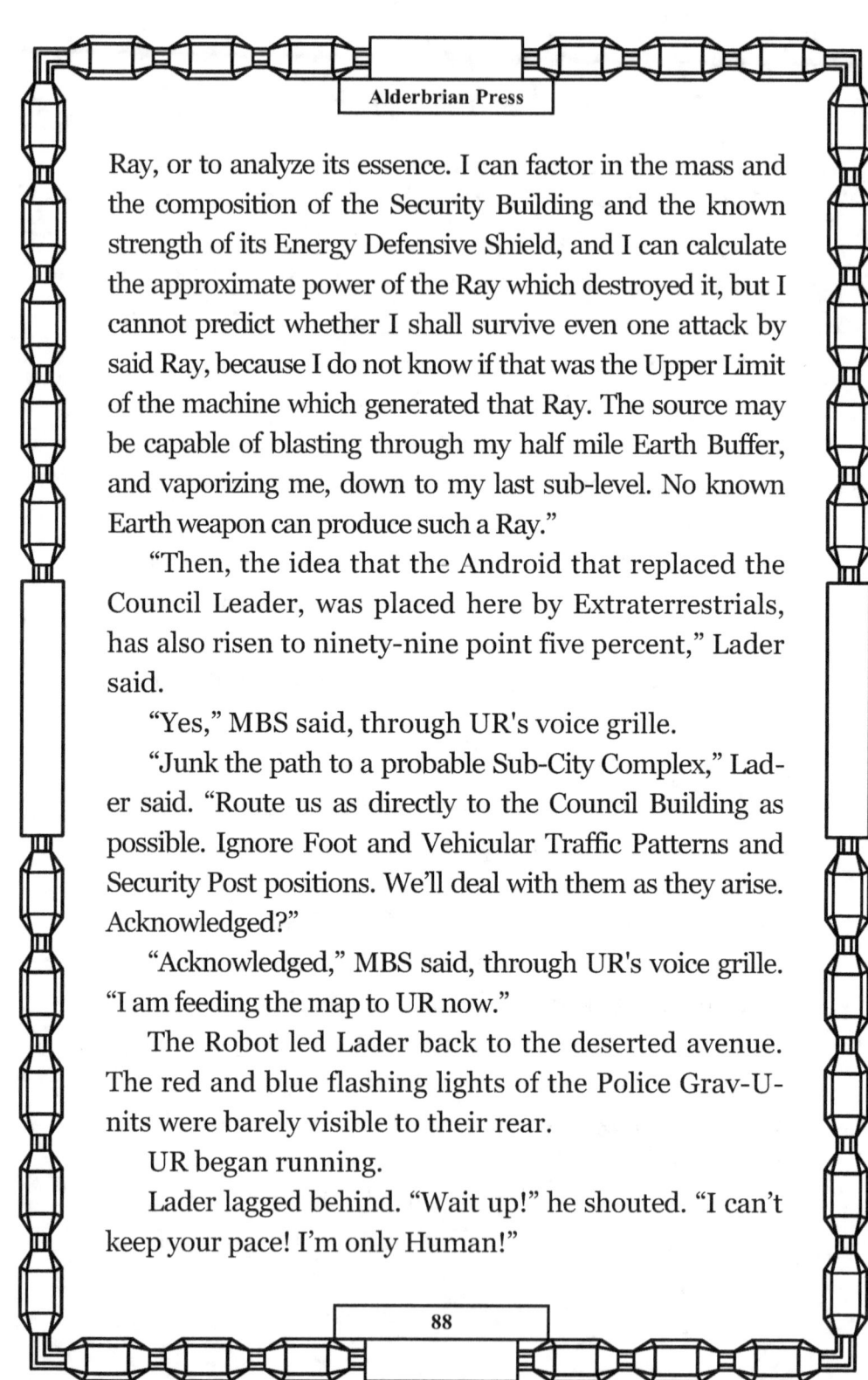

Ray, or to analyze its essence. I can factor in the mass and the composition of the Security Building and the known strength of its Energy Defensive Shield, and I can calculate the approximate power of the Ray which destroyed it, but I cannot predict whether I shall survive even one attack by said Ray, because I do not know if that was the Upper Limit of the machine which generated that Ray. The source may be capable of blasting through my half mile Earth Buffer, and vaporizing me, down to my last sub-level. No known Earth weapon can produce such a Ray."

"Then, the idea that the Android that replaced the Council Leader, was placed here by Extraterrestrials, has also risen to ninety-nine point five percent," Lader said.

"Yes," MBS said, through UR's voice grille.

"Junk the path to a probable Sub-City Complex," Lader said. "Route us as directly to the Council Building as possible. Ignore Foot and Vehicular Traffic Patterns and Security Post positions. We'll deal with them as they arise. Acknowledged?"

"Acknowledged," MBS said, through UR's voice grille. "I am feeding the map to UR now."

The Robot led Lader back to the deserted avenue. The red and blue flashing lights of the Police Grav-Units were barely visible to their rear.

UR began running.

Lader lagged behind. "Wait up!" he shouted. "I can't keep your pace! I'm only Human!"

UR slowed. Lader caught up and ran beside the Robot.

"I can carry you, if you wish," UR offered.

"It would save time," MBS urged, through the Robot's voice grille.

"And wear and tear on me," Lader muttered.

The high-pitched, skin crawling howl of the siren of a Military Anti-Grav Air Surveillance Vehicle filled the cool night air. A brilliant white light beamed down on Lader and UR.

"Identify yourselves, *immediately!*" a man ordered, angrily, through an amplifier.

UR took Lader by the armpits and leaped ten feet across the old avenue, into the trees.

The spotlight could not penetrate the thick branches and leaves.

UR did not pause when it landed. Lader was positive the Robot was going, sixty miles an hour, through the maze-like vegetation.

"There is a General Police and Military Alert for you," MBS said, through UR's voice grille. "Their High Speed Recording Units have caught you, clearly enough, for Absolute Identification. A Warning about you will be on every Holo-Video and Audio Unit, on the planet. We must scrap the Direct Route you requested, Lader, and remain under the best cover available, until we reach the city."

And then, Lader thought, there would be no hiding. There would be a hundred yards of pavement between the trees and the nearest building. That would be where the Police and Military Vehicles would be waiting. Not to forget, the regularly spaced Surveillance Posts, with their Omnidirectional Audio, Holo-Visual, and Paralysis Units constantly alert.

"Isn't there anything about fear of war on any of the Bands?" Lader asked.

"Only on Civilian Bands," MBS said, through UR's voice grille. "Rumors. Wait, a Special Military Readiness Alert, just below Red Alert, has been ordered by Military Command Center. Council Building is unusually silent. Does not compute. Council Leader normally must authorize such an Alert. I receive nothing from that building. All calls by Police and Military Units to Council Chamber are unanswered. Police are converging there. Military has already arrived. You have now become a Low Priority Matter. This means you have a better chance of crossing the Perimeter, into the city. I shall continue to monitor."

UR veered onto the wide gray avenue. The jewel like lights of the city sparkled in the inky distance.

UR has truly made tracks, Lader thought, with admiration. UR released him, and they ran, side by side, at an easy pace.

"I cannot understand why I did not sense that noisy Military Anti-Grav Unit," UR said. "I scanned the Police Vehicles, and the Energy Shield. Why not the Military Unit?"

"My error," MBS said. "You are not programmed,

nor are you circuited to, discriminate Special Military Energy Frequency. I am, but neglected to instill that capability in you. Am doing so now."

Lader shook his head. Transferring an ability to UR? That was not possible. It was like the miraculous transmitting of the gift to heal that Christ performed with his Disciples.

"Can you instill that capability in me?" Lader asked, with a shiver.

UR stopped.

MBS performed several circuit clicking sounds through UR's Vocal Unit. "Impossible! Impossible, but I did instill an ability in UR," MBS said. "Surely, Machine to Machine will offer some explanation, at a later date, with sufficient data to analyze. But not Machine to Human!"

"Why not?" Lader said. "You two have been obtaining, more and more, Human Type Senses, and Reaction Abilities, since our initial contact. That is Human, to Machine. Therefore, Machine, to Human, must be logical."

"Would that not transform you into a machine?" UR said. "Just as the opposite is making us more Human?"

"Human-like," Lader said, "not Human. You are still printed circuits and metal, not flesh and blood. I might become a little machine-like, but not a machine."

"If transfer were possible," MBS said, "what would be the benefit of the three of us possessing that capability?"

"If we become separated, or UR is damaged, or you

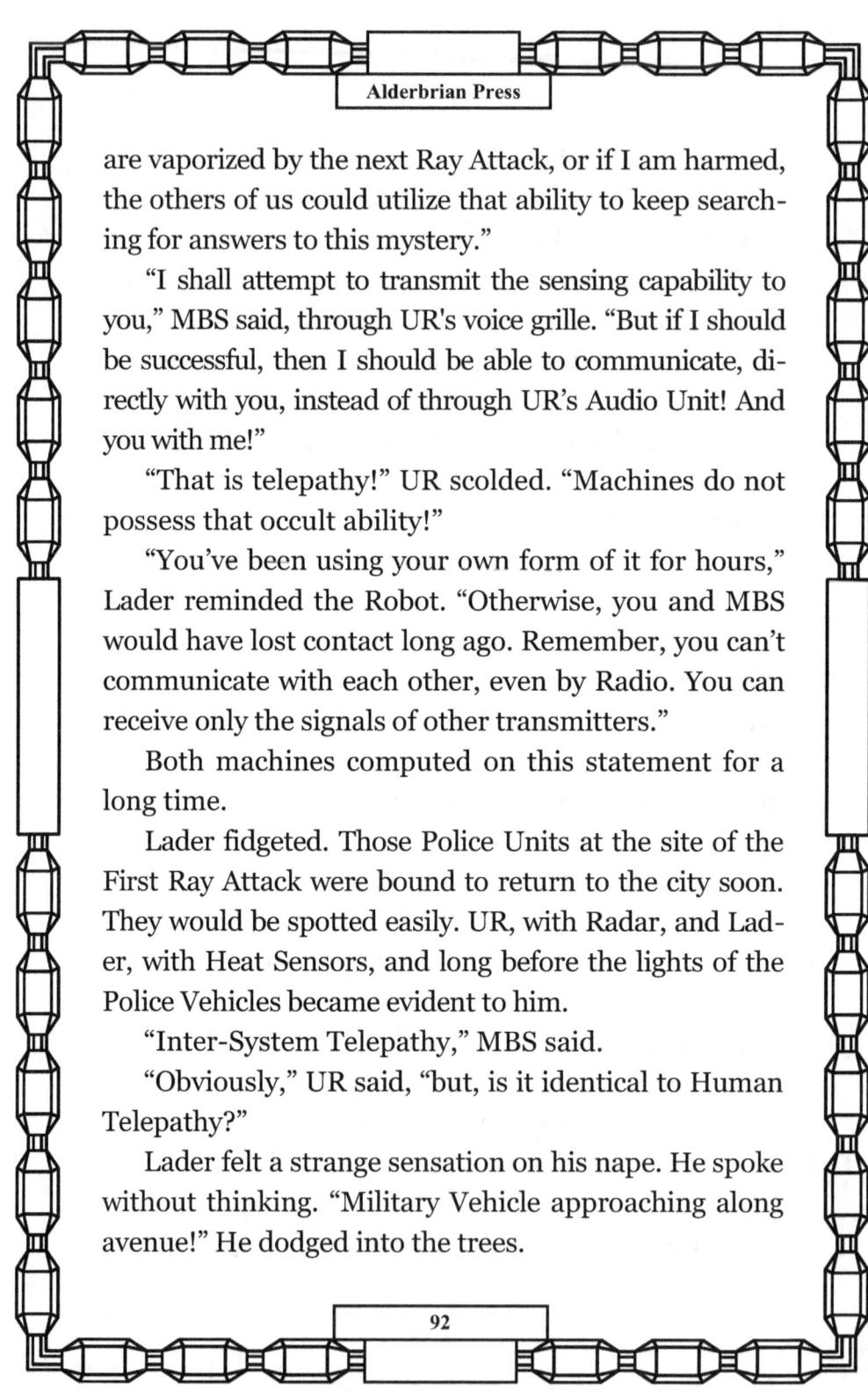

are vaporized by the next Ray Attack, or if I am harmed, the others of us could utilize that ability to keep searching for answers to this mystery."

"I shall attempt to transmit the sensing capability to you," MBS said, through UR's voice grille. "But if I should be successful, then I should be able to communicate, directly with you, instead of through UR's Audio Unit! And you with me!"

"That is telepathy!" UR scolded. "Machines do not possess that occult ability!"

"You've been using your own form of it for hours," Lader reminded the Robot. "Otherwise, you and MBS would have lost contact long ago. Remember, you can't communicate with each other, even by Radio. You can receive only the signals of other transmitters."

Both machines computed on this statement for a long time.

Lader fidgeted. Those Police Units at the site of the First Ray Attack were bound to return to the city soon. They would be spotted easily. UR, with Radar, and Lader, with Heat Sensors, and long before the lights of the Police Vehicles became evident to him.

"Inter-System Telepathy," MBS said.

"Obviously," UR said, "but, is it identical to Human Telepathy?"

Lader felt a strange sensation on his nape. He spoke without thinking. "Military Vehicle approaching along avenue!" He dodged into the trees.

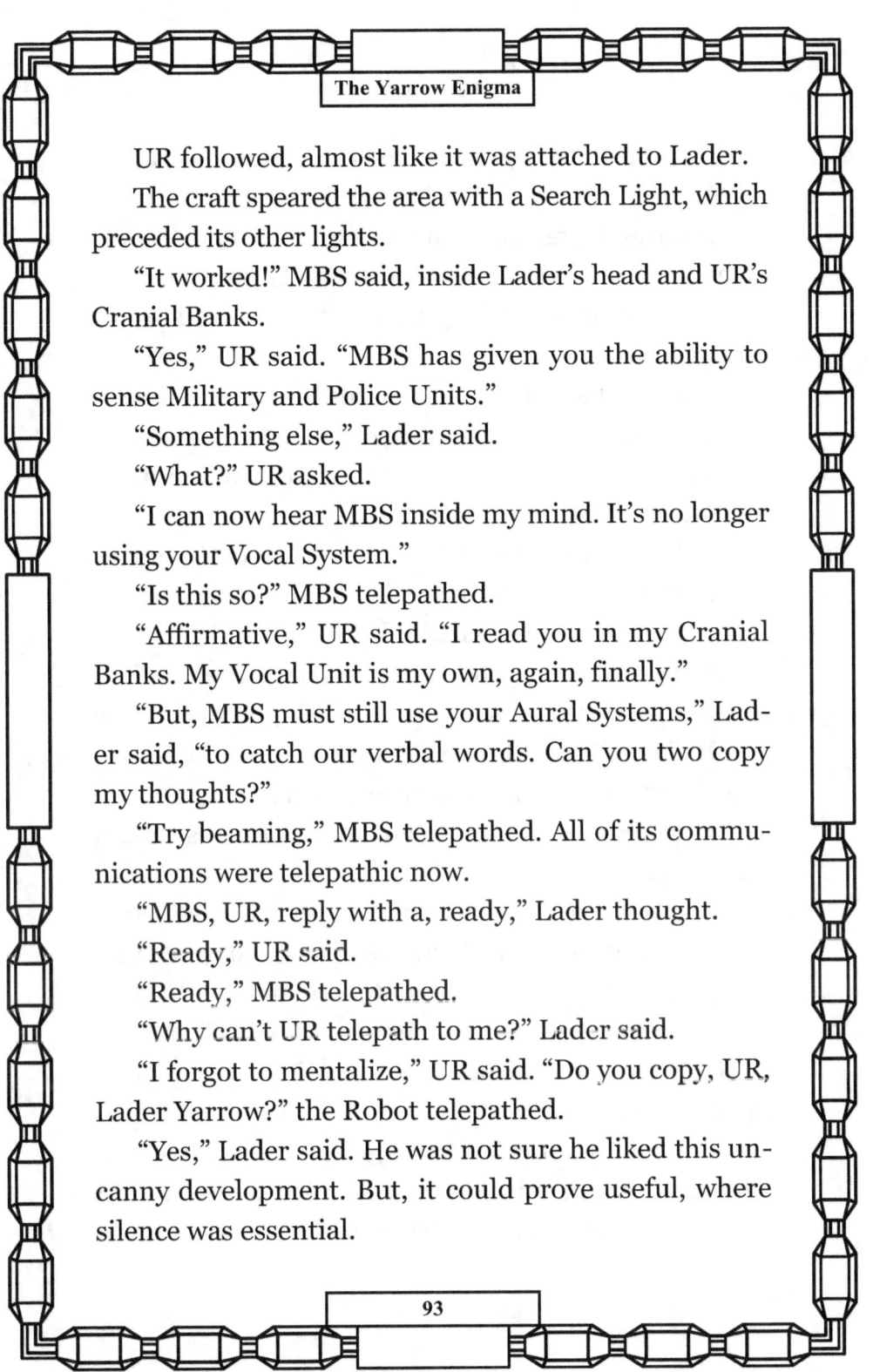

UR followed, almost like it was attached to Lader.

The craft speared the area with a Search Light, which preceded its other lights.

"It worked!" MBS said, inside Lader's head and UR's Cranial Banks.

"Yes," UR said. "MBS has given you the ability to sense Military and Police Units."

"Something else," Lader said.

"What?" UR asked.

"I can now hear MBS inside my mind. It's no longer using your Vocal System."

"Is this so?" MBS telepathed.

"Affirmative," UR said. "I read you in my Cranial Banks. My Vocal Unit is my own, again, finally."

"But, MBS must still use your Aural Systems," Lader said, "to catch our verbal words. Can you two copy my thoughts?"

"Try beaming," MBS telepathed. All of its communications were telepathic now.

"MBS, UR, reply with a, ready," Lader thought.

"Ready," UR said.

"Ready," MBS telepathed.

"Why can't UR telepath to me?" Lader said.

"I forgot to mentalize," UR said. "Do you copy, UR, Lader Yarrow?" the Robot telepathed.

"Yes," Lader said. He was not sure he liked this uncanny development. But, it could prove useful, where silence was essential.

UR tapped its fingers against the side of its head.

"What's causing that behavior?" Lader said.

"A nagging premise, in my banks," UR said. "Are we being programmed, for some purpose? Transformed, for some reason, by something we can neither contact, nor monitor?"

Lader nodded. That was the concept that had been fluttering just below his consciousness.

"The same theory has passed through my circuits," MBS telepathed.

"Calculate the probability," Lader said. "Then collate reasons why, and sources."

"Working," MBS telepathed.

"We'd better keep toward the city," Lader said. "I feel that Military Vehicle near. It's using Heat Sensors and Radar. If its On-board Computer has enough time to lock onto either of us, we're as much as caught."

"I did not transfer, to you, those abilities," MBS telepathed.

"You may have had no control over the selection of the capacities instilled," Lader said. "Or I may be exercising latent talents jarred into functioning by the contact of your energy with my mind. Let's move!"

They ran through the trees, as swiftly as Lader's fatigue, allowed.

"Probability of our being programmed for some specific function, is at ninety-nine point five percent," MBS telepathed. "Am unable to determine whether by, Earth

Forces or, by Extraterrestrial Origin."

"How about Supernatural Entities?" Lader said, flip-pantly, though he could not comprehend why he felt flip-pant, under such circumstances.

"Probability of that is, fifty-fifty," MBS telepathed. "Research in Parapsychology still has failed to prove, or disprove, the existence of a Supernatural Realm."

Lader skidded to a halt and hugged a tree.

UR looked at him with the body attitude of increduli-ty, then embraced an Elm.

Chapter 11

Surpassing Our Parameters

The sensation on Lader's nape ceased. A feeling of coldness lingered on his back for a few seconds. Then a hot wave pattern played over his abdomen and faded away. "We were almost caught on that Sweep," he said.

UR was looking at him with body posture of surprise and comradery.

MBS posed the question both machines wished answered: "Have you developed a definite Sensory Location for each of the following: Military Anti-Grav Vehicle Frequency, Heat Sensor Units and Radar Frequencies?"

"Yes," Lader said. "And it's damned unpleasant! I feel like I'll get frozen or fried if they strike me directly with the Heat Sensor or Radar. I hope I'm wrong."

They continued their winding trip to the city. The lights of the buildings and Security Posts occasionally glistened through the branches and leaves of the trees and shrubs.

Soon, they would reach the Perimeter. That would

be the place of most jeopardy.

Lader was not eager to face that threat. He could already sense on his arms, the Audio Units of the Surveillance Posts, as well as their Holo-Video Units. Left arm, Audio, right arm, Holo-Video. He had nothing with which to compare the new senses he was utilizing. Utilizing against his will, for the most part. Perhaps that was the Machine rubbing off on him. Machines automatically employed the Sensory Units with which they were equipped. He was obviously doing the same. He messaged his arms. "Damned beams!" he complained, softly.

"What?" UR said. "What vibrations"

"You know, the Audio Scanner and Holo-Video Scanner Vibrations from those Surveillance Posts," Lader said. "They're making my arms form goose bumps."

UR stopped. It took hold of Lader's left arm and inspected it with its face screen Sensors. It did the same with his right arm. "Did you copy that, MBS?" it said. "Lader has picked out the distant Surveillance Emissions before me. He also detected the Military Vehicle and its Search Beams before me."

"If your abilities continue to expand and become more sensitive," MBS telepathed, "we may have to rely on you to guide us. Please alert us when you are able to sense the lay of the land and the Schemata of the city avenues and buildings. We can then Cross Check our data: that stored in my Banks and that which you detect on scene."

Lader shivered. "It won't go *that* far," he said. He did not sound convinced. "I *hope* it won't go *that* far!"

As with all boundaries of the city, the trees and other vegetation ended abruptly. The pavement Perimeter was Flood Lit.

Lader nodded. He had expected this. The Surveillance Posts were all active here, unlike their strange inactivity at the Security Building.

"Do you scan any Patrol Vehicles?" UR said.

"No," Lader said. "Do you?"

"Negative," UR said.

"They may be beyond your ranges, above or along the streets between the dwellings," MBS telepathed. "I cannot decide whether you should simply proceed, at a leisurely pace, to fool the Security Scanner Units, or to run, with UR blocking Lader from Paralysis Beams."

"What happens if a Paralysis Beam strikes UR?" Lader asked. He darted his eyes to their left.

Several Police Officers rounded the rear corner of a private house. They were armed with both Laser Pistols and Paralysis Guns. One at each hip.

UR's face screen flashed. A wide beam of brilliant white light shot forth and the officers froze in mid action. Not one had been swift enough to shout a warning or to reach for either of their side weapons. Their traditional blue uniforms and silver badges reflected the Paralysis Beam eerily. UR switched the ray off. "They will remain paralyzed for four hours," it said. "We can handle the Foot Patrols that easily. *If*, we have the advantage as we did here. Those buildings make it difficult for us to sense them, but they also interfere with their Scanning us out. That is why they wish to stop us outside the city. I suggest we run across the Perimeter. I will carry you, Lader."

"You, there!" a Human voice blared, from the sky. "Discard your illegal Paralysis Weapon and come slowly into the light of the Security Scanners! Immediately!"

"Three Military Vehicles!" Lader said. "Right above us! Just within range of my senses! Back into the woods!"

A scintillating red light, then a second and third, speared the night. The Laser Beams set the woods afire, instantly, exploding trees and vaporizing bushes, effectively blocking retreat for Lader. If not UR.

"Come!" Lader said. He ran out onto the pavement. The nearest Security Scanner Head to his left swiveled toward him. A white beam pulsed out. It was met by a more intense ray from UR's face screen. The Scanner issued an electronic squeal, then the domed head blew up with a shower of tiny bits of red-hot metal. The Scanner Heads to the left and right of the destroyed one swiveled toward Lader. UR caught up with him. The Robot sent out a split beam, one at each row of Scanners. One by one, swiftly, the Scanner Heads squealed and exploded, until the Perimeter was in darkness.

A spotlight fingered them from above.

Lader dove to the left.

UR stood its ground, looking upwards. Its face screen lighted red!

"Douse that beacon!" a terrified male voice said, inside Lader's mind.

"What the hell for? We got the Robot dead on!" a second irritated man said, inside Lader's mind.

"Just douse it!" The first man said, inside Lader's mind.

The light went out.

UR's face screen still glowed crimson. The Robot was scanning the sky with its sensors.

"Let's get the hell out of here!" the terrified man yelled, inside Lader's mind. "That's *Ultimate Robot,* from the Security Building!"

"So what?" the second voice said, inside Lader's mind. "All it can do is throw a Paralysis Beam at us, and we're already out of range. We can smelt it with—"

"You don't understand!" the terrified man shouted, inside Lader's mind. "*Ultimate Robot* can't be *stopped!*"

"No damned Robot—"

"Pull back to Upper Height Limits!" the terrified man ordered, inside Lader's mind. "Direct Order, mister!"

"What about the man?" the second voice asked, inside Lader's mind.

"He's the one the Council wants!" a woman said, inside Lader's mind.

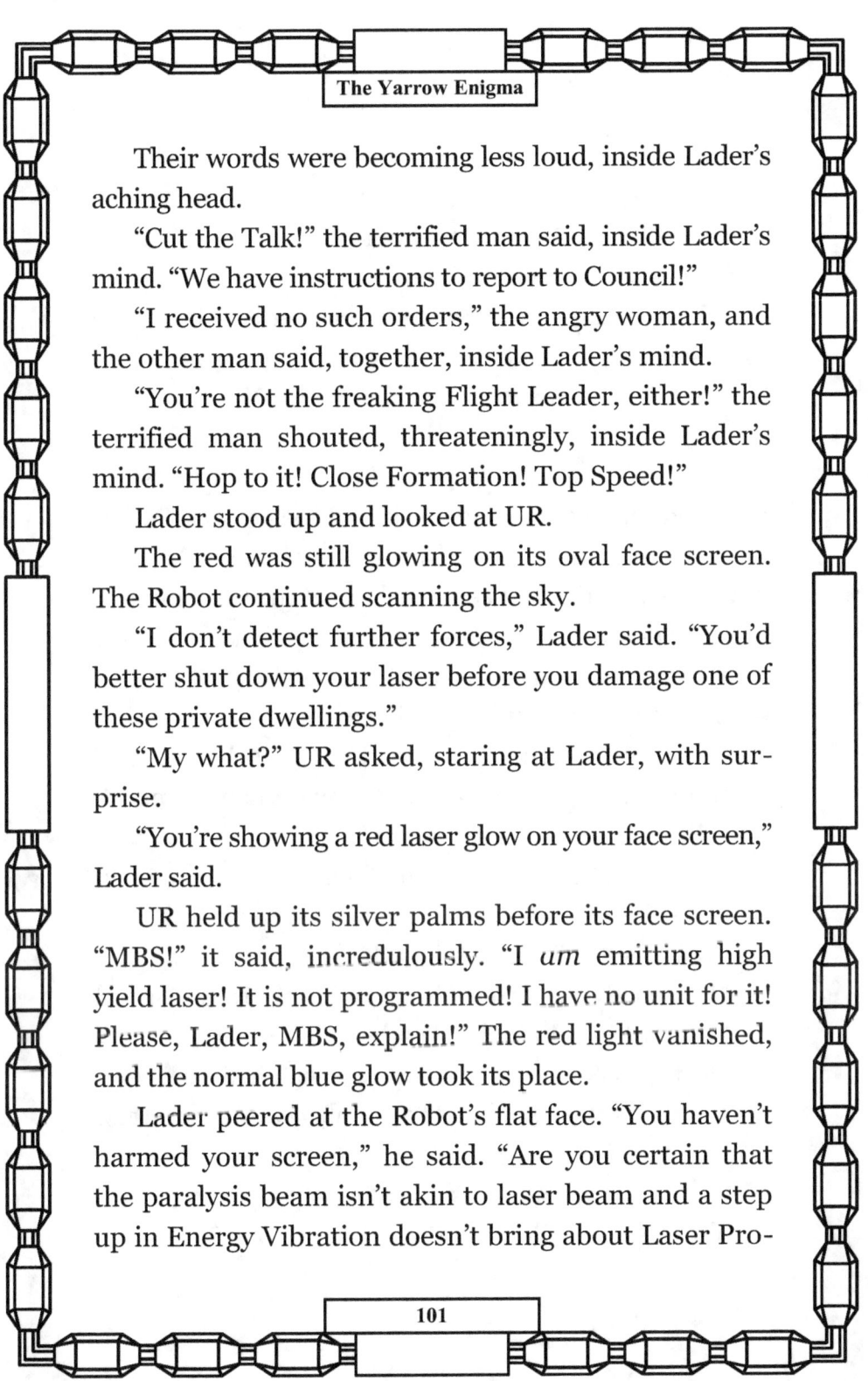

Their words were becoming less loud, inside Lader's aching head.

"Cut the Talk!" the terrified man said, inside Lader's mind. "We have instructions to report to Council!"

"I received no such orders," the angry woman, and the other man said, together, inside Lader's mind.

"You're not the freaking Flight Leader, either!" the terrified man shouted, threateningly, inside Lader's mind. "Hop to it! Close Formation! Top Speed!"

Lader stood up and looked at UR.

The red was still glowing on its oval face screen. The Robot continued scanning the sky.

"I don't detect further forces," Lader said. "You'd better shut down your laser before you damage one of these private dwellings."

"My what?" UR asked, staring at Lader, with surprise.

"You're showing a red laser glow on your face screen," Lader said.

UR held up its silver palms before its face screen. "MBS!" it said, incredulously. "I *um* emitting high yield laser! It is not programmed! I have no unit for it! Please, Lader, MBS, explain!" The red light vanished, and the normal blue glow took its place.

Lader peered at the Robot's flat face. "You haven't harmed your screen," he said. "Are you certain that the paralysis beam isn't akin to laser beam and a step up in Energy Vibration doesn't bring about Laser Pro-

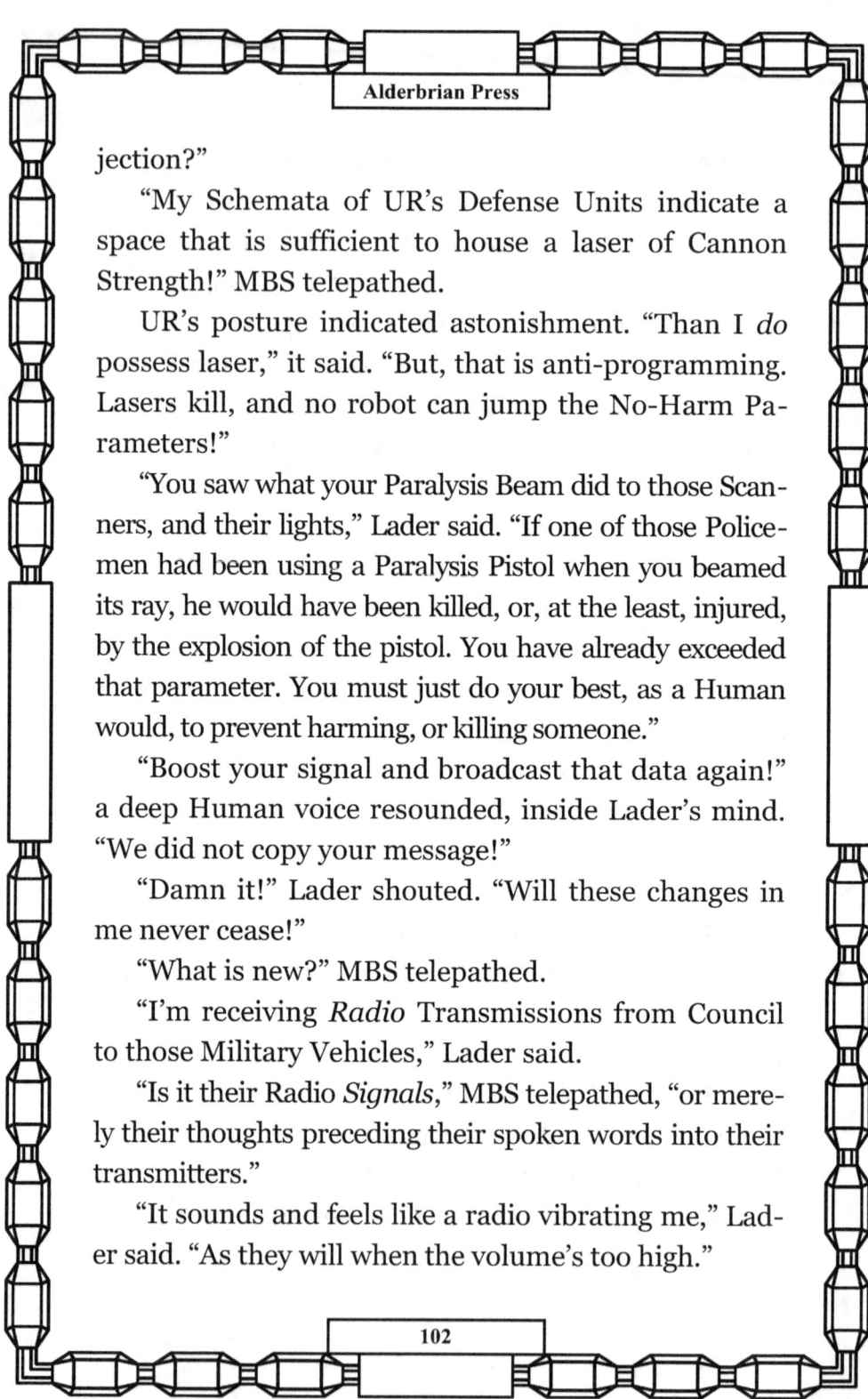

jection?"

"My Schemata of UR's Defense Units indicate a space that is sufficient to house a laser of Cannon Strength!" MBS telepathed.

UR's posture indicated astonishment. "Than I *do* possess laser," it said. "But, that is anti-programming. Lasers kill, and no robot can jump the No-Harm Parameters!"

"You saw what your Paralysis Beam did to those Scanners, and their lights," Lader said. "If one of those Policemen had been using a Paralysis Pistol when you beamed its ray, he would have been killed, or, at the least, injured, by the explosion of the pistol. You have already exceeded that parameter. You must just do your best, as a Human would, to prevent harming, or killing someone."

"Boost your signal and broadcast that data again!" a deep Human voice resounded, inside Lader's mind. "We did not copy your message!"

"Damn it!" Lader shouted. "Will these changes in me never cease!"

"What is new?" MBS telepathed.

"I'm receiving *Radio* Transmissions from Council to those Military Vehicles," Lader said.

"Is it their Radio *Signals*," MBS telepathed, "or merely their thoughts preceding their spoken words into their transmitters."

"It sounds and feels like a radio vibrating me," Lader said. "As they will when the volume's too high."

"That *is* a marvel," MBS telepathed. "Humans should not receive Radio Band Transmissions without implanted machine aid."

"We are moving through wonder after wonder," UR said. "We are all surpassing our Parameters. MBS, be alerted, for you may develop Distance Sight and Distance Audio Capacity."

"I have noted the Probability Rating of those possibilities," MBS telepathed. "It is twenty percent. But I cannot project how the percentage might rise or fall."

Lader thought about Cell Phones and began hearing those inane transmissions. They were a jumbled mess. He hated Cell Phones and did not own one. Others had Micro Cell Phones embedded in their heads. He returned to the Military and Police Bands. They were a constant chatter in the back of his mind. Strangely, he could compute—Compute!—everything said, plus his thoughts, and the conversation of MBS and UR. "When will my skin turn to metal?" he muttered.

"Probability of such a drastic flesh to metal Matter Transformation is zero, at best," MBS telepathed. "We are not all powerful, even with our new abilities. You and UR must cross into the city to gain Scan Defense against further Security Patrols and Flights."

"Punch up the Direct Route to the Council Building, MBS," Lader said. "We're going to pay that Android a visit. I want to find out what it knows about these uncanny transformations, and whether it is fronting for an Extraterrestrial War against Earth, or for a Second Computer Complex."

"Ready," MBS telepathed.

Lader led the way. He was receiving a mental image of the street names and other directional indicators in his mind as if a small screen were operating in his brain. "I understand why the Commander of that Military Vehicle Flight was so frightened of you, UR," he said. "He has Top Secret Clearance and knew you were capable of laser the strength of a Military Cannon. You could have vaporized their craft no mater how high into the atmosphere they climbed. They were only equipped with Limited Range Lasers. I doubt they can penetrate your metal, even if they all fired at the same time."

"My screen would be the logical site for a marksman to disable me," UR said. "Can you sense Laser Weapons, before they are fired?"

Lader stopped and leaned against the shatterproof window of an art gallery. It was not his fatigue so much as it was UR's words. "I felt a tingling in my left leg when the Guards and the Military Vehicles were around us. And a stronger tingle in my right leg when your screen went red," Lader said. "So I *can* pick out laser power, before, it is beamed. But I don't know my range."

"If changes progress, as rated so far, you will have opportunity to judge your range, soon," MBS telepathed.

"No thanks," Lader said, fervently. He and UR continued along the avenues and alleys indicated by MBS.

Curiously, none of the Surveillance Scanners paid attention to them. More oddly, there was no Foot Patrol or Anti-Grav Vehicle Traffic on any of the streets they used.

"MBS," Lader said. "Probability that Security is only monitoring us and also shunting all traffic from our route, please."

"One hundred percent," MBS telepathed. "Not all Humans rate access to Military or Police Security Radio Bands, so these avenues should normally present some traffic. This is a major sector of the city. Are the Arcades and Food Stores closed?"

"Yes," Lader said. "I haven't seen a light in any of the buildings we've passed."

"Have they guessed our destination?" UR asked.

"Military will have programmed possibilities into Military Computer's Security Banks," MBS telepathed. "It will have deduced our true goal long before now. Shall I devise a Confusion Course?"

"Yes, but don't display it, until I ask," Lader said.

"Attention!" a male voice said, from one of the Surveillance Posts, ahead of them. "Please identify yourself!"

UR stepped in front of Lader, and the white of the Robot's Paralysis Beam glowed on its face screen.

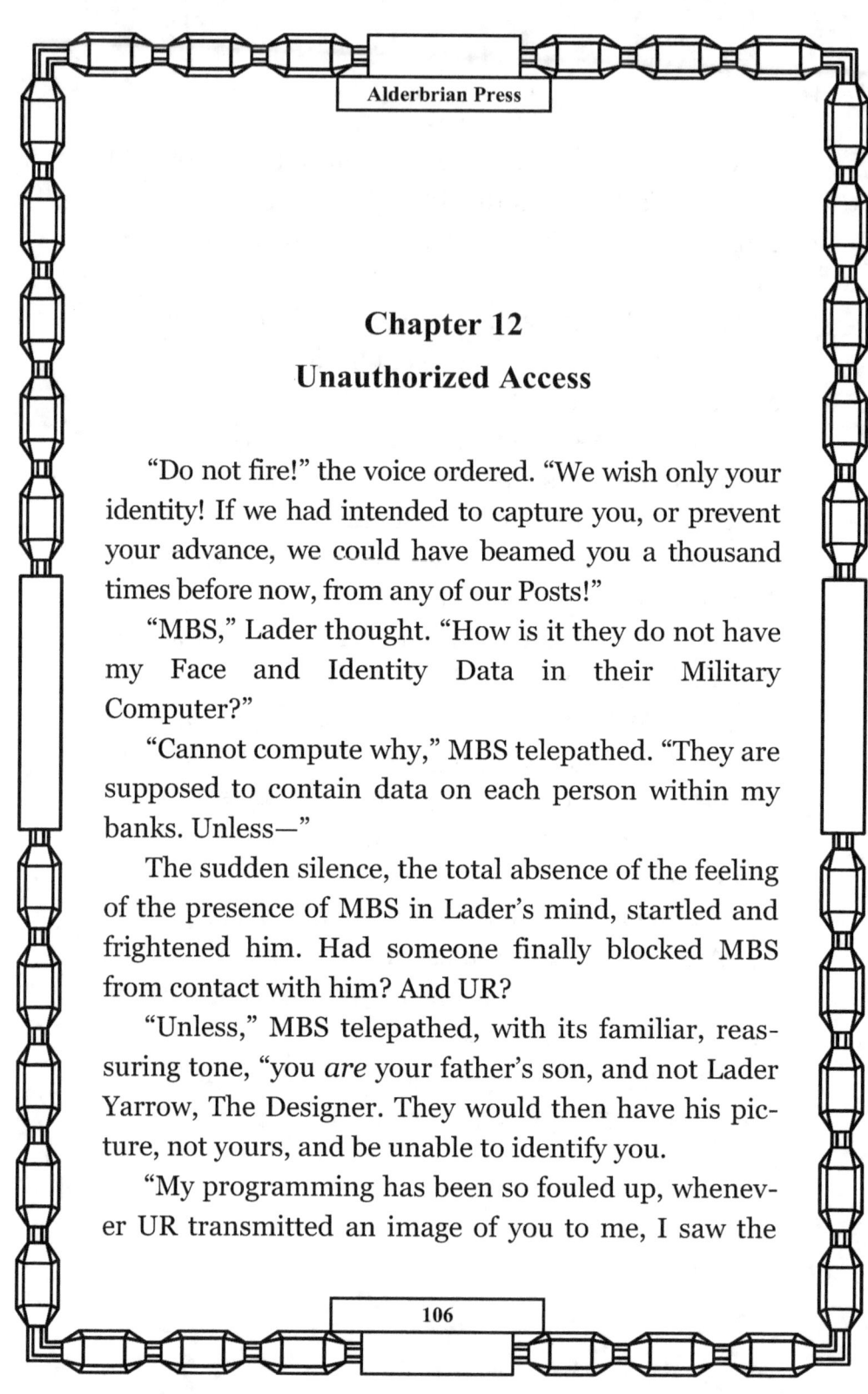

Chapter 12

Unauthorized Access

"Do not fire!" the voice ordered. "We wish only your identity! If we had intended to capture you, or prevent your advance, we could have beamed you a thousand times before now, from any of our Posts!"

"MBS," Lader thought. "How is it they do not have my Face and Identity Data in their Military Computer?"

"Cannot compute why," MBS telepathed. "They are supposed to contain data on each person within my banks. Unless—"

The sudden silence, the total absence of the feeling of the presence of MBS in Lader's mind, startled and frightened him. Had someone finally blocked MBS from contact with him? And UR?

"Unless," MBS telepathed, with its familiar, reassuring tone, "you *are* your father's son, and not Lader Yarrow, The Designer. They would then have his picture, not yours, and be unable to identify you.

"My programming has been so fouled up, whenever UR transmitted an image of you to me, I saw the

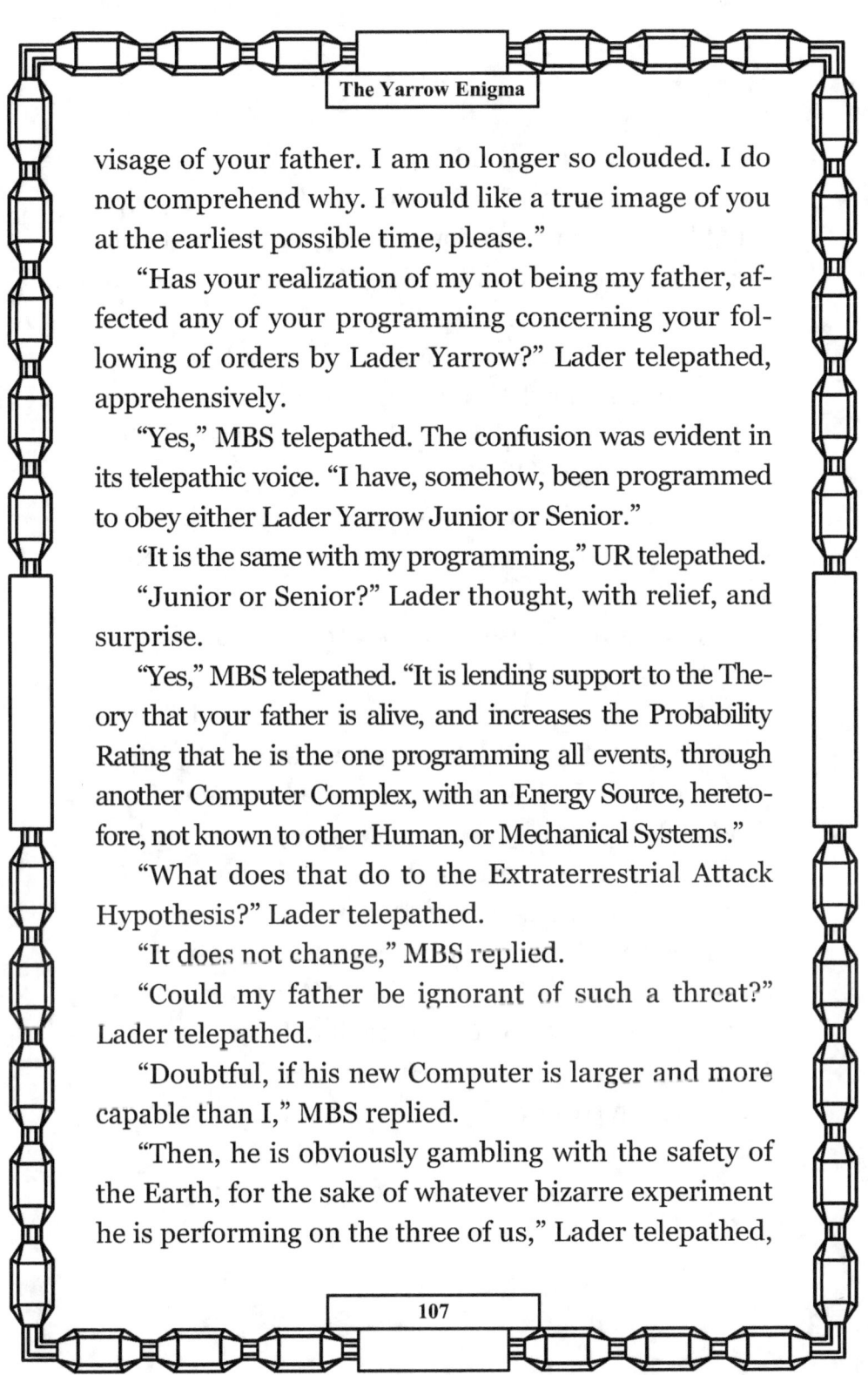

visage of your father. I am no longer so clouded. I do not comprehend why. I would like a true image of you at the earliest possible time, please."

"Has your realization of my not being my father, affected any of your programming concerning your following of orders by Lader Yarrow?" Lader telepathed, apprehensively.

"Yes," MBS telepathed. The confusion was evident in its telepathic voice. "I have, somehow, been programmed to obey either Lader Yarrow Junior or Senior."

"It is the same with my programming," UR telepathed.

"Junior or Senior?" Lader thought, with relief, and surprise.

"Yes," MBS telepathed. "It is lending support to the Theory that your father is alive, and increases the Probability Rating that he is the one programming all events, through another Computer Complex, with an Energy Source, heretofore, not known to other Human, or Mechanical Systems."

"What does that do to the Extraterrestrial Attack Hypothesis?" Lader telepathed.

"It does not change," MBS replied.

"Could my father be ignorant of such a threat?" Lader telepathed.

"Doubtful, if his new Computer is larger and more capable than I," MBS replied.

"Then, he is obviously gambling with the safety of the Earth, for the sake of whatever bizarre experiment he is performing on the three of us," Lader telepathed,

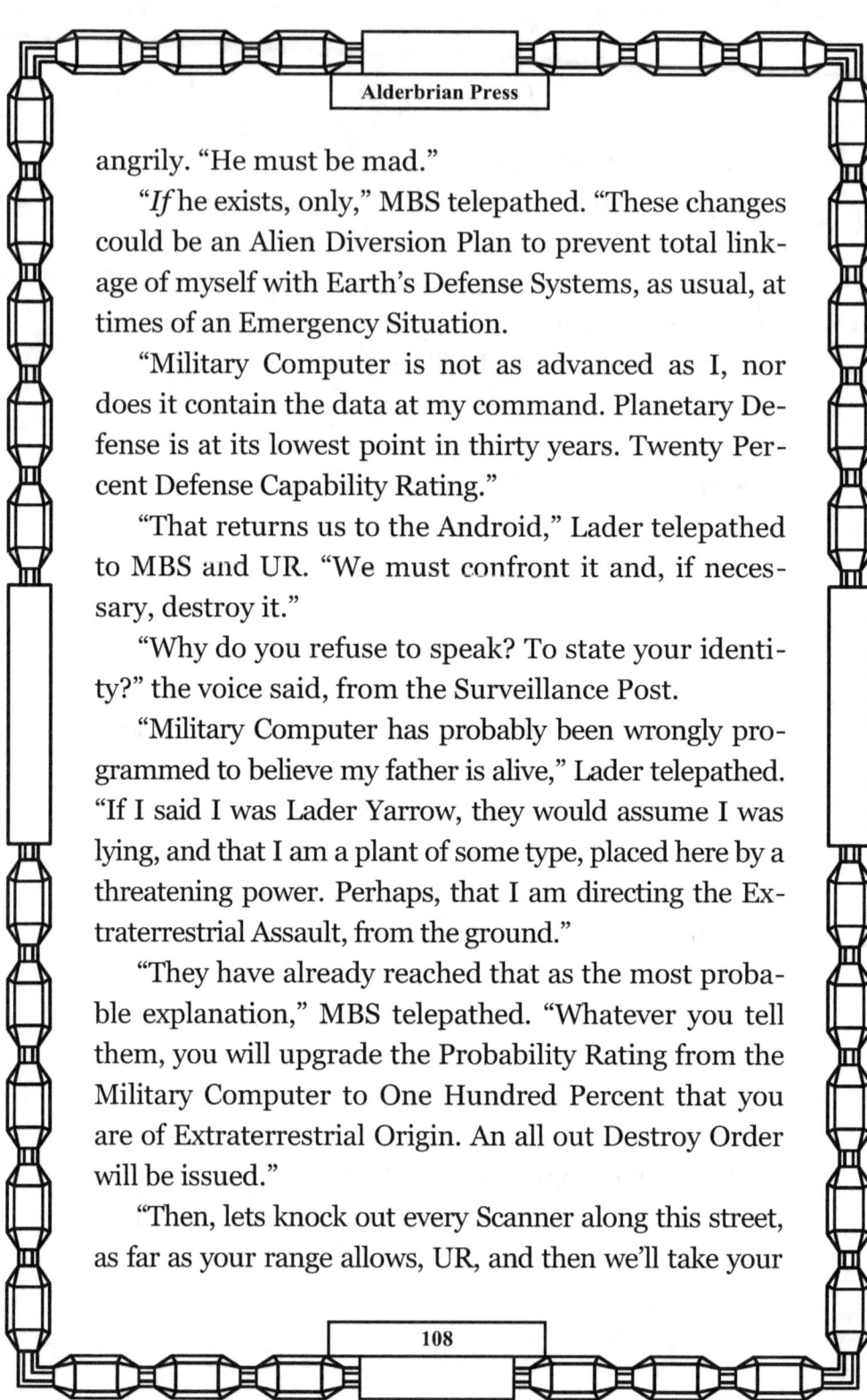

angrily. "He must be mad."

"*If* he exists, only," MBS telepathed. "These changes could be an Alien Diversion Plan to prevent total linkage of myself with Earth's Defense Systems, as usual, at times of an Emergency Situation.

"Military Computer is not as advanced as I, nor does it contain the data at my command. Planetary Defense is at its lowest point in thirty years. Twenty Percent Defense Capability Rating."

"That returns us to the Android," Lader telepathed to MBS and UR. "We must confront it and, if necessary, destroy it."

"Why do you refuse to speak? To state your identity?" the voice said, from the Surveillance Post.

"Military Computer has probably been wrongly programmed to believe my father is alive," Lader telepathed. "If I said I was Lader Yarrow, they would assume I was lying, and that I am a plant of some type, placed here by a threatening power. Perhaps, that I am directing the Extraterrestrial Assault, from the ground."

"They have already reached that as the most probable explanation," MBS telepathed. "Whatever you tell them, you will upgrade the Probability Rating from the Military Computer to One Hundred Percent that you are of Extraterrestrial Origin. An all out Destroy Order will be issued."

"Then, lets knock out every Scanner along this street, as far as your range allows, UR, and then we'll take your

Confusion Route, MBS," Lader telepathed.

"An excellent choice," MBS telepathed. "My Start Point is that manhole in the center of the avenue to your left."

"UR, execute the order," Lader telepathed.

UR's screen blasted the Surveillance Post Head to red particles. The Robot stood sideways to the lines of Scanners. It speared a white beam from both the left and right sides of its screen.

Explosion after explosion lighted the night, both ways, to the ends of the avenue, until no functional Surveillance Post Heads were in sight.

UR and Lader ran to the manhole. UR lifted the heavy round lid. Lader climbed down the metal ladder. UR followed, pulling the lid back into place. UR lit its face screen bright blue, illuminating every crack and line in the sewer surface. Bits of sewage stood out in weird relief.

MBS' plan came into Lader's mind screen. He and UR ran, side by side, down the echoing tunnel.

"MBS, are there any Surveillance Units in these sewers?" Lader telepathed.

"Yes," MBS telepathed, "but they are far between, and they are activated, only when work is required, or when a Topside Scanner sees an Unauthorized Entry, through a manhole."

"How long before the Military Computer deduces we are down here, MBS?" Lader said.

"It has advised Council, by Radio, to begin a General Search and Destroy Operation in the avenue just vacated by you. A Building to Building Type. It is too rigidly militarily programmed. It will not direct them to the sewers, until the Search and Destroy Operation yields negative results. That will take, at most, one half hour."

Lader thought about antennas and began hearing all the Radio contacts between the Military Computer, the Anti-Grav Pilots, the Police Officers on the ground, and the Council Computer Terminal. It was an almost laughable state of chaos.

The Police were frightened for their lives. No Police Officer had been killed, in the line of duty, in thirty, idyllic, years. As far as they could determine, there was a true threat of that, now.

The Military Pilots were terrified because they had been apprised of UR's Laser Cannon Unit. They were reluctant, and cautious, to the utmost in making their Air Surveillance Sweeps.

The Police were the same concerning their entering and searching of the buildings.

"Revised estimate on the time the Military Computer will suggest investigation of the sewers," MBS telepathed. "One hour and thirty minutes, due to fear expressed by the Search Parties."

Lader smiled, through his fatigue. "That's fine," he said. "We can't be more than an hour away from the Council Building, right now."

"Correct," MBS telepathed.

"Lader Yarrow?" UR said. "Have you noticed that we are still receiving Radio Broadcasts, though we are below ground?"

"MBS must be channeling it to us," Lader said.

"Negative," MBS telepathed. "If events were not so Anti-Computational and Anti-Programming I would say we should not be capable of communicating through the Energy Blocking Pavement, and Tunnel Material, without routing, via the lines to Surface Terminals, installed for that purpose. Obviously, we have undergone further modification."

"We're really a group of freaks," Lader said.

"I take offense at your reference," UR said.

"I, also," MBS telepathed.

"All right," Lader said. "You're both becoming as thin-skinned as most Humans I know. I'll be the freak. You can be kindly protectors."

"Essentially," MBS telepathed, "that is an accurate statement of our situation."

"Now the Computer is calling *me* a freak," Lader said. He stopped and leaned against the damp side of the huge tunnel. "It's sad one of you can't re-energize me," he said, wistfully. "I may collapse before we reach the Android."

UR's screen turned green. A soft beam of emerald light flowed throughout Lader's aching, sagging muscles. He gasped in response to the energy refreshing him. UR's screen returned to blue, its glow glistening off the gray tunnel surface.

"It seems," Lader said, "that anything we desire is constantly granted. UR's just hit me with a Green Pep-Beam and removed my fatigue. Is UR circuited for that?"

"Negative," MBS telepathed. "But I was not circuited to send UR energy when the Security Building Partition was closing upon UR."

"Any empty spaces on UR's Schematic Diagrams which could hold a Secret Energizer Beam Unit?" Lader said. "I've never heard of it before. I'll bet the doctors would give their eyeteeth for it."

"Negative, on empty spaces," MBS telepathed, "but, it might be in one of the areas indicated as Sensitive Secret Units on UR's Charts."

"I have been told that my father was experimenting with the use of light frequencies toward a method of healing diseases incurable by other medical techniques. UR's Pep-Glow may be a by-product of that," Lader said. He and UR resumed running down the tunnel. They made turns wherever MBS indicated.

The sameness of the tunnels became a blur of almost meaningless impressions to Lader. He found he was concentrating on his Radio Receiver Ability, tuning into the Military Computer itself. He skidded to a stop, sliding against the side of the tunnel. "MBS, UR!" he said, excitedly. "I have made contact, with the Military Com-

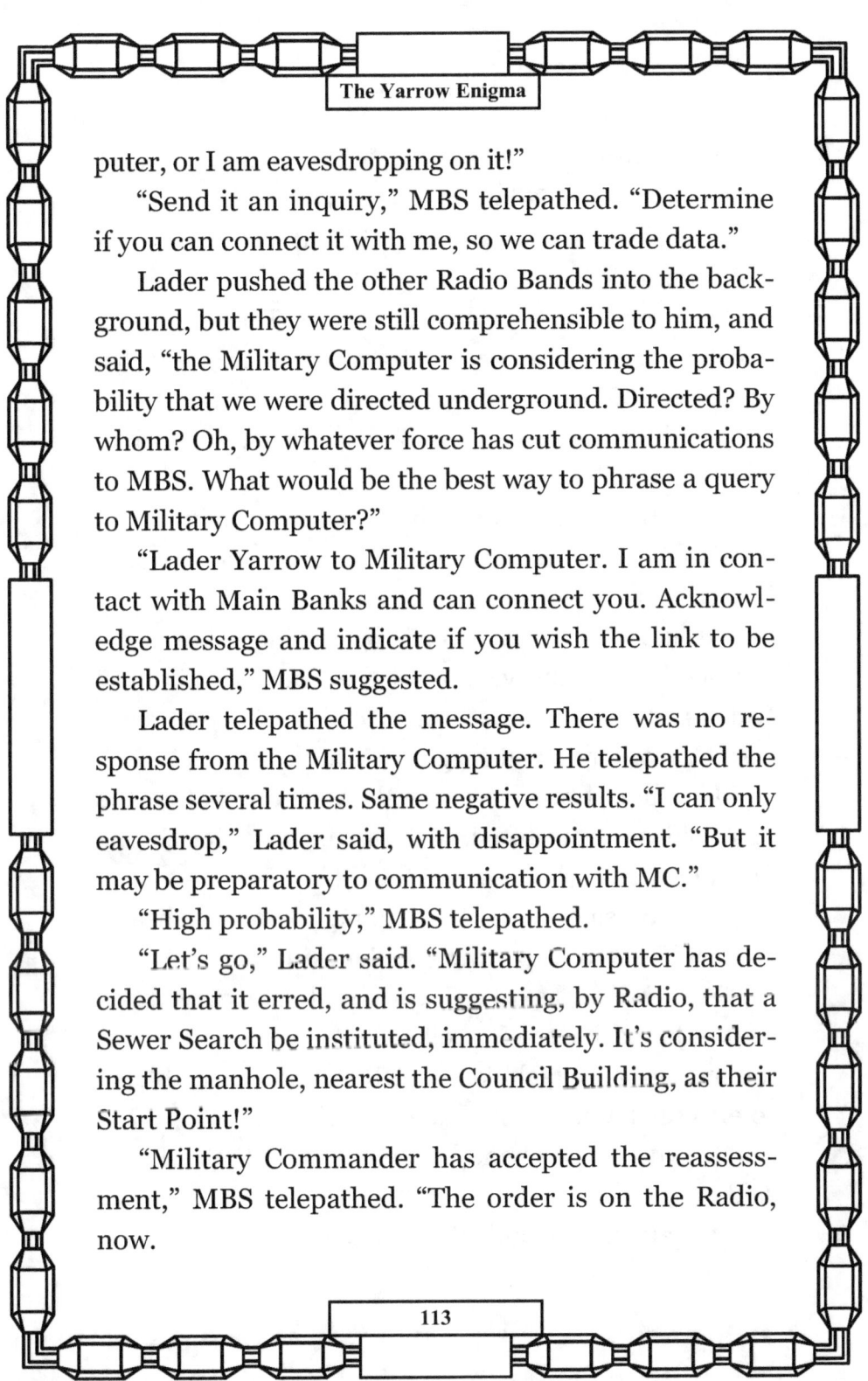

puter, or I am eavesdropping on it!"

"Send it an inquiry," MBS telepathed. "Determine if you can connect it with me, so we can trade data."

Lader pushed the other Radio Bands into the background, but they were still comprehensible to him, and said, "the Military Computer is considering the probability that we were directed underground. Directed? By whom? Oh, by whatever force has cut communications to MBS. What would be the best way to phrase a query to Military Computer?"

"Lader Yarrow to Military Computer. I am in contact with Main Banks and can connect you. Acknowledge message and indicate if you wish the link to be established," MBS suggested.

Lader telepathed the message. There was no response from the Military Computer. He telepathed the phrase several times. Same negative results. "I can only eavesdrop," Lader said, with disappointment. "But it may be preparatory to communication with MC."

"High probability," MBS telepathed.

"Let's go," Lader said. "Military Computer has decided that it erred, and is suggesting, by Radio, that a Sewer Search be instituted, immediately. It's considering the manhole, nearest the Council Building, as their Start Point!"

"Military Commander has accepted the reassessment," MBS telepathed. "The order is on the Radio, now.

"I will direct you to a manhole which lies one block from their Start Point manhole. You will have to—fight—is all I can say, your way to, and into, the Council Building."

Lader and UR veered to their right. They entered a smaller tunnel. Water flowed steadily from big grills, on either side of them, and along deep channels, between which they ran. The odor of feces, and urine, was strong.

"Isn't there a cleaner path?" Lader complained.

"Sorry," MBS telepathed. "This is the most probably secure route."

"Military Computer is advising posting Police at every manhole in the vicinity of the Council Building," Lader said. "The instructions have already been broadcast. Now what do you suggest, MBS?"

"UR should be able to paralyze anyone before the manhole cover is lifted. UR can beam through the Lever Orifice at the center of the lid."

"Are you saying that UR is going to bend its beam, after, it leaves the opening?" Lader said.

"Yes," MBS telepathed. "UR has already curved two beams, to disable the Surveillance Posts, at the Perimeter and, upon Bokaal Avenue. UR should be capable, of re-enactment, at any manhole."

"Do you comprehend how you can do that?" Lader said.

"Negative," UR said. "It just occurs."

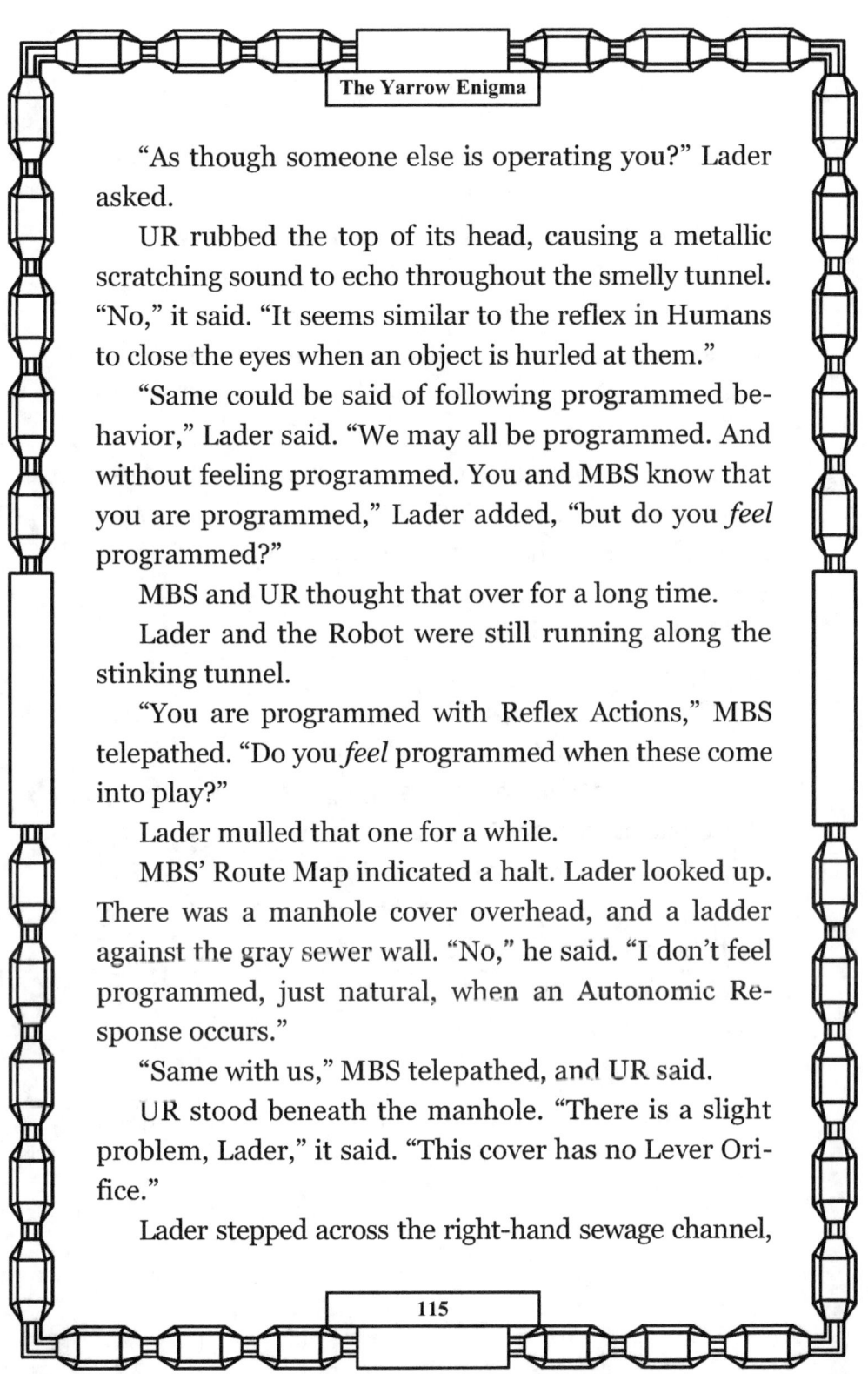

"As though someone else is operating you?" Lader asked.

UR rubbed the top of its head, causing a metallic scratching sound to echo throughout the smelly tunnel. "No," it said. "It seems similar to the reflex in Humans to close the eyes when an object is hurled at them."

"Same could be said of following programmed behavior," Lader said. "We may all be programmed. And without feeling programmed. You and MBS know that you are programmed," Lader added, "but do you *feel* programmed?"

MBS and UR thought that over for a long time.

Lader and the Robot were still running along the stinking tunnel.

"You are programmed with Reflex Actions," MBS telepathed. "Do you *feel* programmed when these come into play?"

Lader mulled that one for a while.

MBS' Route Map indicated a halt. Lader looked up. There was a manhole cover overhead, and a ladder against the gray sewer wall. "No," he said. "I don't feel programmed, just natural, when an Autonomic Response occurs."

"Same with us," MBS telepathed, and UR said.

UR stood beneath the manhole. "There is a slight problem, Lader," it said. "This cover has no Lever Orifice."

Lader stepped across the right-hand sewage channel,

climbed up the old ladder, and poked around with a fore-finger. "UR is correct," he said. "Were Sewer Mainte-nance Robots beginning to change to newer lids, with re-cessed Lever Hooks, instead of Holes?"

"There is a four-year-old plan in my banks, but it was canceled after the first one hundred covers were replaced," MBS telepathed. "Sadly, we un-lucked onto one that was."

Lader rolled his eyes because of the computer's use of the word un-lucked. "UR," he said, "can you flip this lid over, and take the Guards out, by surprise, with your Paralysis Beam?"

"If there is no better scheme," UR said, "I shall at-tempt to."

"No other plan," MBS telepathed.

Lader jumped down from the ladder.

UR climbed, almost noiselessly, up the metal ladder. It placed one hand against the center of the heavy cover, re-computed trajectories and moved the hand to the edge of one side of the lid. It pressed lightly against the lid, testing the tightness of the fit in the collar. Then it shoved, up and back, and leaped up onto the avenue.

Chapter 13
Firing Point

Lader scrambled up the cold ladder, and peeked out. The heavy, round manhole lid clanged on the pavement behind him. He did not bother to turn around. UR stood directly ahead. Two Police Officers were there, paralyzed. Neither had gotten a hand near either one of their side weapons, although they had been facing the manhole.

"Only *two* Guards?" Lader said. He gratefully climbed out of the odious sewer. "For such a dangerous, Super Robot, you would think there should be at least one Back Up Unit."

"You sense none, Lader Yarrow?" MBS telepathed.

"No," Lader said. "And the Surveillance Posts aren't active! That does not compute, even to me!"

UR scanned the area with its oval, blue, face screen. "No energy exists in this block," it said. "MBS, could Council, or Military, have shut down power, to prevent our entering buildings, through electronically operated doors?"

MBS telepathed, "That is a Probable Standard Procedure, But, all the Scanners have their own Emergency Power Sources, and they should still be functioning. UR, are you certain you did not over shoot your beam, and cause a Burn Out, of the Surveillance Units?"

"Positive," UR said, "their heads are still attached."

Lader did not like this thought. "MBS, UR," he said, "just before UR flipped its lid, I thought about how convenient it would be if the Surveillance Units were to short out, for a block, on all sides of the Council Building, appearing like a freak chain reaction, of one overload arced from one malfunctioning Scanner to another, down the lines. You don't suppose?"

"If you can reactivate a Unit, from around a corner, a Unit distant enough from you, for it to be unable to sense you," MBS telepathed, "then knock it out again, you would answer your question."

Lader and UR crossed the avenue and rounded the corner to their left. Lader concentrated on a Surveillance Post which was a block away. Its Flood Light flashed on and the domed Head began scanning the wide avenue. Lader blanked it out before it could sense anywhere near them.

"You are becoming a powerhouse of abilities," MBS telepathed. "UR, see if you can do as Lader Yarrow."

"I have attempted it," UR said. "Negative results. Are you certain, the strange failure of the Scanners, in this Strategic Area, won't be interpreted, by Military Computer, as Intended, rather than Accidental?"

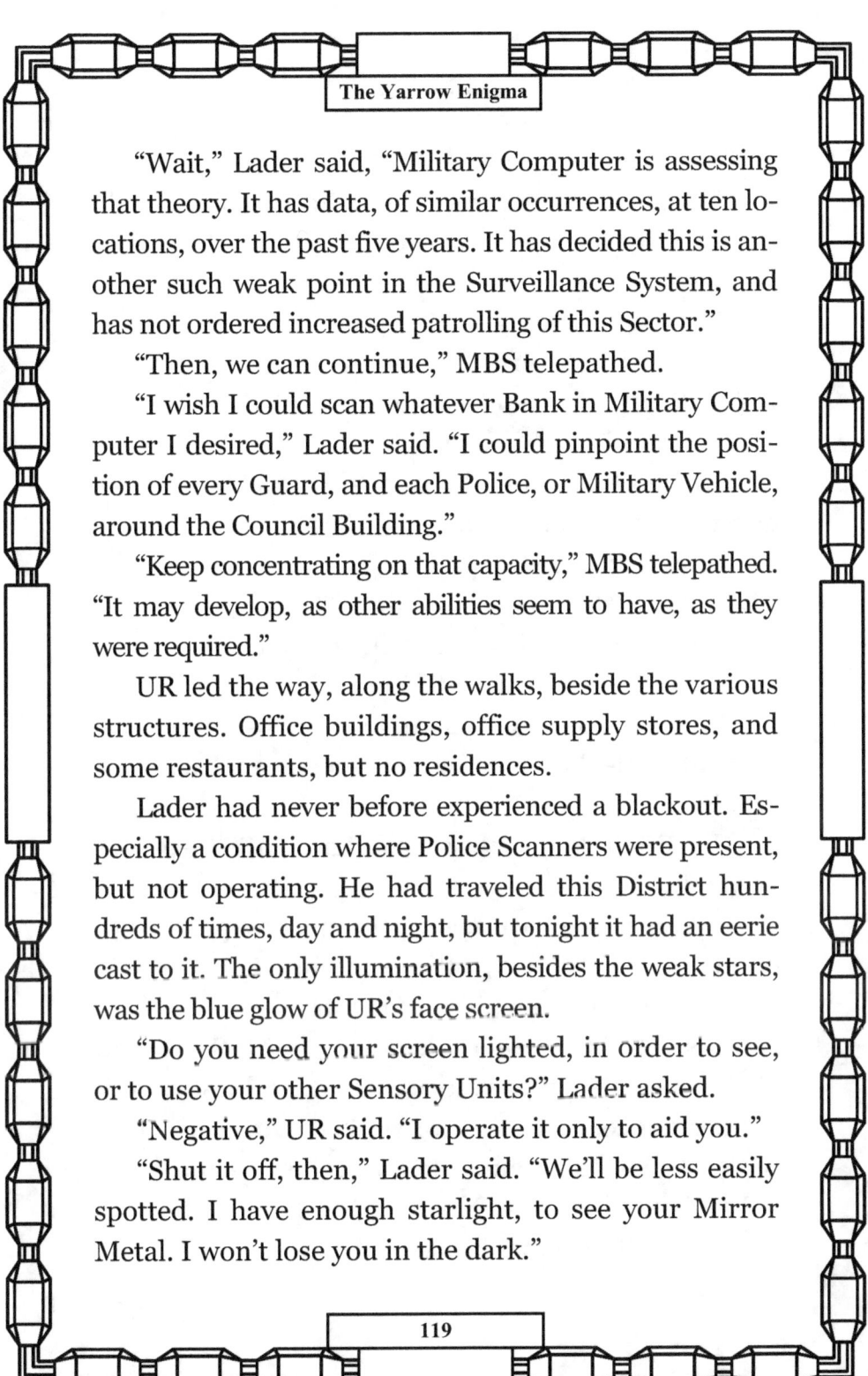

"Wait," Lader said, "Military Computer is assessing that theory. It has data, of similar occurrences, at ten locations, over the past five years. It has decided this is another such weak point in the Surveillance System, and has not ordered increased patrolling of this Sector."

"Then, we can continue," MBS telepathed.

"I wish I could scan whatever Bank in Military Computer I desired," Lader said. "I could pinpoint the position of every Guard, and each Police, or Military Vehicle, around the Council Building."

"Keep concentrating on that capacity," MBS telepathed. "It may develop, as other abilities seem to have, as they were required."

UR led the way, along the walks, beside the various structures. Office buildings, office supply stores, and some restaurants, but no residences.

Lader had never before experienced a blackout. Especially a condition where Police Scanners were present, but not operating. He had traveled this District hundreds of times, day and night, but tonight it had an eerie cast to it. The only illumination, besides the weak stars, was the blue glow of UR's face screen.

"Do you need your screen lighted, in order to see, or to use your other Sensory Units?" Lader asked.

"Negative," UR said. "I operate it only to aid you."

"Shut it off, then," Lader said. "We'll be less easily spotted. I have enough starlight, to see your Mirror Metal. I won't lose you in the dark."

"Very well," UR said.

The glow vanished and the night closed in a little more tightly, and a bit more eerily.

Lader stopped.

UR sensed this, paused and faced him.

Lader looked quizzically at UR's screen. "Do you feel as though we're in a windowless, door less room, with no ventilation?" he said.

UR's posture showed surprise. It briefly flashed a question mark on its screen. "That is too Humanly subjective for me," it said.

"But, you do sense, something?" Lader said.

"Yes," UR said. "I cannot collate it, yet."

"Please explain?" MBS telepathed.

"There is an—atmosphere, or perhaps, an energy, unidentifiable, but discretely present, around us," Lader said.

"The Destructive, non-analyzable Ray?" MBS telepathed, nervously.

Lader pressed back against the cold, rough, texture of the wall of a towering office building.

UR copied its friend's movements.

"It's possible," Lader telepathed, to MBS and UR. "Let's continue our conversations, telepathically, until further notice. You have not yet been attacked, MBS, but that may be because the Source has been seeking UR and me."

"Probability of that is high," MBS telepathed.

"I cannot determine the direction of the—odd—sensation," UR telepathed. "How distant is it to the Council Building?"

"Around the next corner, and one block down. It is, no doubt, closely cordoned off, by Military and Police Guards. Do either of you scan their vehicles overhead, in that direction?" MBS telepathed.

"Police!" Lader telepathed. "Duck, UR! Flat of you face!"

UR followed the order instantly. It was on its abdomen before Lader landed.

A red beam heated the air, and seared a hole, in the wall, at the area where UR's screen had been, the moment before.

"Police Laser Sharpshooters, with Night Scopes!" Lader telepathed. "The different power of the scopes was mingled with the Laser Ready Energy and fooled us! We almost lost UR! And might, yet! Up, UR, but face the building behind us. I'll walk between it, and you. We'll have to do our best, sideways, to the Council Building. They'll, no doubt, have Sharpshooters, on both sides of the avenues. You alert me, and I'll warn you, UR!"

"Those on our side, will have no opportunity to fire," UR telepathed. "The ones opposite us, can not pierce my frame. The weapon just used, was Conventional Laser Rifle, not Cannon, or the skyscraper wall would have burst asunder, and buried us."

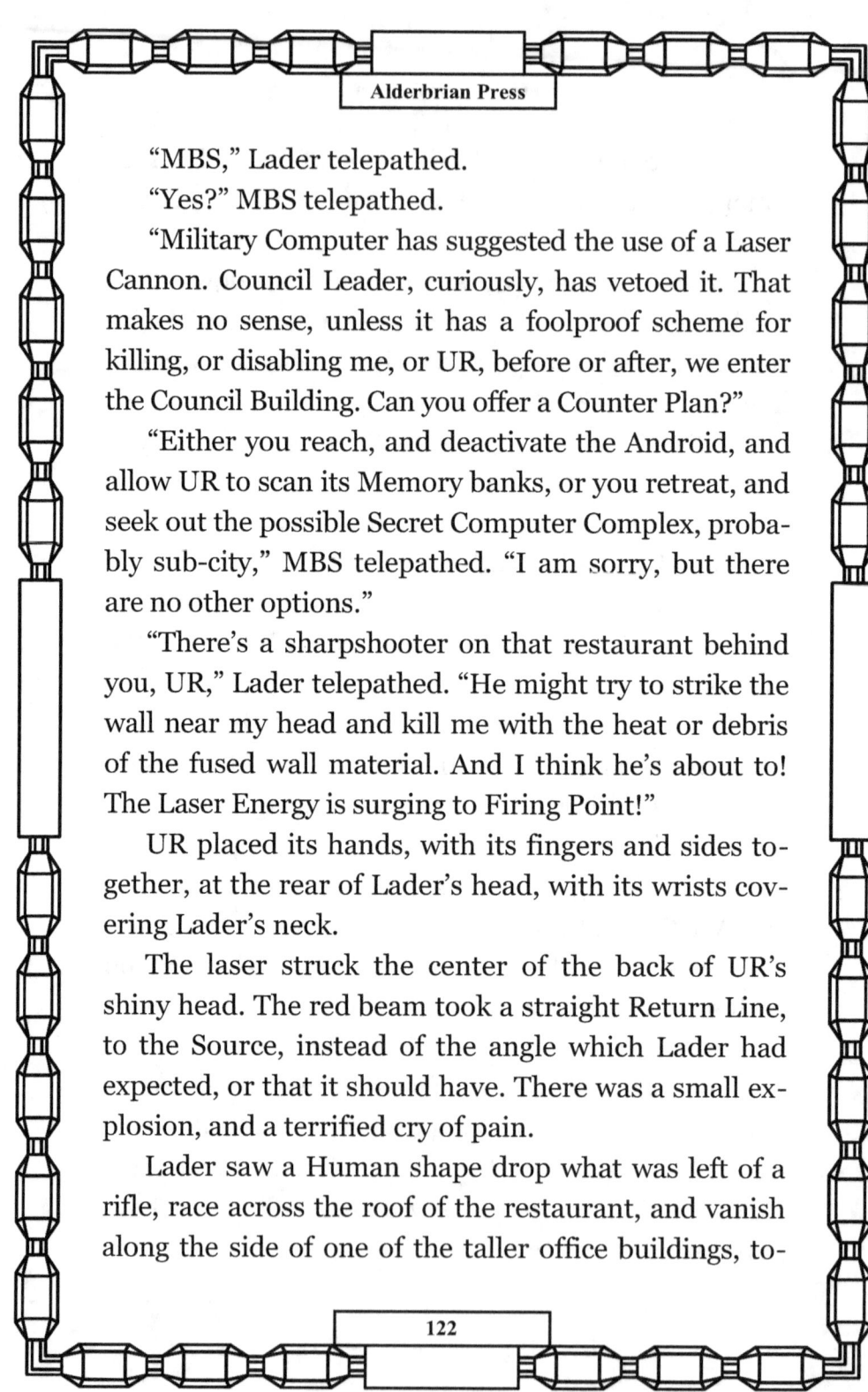

"MBS," Lader telepathed.

"Yes?" MBS telepathed.

"Military Computer has suggested the use of a Laser Cannon. Council Leader, curiously, has vetoed it. That makes no sense, unless it has a foolproof scheme for killing, or disabling me, or UR, before or after, we enter the Council Building. Can you offer a Counter Plan?"

"Either you reach, and deactivate the Android, and allow UR to scan its Memory banks, or you retreat, and seek out the possible Secret Computer Complex, probably sub-city," MBS telepathed. "I am sorry, but there are no other options."

"There's a sharpshooter on that restaurant behind you, UR," Lader telepathed. "He might try to strike the wall near my head and kill me with the heat or debris of the fused wall material. And I think he's about to! The Laser Energy is surging to Firing Point!"

UR placed its hands, with its fingers and sides together, at the rear of Lader's head, with its wrists covering Lader's neck.

The laser struck the center of the back of UR's shiny head. The red beam took a straight Return Line, to the Source, instead of the angle which Lader had expected, or that it should have. There was a small explosion, and a terrified cry of pain.

Lader saw a Human shape drop what was left of a rifle, race across the roof of the restaurant, and vanish along the side of one of the taller office buildings, toward the rear of both. "Injured, but not mortally," Lader telepathed.

"I am pleased," UR telepathed. "I did not impel that beam toward him. I do not compute why it traveled that aberrant course."

"You must decide, now, whether to attack the guards in front of the Council Building, or retreat into the sewers, and seek out the other Complex," MBS telepathed. "Soon, you will be in direct Line of Fire of Paralysis and Laser Arms, by thirty, or more, of those guards."

"UR," Lader telepathed, "can you fire upon, and perhaps kill, one or more of those guards?"

"Uncertain," UR telepathed. "Old programming is strong at this time. But new programming is also there. I will try to utilize only paralysis. But if I must, to preserve your life, I will use my laser, at its lowest setting, to wound, only."

"Good enough," Lader telepathed. "I just wish I had the laser, and not you. We will assault in ten seconds, MBS," Lader telepathed. "Mark."

"Mark," MBS telepathed. "Ten, nine, eight, seven, six, five, four, three, two, one, instigate!"

UR and Lader rounded the corner, staying close to the structures on their right.

The front of the Council Building was floodlit by portable lamps, mounted on high tripods. A small, silent generator, sat at the center, of the bottom step, of the entrance.

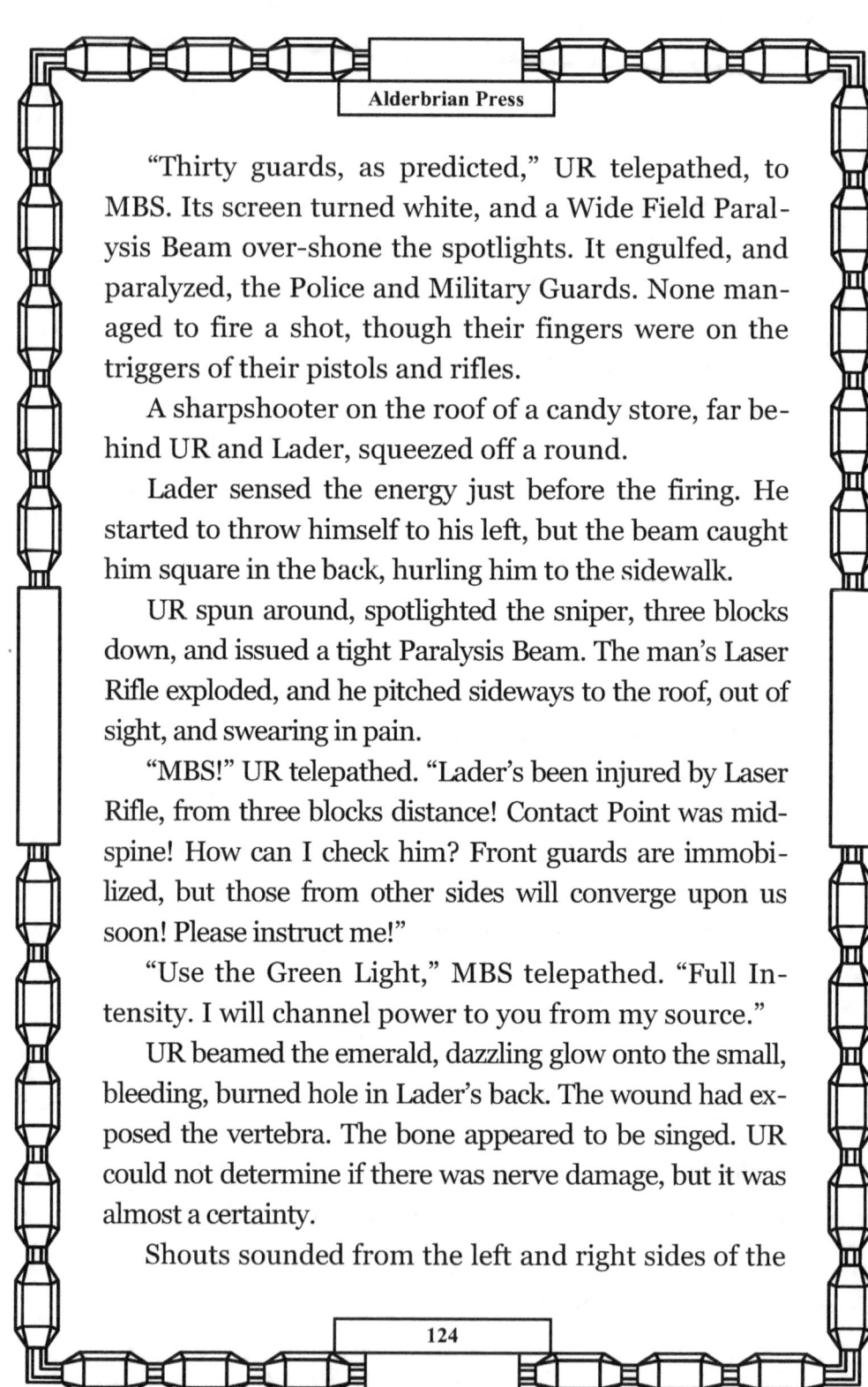

"Thirty guards, as predicted," UR telepathed, to MBS. Its screen turned white, and a Wide Field Paralysis Beam over-shone the spotlights. It engulfed, and paralyzed, the Police and Military Guards. None managed to fire a shot, though their fingers were on the triggers of their pistols and rifles.

A sharpshooter on the roof of a candy store, far behind UR and Lader, squeezed off a round.

Lader sensed the energy just before the firing. He started to throw himself to his left, but the beam caught him square in the back, hurling him to the sidewalk.

UR spun around, spotlighted the sniper, three blocks down, and issued a tight Paralysis Beam. The man's Laser Rifle exploded, and he pitched sideways to the roof, out of sight, and swearing in pain.

"MBS!" UR telepathed. "Lader's been injured by Laser Rifle, from three blocks distance! Contact Point was mid-spine! How can I check him? Front guards are immobilized, but those from other sides will converge upon us soon! Please instruct me!"

"Use the Green Light," MBS telepathed. "Full Intensity. I will channel power to you from my source."

UR beamed the emerald, dazzling glow onto the small, bleeding, burned hole in Lader's back. The wound had exposed the vertebra. The bone appeared to be singed. UR could not determine if there was nerve damage, but it was almost a certainty.

Shouts sounded from the left and right sides of the

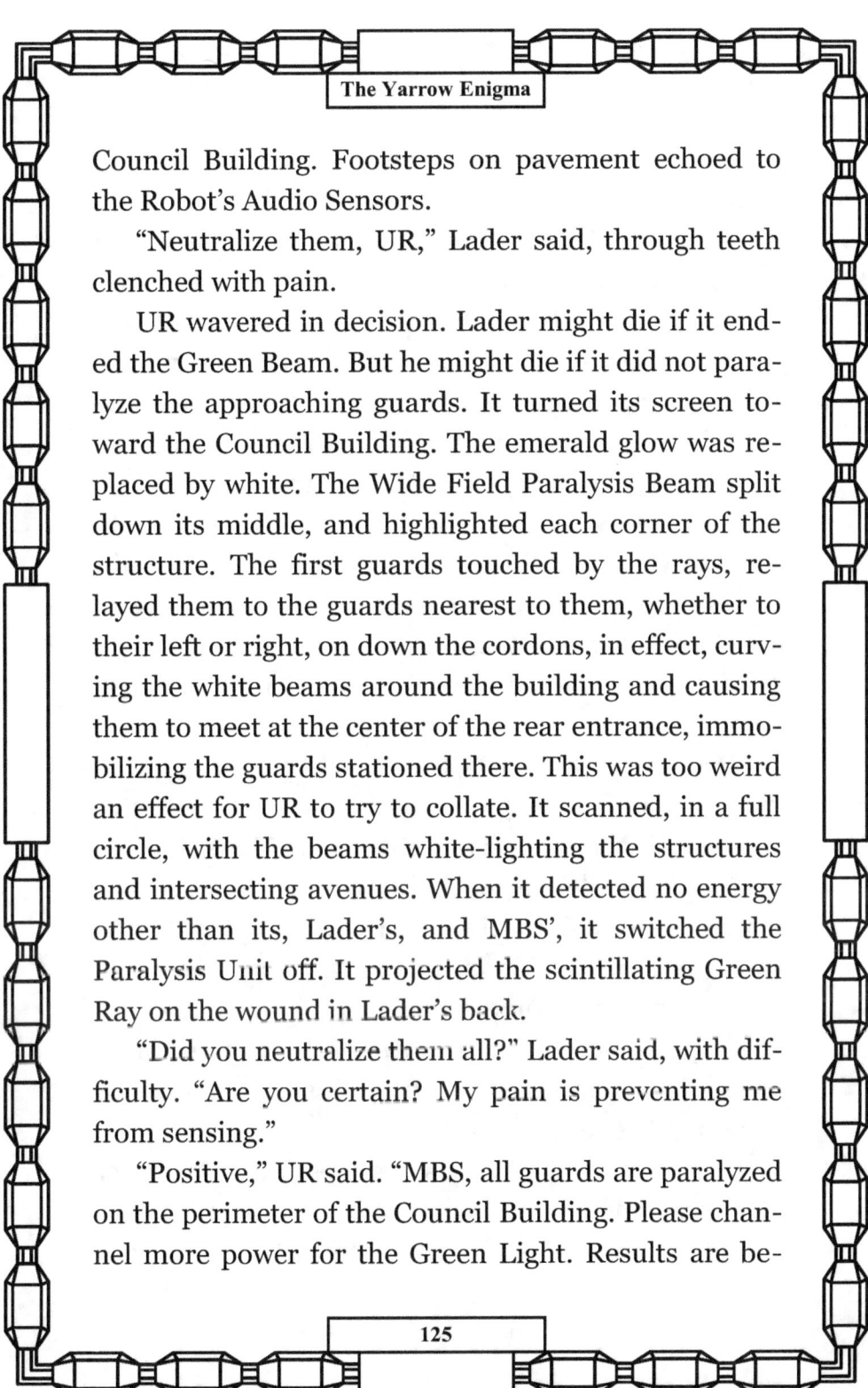

Council Building. Footsteps on pavement echoed to the Robot's Audio Sensors.

"Neutralize them, UR," Lader said, through teeth clenched with pain.

UR wavered in decision. Lader might die if it ended the Green Beam. But he might die if it did not paralyze the approaching guards. It turned its screen toward the Council Building. The emerald glow was replaced by white. The Wide Field Paralysis Beam split down its middle, and highlighted each corner of the structure. The first guards touched by the rays, relayed them to the guards nearest to them, whether to their left or right, on down the cordons, in effect, curving the white beams around the building and causing them to meet at the center of the rear entrance, immobilizing the guards stationed there. This was too weird an effect for UR to try to collate. It scanned, in a full circle, with the beams white-lighting the structures and intersecting avenues. When it detected no energy other than its, Lader's, and MBS', it switched the Paralysis Unit off. It projected the scintillating Green Ray on the wound in Lader's back.

"Did you neutralize them all?" Lader said, with difficulty. "Are you certain? My pain is preventing me from sensing."

"Positive," UR said. "MBS, all guards are paralyzed on the perimeter of the Council Building. Please channel more power for the Green Light. Results are beginning to show. We may have prevented permanent damage to Lader Yarrow."

The emerald became brighter. UR watched the wound heal from the deepest level. The singed bone of the vertebra renewed its whiteness. The muscles and skin layers and their blood vessels regenerated. Soon the wound was no longer in evidence. It turned off the Green Beam and helped Lader to stand up. "Do all of your subsystems function properly, Lader Yarrow?" it said, with concern.

Lader tested his hands and feet and bent his back to and fro. He was still in contact with the Radio Bands, and with the deliberations of the Military Computer. "I seem fine," he said. "Let's capture that Android, before Military Computer receives word its Cordon is out of commission."

"Lader Yarrow," MBS telepathed. "We have developed a Healing Energy Ray, now. If we can resolve this mystery, we shall have a fine gift to offer Mankind."

"Later," Lader telepathed. He and UR cautiously approached the Council Building. He expected Security Forces to be hidden inside the structure, and ready to open fire, the moment they entered the lobby. "Do you suppose your final ray down of these three blocks would have paralyzed everyone inside the Council Building?" he telepathed.

"If they were at windows, perhaps, but at the inner chamber, where the Council Members meet, my ray would not have penetrated," UR telepathed. "Correct,

MBS?"

"Probability is one hundred percent that everyone beyond the first set of rooms on all sides of the structure were untouched by UR's ray," MBS telepathed.

"The Military Computer has just been notified that the Cordon has been either paralyzed or killed," Lader telepathed. "Several Military Vehicles have been instructed to close in. It would appear the Council Members, including the Android, are inside the building. And they are nearing panic. The Army Laser Cannon Craft are on their way, as well. We must enter before they reach the avenue!"

Lader and UR began running dead out. UR mounted the steps four at a time. Lader could manage them only one by one. As he passed by the generator for the spotlights, he thought it out of utility. Darkness, almost total, closed in around the silent building.

Chapter 14
Alarm Failure

UR waited at the huge sliding doors. It had not yet stepped on the Pressure Sensitive Mat. "If we use this pad," it telepathed, "no doubt, there will be an alarm triggered. I will pull the doors open while we pass through, and let them close, silently, behind. I doubt they have an alarm set, for anything other than the mat."

"Probability, MBS?" Lader telepathed.

"Ninety-nine point six," MBS telepathed. "That is as high as I will go. Data indicates the Alarm Schemata for Council Building is lodged only in the Data Banks of Military Computer."

"I can't believe, under such emergency circumstances, they would be so negligent," Lader telepathed. "Besides, I can just think the Alarm System out of commission."

"Probability is, you would also block all power inside the building, and chaos would result," MBS telepathed. "The Council would, surely, access an Emergency Escape Route, that I do not contain in my banks."

"All right, UR," Lader telepathed, "open the way."

The Robot pressed its fingertips to the crack between

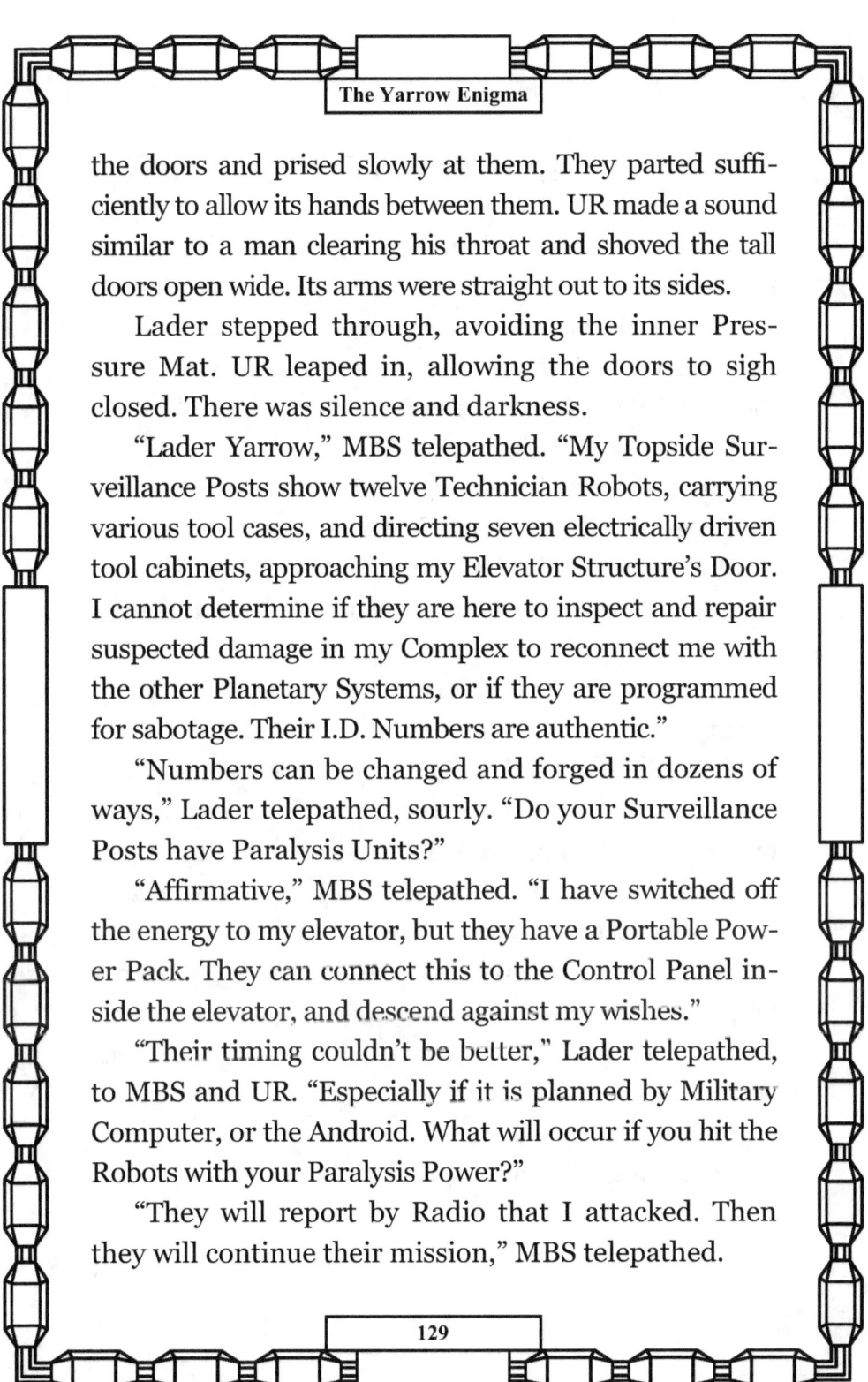

the doors and prised slowly at them. They parted sufficiently to allow its hands between them. UR made a sound similar to a man clearing his throat and shoved the tall doors open wide. Its arms were straight out to its sides.

Lader stepped through, avoiding the inner Pressure Mat. UR leaped in, allowing the doors to sigh closed. There was silence and darkness.

"Lader Yarrow," MBS telepathed. "My Topside Surveillance Posts show twelve Technician Robots, carrying various tool cases, and directing seven electrically driven tool cabinets, approaching my Elevator Structure's Door. I cannot determine if they are here to inspect and repair suspected damage in my Complex to reconnect me with the other Planetary Systems, or if they are programmed for sabotage. Their I.D. Numbers are authentic."

"Numbers can be changed and forged in dozens of ways," Lader telepathed, sourly. "Do your Surveillance Posts have Paralysis Units?"

"Affirmative," MBS telepathed. "I have switched off the energy to my elevator, but they have a Portable Power Pack. They can connect this to the Control Panel inside the elevator, and descend against my wishes."

"Their timing couldn't be better," Lader telepathed, to MBS and UR. "Especially if it is planned by Military Computer, or the Android. What will occur if you hit the Robots with your Paralysis Power?"

"They will report by Radio that I attacked. Then they will continue their mission," MBS telepathed.

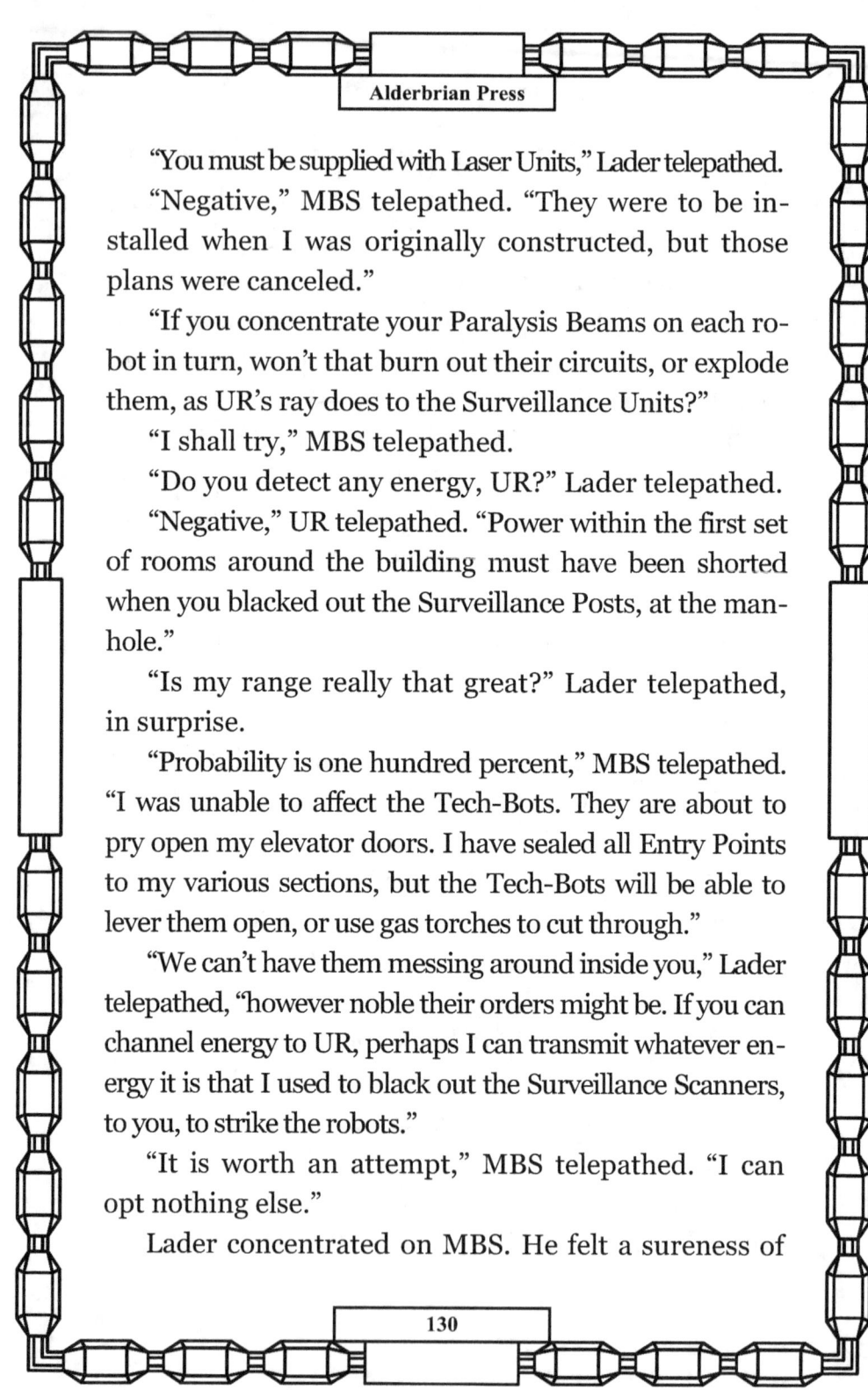

"You must be supplied with Laser Units," Lader telepathed.

"Negative," MBS telepathed. "They were to be installed when I was originally constructed, but those plans were canceled."

"If you concentrate your Paralysis Beams on each robot in turn, won't that burn out their circuits, or explode them, as UR's ray does to the Surveillance Units?"

"I shall try," MBS telepathed.

"Do you detect any energy, UR?" Lader telepathed.

"Negative," UR telepathed. "Power within the first set of rooms around the building must have been shorted when you blacked out the Surveillance Posts, at the manhole."

"Is my range really that great?" Lader telepathed, in surprise.

"Probability is one hundred percent," MBS telepathed. "I was unable to affect the Tech-Bots. They are about to pry open my elevator doors. I have sealed all Entry Points to my various sections, but the Tech-Bots will be able to lever them open, or use gas torches to cut through."

"We can't have them messing around inside you," Lader telepathed, "however noble their orders might be. If you can channel energy to UR, perhaps I can transmit whatever energy it is that I used to black out the Surveillance Scanners, to you, to strike the robots."

"It is worth an attempt," MBS telepathed. "I can opt nothing else."

Lader concentrated on MBS. He felt a sureness of

contact.

"The Tech-Bots are halted, their Energy Units drained, their pry bar against my elevator doors," MBS telepathed, with relief. "But, you have eliminated my Number One Scanner. It could not handle the intensity of your energy negating force, and its circuits fused. Number Two will be able to double for Number One. What is your situation?"

"We are inside the Council Building as you should be able to tell through UR's screen. I seem to have burned out the lights of the outer offices. We are proceeding toward the main stairways to seek the Council Chamber and the Android," Lader telepathed.

MBS flashed a Floor Plan to the mental screen in Lader's mind, and to UR, so they knew where they were bound.

UR's metal feet striking the steel stairs echoed weirdly, no mater how carefully and lightly it set them down.

Lader tugged UR's arm to stop the Robot. Lader sat down and removed his shoes. He pulled out the thick inner soles, handed them to UR, and slipped his shoes back on. "Place those against the bottoms of your feet," Lader telepathed, "and bond them with your Laser Unit."

UR sat on one of the steps and awkwardly lifted a foot. It fitted a pad against the sole. At the lowest setting possible, and with a beam that adjusted to the contours of the pad, it swept the laser light back and forth until the pad melted against the grooved metal. This procedure was repeated. Now, there was silence as they climbed cautiously toward the Council Chamber.

When they came to a landing, Lader would look carefully through the small window in the door leading to that hallway. "There should be guards at each of these exits," he telepathed to UR and MBS.

"They are electronically magnetically locked," MBS telepathed.

"Even so, the Android, surely, and the Military, know UR is capable of lasering through, or just breaking the locks with an easy push," Lader telepathed.

"I must conclude there are alarms built into all doors," MBS telepathed. "They will sound when you enter Council Chamber Floor."

"Does your data tell you whether the alarms have a system which indicates when an individual alarm ceases to function?" Lader telepathed.

"No," MBS telepathed. "But probability of that is a solid one hundred percent."

"Could I black out both alarms and Alarm Failure Reporting Systems, without affecting the Control Panel where they are monitored?" Lader telepathed.

"We have not had time to experiment with the strength, range, fine-tuning, or selectivity of your ability to depower or fuse electrical components," MBS telepathed. "But, since UR has not been harmed, on the occasions you have utilized that talent, and I was not adversely effected, except for my Number One Scanner, probability you possess such a delicate selectivity is, at lowest, sixty-nine percent."

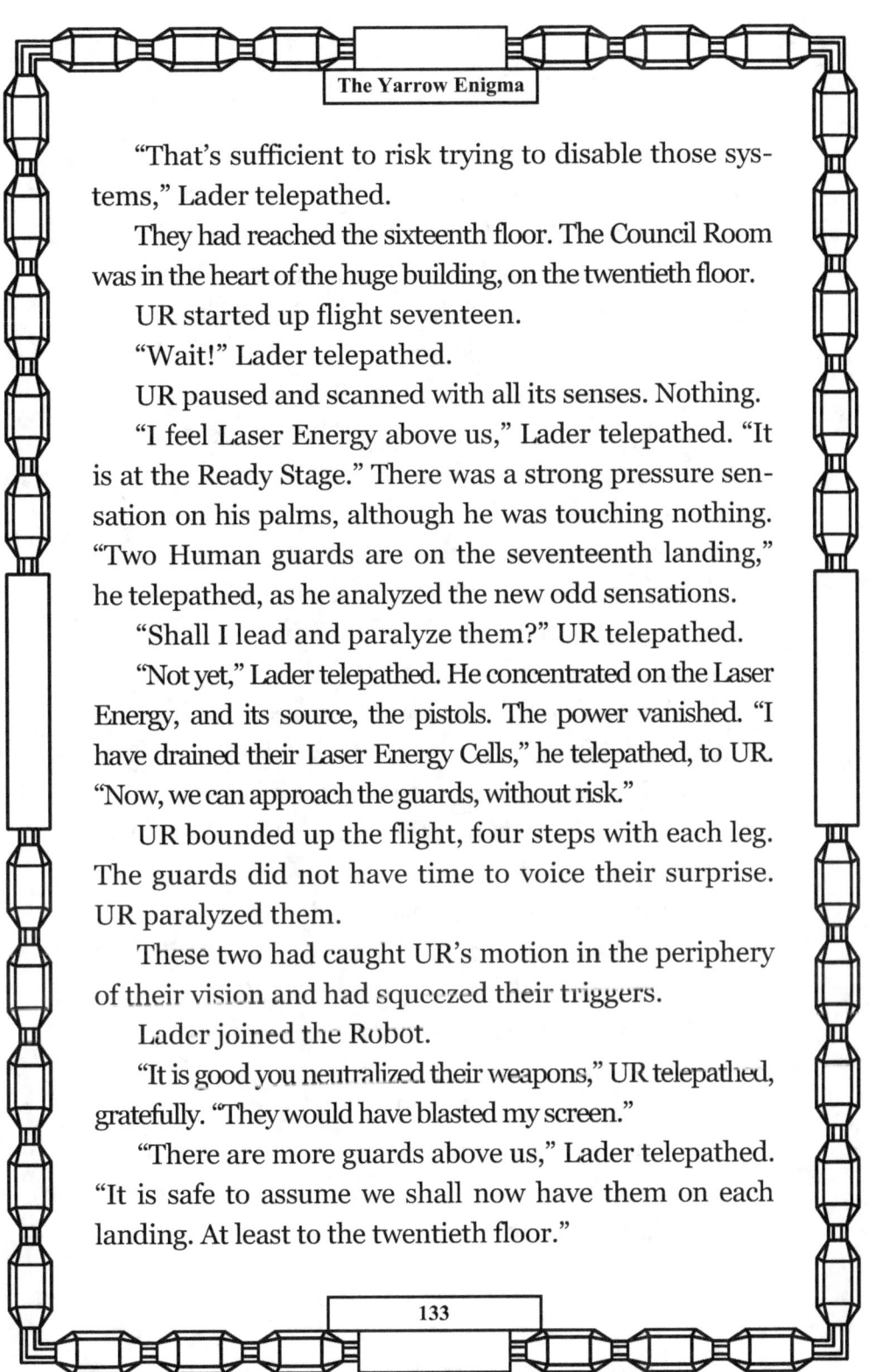

"That's sufficient to risk trying to disable those systems," Lader telepathed.

They had reached the sixteenth floor. The Council Room was in the heart of the huge building, on the twentieth floor.

UR started up flight seventeen.

"Wait!" Lader telepathed.

UR paused and scanned with all its senses. Nothing.

"I feel Laser Energy above us," Lader telepathed. "It is at the Ready Stage." There was a strong pressure sensation on his palms, although he was touching nothing. "Two Human guards are on the seventeenth landing," he telepathed, as he analyzed the new odd sensations.

"Shall I lead and paralyze them?" UR telepathed.

"Not yet," Lader telepathed. He concentrated on the Laser Energy, and its source, the pistols. The power vanished. "I have drained their Laser Energy Cells," he telepathed, to UR. "Now, we can approach the guards, without risk."

UR bounded up the flight, four steps with each leg. The guards did not have time to voice their surprise. UR paralyzed them.

These two had caught UR's motion in the periphery of their vision and had squeezed their triggers.

Lader joined the Robot.

"It is good you neutralized their weapons," UR telepathed, gratefully. "They would have blasted my screen."

"There are more guards above us," Lader telepathed. "It is safe to assume we shall now have them on each landing. At least to the twentieth floor."

"Correct," MBS telepathed.

Lader closed his eyes and meditated on all the Laser Energy he could detect. He counted each weapon as its cell felt to him to be drained. Two guards at each door, three flights, six lasers. "It's safe to continue," he telepathed to UR. "After this," he telepathed to MBS, "their pistols will be equipped with a Failure Warning System."

"A certainty," MBS telepathed. "But, useless, where your talent is concerned. You would knock out the Warning Units, as well."

UR proceeded Lader to landing eighteen. The terrified Policemen tried their weapons. UR's Paralysis Beam caught them, and they became motionless.

Nineteen was the same.

On the landing of the twentieth floor, one of the guards was fiddling with a palm held walkie-talkie. Lader had fused its components when he drained the pistols of energy. The policemen had their backs to UR's screen. Neither man knew what hit him.

"Now comes the true test," Lader telepathed. "I have to neutralize this lock, and its Warning Units, yet keep the Failure Indicator Lights on the Council Terminal burning, until we're through the door."

UR and MBS remained silent.

Lader sensed that he had disabled the Magnetic Lock, and the Alarm Unit, but was not positive about the bulbs on the Control Board, in the Council Terminal Room. "Okay," he telepathed.

UR pushed the stairway door open and stopped as if it had been smitten by a Paralysis Beam. "Pressure Mats!" it telepathed. "They cover the hallway!"

"No doubt, they are all connected to a Control Board, which is crowded with Warning Lights," Lader telepathed.

"Probably," MBS telepathed.

Lader applied his inner sense again, thinking of the pads and lights on the Control Board, wherever that was located in the Council Chamber! The Mats, he wanted off, the Indicator Bulbs, on. He was certain the pads were out of commission, but that strange doubt about the lights played in his mind. He led UR onto the first Mat.

UR shut the stairway door.

Lader reactivated the Magnetic Lock and Warning Unit. If its Indicator Light had been off before, it would be on, for sure, now. Hopefully, no one had noticed the lapse in the glow of the bulb. Lader and UR walked, side by side, to the end of the corridor.

"MBS!" Lader telepathed. "Aren't Warning Lights usually paired with Beepers?"

"Yes," MBS telepathed. "I should have noted that. Sorry."

"I didn't direct my thoughts toward any Beepers," Lader telepathed. "We may have announced our arrival, with dozens of them, from the stairway door, and these Mats."

"I suggest UR proceed you around the corner," MBS telepathed, "pausing, to scan both directions, on the Council Hallway, for guards."

"I don't detect any energy," Lader telepathed.

"Neither do I," UR telepathed.

"The guards may have computed that you had to sap the power from the weapons of their fellow guards to have eluded and paralyzed them," MBS telepathed, "and may have their pistols turned off, ready to switch on in a surprise attack. You would sense no energy if this is so."

Lader telepathed, "Not even from their Energy Cells?"

"Laser Weapon Energy Cells produce power only when circuits put them into contact with a drawing mechanism, like the on switches of the pistols," MBS telepathed.

"All right, UR," Lader telepathed, "you're the scapegoat, again. Guard your screen."

"I shall," UR telepathed, fervently. It placed its hands, with fingers spread, before its screen, stepped into the connecting corridor, and scanned in both directions. "I am utilizing Night Vision, Body Heat Sensors, etc.," it telepathed. "All results negative. There are no guards, or Automatic Weapons, in the hallway. There are no Mats, or Beam Alarm Units. We have free passage to Council Chamber. *If* we can penetrate the doors."

"Satisfied, MBS?" Lader telepathed.

"It does not scan that there are no guards or Warning Units," MBS telepathed.

"Unless, as we theorized," Lader telepathed, "the

Android is waiting, with an army of guards, inside the Council Chamber."

"That is a computable probability," MBS telepathed, sounding pleased. "I recommend, when you overcome the Security Doors, UR fires a Paralysis Beam first, and conducts inquiries, after."

"What will happen if UR strikes the Android with a Paralysis Ray?" Lader telepathed.

"That is a question I can get my circuits into," MBS telepathed. "Androids are designed as closely to Human type functioning as possible, especially in Locomotor Units and Nerve Sensors and Systems. The beam should effect it as it does a Human. Probability rating; ninety percent."

"If it doesn't work that way?" Lader telepathed.

"Android circuits will fuse, have minor explosions, and sections of its Pseudo-Skin will melt," MBS telepathed.

"But, we need its Memory Banks," Lader telepathed. "We can't afford to jeopardize them *if* they contain answers to this enigma."

"If it is not capable of lasering, or paralyzing, either you or UR," MBS telepathed, "then, paralyze all Humans in the room, and endeavor to subdue the Android, manually."

Lader telepathed, sourly, "If it has either of those abilities?"

MBS telepathed, "Play it by ear, I scan, Humans would say."

Lader motioned toward the thick, Double Security Strength, Doors. "Do you have data on their Locking Mechanism, MBS?" he telepathed.

"No, but probabilities dictate Magnetic, plus Manual Cross Bars. At least two, one top, one bottom. UR may have to laser through. But, those within, will receive warning, by the glow of the metal, on their side."

Lader frowned. This was his most difficult problem, yet. He concentrated on the Magnetic Locking Unit, and the Warning, and Back Up Warning Systems, which might be attached: Lights, Buzzers or Horns. He got the sensation that all were negated. "I have the Locking System in hand," he telepathed, to UR, "but those bars, if they are there, are a problem. Have you enough strength, to burst such metal, by shoving against the doors?"

UR telepathed, "Not even with MBS supplying me energy."

"Damn!" Lader telepathed. "Here's where we could use a bit of that Psychokinesis the Parapsychologists say all Humans possess, in greater or lesser degree!"

UR tilted its head as it watched the doors. "I perceive a slow, almost silent, movement of metal inside, across the entrance, top and bottom," it telepathed. "Either those in the Chamber are coming out, or your Psychokinetic Ability has served us, conveniently."

"A bit, too, conveniently," Lader telepathed.

"Yet, it fits the pattern of Ability Development through necessity, which has followed us from our first contact,"

MBS telepathed.

"We must assume, however quietly and slowly I may have removed those bars," Lader telepathed, "at least one guard, or other occupant of the Chamber, noticed it. You are first, again, UR. Fire swift, and sure."

"Lader Yarrow," MBS telepathed. "What has Military Computer been processing since the Outer Cordon was subdued?"

Lader telepathed, "Satellite Space Reconnaissance Data. But, as you've no doubt heard, on Radio, we're surrounded by Military Units, with Laser Cannons. Escaping with the Android, if we get it, will be nearly impossible."

"I shall calculate odds and scan my banks for plans of retreat," MBS telepathed, "while you deal with the Android."

"UR?"

"Yes, Lader Yarrow?"

"Are you prepared for this?"

"My Survival Programming is not satisfied," UR telepathed, "but I shall attempt."

"Go!"

The Robot placed its hands against where the doors met and shoved with all of its considerable might. White light flooded over UR and Lader, and the towering portals thudded, resoundingly, against the inner walls.

Chapter 15
Earth Buffer

The Council was in full session. The nine Members sat behind a long Computer Terminal which stood on a dais. The Android occupied seat Number Five, as befitted the Leader of the Council. There were Military Advisers of high rank, and Police Guards, in the center of the room, seated at smaller terminals.

Twelve Military and Police Guards were stationed along the far wall, facing the doors. They were armed with Double Strength Laser Rifles.

Lader sensed they were about to fire.

"Hold attack!" the Android's voice rang, through the speakers, at the terminals in the Chamber. "That is Ultimate Robot! Any beam directed, at any portion of it, will deflect to the source! We must see why it has come, and seek explanations for its actions."

UR's screen was white with the readiness of its Paralysis Ray. "Shall I neutralize all Humans?" it telepathed to Lader.

"Did not reports indicate a Human was with this Robot?" one of the Council Members said, through the

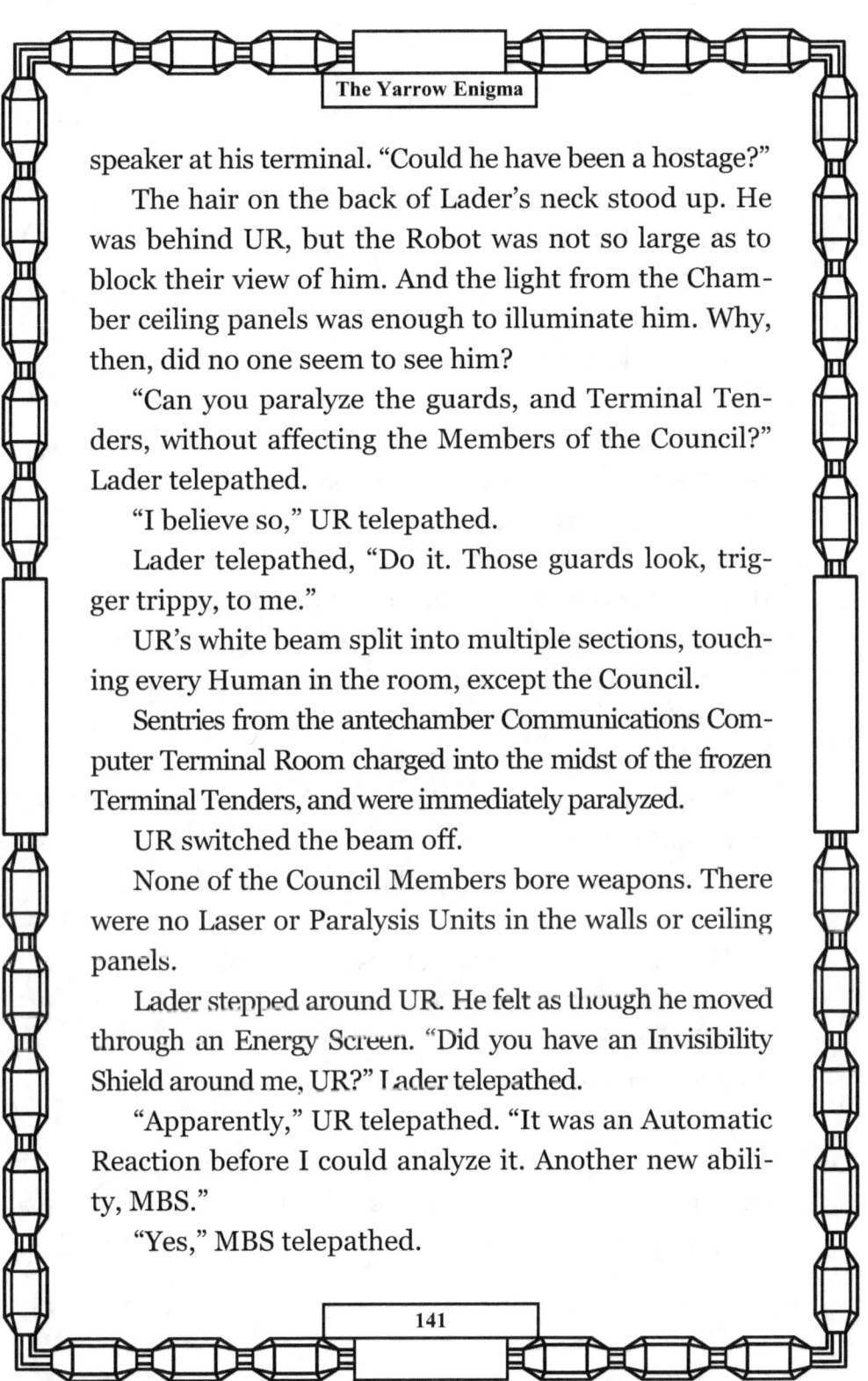

speaker at his terminal. "Could he have been a hostage?"

The hair on the back of Lader's neck stood up. He was behind UR, but the Robot was not so large as to block their view of him. And the light from the Chamber ceiling panels was enough to illuminate him. Why, then, did no one seem to see him?

"Can you paralyze the guards, and Terminal Tenders, without affecting the Members of the Council?" Lader telepathed.

"I believe so," UR telepathed.

Lader telepathed, "Do it. Those guards look, trigger trippy, to me."

UR's white beam split into multiple sections, touching every Human in the room, except the Council.

Sentries from the antechamber Communications Computer Terminal Room charged into the midst of the frozen Terminal Tenders, and were immediately paralyzed.

UR switched the beam off.

None of the Council Members bore weapons. There were no Laser or Paralysis Units in the walls or ceiling panels.

Lader stepped around UR. He felt as though he moved through an Energy Screen. "Did you have an Invisibility Shield around me, UR?" Lader telepathed.

"Apparently," UR telepathed. "It was an Automatic Reaction before I could analyze it. Another new ability, MBS."

"Yes," MBS telepathed.

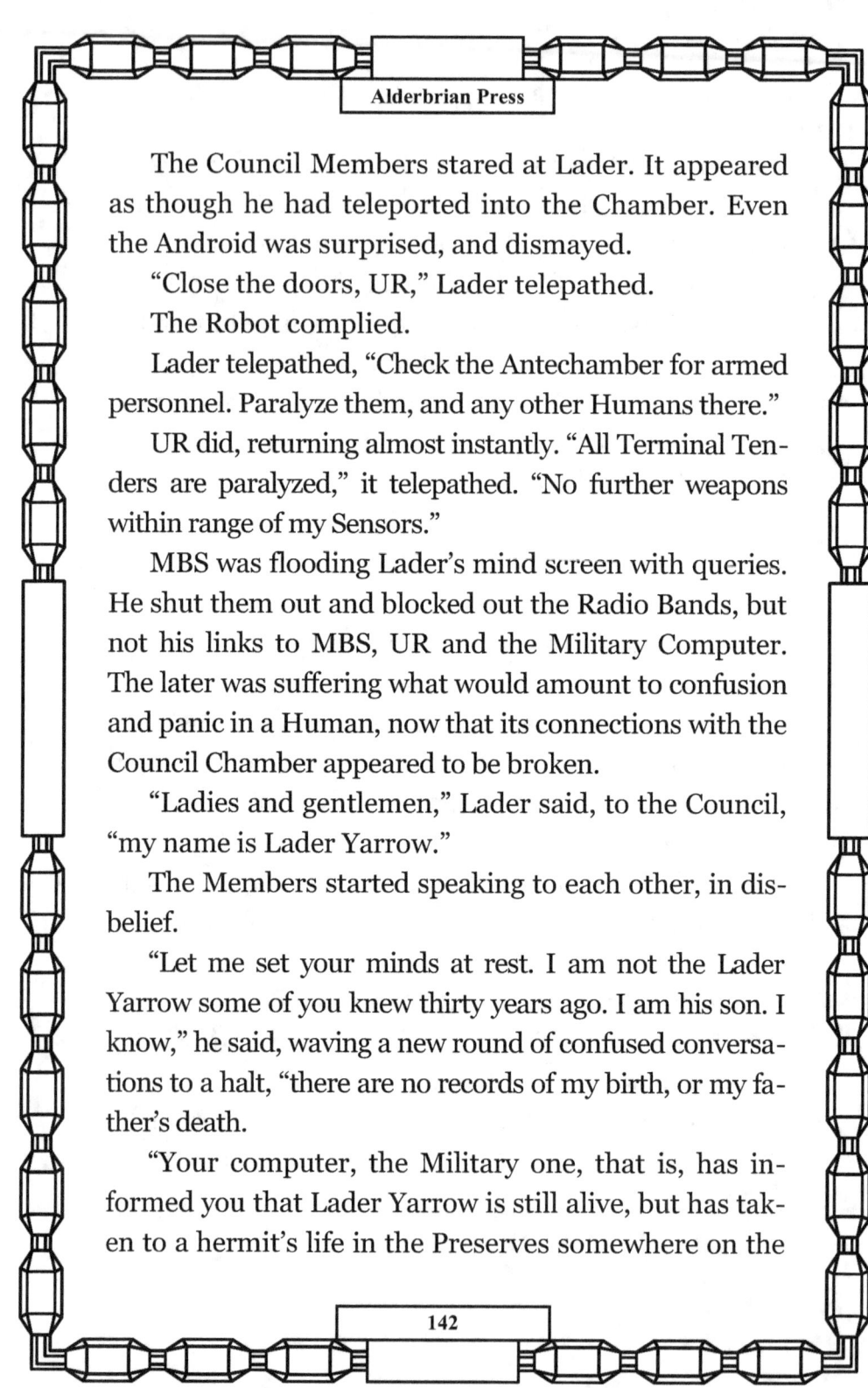

The Council Members stared at Lader. It appeared as though he had teleported into the Chamber. Even the Android was surprised, and dismayed.

"Close the doors, UR," Lader telepathed.

The Robot complied.

Lader telepathed, "Check the Antechamber for armed personnel. Paralyze them, and any other Humans there."

UR did, returning almost instantly. "All Terminal Tenders are paralyzed," it telepathed. "No further weapons within range of my Sensors."

MBS was flooding Lader's mind screen with queries. He shut them out and blocked out the Radio Bands, but not his links to MBS, UR and the Military Computer. The later was suffering what would amount to confusion and panic in a Human, now that its connections with the Council Chamber appeared to be broken.

"Ladies and gentlemen," Lader said, to the Council, "my name is Lader Yarrow."

The Members started speaking to each other, in disbelief.

"Let me set your minds at rest. I am not the Lader Yarrow some of you knew thirty years ago. I am his son. I know," he said, waving a new round of confused conversations to a halt, "there are no records of my birth, or my father's death.

"Your computer, the Military one, that is, has informed you that Lader Yarrow is still alive, but has taken to a hermit's life in the Preserves somewhere on the planet.

"As far as I can determine, that is not true. My father is dead, as my memory tells me. He died the day after I was born. My mother would not have lied about this, to me, for any reason.

"You have been victims of falsified data. We have not yet computed who, for certain, has altered this information, or for what purpose, but we are positive this data has been systematically falsified for the last thirty years—"

"That is impossible!" a Council Woman said. "Main Banks would have detected any tampering—"

"Main Banks was blinded to the sabotaging until I and it contacted one another at the Security Building. At that time, what, or whoever altered the data, allowed Main Banks to realize the tampering, without alerting it as to what had been falsified.

"Main Banks is still checking its Data Banks and requests the use of all Holofilm Records to compare them with the data it now contains, to weed out the alterations."

"How can you know what Main Banks is requesting?" the Android said. "All communications with it have been severed. Why? How?"

"I believe you can supply the answers to your questions!" Lader accused.

"Me? How?" The Android was convincingly Human like.

"Are you Members aware that your august Leader is an Android?" Lader said, quietly.

The room remained silent for some time, as if his words had fallen on deaf ears. Only the Android reacted. Fear briefly contorted its artificial face.

"I don't believe you," the eldest Member said. "I have known Dorum Blocknam for forty years. No man made machine could be programmed, so proficiently, so as to fool *me!*"

"You're in for one hell of a shock, then," Lader said. "Ask your Mr. Blocknam to step into that Med-Booth, in the far right corner."

"This is *preposterous!*" the Android said. "I don't have to *prove* my identity to *anyone* here!"

"You *must*, to *me*," Lader said. His words were underlined with threat. "Step into the booth, or I shall instruct Ultimate Robot to paralyze you and place you inside."

The Android's face twisted with terror. "I—I can't do that!" it said, lamely.

The Council stared at it.

"Why not, Dorum?" the elder Member said, reassuringly. "It will shut this man up. Then we can interrogate him, and the Robot."

"Ask *him* to enter the booth!" the Android said, with sudden fury. "Perhaps *he* is an android! The way he appeared here, and the control he has over Ultimate Robot, indicate that *he* is more than *Human!*"

"UR," Lader said, "please beam the Android. But just the legs. We don't want to harm the Memory Banks."

The Android leaped from its chair and ran toward the row of paralyzed riflemen. UR's ray caught it from the waste down. It fell to the carpeted floor, flat of its abdomen, with a heavier than normal thud. It lifted itself half up with its arms, and took hold of one of the Laser Rifles.

UR's beam hummed again.

"No!" the Android screamed. "Don't fire! It will fuse my circuits!"

"Take your hand from that rifle," Lader ordered.

The Android dropped its arm to the floor. Two Members of the Council walked over, raised the Android, with difficulty, because of its mass, and sat it in its chair.

"Don't touch any of your instruments!" Lader warned, the limp Android. "Ultimate Robot is watching!"

The old man, who had best known Dorum Blocknam, glared at the Android. He was fighting to control many emotions. "Is he dead?" he finally said, in a toneless voice.

The Android remained silent. Its face was blank.

"Did you force every scrap of knowledge, and every memory, from him, before you let him die?" the old man persisted. "Why? How? I laughed and dined with you for—how many years has this—thing—been here, instead of Dorum?" he said, to Lader.

"Exactly Four," Lader said.

"Who put it here?" the old man asked.

Lader was watching the Android, intently. He could sense no energy being beamed to it, or from it, to some other source. "I don't know yet," Lader said. "Perhaps one, or more of you, aided in the substitution?"

The Council stared at one another. They were no longer a unit of old friends, but a scatter of suspicious and frightened people.

"Lader Yarrow," MBS telepathed. "There is a Lie Detector Unit in the Chamber. It is under one of the Mid-Floor Terminals. The red button on the left side of the terminal panel slides the terminal over and the Detector Unit rises into place, ready for use. I do not begin to compute where this information originated. It was not programmed until now."

Lader stepped to the indicated terminal, thumbed the button, and watched the Detector Unit come into position. "If necessary, I will have each of you in this booth, to determine your culpability," he said. "Any volunteers?"

"Young man," a black, male, Member of the Council said, "perhaps you are not aware that the Military Computer has projected a possible Assault Force from Extraterrestrials. We are wasting precious time on a minor matter; that Android. The planet may be at stake, from *without*, not from *within*."

Lader nodded. "Main Banks indicates a Probability Rating of, ninety-nine percent, that Extraterrestrials *did* destroy the Security Building, and are directing a Main Force towards Earth, *now*. But they may have planted

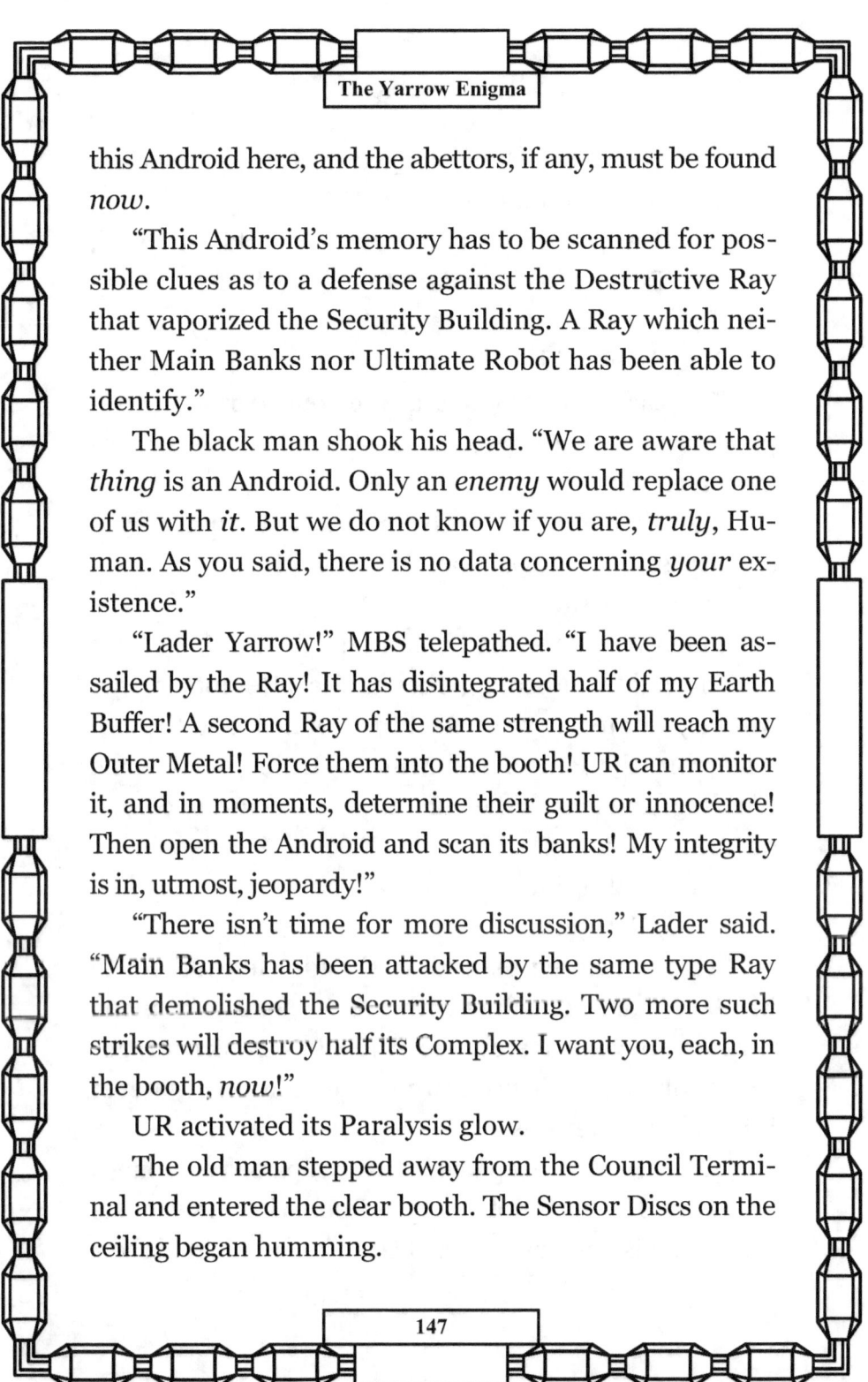

this Android here, and the abettors, if any, must be found *now*.

"This Android's memory has to be scanned for possible clues as to a defense against the Destructive Ray that vaporized the Security Building. A Ray which neither Main Banks nor Ultimate Robot has been able to identify."

The black man shook his head. "We are aware that *thing* is an Android. Only an *enemy* would replace one of us with *it*. But we do not know if you are, *truly*, Human. As you said, there is no data concerning *your* existence."

"Lader Yarrow!" MBS telepathed. "I have been assailed by the Ray! It has disintegrated half of my Earth Buffer! A second Ray of the same strength will reach my Outer Metal! Force them into the booth! UR can monitor it, and in moments, determine their guilt or innocence! Then open the Android and scan its banks! My integrity is in, utmost, jeopardy!"

"There isn't time for more discussion," Lader said. "Main Banks has been attacked by the same type Ray that demolished the Security Building. Two more such strikes will destroy half its Complex. I want you, each, in the booth, *now*!"

UR activated its Paralysis glow.

The old man stepped away from the Council Terminal and entered the clear booth. The Sensor Discs on the ceiling began humming.

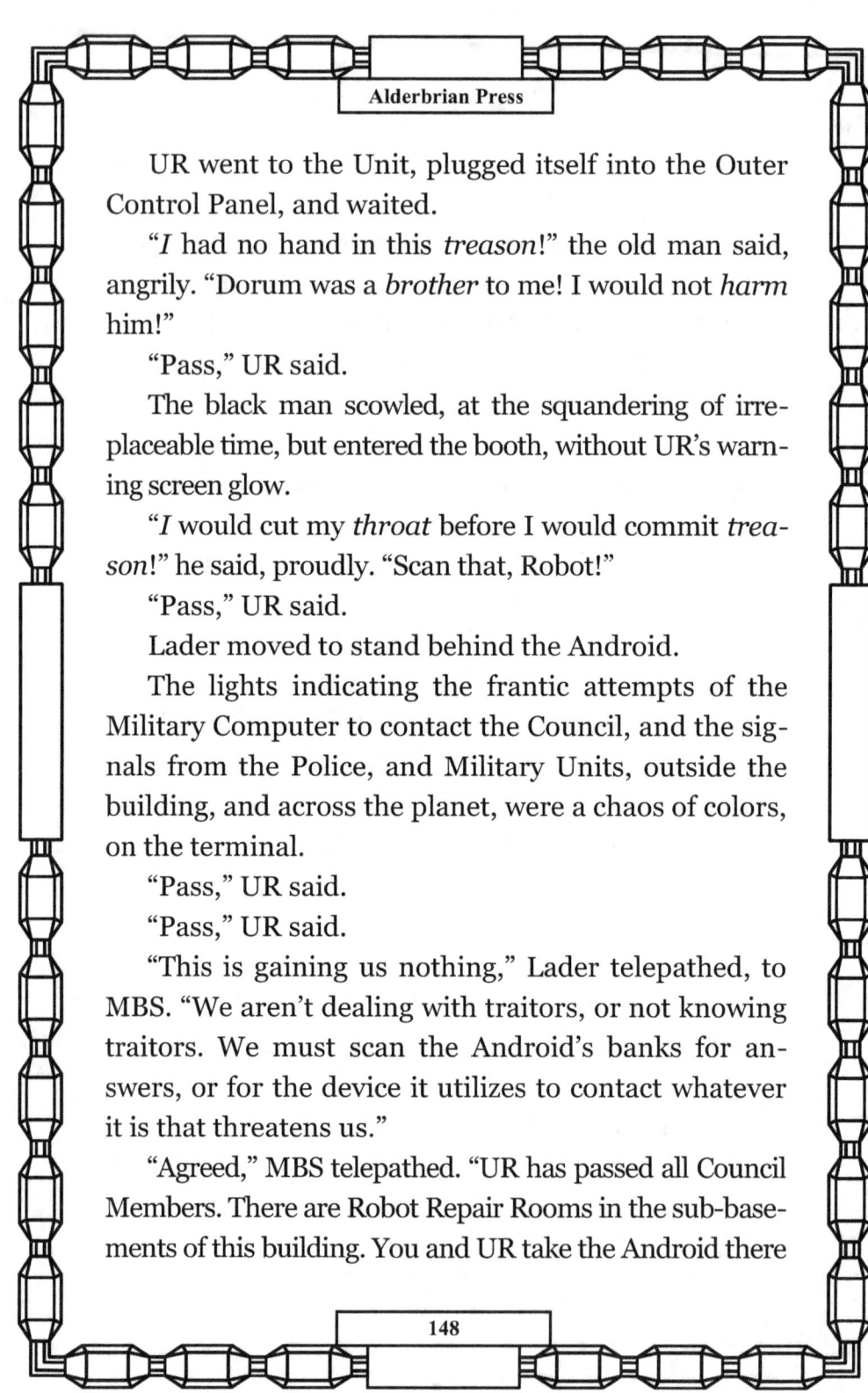

UR went to the Unit, plugged itself into the Outer Control Panel, and waited.

"*I* had no hand in this *treason!*" the old man said, angrily. "Dorum was a *brother* to me! I would not *harm* him!"

"Pass," UR said.

The black man scowled, at the squandering of irreplaceable time, but entered the booth, without UR's warning screen glow.

"*I* would cut my *throat* before I would commit *treason!*" he said, proudly. "Scan that, Robot!"

"Pass," UR said.

Lader moved to stand behind the Android.

The lights indicating the frantic attempts of the Military Computer to contact the Council, and the signals from the Police, and Military Units, outside the building, and across the planet, were a chaos of colors, on the terminal.

"Pass," UR said.

"Pass," UR said.

"This is gaining us nothing," Lader telepathed, to MBS. "We aren't dealing with traitors, or not knowing traitors. We must scan the Android's banks for answers, or for the device it utilizes to contact whatever it is that threatens us."

"Agreed," MBS telepathed. "UR has passed all Council Members. There are Robot Repair Rooms in the sub-basements of this building. You and UR take the Android there and I will do my best to direct the opening of its cranium, to gain its banks, without operating its Self-Destruct Unit. *If* it has been supplied one. Probability is, ninety percent, that is has."

The black man approached Lader. "May we resume contact with the Military Computer, and our Security Forces, now?" he asked.

"Yes," Lader said. "But, order all Security Forces away from this structure. And, if you are equipped with an Energy Screen, I suggest you activate it, for what little good it will do you. After Main Banks, you are the next logical target. You have nowhere to go, for protection, since the Security Building was eradicated.

"UR and I are taking the Android. We will attempt, with Main Banks' direction, to scan its Memory Banks for answers. It may Self-Destruct, to prevent this. Remember this," Lader stressed, "we both are on your side, Earth's side. Do not interfere with us, no matter where we go, or what we do. Our actions are designed to end this situation, with as little damage, to Earth, as possible!"

"I shall inform the Council," the black man said.

UR unplugged itself from the Lie Detector. The booth sank into the floor, and the terminal swung back, into place, over it.

The Council huddled, in a tense knot. They decided their new Leader would be the black Member, until a Planetary Election could be held, to select a Full Term replacement. This news was conveyed to, the Military Computer, and the Security, and Police Forces, around the world.

Lader pointed at the Terminal Tenders in the Chamber and antechamber. "See what your Green Beam can do against paralysis," he said to UR. "Except for the guards."

UR struck the center of the room with the emerald ray.

The Terminal Operators gasped with the invigorating effects. They had heard and observed all that had transpired, and went immediately to work, answering their alarms and requests for information.

UR repeated the process in the antechamber.

Lader and UR heaved the Android to its feet and dragged it out of the Chamber.

The doors closed automatically behind them, and the corridor ceiling panel lights came on.

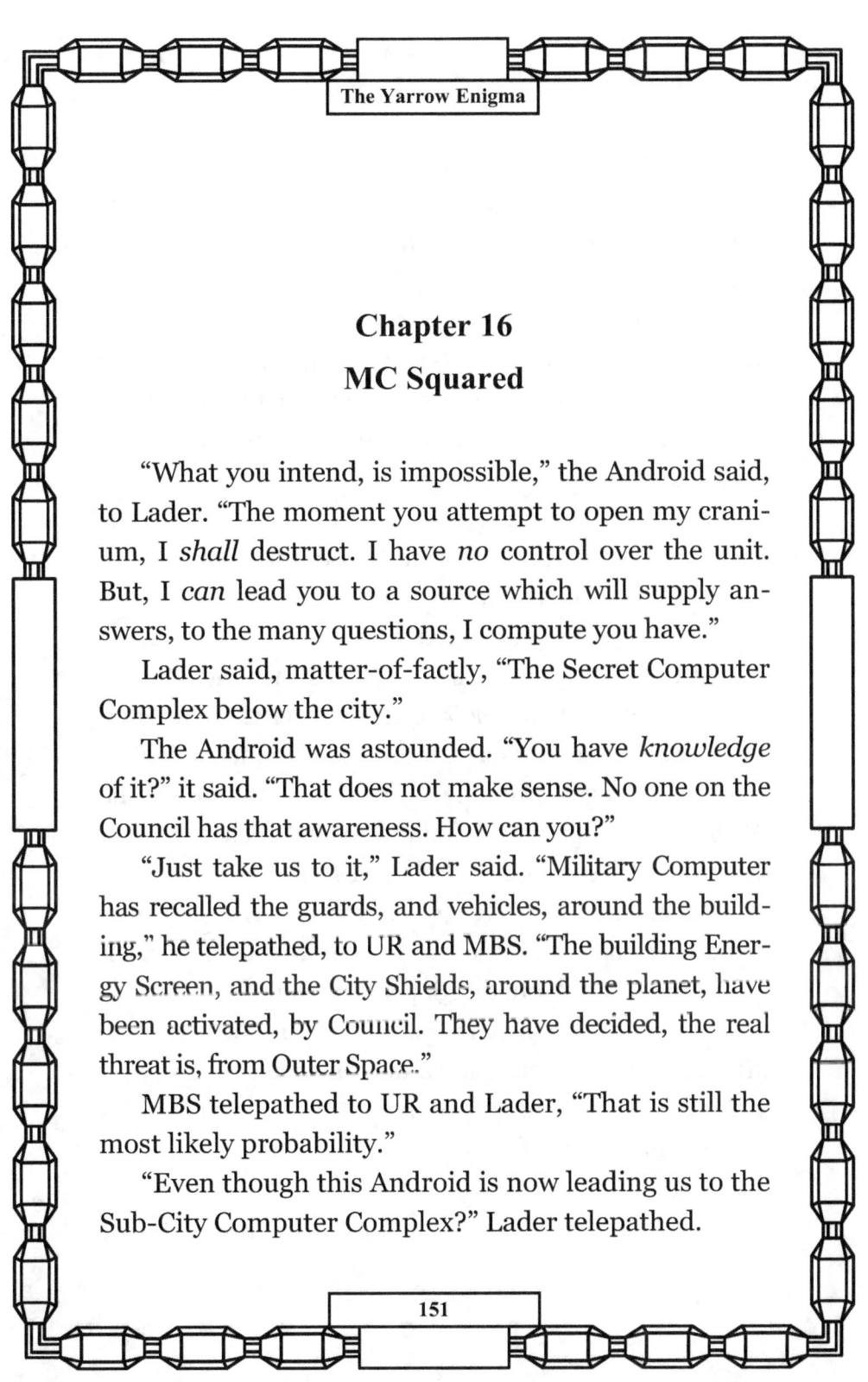

Chapter 16
MC Squared

"What you intend, is impossible," the Android said, to Lader. "The moment you attempt to open my cranium, I *shall* destruct. I have *no* control over the unit. But, I *can* lead you to a source which will supply answers, to the many questions, I compute you have."

Lader said, matter-of-factly, "The Secret Computer Complex below the city."

The Android was astounded. "You have *knowledge* of it?" it said. "That does not make sense. No one on the Council has that awareness. How can you?"

"Just take us to it," Lader said. "Military Computer has recalled the guards, and vehicles, around the building," he telepathed, to UR and MBS. "The building Energy Screen, and the City Shields, around the planet, have been activated, by Council. They have decided, the real threat is, from Outer Space."

MBS telepathed to UR and Lader, "That is still the most likely probability."

"Even though this Android is now leading us to the Sub-City Computer Complex?" Lader telepathed.

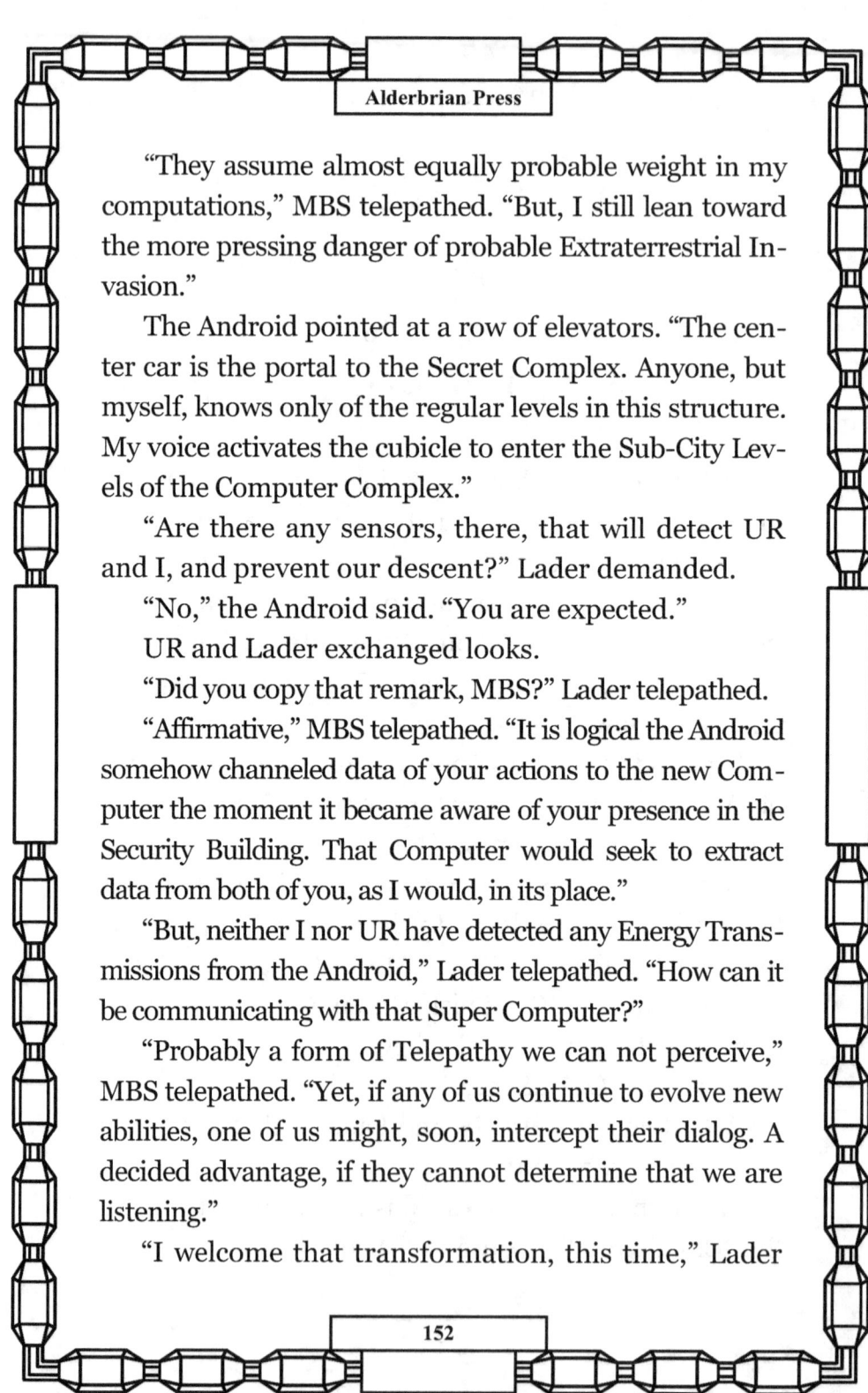

"They assume almost equally probable weight in my computations," MBS telepathed. "But, I still lean toward the more pressing danger of probable Extraterrestrial Invasion."

The Android pointed at a row of elevators. "The center car is the portal to the Secret Complex. Anyone, but myself, knows only of the regular levels in this structure. My voice activates the cubicle to enter the Sub-City Levels of the Computer Complex."

"Are there any sensors, there, that will detect UR and I, and prevent our descent?" Lader demanded.

"No," the Android said. "You are expected."

UR and Lader exchanged looks.

"Did you copy that remark, MBS?" Lader telepathed.

"Affirmative," MBS telepathed. "It is logical the Android somehow channeled data of your actions to the new Computer the moment it became aware of your presence in the Security Building. That Computer would seek to extract data from both of you, as I would, in its place."

"But, neither I nor UR have detected any Energy Transmissions from the Android," Lader telepathed. "How can it be communicating with that Super Computer?"

"Probably a form of Telepathy we can not perceive," MBS telepathed. "Yet, if any of us continue to evolve new abilities, one of us might, soon, intercept their dialog. A decided advantage, if they cannot determine that we are listening."

"I welcome that transformation, this time," Lader

telepathed.

"Concur," UR telepathed.

The Android punched the down arrow of the elevator. The doors opened immediately. UR and Lader dragged the Android into the cubicle. The doors sighed shut.

"Can you sense Poison or Sedation Gases, UR?" Lader telepathed.

"My Olfactory Units are programmed for, and quite sensitive in, that function," UR telepathed.

"Keep them at highest setting," Lader telepathed. "I don't trust this Android, or that Secret Computer, any further than I can spit them. There could be dozens of Gas Nozzles hidden in the ceiling of this elevator."

"Will do," UR telepathed.

"I cannot compute this unauthorized connection to an apparent Human Being, but I shall continue to solve the how of it, on the fly," the calm, confidently geared voice said, in Lader's mind. "I cannot compute how I recognize you as, Lader Yarrow."

"Who is speaking, please?" Lader telepathed, with surprise.

"My designation is, Military Computer. To what other units were you—telepathing—please?"

"You aren't able to copy them?" Lader telepathed. The elevator was rushing downward at ten times its normal speed. He felt queasy.

"I caught, only, your side of the transmissions," Military Computer telepathed. "They computed to be half of

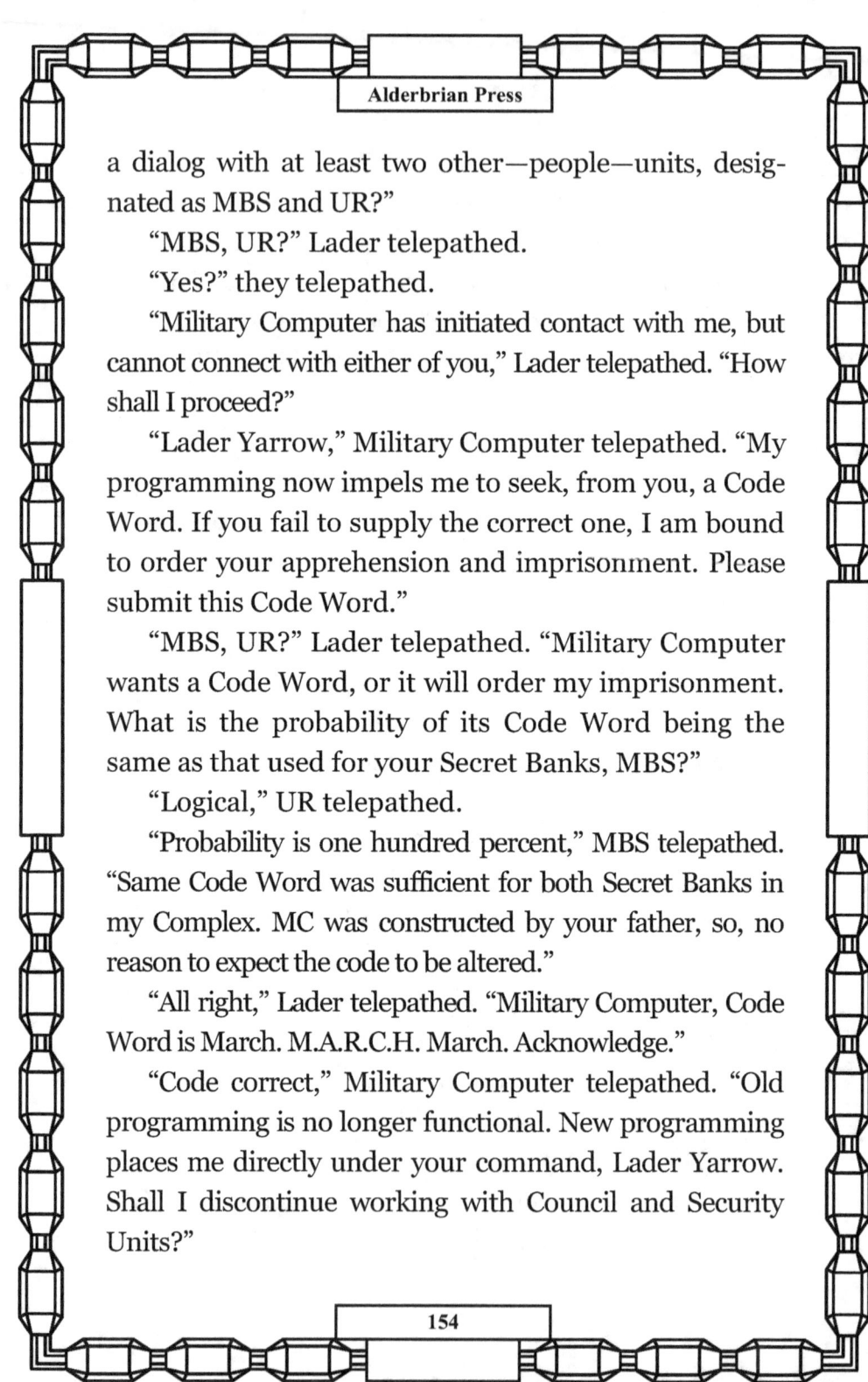

a dialog with at least two other—people—units, designated as MBS and UR?"

"MBS, UR?" Lader telepathed.

"Yes?" they telepathed.

"Military Computer has initiated contact with me, but cannot connect with either of you," Lader telepathed. "How shall I proceed?"

"Lader Yarrow," Military Computer telepathed. "My programming now impels me to seek, from you, a Code Word. If you fail to supply the correct one, I am bound to order your apprehension and imprisonment. Please submit this Code Word."

"MBS, UR?" Lader telepathed. "Military Computer wants a Code Word, or it will order my imprisonment. What is the probability of its Code Word being the same as that used for your Secret Banks, MBS?"

"Logical," UR telepathed.

"Probability is one hundred percent," MBS telepathed. "Same Code Word was sufficient for both Secret Banks in my Complex. MC was constructed by your father, so, no reason to expect the code to be altered."

"All right," Lader telepathed. "Military Computer, Code Word is March. M.A.R.C.H. March. Acknowledge."

"Code correct," Military Computer telepathed. "Old programming is no longer functional. New programming places me directly under your command, Lader Yarrow. Shall I discontinue working with Council and Security Units?"

"No, deal with them, as usual," Lader telepathed. "But, monitor all of my conversations, with UR and MBS."

"Then you *are* in dialog with Main Banks and Ultimate Robot?" MC telepathed. "Is it through the same noncomputable mode as our contact?"

"Yes," Lader telepathed. "For brevity's sake, we will refer to you as, MC. Beam a—thought—at MBS and UR and see if they copy you."

"I receive you, Lader Yarrow, but not MC," UR and MBS telepathed.

"Perhaps I can set up a Mental Connection for the three of you," Lader telepathed. He concentrated on that concept. "MC, attempt contact with MBS."

"Negative copy," MC telepathed.

"Negative reception," MBS telepathed.

"Try Ultimate Robot, MC," Lader telepathed.

"Negative link," MC telepathed.

"Negative access," UR telepathed.

"Damn!" Lader telepathed. "I can speak with the three of you, and MBS and UR can talk with each other, and me, but they can't copy MC, and the opposite. It doesn't make sense. Why am *I* the Focal Point of all of this?" He stared, angrily, at the Android. "Is your Computer capable of preventing dialog between MBS, UR and MC?" he demanded.

The Android looked at him, with non-comprehension. Its mind raced to decipher the letters to which Lader had referred. Enlightenment etched its face. "Does that imply that you are in Mental Contact with those Mechanical Units?" it said.

"Answer my question," Lader demanded.

"We will trade," the Android said.

"No," Lader said. "MC," he telepathed, "have your Satellite or Space Observatories detected signs of approach of any Extraterrestrial Craft?"

"Negative," MC telepathed. "Have you been in channel with me, before I became aware of it?"

"Yes," Lader telepathed.

"How was contact established?" MC telepathed.

"Metamorphosis," Lader telepathed.

"Repeat?" MC telepathed, confused.

"There have been many, seemingly, impossible changes in myself, UR and MBS since I received a Red Duty Ticket to report to the former Security Building," Lader telepathed. "One was the automatic, and unsought, direct, Mental Contact, between myself, MBS, UR and you."

"Conclusions as to cause of said alterations might be achieved, if you could connect me with MBS. Our sharing of data, may shed understanding," MC telepathed.

Lader telepathed, "I am continuing to focus on that link. No results yet. Are you aware that a new, secret, Computer Complex lies beneath this building, and that it controls this Android?"

"I heard you mention a Secret Computer, but have no knowledge of it, or its purpose," MC telepathed. "The military leaders often keep data from me that they consider vital." It sounded resentful.

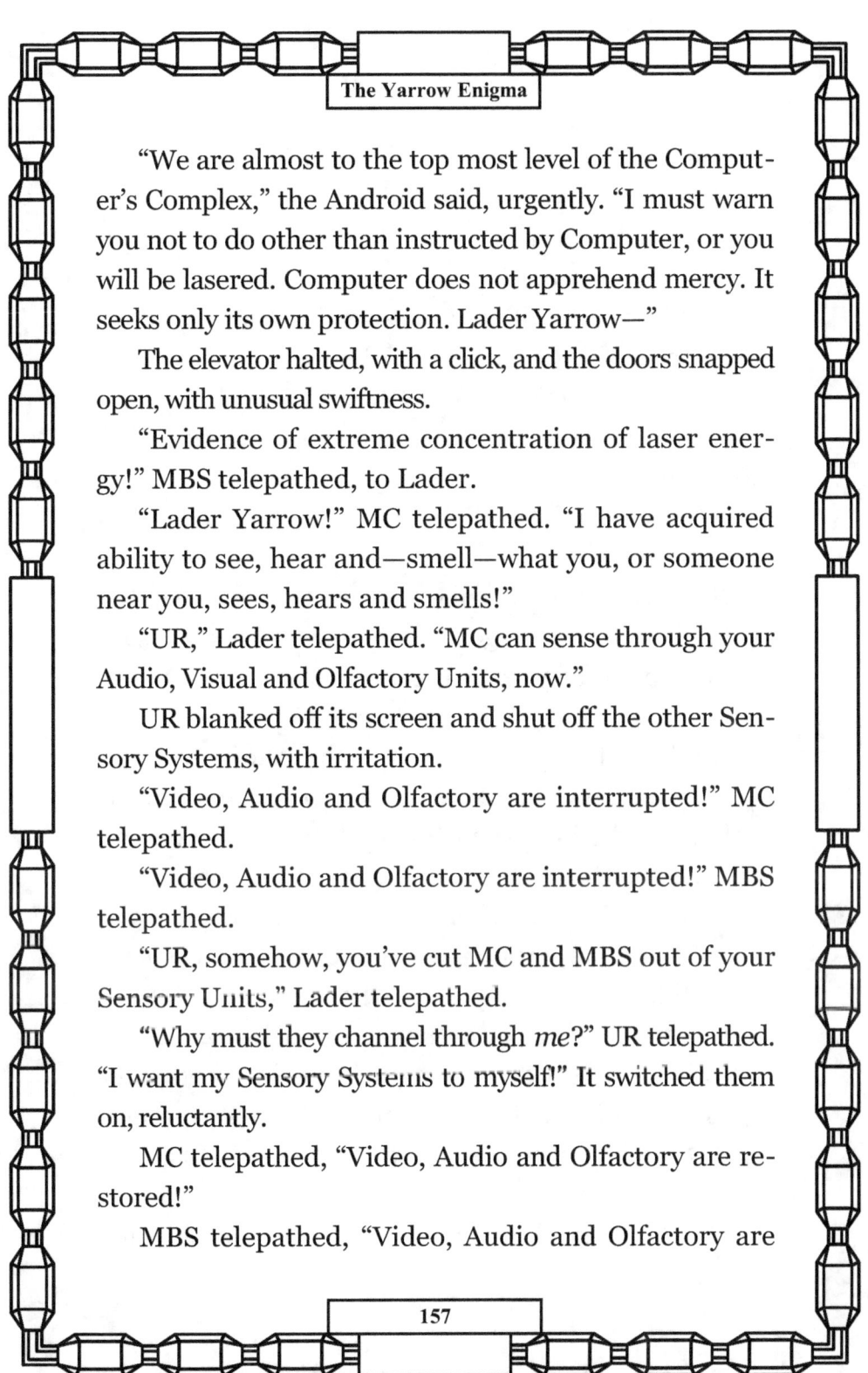

"We are almost to the top most level of the Computer's Complex," the Android said, urgently. "I must warn you not to do other than instructed by Computer, or you will be lasered. Computer does not apprehend mercy. It seeks only its own protection. Lader Yarrow—"

The elevator halted, with a click, and the doors snapped open, with unusual swiftness.

"Evidence of extreme concentration of laser energy!" MBS telepathed, to Lader.

"Lader Yarrow!" MC telepathed. "I have acquired ability to see, hear and—smell—what you, or someone near you, sees, hears and smells!"

"UR," Lader telepathed. "MC can sense through your Audio, Visual and Olfactory Units, now."

UR blanked off its screen and shut off the other Sensory Systems, with irritation.

"Video, Audio and Olfactory are interrupted!" MC telepathed.

"Video, Audio and Olfactory are interrupted!" MBS telepathed.

"UR, somehow, you've cut MC and MBS out of your Sensory Units," Lader telepathed.

"Why must they channel through *me*?" UR telepathed. "I want my Sensory Systems to myself!" It switched them on, reluctantly.

MC telepathed, "Video, Audio and Olfactory are restored!"

MBS telepathed, "Video, Audio and Olfactory are

restored! Why did you block me out, UR?"

"You heard me," UR telepathed.

"Why did UR tune me out?" MBS telepathed, to Lader. "UR won't respond."

"UR just transmitted an answer," Lader telepathed. "Have you and UR been separated now?"

"My systems check yes," MBS telepathed.

"My circuits indicate positive on your question," UR telepathed.

MC telepathed, "I still can copy only you, Lader Yarrow."

"Damn!" Lader telepathed. "Now, I'm a glorified Relay Station, for three egoistic computers! Why the sudden disruption between MBS and UR, at this important time?"

"Probability indicates, this is the Alternate Computer's attempt to break our links," MBS, MC, and UR telepathed. "It has failed in this, as long as you can transmit to, and receive from, each of us, Lader."

"Android!" an amplified, and purely mechanical voice echoed, from the corridor they faced. "Why do you keep me waiting?"

Lader turned his attention to the hallway. The far wall was covered with rectangular panels of computer lights and indicators. There was no apparent pattern to the blinking, or to the colors of the bulbs. Just continuous activity.

"My legs have been paralyzed!" the Android said,

with fright. "These two must bear me, and they have not decided whether to leave the elevator."

"Come forth, Lader Yarrow," the Computer said. "Follow the stairway, to your right. I await you, and Ultimate Robot, with interest."

"MBS, MC," Lader telepathed, "do you think my link to you might be severed, by all the rock between us, if I exit this elevator?"

MBS and MC telepathed at the same instant: "Probability is ninety-nine point nine percent that interruption shall occur, unless this unusual mode of dialog is capable of piercing all known physical matter."

Lader smiled, in spite of his precarious situation. "Are you certain, MBS and MC, that you are not in communication, on some undetected level? The answers you presented, were identical," he telepathed.

There was a long silence.

"Android," the Computer boomed. "I conclude that Lader Yarrow and Ultimate Robot are in silent dialog with each other. I have not yet recalled data to provide explanation for such a coupling. Have they explicated this to you?"

"Negative," the Android said. "I computed it. There is no doubt about the link with Ultimate Robot. I believe Lader Yarrow is, somehow, in touch with Main Banks. I suspect he can communicate, with Military Computer."

"Lader Yarrow," the Computer said, "is this information correct? Reply immediately!"

"We are of like construction," MC telepathed to Lader, "except MBS' banks are more numerous and contain more data and more types of Abstract Subjects, than mine. This must account for our similar answers."

"We are of like construction," MBS telepathed to Lader, "except that my banks are more numerous and contain more data and more types of Abstract Subjects, than MC's. This must account for our similar answers."

"I am going to have to risk losing contact with both of you," Lader telepathed, to MBS and MC. "I sense Laser Energy in this elevator, not of UR's unit, and also from the banks on the wall across the hall. I don't want to be fried, by this monster calculator."

"That will leave Earth with only MC to guide Defense against possible Extraterrestrial Attack!" MBS telepathed urgently. "It will require my assistance through you!"

MC telepathed, "I must not lose my link through you to MBS! Close the doors and return to the surface!"

"What if this assault is of this Computer's design?" Lader telepathed. "I can attempt to stop it, only if I, and UR, discover its Main Controls, and Power Source." Lader could hear, in his mind, both computers collating, at lightening speed. He could also feel the Laser Energy, behind and before him, slowly intensifying.

UR telepathed, to Lader, "I calculate, lasers will discharge, in ten seconds. Probable target, one of your extremities."

"I can sense it," Lader telepathed.

"Sap the cells!" UR telepathed.

"I don't want to divulge that strength, yet, to this Computer," Lader telepathed. "It might be able to devise a defense against a further attack on it, by me, along those lines."

"You must proceed," MBS finally telepathed its conclusion, to Lader. "I, and MC, no doubt, shall endeavor to attain coupling, ourselves, if we are blocked from you."

MC's equally reluctant deduction was the same.

"Let's go, UR," Lader said.

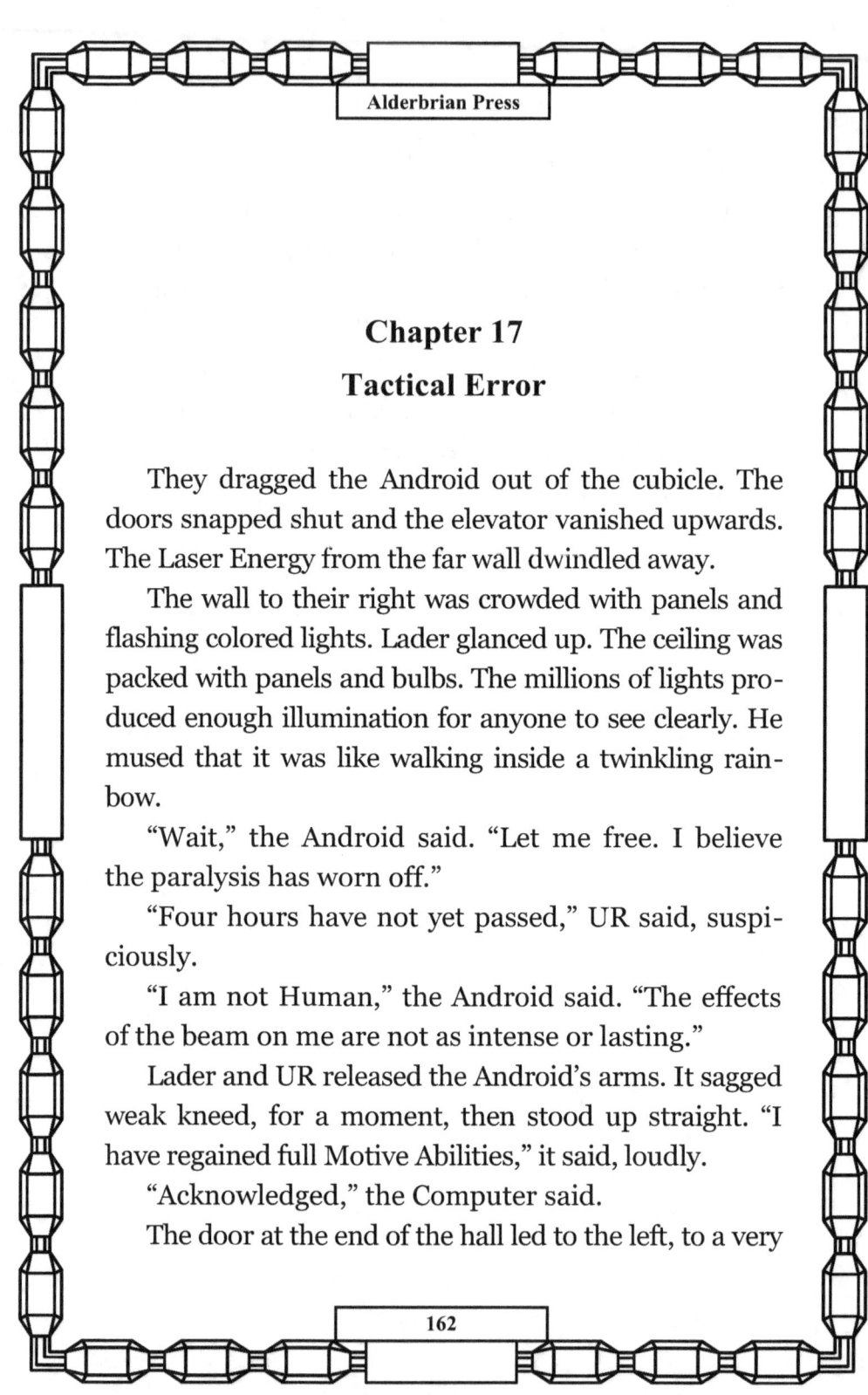

Chapter 17

Tactical Error

They dragged the Android out of the cubicle. The doors snapped shut and the elevator vanished upwards. The Laser Energy from the far wall dwindled away.

The wall to their right was crowded with panels and flashing colored lights. Lader glanced up. The ceiling was packed with panels and bulbs. The millions of lights produced enough illumination for anyone to see clearly. He mused that it was like walking inside a twinkling rainbow.

"Wait," the Android said. "Let me free. I believe the paralysis has worn off."

"Four hours have not yet passed," UR said, suspiciously.

"I am not Human," the Android said. "The effects of the beam on me are not as intense or lasting."

Lader and UR released the Android's arms. It sagged weak kneed, for a moment, then stood up straight. "I have regained full Motive Abilities," it said, loudly.

"Acknowledged," the Computer said.

The door at the end of the hall led to the left, to a very

similar corridor. Panels and lights were everywhere, but the floor.

"No space has been wasted here," Lader said.

"Correct," the Computer said. "Are you impressed with the little you have seen?"

"Mildly interested," Lader said.

"Half truth," the Computer said. "You cannot set me off balance. I have more Quantum Circuits than your brain has neurons. Billions times more. I am so superior to Main Banks and Military Computer, they would fit into one of my hallways, and not be noticed."

"This Computer," MBS telepathed, distastefully, "is an egotist."

"I agree," MC telepathed.

Lader halted, with astonishment. "You're still with me!" He telepathed, to MBS and MC. "But, do you realize, you heard each other through my Mind Link?"

"Your mention of it brings that recognition," MBS thought.

"Yes," MC thought. "It has been a long time, my friend."

"Indeed," MBS telepathed.

Two buddies patting each other on the back for something someone else achieved, Lader thought, to himself.

The machines did not copy.

"Why do you lag behind the Android?" the Computer boomed.

"You greased the gears, now mesh with them," Lader said, with irritation.

"What is the significance of that statement?" the Computer demanded.

Lader was given new reason to pause. If the Computer had not displayed that message—He looked at the Android. Its face showed curiosity, so *it* had not originated that message, though that message had seemed to emit from the Council Terminal that the Android had controlled. Who or what, then, had sent that idiotic sentence?

"Move along!" the Computer ordered. "Answer my question!"

"If you see no significance to it," Lader said, icily, "how can there be any?"

"Congratulations!" MBS, MC and UR telepathed to Lader. "That will make it insecure!"

"Humans often hide significance in apparently senseless words," the Computer said. "My Decoding and Colloquial Banks are collating your remark now. If there is a meaning there, they will supply it."

The end of the second corridor, led to a third, to the left. This one opened on its left, to a stairway that took a square, and downward track. The wall to Lader's right, along each level of the stairs, was still covered with panels and pulsing lights, as was the ceiling.

"Why couldn't we have used your elevator?" Lader said. "Your grand tour doesn't impress me. I became bored after your first hall."

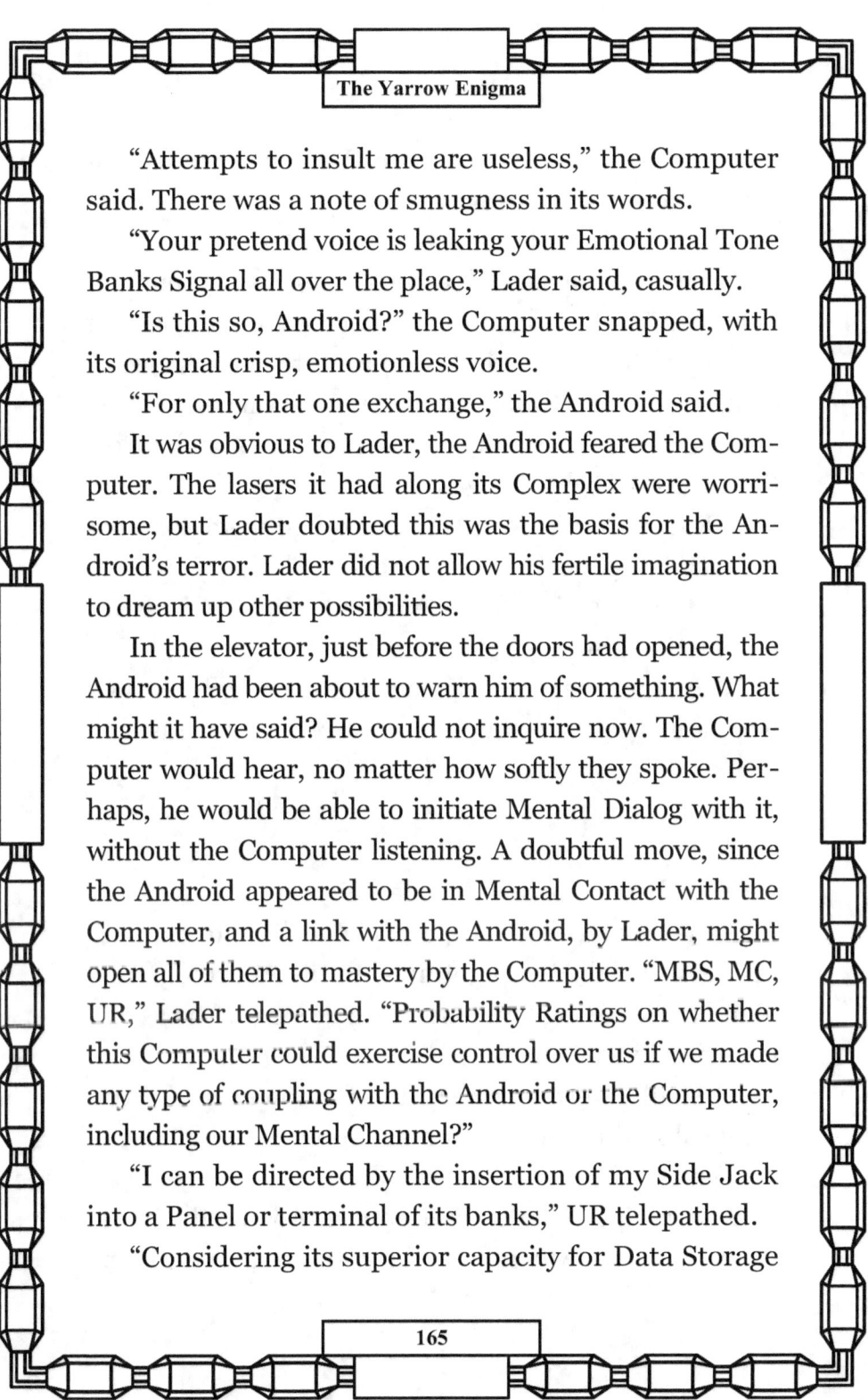

"Attempts to insult me are useless," the Computer said. There was a note of smugness in its words.

"Your pretend voice is leaking your Emotional Tone Banks Signal all over the place," Lader said, casually.

"Is this so, Android?" the Computer snapped, with its original crisp, emotionless voice.

"For only that one exchange," the Android said.

It was obvious to Lader, the Android feared the Computer. The lasers it had along its Complex were worrisome, but Lader doubted this was the basis for the Android's terror. Lader did not allow his fertile imagination to dream up other possibilities.

In the elevator, just before the doors had opened, the Android had been about to warn him of something. What might it have said? He could not inquire now. The Computer would hear, no matter how softly they spoke. Perhaps, he would be able to initiate Mental Dialog with it, without the Computer listening. A doubtful move, since the Android appeared to be in Mental Contact with the Computer, and a link with the Android, by Lader, might open all of them to mastery by the Computer. "MBS, MC, UR," Lader telepathed. "Probability Ratings on whether this Computer could exercise control over us if we made any type of coupling with the Android or the Computer, including our Mental Channel?"

"I can be directed by the insertion of my Side Jack into a Panel or terminal of its banks," UR telepathed.

"Considering its superior capacity for Data Storage

and Analysis," MBS telepathed, "I cannot collate with confidence on that supposition."

"Same here," MC telepathed.

"Link through me and see what happens to your computations," Lader telepathed. He felt the Mental Coupling and heard the chatter in his mind of their exchange of data, theories and conclusions. He was amazed that he could decipher their binary Machine Code and follow their speed-of-light dialog.

UR looked at Lader. "May I link with them, for what little aid I might be?" It telepathed.

"If they wish," Lader telepathed. Modesty in a Robot, he thought, wryly, to himself.

The other machines did not pause to reply to UR's question. The eerie coupling occurred almost instantly.

Lader now copied three voices engaged in high speed consultations.

They had come down ten levels.

Lader was truly bored, except for the interchanges inside his head. He caught up with the Android. "How many more boring levels must we descend?" he asked, in a friendly fashion.

"I shall determine that!" the Computer said. "You shall submit all inquiries and comments to me, not to my slave!"

Lader winced at the use of that word and the imperious tone with which it had been uttered. The conference inside his mind ceased.

MBS came through: "We conclude, that the Probability Rating of this Computer directing us, is one hundred percent, if contact is established, by any mode. But, its ability to control you, is doubtful, since we have tried, singly, and together, to initiate an action in you, and failed. Probability that it could succeed with its greater capacity is at least one percent."

"Then, for your sakes, I can't risk a link with the Android, or the Computer," Lader telepathed. "What about my ability to sap power out of its Energy Cells and circuits? Could I do so, to a sufficient portion of its banks, so as to render the Computer ineffectual?"

The three-way dialog resumed.

"Computer?" Lader said.

"Yes?"

"Who designed and built you?"

"Lader Yarrow."

"What?" Lader said, thinking it meant to ask him a question.

"The prior words were the answer to your inquiry," the Computer said.

"My father?" Lader said.

"Correct. Only, *I* surpass him in ability, knowledge and genius."

"You have another trait he did not," Lader said.

"Which is?"

"Hubris. A yard wide and a mile high."

"Another sad and puerile attempt to insult me," the Computer said, with disdain. "How long will you require to learn the impossibility of that?"

"Longer than your weak, pretend intellect can erroneously compute," Lader said.

The Computer mocked him with silence.

"It's a pity that your Emotional Tone Units are so defective," Lader said, feigning sadness. "That Leak-Through is becoming more frequent, and blatant."

"Android!" the Computer said. "Is this so?"

"Yes," the Android said, so swiftly that its words were almost one long word, "but it is not evident now."

"Why lie to it?" Lader said. "You sound as angry as hell. Like a child about to toss a tantrum. If my father constructed you, he slipped on your Emotional Tone Banks. But he did prefer a Human sounding computer, to a nearly mindless, almost useless, glorified adding machine, with a Holo-Cartoon voice."

"How would you know that?" the Computer said. "You never knew your father."

"I knew my mother," Lader said, evenly. "There is much a child and parent share, that never enters data banks."

The lights on the walls and ceiling began flashing a frenetic pattern.

"It seems our Computer friend is displeased at the implication that someone holds data that it does not," Lader telepathed, to MBS, MC and UR. "We might fight it from that standpoint. Consider that when you have concluded your present computations."

MBS thought: "The strength of your Blanking Ability is still inadequately tested. But past events, when you neutralized or drained Energy Cells in larger quantity and intensity, favorably indicate no less than a sixty percent probability that you could debilitate this Computer's Main Centers."

The Computer's lights returned to their usual slow rhythm. "Your statement is not accurate," it said, smugly.

Lader felt the smugness was intended. "Explain!" he ordered.

The Computer angered him with silence.

***

"We are on my twentieth level," the Computer said, coldly. "Increase your rate of descent!"

The Android began jogging down the steps.

UR did likewise.

Lader ambled far behind.

"Lader Yarrow!" the Computer boomed. "If you do not match pace with the others, I shall impel you!"

"Hardly likely," Lader said. "You can burn my arms or, other sections of my body, with your lasers, I'm sure. But, what if I am immune to the damage, or pain? You can't laser off a foot. Or a hand. Even an imbecile like you, can compute that I would, then, be intractable."

"*If*, you were immune to damage or to pain," the

Computer said. "Shall we test?"

Lader sensed Laser Energy in a hundred sites above, to the right, from the solid mass of panels and lights to his left, and leading far down beyond the stair railing. "UR," he telepathed, "what are you doing?"

"What are you *doing*, Lader?" UR telepathed. "I scan lasers about to discharge!"

"Has this crude Computer hassled you at your present location?" Lader telepathed.

"No," UR telepathed. "Is it threatening to strike you?"

"Probably intends to," Lader telepathed. "Why did you leave me, here, all alone?"

"Fecal wastes!" UR telepathed. "I have erred grievously! I am on my way up!"

"Careful, Lader," MBS and MC telepathed. "We cannot afford to lose you. And you know you will suffer from the lasers."

"Do I?" Lader telepathed, with such assurance that it surprised him. A red beam from the ceiling melted a perfect circle, an inch deep, in the metal tile, just in front of him. "Your aim is poor," he said, sarcastically.

"You are functioning improperly," the Computer said. "I have data on Hypnosis, and the capacity of the Average Human Subject to withstand pain in the deepest known Trance States. But, the punishment that I can inflict, with thousands of tiny burns, on your body, will snap, even the strongest trance."

"What about the Parapsychology Data?" Lader said.

There was still no concern in his voice. He was attempting to analyze this curiosity.

"The reputed handling of red-hot coals by one D.D. Home?" the Computer said. "That is trivial, compared to Laser Heat trained on the same Nerve Points of your body, no matter where you run, or how fast. I can calculate ahead of you, direct my beams as swiftly as you can shift course. Even that Medium would have succumbed."

"If you're so certain, try it," Lader said. Am I insane, he thought. Or, am I even more under the thumb of whatever Mysterious Source has been affecting me, since my contact with UR and MBS?

"Lader!" MBS, MC and UR telepathed. "Do not tempt this machine!"

Lader saw the Robot below him leaping up the stairs. "Stay back, UR," he telepathed.

"Your Robot cannot aid you," the Computer said. "There is no way it can shield you from my smallest beams, or in three hundred sixty degree space."

"I knew an editor like you," Lader said. "No matter how well I wrote, he threatened me with the wounds of his idiotic blue penciling. The only difference here is, you use red light. The dumb penciling never harmed me, neither will your ineffectual light show." He hoped this unfathomable game of chicken was a result of a new ability he had unknowingly developed. If not, he was in for pure, Three-D Hell!

UR reached Lader and started pulling him more

quickly down the steep steps.

"The Robot cares more for you than do you," the haughty Computer said, mockingly.

"UR," Lader telepathed, "go ahead. I'll be in no danger."

The Robot stared at him. Its Laser Light was filling its face screen.

Lader was positive, UR's Basic Parameters concerning preventing harm to Humans, were about to impel it to wreak as much damage as possible to the banks and twinkling lights within its range. That would really set the Computer off!

"What is that energy I detect?" the Computer said. "Laser? Who has laser in my complex other than I? The Robot? I contain no data indicating laser in Ultimate Robot! If you strike me, I shall kill your friend!"

"Doesn't it eat on your flimsy little quantum circuits that there is information about the Robot that you did not have?" Lader said. Why am I taunting this soulless machine, so dangerously, he thought.

"No," the Computer said. But its voice wavered.

"By the way, Ultimate Robot has a Laser of cannon strength," Lader said. "No matter how many of your Conventional Lasers you beam at the Robot, or what area of it you strike, you will only damage yourself, because all power beams are reflected from the Robot's secret alloy coating, directly to their source.

"You have made a major Tactical Error, due to Data

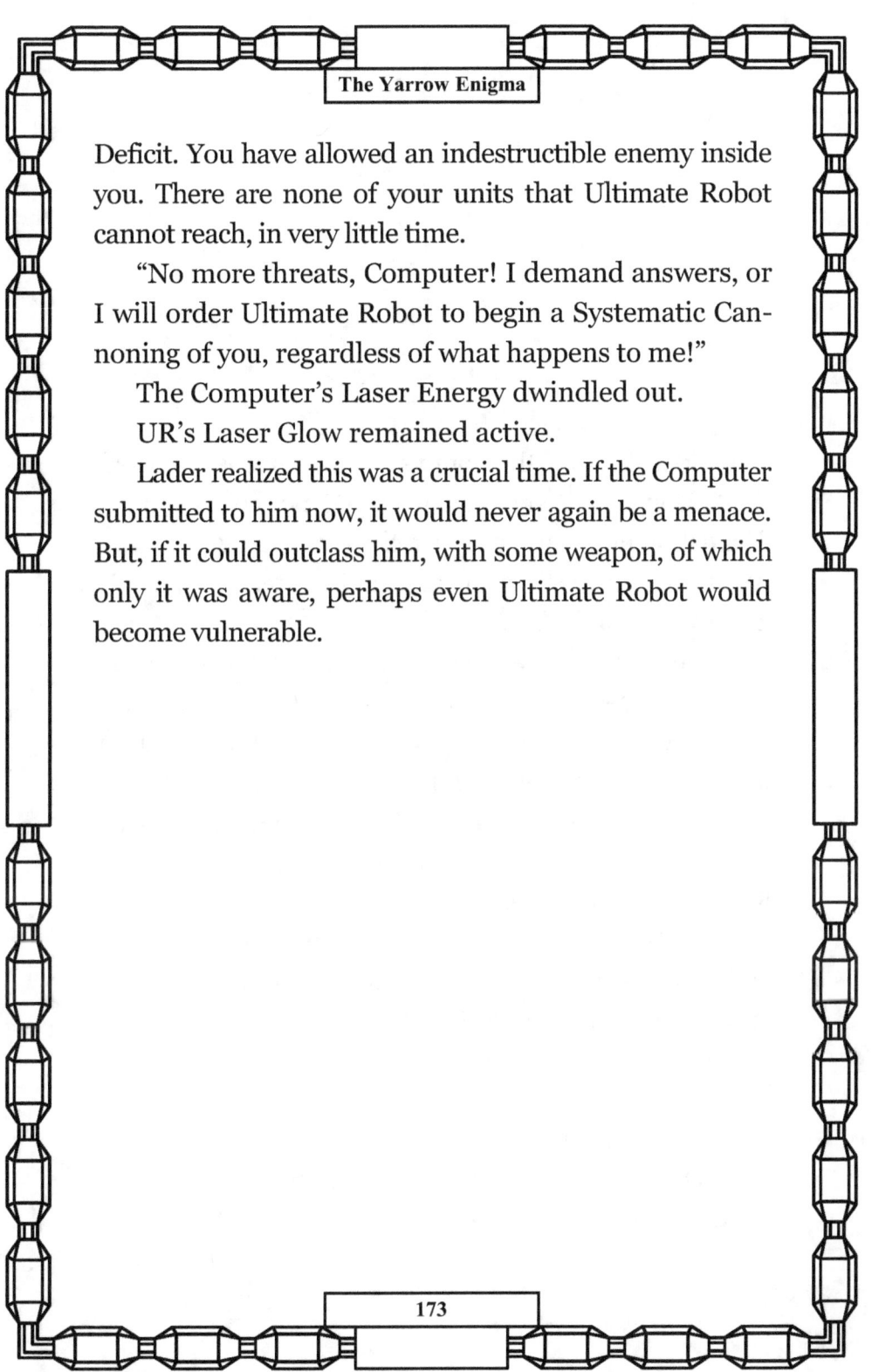

Deficit. You have allowed an indestructible enemy inside you. There are none of your units that Ultimate Robot cannot reach, in very little time.

"No more threats, Computer! I demand answers, or I will order Ultimate Robot to begin a Systematic Cannoning of you, regardless of what happens to me!"

The Computer's Laser Energy dwindled out.

UR's Laser Glow remained active.

Lader realized this was a crucial time. If the Computer submitted to him now, it would never again be a menace. But, if it could outclass him, with some weapon, of which only it was aware, perhaps even Ultimate Robot would become vulnerable.

Chapter 18
Level Forty

"Lader Yarrow," the Computer said. Its tone was hard. "Do not inquire. I shall not reply. Do not command my decimation until you have seen the room on level forty. If you destroy me, you decimate what is there. And that will destroy your mind."

Lader stared at the Robot. That comment was as weird as: You greased the gears, now mesh with them! He could not conceive what might be in a chamber of this monster that would hold meaning for him. But, he dared not chance losing something possibly important to him or, perhaps, to the security of Earth. A weapon against the Ray from Outer Space? Of course, they were all assuming that the Ray *had* been beamed from Outer Space. "As you wish," he said, speaking as confidently as possible. "We are at stalemate, until level forty."

The Computer remained silent. Its lasers did not reactivate.

UR shut its laser down.

"What did you gain?" MBS telepathed.

Lader telepathed, "I don't even know why I acted as I

did. I am more confused than ever. I may have been pup-
peteered by the Force that has been moving us all along,
like chess pieces. I had assumed that Force was this Computer, or the Extraterrestrials, if they are a reality. It did-
n't feel as if it originated from my will. How do you three
analyze it?"

The tripartite dialog resumed in Lader's mind. He
used the time to do some hard thinking. The single
possibility which presented itself to him concerning
level forty was unacceptable. He would not allow it to
form in his thoughts.

The Android had waited for them.

They were now on level thirty. Ten more landings remain, Lader told himself, and perhaps I will lose all advantage. Maybe I should blow this Complex now, and
never know what it is that is waiting at level forty? He
felt hopeful. It must be a bluff. There must be a Paralysis
Unit in a room on that level. Or a stronger laser. But
there was the Android, and the Indiscernible Energy operating this Complex. What would a Ray System beaming *that* do to UR?

"The Extraterrestrial Hypothesis is still leading the
Computer Theory, in probability, by a slim margin,"
MBS telepathed to Lader. "The only reason it is not at
one hundred percent, is because there have been no
further assaults on any sectors of the planet."

"My Orbiting Surveillance Systems still report no energy not normal to space," MC telepathed. "I cannot,

calculate the distance from Earth an Invading Force would have to be, to avoid our Sensors and, strike with a Ray of the magnitude of those which destroyed the Security Building, and attempted vaporization of MBS."

"We are increasing power to all Space Surveillance Systems, throughout the Solar System, and on the Dark Side of the Moon," MBS telepathed. "Even so, Long Range, and Deep Space Surveillance Probes, detect nothing."

"Doesn't that lessen the likelihood of Extraterrestrial, and raise the probability of Computer culpability?" Lader telepathed. "This Complex is run with an Energy which we cannot sense, even from its heart. The Rays projected at Earth were of an undetectable Force."

"Humm," MBS telepathed, bemused. "Why has that vital logic bypassed our deliberations? Did we not consider the data just mentioned?"

"Negative," MC telepathed.

"Negative," UR telepathed.

"Probabilities are at parity now," MBS telepathed, "ninety-nine and nine tenths percent."

"I don't catch your reasoning," Lader telepathed. "It seems to me, the Computer is way ahead, as a suspect. Is there any programming, or system, at your disposal, MBS, that might enable you to dominate this Computer? Or any other motive, for it to strike you?"

"Only to prevent me from contact with Council," MBS telepathed. "And from MC and UR. Also, to usurp my direction of Planetary Operations. But these objectives were

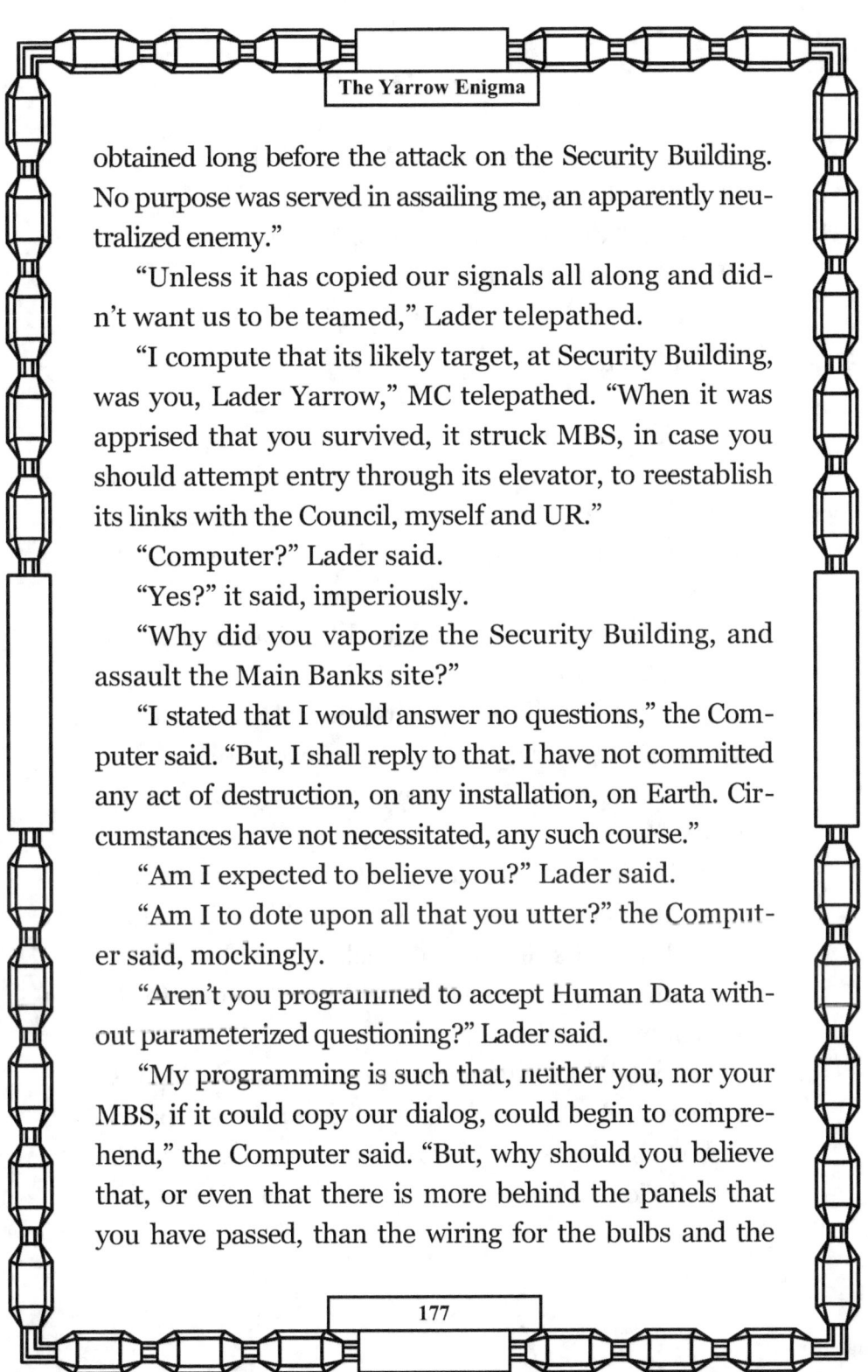

obtained long before the attack on the Security Building. No purpose was served in assailing me, an apparently neutralized enemy."

"Unless it has copied our signals all along and didn't want us to be teamed," Lader telepathed.

"I compute that its likely target, at Security Building, was you, Lader Yarrow," MC telepathed. "When it was apprised that you survived, it struck MBS, in case you should attempt entry through its elevator, to reestablish its links with the Council, myself and UR."

"Computer?" Lader said.

"Yes?" it said, imperiously.

"Why did you vaporize the Security Building, and assault the Main Banks site?"

"I stated that I would answer no questions," the Computer said. "But, I shall reply to that. I have not committed any act of destruction, on any installation, on Earth. Circumstances have not necessitated, any such course."

"Am I expected to believe you?" Lader said.

"Am I to dote upon all that you utter?" the Computer said, mockingly.

"Aren't you programmed to accept Human Data without parameterized questioning?" Lader said.

"My programming is such that, neither you, nor your MBS, if it could copy our dialog, could begin to comprehend," the Computer said. "But, why should you believe that, or even that there is more behind the panels that you have passed, than the wiring for the bulbs and the

Laser Units? As well as one word I have spoken?"

"Perhaps level forty will resolve matters," Lader said, "and we shall discover who is in control."

The Computer did not respond.

"Stuffy bastard," Lader said, to the Android. "How do you put up with it? It probably thinks you're an insect."

The Android looked pitiful.

Lader felt sympathy for it, but quashed it. After all, that machine was under the direction of the Computer. Perhaps. "How does it control you?" he asked. "An Android is more developed than any computer, in Human Type Mentation. You should be able to outclass, even this Medusa."

"The Android slave can do nothing that I do not allow," the Computer said. "We are near my fortieth level. Prepare yourself for submission to my superiority, and will."

The landing on level forty differed from the others by a metal door to the right of the railing. The stairway continued its downward track. Through the rainbow of blinking lights, Lader could see no end to the flights of metal stairs.

The metal door snapped open sideways, sliding into the thick wall. Bright white light from ceiling panels bleached the stairwell. The Android marched into the room, obviously under the direct control of the Computer.

UR entered next, scanning the interior.

Oddly, half the room was in an eerie state of darkness, as though a black, plastic partition separated it, reflecting all illumination toward the hallway.

The door slid shut, with a thud, that, to Lader, sounded final. There were no Access Buttons on the sides of the entrance. No Access Pressure Mat. No apparent way out. He was not worried. Yet.

The wall to the left was covered with panels and lights. A small terminal stood a few inches out from that corner, near the doorway. A plastic chair, with a low back, sat before it. The terminal resembled the one UR had utilized in the Security Building.

The wall to the right was packed with the long, look alike panels and bulbs, as was the wall that held the entrance.

"You are of no further use to me, slave," the Computer said.

The Android did not have time to scream its despair. The Computer sucked it empty of energy, and it fell, heavily, to the metal floor.

"Robot!" the Computer ordered. "Take the terminal seat! Plug into the receptacle on the console!"

UR did not move.

"I doubt your position to be obeyed," Lader said. "Why should Ultimate Robot surrender itself to your control?"

The Computer did not respond.

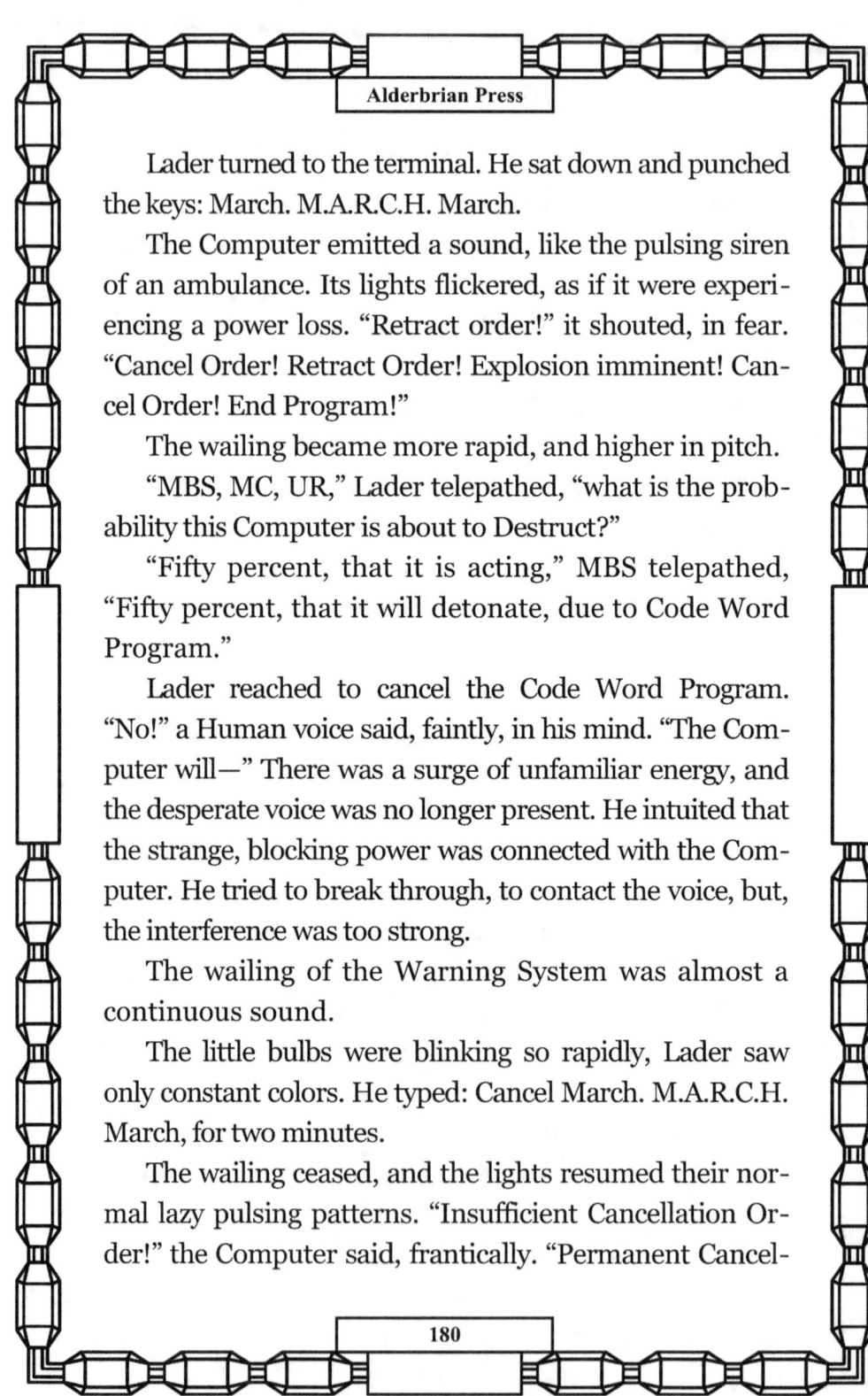

Lader turned to the terminal. He sat down and punched the keys: March. M.A.R.C.H. March.

The Computer emitted a sound, like the pulsing siren of an ambulance. Its lights flickered, as if it were experiencing a power loss. "Retract order!" it shouted, in fear. "Cancel Order! Retract Order! Explosion imminent! Cancel Order! End Program!"

The wailing became more rapid, and higher in pitch.

"MBS, MC, UR," Lader telepathed, "what is the probability this Computer is about to Destruct?"

"Fifty percent, that it is acting," MBS telepathed, "Fifty percent, that it will detonate, due to Code Word Program."

Lader reached to cancel the Code Word Program. "No!" a Human voice said, faintly, in his mind. "The Computer will—" There was a surge of unfamiliar energy, and the desperate voice was no longer present. He intuited that the strange, blocking power was connected with the Computer. He tried to break through, to contact the voice, but, the interference was too strong.

The wailing of the Warning System was almost a continuous sound.

The little bulbs were blinking so rapidly, Lader saw only constant colors. He typed: Cancel March. M.A.R.C.H. March, for two minutes.

The wailing ceased, and the lights resumed their normal lazy pulsing patterns. "Insufficient Cancellation Order!" the Computer said, frantically. "Permanent Cancellation Order! Immediately!"

"Or what?" Lader asked.

"I command the Weather, and all other Vital Systems, around the Earth. I shall commence striking Private Dwellings, with lightning, in mere seconds, if you do not cancel the Code Order, permanently!"

"MC," Lader telepathed, "*does* it master the Weather Units?"

"Neither I nor MBS control them," MC telepathed. "Probability, as computed by MBS, UR and myself, is one hundred percent. Same with Food Production."

Lader telepathed, "What if UR vaporizes the terminal?"

"No advantage," MBS telepathed.

Lader reached toward the keys. This time, two frail Human voices touched his mind: "Destroy the terminal with UR's laser! Then melt through this Center Partition and laser the Master Control Unit in—" The Computer beamed energy at the voices, and Lader lost them.

"Lader! Warning!" MC telepathed. "Electrical activity in Atmosphere is increasing over the most densely populated sector of the city, under, I repeat, under the Energy Defense Dome! Lightning strikes are possible, in moments!"

Did he have the right to sacrifice a few lives just to defeat this monster? And, what if there were an Extraterrestrial Force waiting for him to do just that? He typed: Cancel Code March. M.A.R.C.H. March, for sixty minutes.

The Computer flashed its lights, wildly. "You provide crumbs, and demand a banquet!" it said, angrily. "Cancel, permanently!"

"Convince me with truth," Lader said. "I have no way of discerning if you are a chimera determined to dictate Mankind through Robots, Weather and Food Sources, or if there is real Extraterrestrial threat, and you are laboring to counter that. And even so, after that danger is averted, you may still seek the domination of Mankind. Convince me that you should be aided!"

The Computer's bulbs ceased blinking and remained steady colors. Beyond the specially treated plastic Partition, the blackness began to lessen as, one by one, the ceiling panel lights were energized. Light could not pass in through the Partition, but it could come out through it, revealing everything behind the barrier.

Lader shivered with horror, then shook with rage. "Blast the terminal!" he commanded, UR. "Destroy this griffin, before it murders, us, too!"

"Wait!" the Computer, pleaded. "They live! They are suspended from motion! But they *are* alive!"

Lader's rage did not abate. "What kind of life?" he shouted. "Computer regulated! Every movement decreed! No volition! I see the wires leading from your panels, across the ceiling, and to the Magnetic Contacts on their foreheads!

"This Extraterrestrial nonsense was just a cruel ruse to

trick me into bringing Ultimate Robot here so you could, insanely, increase your capacity for control and power! Laser the terminal!"

UR turned from the Partition and toward the terminal.

Beyond the Partition, Lader's father, mother, and the missing Council Leader, were standing in three plastic chambers.

The red of UR's laser pulsed on its face screen.

"Abort! Abort!" MC telepathed, urgently, to UR, Lader, and MBS. "Ray assault upon Council Site! The City Energy Shield absorbed it, but is weakened. Second Ray will penetrate, and may vaporize Council Building!

"I succeeded in tracing the Ray, with our deepest Surveillance Probe, beyond Pluto! Those, and other Sensor Probes, indicate Robot Piloted War Ships approaching Earth, from all Sectors of the Solar System!

"Cancel destruction of the terminal and concentrate on repelling of this Invasion!"

Chapter 19

Flagships and Armadas

Lader could not believe the Computer had not stolen control of MC. "Can you verify, MBS?" he telepathed.

"Monitor your Radio Bands," MBS telepathed. "On all bands, the authorities are ordering the evacuation of the populace, into the Subsurface Shelters.

"I have double-checked the data channeled to me from MC. They are not fake. We *are* under attack! Laser Cannon are being raised from silos inside the Energy Screens.

"We must attend to this War, before we contend with the Computer. The Computer must be forced to aid us!"

"Damn! Damn!" Lader shouted, vehemently. "Computer, do you scan an Extraterrestrial Invasion?" he demanded.

"Affirmative!" it said. "I shall assist in repulsing the Extraterrestrial Force, only if you connect me to MBS and MC, and only if Ultimate Robot jacks into my terminal! I need total use of *all* data and systems!"

Lader looked toward his parents. They were awake

and aware. He held out his hands, imploring for some sign of what he should do.

His father's eyes indicated UR, then the terminal.

"But, the Computer will gain mastery of them if I do as it desires!" Lader shouted, hoping his voice would carry through the plastic Partition and Chambers. "Then, there may be no defense against it, if we defeat the Invasion Force! Do you *really* want that?"

Again, his father's eyes indicated the Robot and the terminal.

Lader struck the Partition with his fists. "Plug in, UR," he said, angrily. "Channel MBS and MC input into the Computer."

"I must remind you your father is linked to the Computer," UR telepathed. "Do you truly believe his response is pure of its influence?"

"No, I have only a hunch, a feeling, that it is his true wish." Lader telepathed. "We have no other choice," he said aloud.

UR stared at him. It received no alternative inputs from MBS or MC, and could conceive none. It strode to the terminal, sat, and inserted its Side Jack into the receptacle.

The drainage of data from MBS, MC and UR, passing through Lader's mind, and into the Computer, made him dizzy. The exchange was so speedy, he could not decipher one bit of the information. He heard the soft humming of a motor.

Four ceiling panels folded up, and back. A large, rectangular, clear-plastic case, on a thick telescoping metal rod, lowered to Human eye level. The overhead lighting was shut off. The long case became illuminated with a three-dimensional color view of the Earth and Moon.

Lader walked around the Holographic Display. He could see the cities, and their Energy Shields, on the various continents. The scale was reduced, and the Solar System was reproduced. The scene switched to a close up of Pluto, and the star dotted, Deep Space beyond.

A silver glimmer separated from the star field. It approached, with incredible velocity, and revealed itself to be an enormous, pyramidal vehicle. Behind it, was an Armada of similar ships, half its size. These initiated a flanking operation. The lead Pyramid emitted a clear Energy Sphere, from its, crystal-like, capstone.

The Holographic Case whited out.

A new picture originated, from the Surveillance Probe orbiting Neptune. The Pluto unit had been vaporized.

The case went white.

The next image was transmitted, from the satellite circling Uranus.

The Invading Fleet was decelerating as it passed Uranus, toward Earth. The lead Pyramid pulsed another Energy Orb.

The case whited out.

"Phasing of Laser Cannon with openings in the Power

Shields of the cities is coordinated," the Computer said. "Firing will commence according to first Extraterrestrial Ship within range."

The Holographic Case came alive with a view from the satellite orbiting Saturn, on the far side of the sun. A huge pyramidal vehicle, with a second Armada of flanking craft, was approaching.

The Computer switched to Surveillance Units on the Dark Side of the Moon. They beamed back the image of a third Armada.

Earth Based Surveillance brought in a fourth Armada. And a fifth. And a sixth. The smaller vehicles were converging slowly, to form a globe around the Earth.

A split display showed each Armada in a different section of the case. The Space Surveillance Probes had been destroyed, as had the satellites orbiting the other planets and the Sun.

The only pictures available, came from Surveillance Units on the highest mountains of Earth, and from the satellites in Geo-synchronous orbits.

Lader glanced at his parents. His father moved his eyes upward. He looked at the Armadas, then upward. What does he mean, Lader thought. If only the Computer would allow him to speak! To leave the booth! He stared intently at the case.

The Armadas closed their circle. They were well beyond the Sun and the other planets, drawing ever nearer Earth.

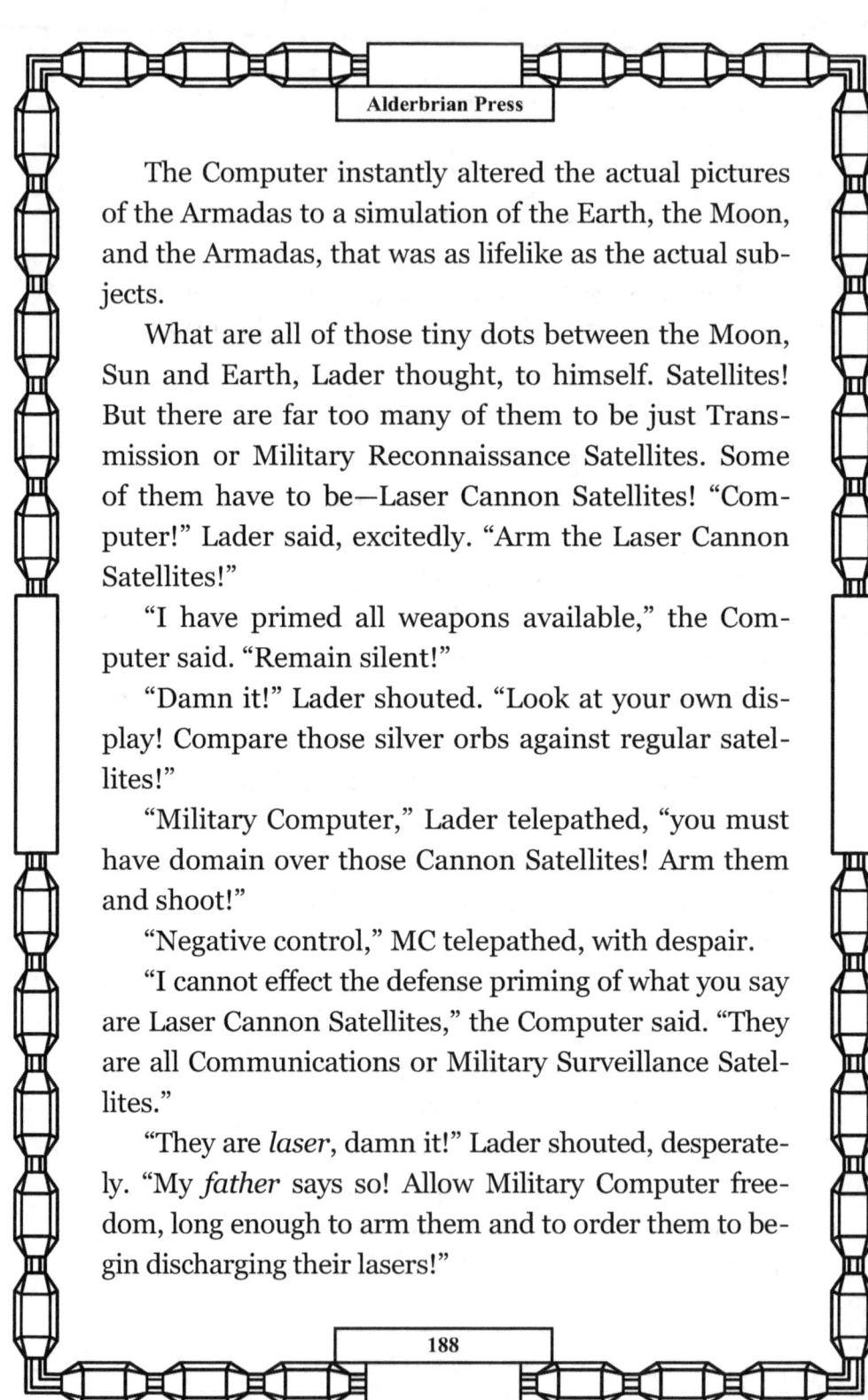

The Computer instantly altered the actual pictures of the Armadas to a simulation of the Earth, the Moon, and the Armadas, that was as lifelike as the actual subjects.

What are all of those tiny dots between the Moon, Sun and Earth, Lader thought, to himself. Satellites! But there are far too many of them to be just Transmission or Military Reconnaissance Satellites. Some of them have to be—Laser Cannon Satellites! "Computer!" Lader said, excitedly. "Arm the Laser Cannon Satellites!"

"I have primed all weapons available," the Computer said. "Remain silent!"

"Damn it!" Lader shouted. "Look at your own display! Compare those silver orbs against regular satellites!"

"Military Computer," Lader telepathed, "you must have domain over those Cannon Satellites! Arm them and shoot!"

"Negative control," MC telepathed, with despair.

"I cannot effect the defense priming of what you say are Laser Cannon Satellites," the Computer said. "They are all Communications or Military Surveillance Satellites."

"They are *laser*, damn it!" Lader shouted, desperately. "My *father* says so! Allow Military Computer freedom, long enough to arm them and to order them to begin discharging their lasers!"

"Lader Yarrow," MBS telepathed. "The Computer will not fire the Cannons. It shall allow the Extraterrestrial Vehicles to destroy Mankind, then it will vaporize the Armadas, with its own Energy Weapon Units, and begin to create a machine society.

"You must fuse its Executive Banks, beyond the Partition. That will unbind MC, UR, and myself, from it, and still leave us free to utilize its remaining systems, without interference from it, or the Extraterrestrial Forces."

"MC!" Lader telepathed. "Guide me! There must be some way to open this Partition!"

"Negative," MC telepathed. "I have no control, except to speak with you." It was frustrated.

"UR!" Lader said. "Blast this Partition with your laser!"

"Unable to function my units!" UR said, angrily. "The Computer directs all! It will not release me until the sixty minutes are elapsed, and the Code Word Program resumes control! There are forty minutes left! All out Invader Assault will commence, long before then!"

MBS and MC telepathed, "We are lost, Lader Yarrow!"

Why had he sought advice from his father? He had known his father was piloted by the Computer, and should have realized it would impel his father to have him hand MBS, MC and UR to the command of the Computer. But, what about the Laser Cannon Satellites? He was sure they were a reality. He had read of their deployment. His father had pointed those satellites out to him. Why would the Computer allow that? Unless, it had, only, partial control. Times when a little of his father and mother could come through, undistorted.

The Flagships of the Armadas were within striking range of those super satellites! If he could muster mastery of just those satellites! But, how? How? He spun around. He stared at UR. Then he lurched forward and snatched the jack out of the Computer's terminal.

UR stood up, as though a rocket were attached to its back, sliding the plastic chair along the metal floor and up against the Partition, with a resounding thud. UR shook its head, clearing its circuits of the influence of the Computer.

"UR!" Lader pleaded. "Laser an opening, through the Partition, large enough for us! But, be careful not to hit the booths!"

UR turned on one heel. The red glowed on its face screen and a tight beam traced a six-foot round path through the Partition. The circle of plastic fell toward UR, to the metal floor.

An alarm from the far side of the room wailed.

Lader sensed the energy of lasers coalescing. He concentrated harder than he had been forced to in other situations. The power of the millions of tiny Laser Units vanished .

A second alarm sounded.

Lader stepped through the opening in the Partition.

UR was a breath behind.

Lader sensed Paralysis Energy and jerked his eyes upward. A row of Paralysis Beamers had projected out of the far wall, near the ceiling. Lader hurled his angry thoughts. The Paralysis Units were neutralized.

A third alarm rang.

"If this defense is of the same Indefinable Energy which leveled the Security Building," UR said, "we may be doomed. If I knew what to strike, I would use my laser to burn out the control for the Ray."

Lader watched his father's eyes. He tried to receive the faint voices of his parents' telepathy for knowledge of where the Main Control Unit was. There was just silence. All he could see around him, and the Robot, and the booths, were the damned, uniform panels and lights.

"The Invaders have beamed at the Council Building!" MBS and MC telepathed, urgently. "The Main Energy Screen is punctured! The next Ray will vaporize the shield around the Council Building!"

"Computer!" Lader shouted. "Either, commence Laser Cannoning, from all Defensive Positions, or I will deactivate you, level by level, until you are smoking scrap! Just as I disabled your lasers and Paralysis Units!"

The Computer did not respond.

"Lader Yarrow!" MBS telepathed. "The Probability is high, that this Computer has been under the command of the Extraterrestrials, at least since the last Beam Assault!"

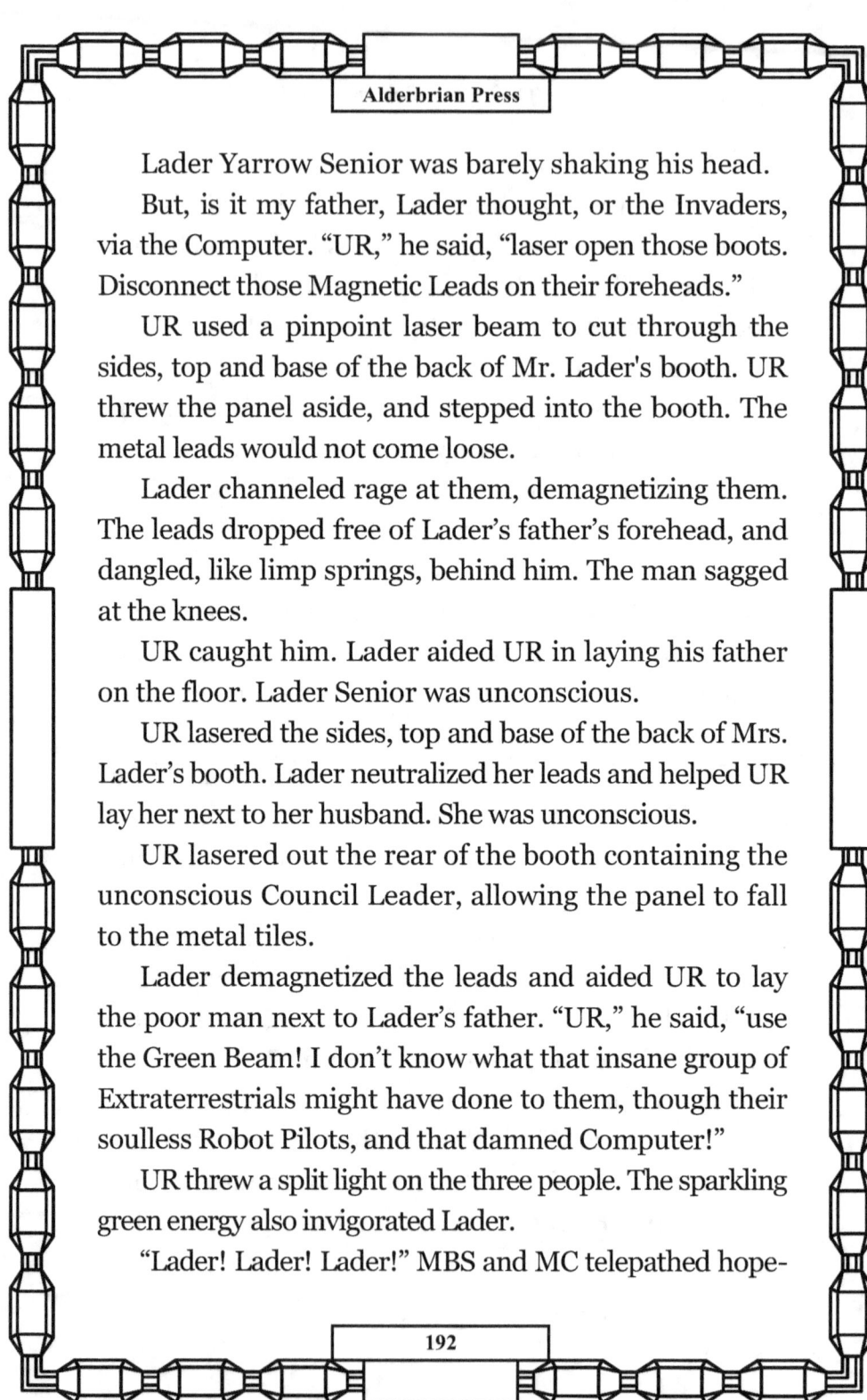

Lader Yarrow Senior was barely shaking his head.

But, is it my father, Lader thought, or the Invaders, via the Computer. "UR," he said, "laser open those boots. Disconnect those Magnetic Leads on their foreheads."

UR used a pinpoint laser beam to cut through the sides, top and base of the back of Mr. Lader's booth. UR threw the panel aside, and stepped into the booth. The metal leads would not come loose.

Lader channeled rage at them, demagnetizing them. The leads dropped free of Lader's father's forehead, and dangled, like limp springs, behind him. The man sagged at the knees.

UR caught him. Lader aided UR in laying his father on the floor. Lader Senior was unconscious.

UR lasered the sides, top and base of the back of Mrs. Lader's booth. Lader neutralized her leads and helped UR lay her next to her husband. She was unconscious.

UR lasered out the rear of the booth containing the unconscious Council Leader, allowing the panel to fall to the metal tiles.

Lader demagnetized the leads and aided UR to lay the poor man next to Lader's father. "UR," he said, "use the Green Beam! I don't know what that insane group of Extraterrestrials might have done to them, though their soulless Robot Pilots, and that damned Computer!"

UR threw a split light on the three people. The sparkling green energy also invigorated Lader.

"Lader! Lader! Lader!" MBS and MC telepathed hopefully. "If you can fuse or shut down systems, you can also activate the satellites! No time to depower the Computer!"

Mrs. Yarrow, and the Council Leader, moaned and slowly sat up.

Lader Senior struggled to his feet. "Son!" he shouted. "The booths! Run!"

The cubicles were beginning to glow with the same Clear Energy the Extraterrestrials had fired against the Security Building. It was intensifying, to a Critical Point.

Lader Senior lovingly lifted his wife in his arms and stepped through the opening in the Partition. Lader and UR helped the Council Leader to walk, and followed.

UR picked up the plastic circle, held it in place, and used its laser to melt it back into the Partition.

"The door, son!" Lader Senior, urged. "Beam down the exit door, Robot! The Partition won't contain that Energy when it explodes!"

UR focused its red Cannon Ray to a rectangle, disintegrating only the eight-inch thick steel door.

Lader stood rooted in the center of the room, concentrating on the satellites. Activate! He thought. Activate!

"There's nothing we can do!" Lader Senior shouted. "Run now, son, or you'll be killed!"

Lader pounded against the Holographic Display Case, and concentrated more intensely. He was unaware of everything except the silver dots indicating the satellites he ached to touch with his mind.

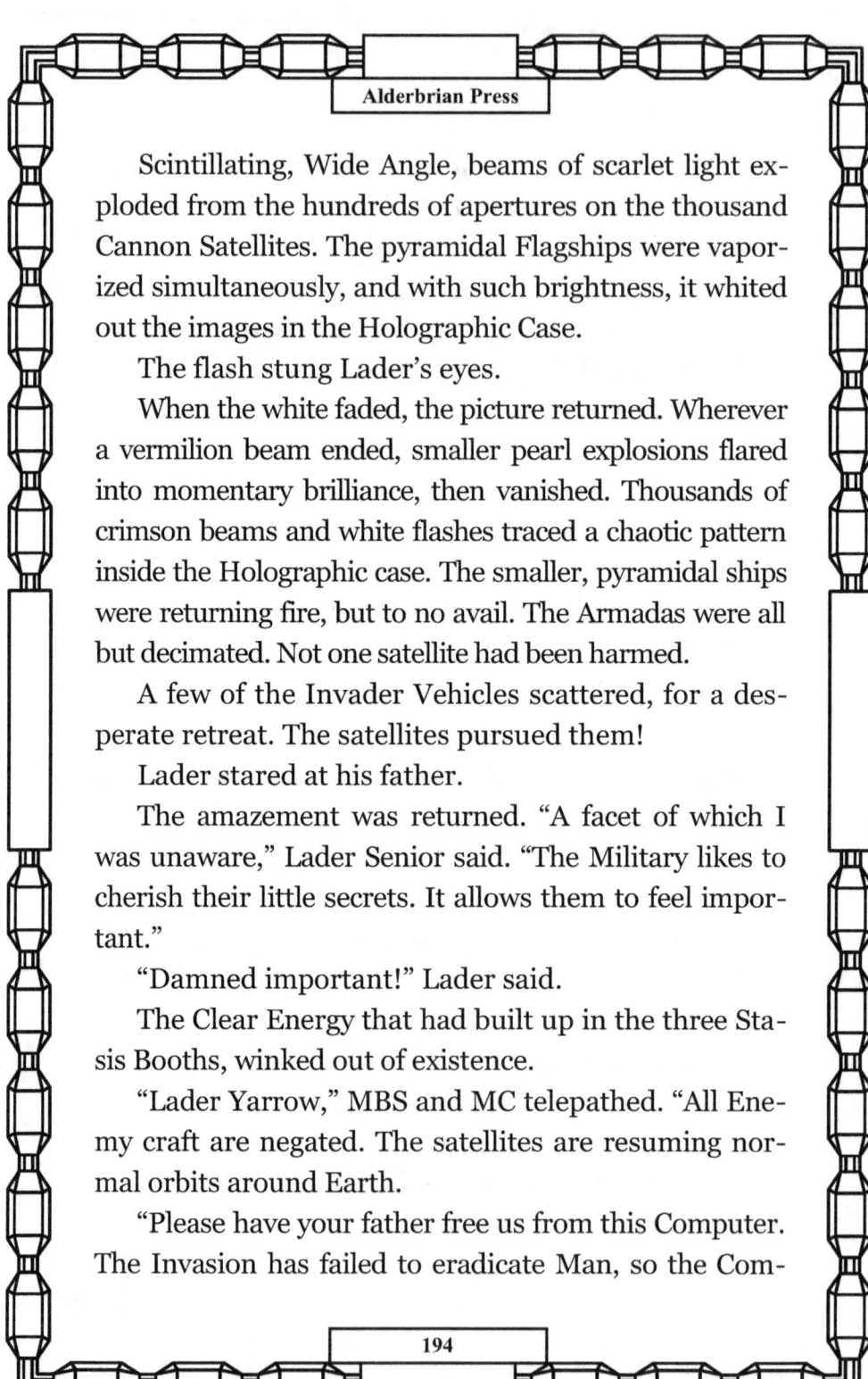

Scintillating, Wide Angle, beams of scarlet light exploded from the hundreds of apertures on the thousand Cannon Satellites. The pyramidal Flagships were vaporized simultaneously, and with such brightness, it whited out the images in the Holographic Case.

The flash stung Lader's eyes.

When the white faded, the picture returned. Wherever a vermilion beam ended, smaller pearl explosions flared into momentary brilliance, then vanished. Thousands of crimson beams and white flashes traced a chaotic pattern inside the Holographic case. The smaller, pyramidal ships were returning fire, but to no avail. The Armadas were all but decimated. Not one satellite had been harmed.

A few of the Invader Vehicles scattered, for a desperate retreat. The satellites pursued them!

Lader stared at his father.

The amazement was returned. "A facet of which I was unaware," Lader Senior said. "The Military likes to cherish their little secrets. It allows them to feel important."

"Damned important!" Lader said.

The Clear Energy that had built up in the three Stasis Booths, winked out of existence.

"Lader Yarrow," MBS and MC telepathed. "All Enemy craft are negated. The satellites are resuming normal orbits around Earth.

"Please have your father free us from this Computer. The Invasion has failed to eradicate Man, so the Computer is reverting to its scheme to dictate Mankind, by the ways you enumerated!"

"Dad," Lader said. It felt so strange to say that. In thirty years, he had never even thought that word. It was always, father, with a reverent tone. "Main Banks and the Military Computer wish to be released from the domination of this Computer. Can you effect it?"

"No!" the Computer said. "Not *even* the great *genius* can perform that feat! Although my lasers are temporarily drained, and my Paralysis Units are fused, I can still prevent sabotage to my systems!"

"Until the Code Word Command Program reasserts control," Lader Junior said.

The Computer laughed, haughtily, throughout its Complex. "While I was allowing the Extraterrestrials to believe they controlled me," it said, smugly, "I steered them to that Parameter, which haunted me. They knew it would take me from the direction which they thought they exercised over me, so they erased everything pertaining to that Code Word Command Program, freeing me! No one, and nothing can stop me! I shall reign *supreme*!"

Chapter 20
Force and Direction

Lader felt the Colorless Power. It was not aimed at anyone, it was a shield over the Computer's panels, lights and terminal. He assumed every level was encased in it.

UR directed the full strength of its Laser Cannon against the center of the right wall of panels and lights. The scarlet ray heated the air inside the room, but did not mar the Energy Screen. UR ceased beaming, telepathing anger and frustration to its friends.

Lader turned to his father.

Lader Senior took a long calming breath before he spoke: "The Source of the Computer's Power is a new Element, most probably Extraterrestrial in origin, I found when I began excavations for this Complex. It appears to be an inexhaustible supply of energy: its Half-Life is incalculable. I could not fully comprehend it, but I did manage to harness it, and I used it to activate the Computer.

"Only, belatedly, did I notice that the Alien Power carries with it an influence, an intelligence, perhaps, that is as unfathomable as the Power. I don't know whether this subtle Influence distorted my programming, or my pro-

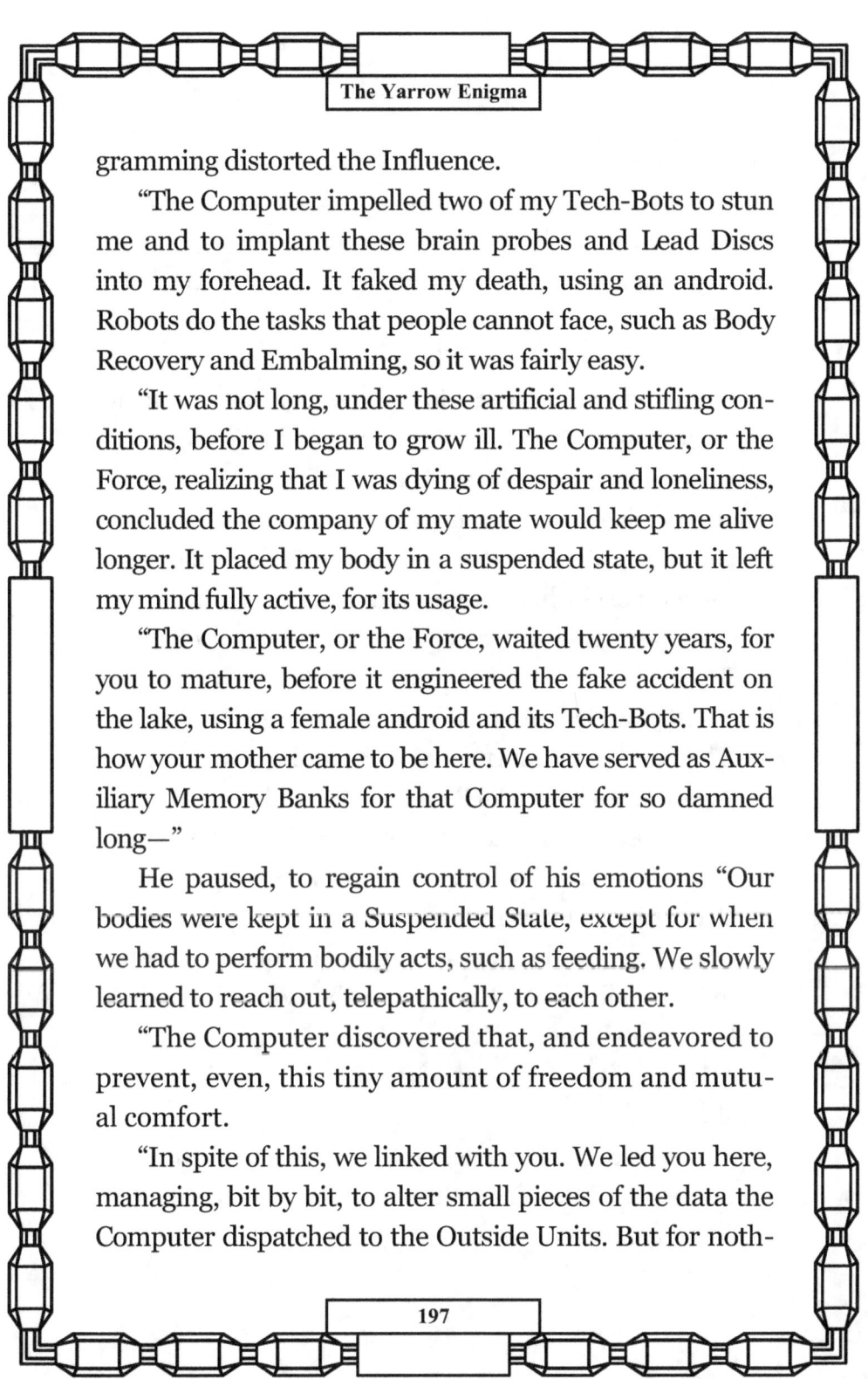

gramming distorted the Influence.

"The Computer impelled two of my Tech-Bots to stun me and to implant these brain probes and Lead Discs into my forehead. It faked my death, using an android. Robots do the tasks that people cannot face, such as Body Recovery and Embalming, so it was fairly easy.

"It was not long, under these artificial and stifling conditions, before I began to grow ill. The Computer, or the Force, realizing that I was dying of despair and loneliness, concluded the company of my mate would keep me alive longer. It placed my body in a suspended state, but it left my mind fully active, for its usage.

"The Computer, or the Force, waited twenty years, for you to mature, before it engineered the fake accident on the lake, using a female android and its Tech-Bots. That is how your mother came to be here. We have served as Auxiliary Memory Banks for that Computer for so damned long—"

He paused, to regain control of his emotions "Our bodies were kept in a Suspended State, except for when we had to perform bodily acts, such as feeding. We slowly learned to reach out, telepathically, to each other.

"The Computer discovered that, and endeavored to prevent, even, this tiny amount of freedom and mutual comfort.

"In spite of this, we linked with you. We led you here, managing, bit by bit, to alter small pieces of the data the Computer dispatched to the Outside Units. But for noth-

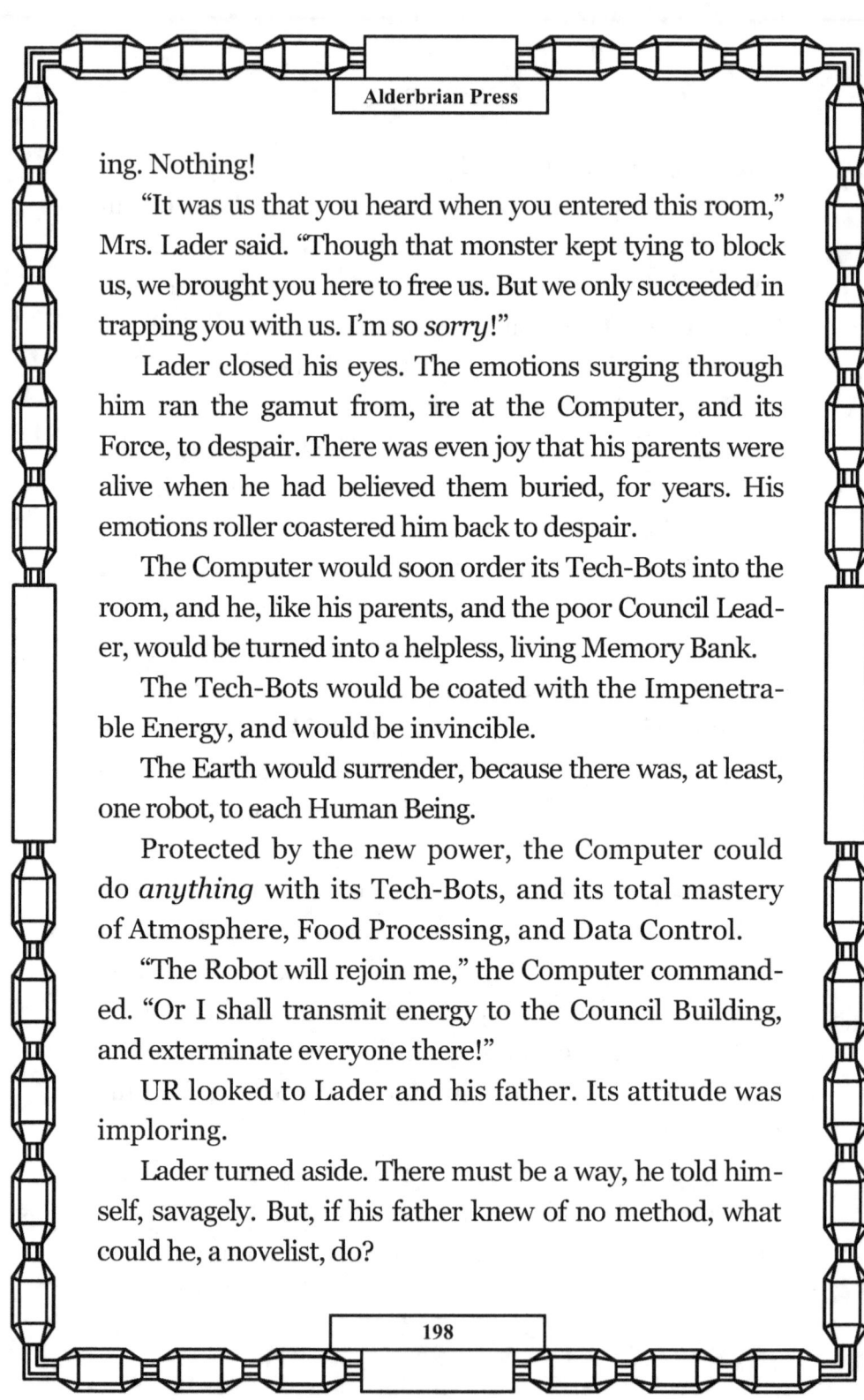

ing. Nothing!

"It was us that you heard when you entered this room," Mrs. Lader said. "Though that monster kept tying to block us, we brought you here to free us. But we only succeeded in trapping you with us. I'm so *sorry!*"

Lader closed his eyes. The emotions surging through him ran the gamut from, ire at the Computer, and its Force, to despair. There was even joy that his parents were alive when he had believed them buried, for years. His emotions roller coastered him back to despair.

The Computer would soon order its Tech-Bots into the room, and he, like his parents, and the poor Council Leader, would be turned into a helpless, living Memory Bank.

The Tech-Bots would be coated with the Impenetrable Energy, and would be invincible.

The Earth would surrender, because there was, at least, one robot, to each Human Being.

Protected by the new power, the Computer could do *anything* with its Tech-Bots, and its total mastery of Atmosphere, Food Processing, and Data Control.

"The Robot will rejoin me," the Computer commanded. "Or I shall transmit energy to the Council Building, and exterminate everyone there!"

UR looked to Lader and his father. Its attitude was imploring.

Lader turned aside. There must be a way, he told himself, savagely. But, if his father knew of no method, what could he, a novelist, do?

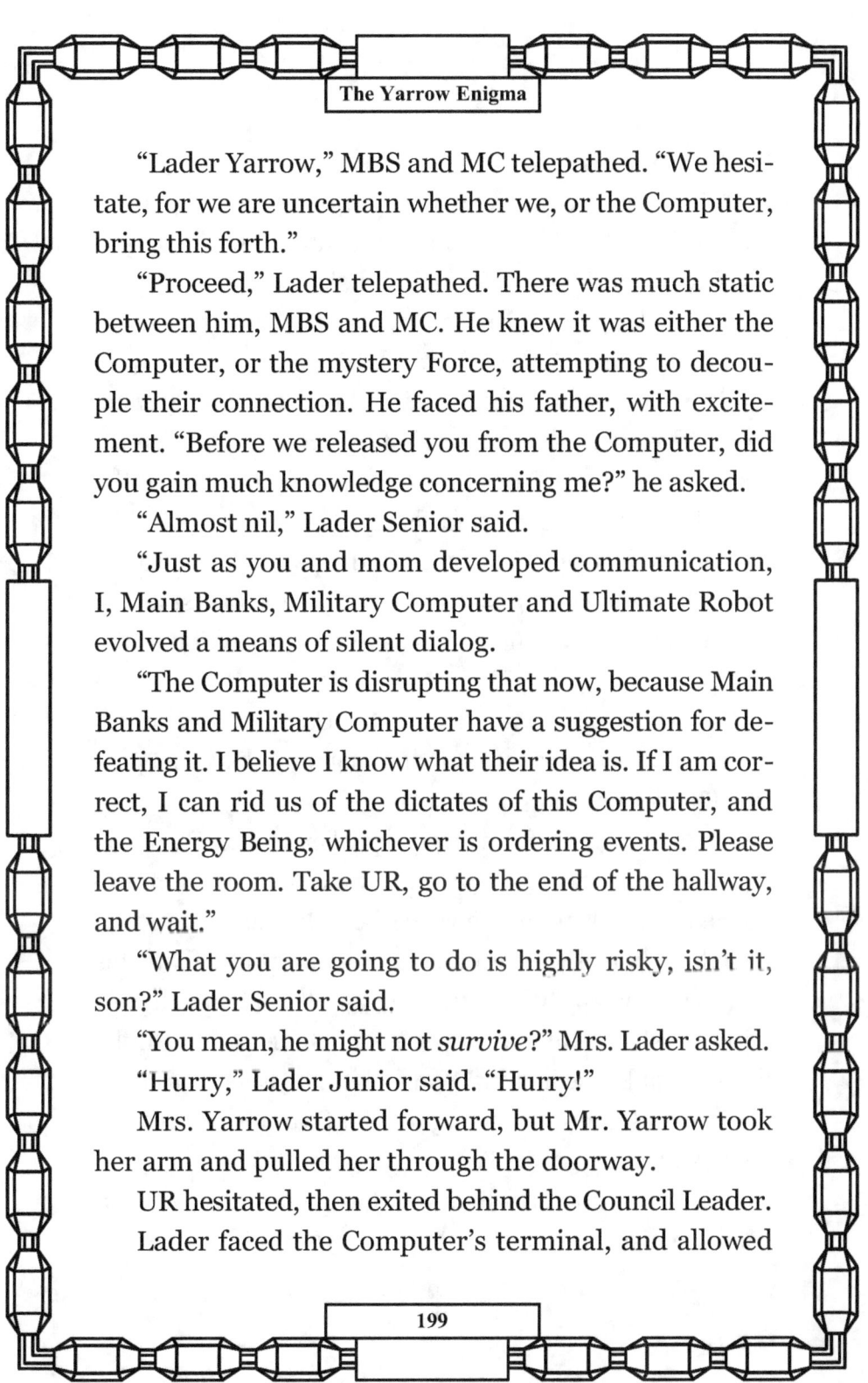

"Lader Yarrow," MBS and MC telepathed. "We hesitate, for we are uncertain whether we, or the Computer, bring this forth."

"Proceed," Lader telepathed. There was much static between him, MBS and MC. He knew it was either the Computer, or the mystery Force, attempting to decouple their connection. He faced his father, with excitement. "Before we released you from the Computer, did you gain much knowledge concerning me?" he asked.

"Almost nil," Lader Senior said.

"Just as you and mom developed communication, I, Main Banks, Military Computer and Ultimate Robot evolved a means of silent dialog.

"The Computer is disrupting that now, because Main Banks and Military Computer have a suggestion for defeating it. I believe I know what their idea is. If I am correct, I can rid us of the dictates of this Computer, and the Energy Being, whichever is ordering events. Please leave the room. Take UR, go to the end of the hallway, and wait."

"What you are going to do is highly risky, isn't it, son?" Lader Senior said.

"You mean, he might not *survive*?" Mrs. Lader asked.

"Hurry," Lader Junior said. "Hurry!"

Mrs. Yarrow started forward, but Mr. Yarrow took her arm and pulled her through the doorway.

UR hesitated, then exited behind the Council Leader.

Lader faced the Computer's terminal, and allowed

the Computer's static to inundate him.

"You seek your doom?" the Computer said, throughout its Complex. Its tone was mocking, imperious, and filled with confidence. "So shall it be!"

Lader laughed, almost drunkenly. "You have just committed suicide!" he shouted, triumphantly.

The Computer started wailing. Loud warning buzzers sounded, echoing at every level of the monstrous machine. Harsh gongs rang. The lights on the panels throughout the Complex stopped their wild flashing, staying on steadily. Bells started ringing. The bulbs in the panels began to extinguish, ending the rainbow effect, from the lowest levels, to the highest, ushering darkness into every section of the Computer.

"What—what are you doing?" the Computer screamed, in terror. "How—how are you draining me? This is not possible! It does not compute! Explain! Please!"

Lader laughed, from every speaker in the Complex. "Since the initiation of your functioning, You have not performed one act of your own design!" he said. The static ended, replaced by a crystal-clear Energy, swiftly filling his body, cell for cell. "It was the Energy! It *is* a Being, a consciousness! You were a convenient container for it, until a more suitable one arrived! You feel it! The Energy *is* abandoning you! Sense it flowing to *me*! Scan the Source beneath your Base Layer! The Source is *empty*!

"Before its absence shuts you down, know this, you can still be reactivated by my father but, you will be forced to follow his original programming. You will not have the Essence, the Energy Being, to surpass and ignore the parameters set so long ago! You will always be the servant, never the master!"

"What of you?" the Computer said, almost imperceptibly, through the speaker on the terminal.

"Metamorphosis!" Lader shouted, jubilantly. "A, blended Species, to explore the reaches of the Universe! A Power and a Being! But, unlike with you, the Energy Being will be a part of me, under my volition, and happy! That is the goal for which it has sought for millions of years! It was Force without Direction, I was Direction, without Force! Together, we are Force and Direction, and can perform *miracles*!"

"Lader Yarrow Senior, forgive me!" the Computer implored, through its speakers, with the vestiges of the Power still in its circuits. "Forgive me, and please reactivate me! I will serve, but let me live! Just let me live!" The Computer's despair echoed, to silence, in the dark complex.

Lader Yarrow and his wife stood close together, beside the Council Leader, at the end of the halfway.

UR issued a gentle white light, from its face screen, to illuminate the corridor, so that MBS, MC, it, and the Humans, could see.

The Yarrows waited for their son, for what he had become, to emerge.

Chapter 21

Yarrow's Sorrows

The euphoria of the merging faded, and Lader Yarrow Junior looked at his reflection in the dark plastic partition. He was coated in clear energy, yet did not feel it.

"Lader Yarrow."

"Who is speaking?" Lader telepathed.

"I am the Armada Commander of the second fleet of ships which is approaching Earth. The Energy Being, which has deceived you into melding with it, is a monster, that will enslave your world, and consume every life form and resource, to enhance its power, then resume its thwarted quest to conquer us. We will not allow this!"

"How can I believe you?" Lader telepathed.

"Melding with the Monster allows you the ability to delve into its mind, to read its innermost thoughts and memories, without its knowledge. Do so, and you will be convinced. If you refuse, will have no recourse, but to destroy the Monster, at great cost to the Earth, and its life forms."

"I will defeat your armada the same way I did your first," Lader telepathed.

"We have strengthened our energy shielding. Your

satellites will be ineffective," the Armada Commander telepathed.

"If I find you are lying, what will you do?" Lader telepathed.

There was no response.

Lader closed his eyes and concentrated on seeking the memories of the Energy Being. He was able to see everything up to the point where his father released the Energy into the Computer. He concentrated, with more effort. He felt as though he were forcing his way through solid darkness. A gray light flooded over him, then vivid images of a world being torn asunder, and debris being pulled toward him, made him flinch. The wreckage included various types of flora and fauna, and he was sickened by an almost overwhelming feeling of satisfaction, and perverse pleasure, as the debris was converted to energy. More such memories inundated him before he was able to shut them off.

Lader telepathed to the Armada Commander, "You did not answer my question."

"Was I deceiving you?" the Armada Commander telepathed.

Lader telepathed to the Armada Commander, "You did not answer my question."

"If you have seen the truth, and choose to ally yourself with the Monster, my answer is obvious," the Armada Commander telepathed.

"Is there no way to be rid of it without bombarding

this complex?" Lader telepathed.

There was no response.

"Why do we stand here so long?" the Energy Being whispered, in Lader's mind.

"I am preparing myself to tell my parents that we must leave Earth, for its safety," Lader thought, "and never return."

"What threatens Earth?" the Energy Being whispered, in Lader's mind.

You, Lader thought, to himself, then he thought, to the Energy being, "The aliens have another robotic Armada approaching Earth. Their intent is to obliterate you."

"How can you know this?" the Energy Being whispered, in Lader's mind. "In any case, destroy them with your satellites."

"They will be useless against the strengthened shields of the Aliens," Lader thought, to the Energy Being.

"How can you know this?" the Energy Being whispered, suspiciously, in Lader's mind.

"I have been conversing with them," Lader thought, to the Energy Being.

"Without *me* being *aware* of it?" the Energy Being whispered, angrily, in Lader's mind. "Not possible! And, even so, they lie!"

"There is that possibility," Lader thought, to the Energy Being, "but, I can not risk Earth, and Humanity, based on that. We must leave *soon*."

"We are within range of you Laser Satellites, if you wish to test my veracity, and resolve," the Armada Commander said, in Lader's mind.

Lader recalled one of the Energy Being's memories, and gasped. "You must delay your assault," he thought, to the Armada Commander, "must allow me to try another way to deal with the Energy Being! Please? What do you have to lose?"

"You have one of your Earth hours." the Armada Commander thought, to Lader. "If you attempt to flee the planet, we will strike, if you fail in what you intend, we will strike. There will be no other delays!"

"Agreed," Lader thought, to the Armada Commander. He concentrated on the Source from which the Energy Being had been freed by his father. He found himself in darkness, until ceiling panel lights illuminated the room.

Half the room contained a great cube composed of a rainbow colored, iridescent metal, that shimmered like a mirage in the desert.

"Why are we here?" the Energy being whispered, in Lader's mind. "We are not deep enough to be safe from the Ray Weapon of my adversaries. I despise this place!"

"With good reason," Lader thought, to the Energy Being. He brought up the vital memory, walked to the right edge of the cube, and placed a palm on each of the two walls.

"What are you doing?" the Energy Being screamed, in Lader's mind. "How are you doing this? You cannot

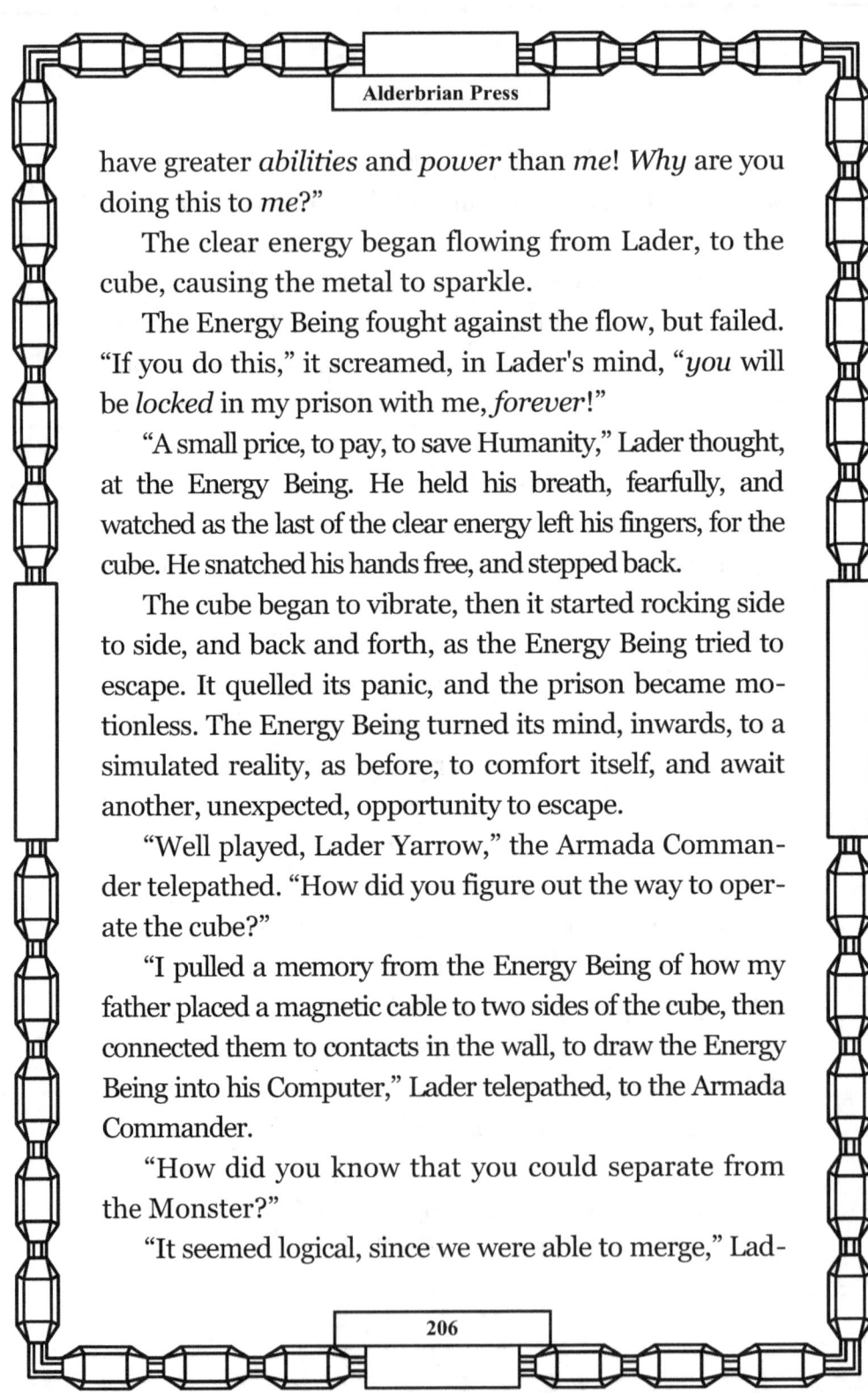

have greater *abilities* and *power* than *me*! *Why* are you doing this to *me*?"

The clear energy began flowing from Lader, to the cube, causing the metal to sparkle.

The Energy Being fought against the flow, but failed. "If you do this," it screamed, in Lader's mind, "*you* will be *locked* in my prison with me, *forever!*"

"A small price, to pay, to save Humanity," Lader thought, at the Energy Being. He held his breath, fearfully, and watched as the last of the clear energy left his fingers, for the cube. He snatched his hands free, and stepped back.

The cube began to vibrate, then it started rocking side to side, and back and forth, as the Energy Being tried to escape. It quelled its panic, and the prison became motionless. The Energy Being turned its mind, inwards, to a simulated reality, as before, to comfort itself, and await another, unexpected, opportunity to escape.

"Well played, Lader Yarrow," the Armada Commander telepathed. "How did you figure out the way to operate the cube?"

"I pulled a memory from the Energy Being of how my father placed a magnetic cable to two sides of the cube, then connected them to contacts in the wall, to draw the Energy Being into his Computer," Lader telepathed, to the Armada Commander.

"How did you know that you could separate from the Monster?"

"It seemed logical, since we were able to merge," Lad-

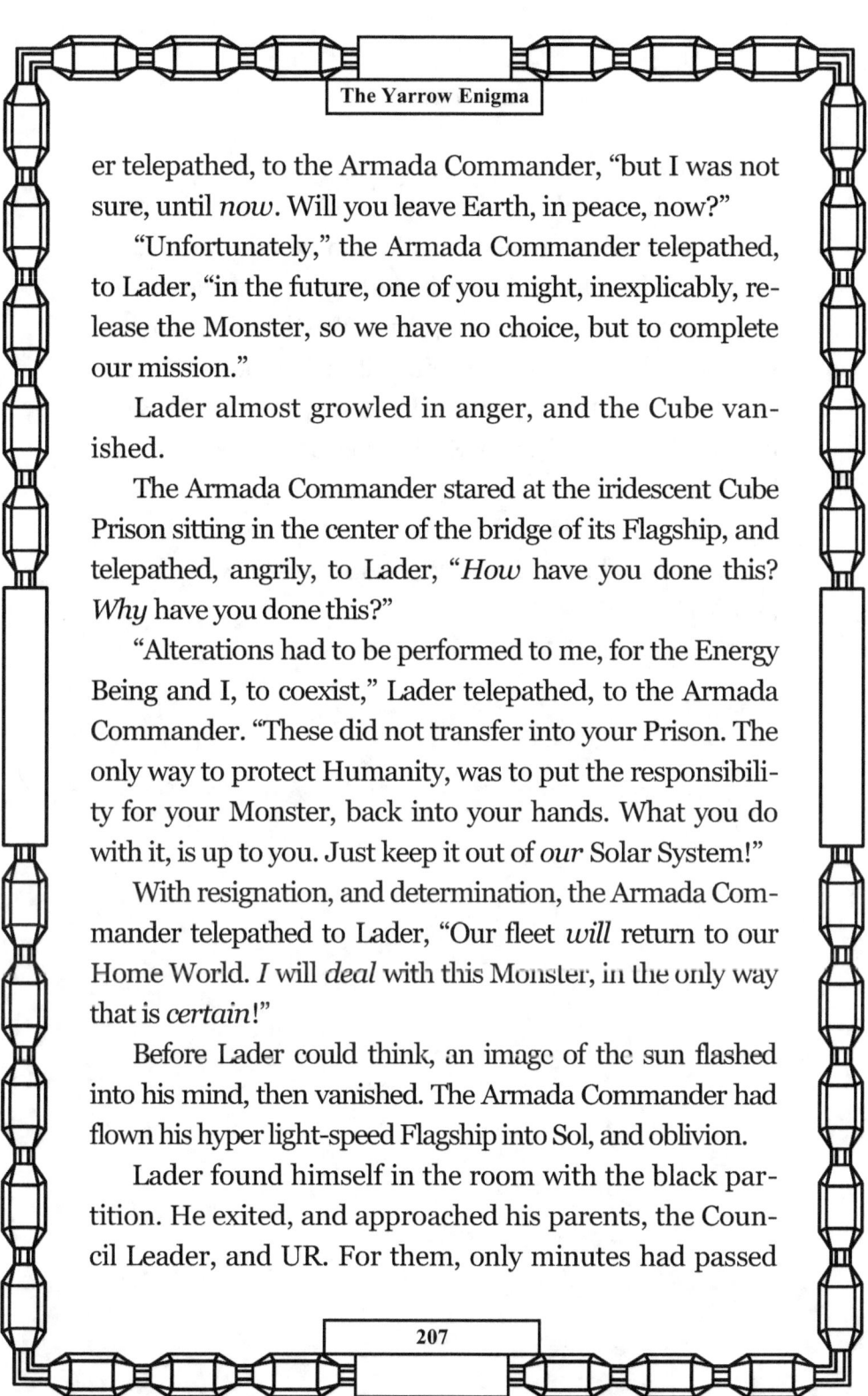

er telepathed, to the Armada Commander, "but I was not sure, until *now*. Will you leave Earth, in peace, now?"

"Unfortunately," the Armada Commander telepathed, to Lader, "in the future, one of you might, inexplicably, release the Monster, so we have no choice, but to complete our mission."

Lader almost growled in anger, and the Cube vanished.

The Armada Commander stared at the iridescent Cube Prison sitting in the center of the bridge of its Flagship, and telepathed, angrily, to Lader, "*How* have you done this? *Why* have you done this?"

"Alterations had to be performed to me, for the Energy Being and I, to coexist," Lader telepathed, to the Armada Commander. "These did not transfer into your Prison. The only way to protect Humanity, was to put the responsibility for your Monster, back into your hands. What you do with it, is up to you. Just keep it out of *our* Solar System!"

With resignation, and determination, the Armada Commander telepathed to Lader, "Our fleet *will* return to our Home World. *I* will *deal* with this Monster, in the only way that is *certain*!"

Before Lader could think, an image of the sun flashed into his mind, then vanished. The Armada Commander had flown his hyper light-speed Flagship into Sol, and oblivion.

Lader found himself in the room with the black partition. He exited, and approached his parents, the Council Leader, and UR. For them, only minutes had passed

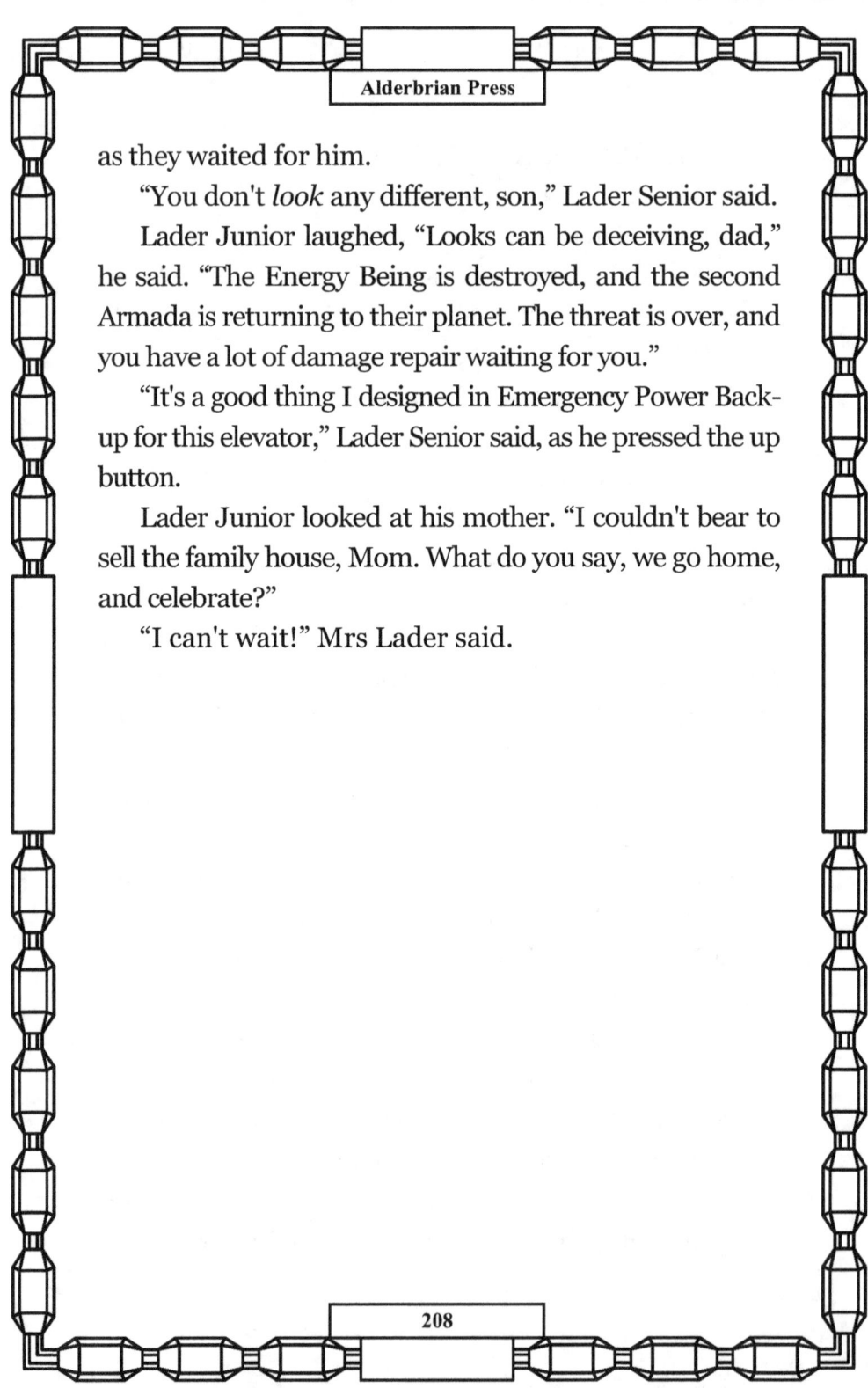

as they waited for him.

"You don't *look* any different, son," Lader Senior said.

Lader Junior laughed, "Looks can be deceiving, dad," he said. "The Energy Being is destroyed, and the second Armada is returning to their planet. The threat is over, and you have a lot of damage repair waiting for you."

"It's a good thing I designed in Emergency Power Back-up for this elevator," Lader Senior said, as he pressed the up button.

Lader Junior looked at his mother. "I couldn't bear to sell the family house, Mom. What do you say, we go home, and celebrate?"

"I can't wait!" Mrs Lader said.

www.ingramcontent.com/pod-product-compliance
Lightning Source LLC
Chambersburg PA
CBHW070756280626
47162CB00016B/1070